Cordelia Strube

Miłosz

Coach House Books, Toronto

first edition

 Canada Council **Conseil des Arts** for the Arts du Canada    ONTARIO ARTS COUNCIL CONSEIL DES ARTS DE L'ONTARIO   Canadä

Published with the generous assistance of the Canada Council for the Arts and the Ontario Arts Council. Coach House Books also acknowledges the support of the Government of Canada through the Canada Book Fund and the Government of Ontario through the Ontario Book Publishing Tax Credit.

The author gratefully acknowledges the support of the Canada Council for the Arts and the Ontario Arts Council.

LIBRARY AND ARCHIVES CANADA CATALOGUING IN PUBLICATION

Strube, Cordelia
    Milosz / Cordelia Strube.

Issued also in an electronic format.
ISBN 978-1-55245-265-3

    I. Title.

PS8587.T72975M53 2012   C813'.54   C2012-904683-3

Miłosz is available as an ebook: ISBN 978-1-77056-329-2.

Purchase of the print version of this book entitles you to a free digital copy. To claim your ebook of this title, please email sales@chbooks.com with proof of purchase or visit chbooks.com/digital. (Coach House Books reserves the right to terminate the free digital download offer at any time.)

for Carson

1

*m*ilo hears more noise than usual coming through the wall. A thumping sound: Robertson's head? Didn't Tanis say he had outgrown head banging?

'I hate you! I hate you! I hate you!' Strapped into his protective helmet, Robertson can go on like this for hours, spacing his words at regular intervals, using the same inflections. Tanis's response is inaudible through the wall but is probably, 'You don't hate me, possum. You've just had a bad day.' She will sit with her son for however long it takes, steadily offering soothing words. If she's lucky, he'll allow her to put her hand on his shoulder. When he lets her touch him, she says, it all feels manageable again. For five minutes. Her love for him can be painful to watch. Milo has walked them to school and seen the open wound of her need to protect her child. Half a block from the schoolyard Robertson insists she let him walk alone. Tanis obeys, smiling brightly and calling out, 'Have a good day, possum!' Stooped, without looking back, Robertson shuffles into the mob, a lone target. Turning from the yard, Tanis's face ages, the forced cheer fading into haggard determination.

'Don't start that or I'll eat you for fucking breakfast!' Robertson shouts. He frequently says he'll eat people for fucking breakfast. What's different about tonight is that his father shouts back. 'Can you for one second think about anyone but yourself? Look what you're doing to your mother. You're destroying your mother!'

Robertson's father doesn't normally shout. He cuts his grass and edges his flower beds. He wants to resurrect the fence dividing his lawn from Milo's weed patch but Tanis insists it would make her feel cramped. 'I don't want to look out my window and stare at a fence.' She has confided to Milo that the real reason she opposes Christopher on the fence is that she wants Robertson to feel free to 'hang' with Milo. She is the only person in living memory who considers him a good influence.

'I hate you! I hate you! I hate you!'

'Look at her,' Christopher screams. 'You're killing her, you're killing your mother!'

'I'll eat you for fucking breakfast!'

Milo can't listen anymore. He hurries downstairs, away from their torment.

'One of these days somebody's going to get hurt,' Wallace says, practising his golf swing in the living room.

'Don't say that.' Milo waters the spider plants.

'Might be better for all parties. Two's company, three's a crowd.'

'He needs both his parents.'

'Do they need him?'

Wallace shakes the crumbs from a chip package into his mouth, crumples the bag and pitches it into the wastebasket. Nothing bothers Wallace. Nuclear war could be declared and Wallace would say, 'More junk removal.' His business is junk removal, is, in fact, called Friendly Junk Removal. There's no end of work, no end of junk, particularly with recession house foreclosures. Wallace tosses the remnants of the evictees' personal belongings, photo albums and birthday cards into the truck without a hint of a wistful sigh. Milo, chronically short of cash, assists Wallace when Pablo isn't available. As Wallace forces his way into what they hope will be unoccupied houses – some evictees resist evacuation despite repeated notices – Milo is frequently stalled in the kitchen, staring at a fridge festooned with lists and recipes, children's drawings, graduation and baby photos, vet bills. 'Get a move on,' Wallace will command, 'we got two hours to clear this fucking shithole.'

Wallace takes another swing. 'That kid's fucked up. I mean, seriously.'

'Who isn't?'

'You want to work tomorrow?'

Milo hasn't worked as an actor for over a year if you disregard his silent appearances in commercials – he's currently moderately popular as set dressing for fast food and big box chain campaigns. Last month he screwed in a light bulb in a Canadian Tire ad. His agent says Milo is experiencing a renaissance as *Everyman*. 'Spreading gut, losing hair, it's all working for you,' his agent says. But Milo knows the reason he hasn't gotten a decent part for over a year is that he no longer knows how to act.

'Isn't Pablo available?' he asks.

'He's getting a tooth pulled.'

'Why?'

'Fuck if I know.'

'Nobody gets their teeth pulled anymore.'

'He's fucking Mexican. You want the gig or not?'

In Milo's last stage role, as Konstantin in *The Seagull*, he began to think too much and was conscious of every movement he made onstage. It was an Equity Showcase production for which he wasn't paid but given the opportunity to showcase his magic. Milo would arrive at the theatre three hours before curtain in an effort to inhabit Konstantin, to work up a desire for Nina and the compulsion to blow his brains out. He'd skip rope for an hour to induce Konstantin's weariness, drink black coffee to attain his edginess, dredge personal experience to suffer his despair. As the curtain rose and his cue came closer, he waited to exit Milo's world and enter Konstantin's. This had always happened in the past: he would forget who he was and become who he was supposed to be. But that was before his father deserted him, leaving Milo steeped in shame although clueless as to what he had done to make his father bail on him. He preferred his father's wrath to the resounding rejection of abandonment. What little self-worth he had managed to nurture in adulthood left him, because a father only abandons a worthless son. And so the futility that began onstage became pervasive. Now Milo acts badly 24/7.

'Whose house is it?'

'What do you mean "whose house"? Some fucking loser.'

'Is it a family house, a single occupant, a childless couple?'

'What's the fucking difference?'

Milo can't think of the difference. It's all lives lost to landfill.

'Fine,' Wallace says. 'I'll ask Jorge.'

'No, I'll do it.'

'Suit yourself,' Wallace says, 'just don't spend six hours staring at the fridge for fuck's sake.'

The banging stops at two a.m. Milo lifts the pillow off his head but still can't sleep and considers going next door to ensure that no one has been hurt. They can seem so comfortable, the three of them, in the backyard flipping burgers, tossing the ball for the dog. Sometimes Milo sits in darkness, undetected, on his side of the yard, and looks in their windows. Tanis and Christopher often share a bottle of wine at the kitchen table, conversing easily. Milo envies their intimacy, their shared troubles, their abnormal son. When he moved back in after his father disappeared, he could hear them making love. It sounded as though they were trying to save each other from drowning. Not anymore. Now the only noise coming through the wall is the TV. Or screams.

He climbs their deck and peers through the sliding glass doors. An old lady hoarder occupied this house while Milo was growing up. Her porch was stacked with newspapers, broken toys, bikes, pots, lawn mowers, chairs. Milo's father referred to her as 'the fire hazard.' The old woman never made a sound on her side of the wall. When she died, Christopher and Tanis bought and gutted the place, filling it with colour and their angel-faced son, who seemed normal, although Milo's father declared him 'backward.' Milo didn't argue because no matter what his rebuttal, his father would argue it. Gustaw had argued himself out of a business and out of a wife. He argued with Christopher about the fence, and with Tanis about her 'shit machine of a mutt.' Towards the end, none of the neighbours would venture into a conversation with Gustaw for fear of becoming embroiled. Milo was able to endure his father only for short visits. The long-suffering, despised adult son caring for his elderly father was a role he could play. With the rebelliousness of youth gone, Milo took pride in his ability to withstand the blows, to resist being drawn into battles he could not win. 'I don't know how you put up with your father,' neighbours confided, and Milo smiled benignly, so secure was he in his role as the misunderstood, underappreciated son.

Of course he still yearned for the old man's approval. On the opening night of *The Seagull*, Milo peered through the slit in the curtains, scanning the audience for Gustaw. His father would see, finally, the scope of Milo's talent. He imagined him jolting at the sound of the gunshot, and possibly a tear rolling down his cheek. After the final curtain Milo waited for the tentative knock on the dressing room door, the awkward embrace, the bewilderment, 'Son, I didn't know you had it in you. You have a gift.' But Gustaw never made the performance or, if he did, never admitted it, and decamped soon after, leaving Milo without the force of his father's loathing to resist. Thrown off balance, he has been stumbling ever since.

Only the light above the Wedderspoons' kitchen sink is on. The table has not been cleared; spaghetti hardens on the plates. This is highly unusual. Tanis always clears the table and does the dishes. Formerly a director of human resources, she became a full-time homemaker to look after Robertson and drive him to appointments with doctors, psychologists and behavioural therapists.

It's not surprising that the sliding doors are unlocked. Tanis and Christopher are Block Parents and rarely lock their doors. Milo finds her in the living room on the rocking chair, watching a muted samurai movie.

'Are you all right?' he asks.

'You heard?'

'Maybe I should've come over sooner.'

'He's asleep on the floor. Can you help me lift him?'

'Of course.' He follows her up the stairs, wondering why she hasn't asked Christopher to lift their son.

Robertson lies prone, his head inches from the wall. Tanis carefully removes the helmet. Freed of consciousness, Robertson could be any pink-cheeked boy on the threshold of life. Tanis steps back, allowing Milo room to manoeuvre. He slides his arms under Robertson's knees and back. Tanis cradles the boy's head as Milo transfers him to the bed. They lay him down gently, pulling the comforter around him. Tanis kisses his forehead, holding her lips against his skin. She has told Milo that the only time she can be sure Robertson won't recoil from her is when he is unconscious.

Back downstairs she resumes rocking and staring at the muted samurai movie. Voiceless warriors swing blades at intruding ninjas. Milo tries to think of encouraging words but knows they have tried everything: drugs, psychotherapy, dietary changes, chelation therapy, supplements, herbs, homeopathics. They have spent their life savings on their son.

'Christopher thinks he's turning into a juvenile delinquent.'

'He's only eleven,' Milo says.

'Next year he'll have a different teacher for every subject. I won't be able to kiss all their asses.'

Tanis has devoted countless hours to the chores Robertson's teachers prefer to avoid: arts and crafts prep and clean-up, flash-card duty, one-on-one reading, vomit mop-up.

A samurai thrusts his sword into a ninja's neck, causing blood to spurt from the ninja's mouth. Tanis's relentlessly curly hair, usually restrained with clips, tumbles over her face, hiding her expression.

'Christopher's leaving,' she says.

'Where's he going?'

'Away.'

'For how long?'

'Forever.'

This information catapults Milo. This couple that he has admired, that talk to each other, that work things out and love their son, cannot separate.

'Does Robertson know?' he asks.

'Not yet.'

'Maybe you should talk about it in the morning.'

'He hit Robertson.'

'When?'

'Tonight.'

'Hard?'

'What do you mean "hard"? He hit him.'

'But people do that,' Milo says.

'What people?'

'My father.'

'Oh, well, that's different. Your father was ... your father wasn't normal.'

'What's normal?'

'A father who doesn't hit his child.' She begins to twirl some of her hair so hard it looks as though it hurts.

'Why don't you see how you feel in the morning?' Milo suggests, standing as though trapped in netting, understanding he has no place here.

'A ten-year-old boy was abducted and sexually assaulted for six hours,' she says. 'What could be worse than that? Death, I suppose. I worry about Robertson. He'll talk to anybody.'

Milo has witnessed Robertson speaking with total strangers. He'll ask them abruptly about things most people would only ponder. Deformity fascinates him and he won't hesitate to ask the disabled what it's like to have flaps for arms or a misshapen head. He reprimands anyone who litters, regardless of their size. And, of course, if he overhears a conversation in which he feels he should take part, he will, in that too-loud voice of his.

'They were bouncing a basketball off his head,' Tanis says. 'Usually he manages to avoid them, pretends to be tying a shoelace or something. When a group of kids starts to pass he jumps up and tries to blend in. It didn't work today.'

'Was he hurt?'

'Not physically.'

'Is he going to school tomorrow?'

'I don't know.' She twirls her hair. 'They win if he doesn't go.'

Milo would like to ask, 'Don't they win anyway? Has Robertson *ever* won?' But Tanis seems scarily fragile, and her husband is leaving her. A samurai warrior, dishonoured in defeat, kneels and commits hara-kiri.

'Sorry if we kept you awake,' she says.

'Don't worry about it.'

'You should get some sleep.'

'Ditto,' he says.

She nods as the warrior falls forward over his dagger and blood pools around him.

'Till tomorrow then,' Milo says.

Closing the sliding doors, he can still hear her rocking.

2

'*H*ope there aren't any fucking Rottweilers,' Wallace says. 'Last house I did there were *two* fucking Rottweilers. Black.'

'All Rottweilers are black,' Milo says.

'These were, like, *totally* fucking black.' Wallace slides a flathead screwdriver between the door and frame, and then leverages the cylinder out of the lock as he twists the doorknob with a clamp wrench. 'We're in,' he says. 'Get a fucking move on. And no way do you read their fucking mail.'

The rancid stench of abandonment greets them. Wallace immediately starts taking photos of the contents and condition of the house while Milo shakes out a garbage bag and begins to toss in the mail. It's mostly bills, easy to ignore. It's the personal letters that stop him, carefully penned and sent. When his father disappeared, Milo felt obliged to respond to Gustaw's personal mail. It was Christmas, which meant greeting cards from relatives his father couldn't stand. Gustaw wanted to forget Poland, the Nazi invasion, the raping and pillaging, the betrayal of Jews and the theft of their property, the mass graves, the Russian invasion, the raping and pillaging, the slaughter of priests. Gustaw remade himself in Canada, became Gus and atheist, learned English and, with much practice, removed all traces of Polish from his accent, even mastering the 'th' sound. Reborn as a Canadian, he married a bubbly Canadian girl and then argued her to death. Milo remembers the soft hairs on her forearms, the smell of Bailey's Irish Cream on her breath and the ragged sound of her sobs, but little else, except the arguing.

Pablo stumbles through the front door.

'I thought you had to go to the dentist,' Milo says.

'I been already,' Pablo mumbles through gauze.

'Did he say it was okay for you to work?'

'He don't know shit.' He pulls a piece of gauze out of his mouth, sees blood on it and shoves it back in. 'That *hijo de puta* charge me two hundred bucks, can you believe that?'

'What the fuck are *you* doing here?' Wallace demands, clutching his sledge-hammer. Any furniture too big for the truck gets demolished in seconds.

'I need cash,' Pablo says.

'No fucking slacking, asswipe, you read me?'

'*Sí, sí.*'

Pablo, although short, can lift entire couches. He spends hours body-building and comes to cause destruction wearing a bodybuilding belt. For this reason, Milo leaves the heavy lifting to the boys. Upstairs he empties a closet of a mildewed fake fur coat and a wedding dress covered in plastic, several pairs of high-heeled shoes moulded to the shape of a small foot, boxes of obsolete PC technology, exercise equipment and numerous garbage bags filled and labelled. Presumably the evictees had intended to take the bags of *summer clothes* and *winter hats/gloves* but had, at the last moment, realized they had nowhere to store them.

'Milo,' Pablo calls. 'Check this out.' He beckons Milo to a pink and blue room undisturbed by the evacuation. 'This is a baby's room, man.'

'So?'

'Nothing's been used, man. Everything's, like, still wrapped up. There's never been no baby here.'

Milo looks at basket of baby toys wrapped in cellophane. 'What's your point?'

'They couldn't have no *bambinos*. They got the house and the nursery but no babies. That's sad, man. They just left everything.'

'What else are they supposed to do with it?'

The upstairs back room of Milo's house was intended for a baby. His parents referred to it as *the baby's room*. But after repeated miscarriages the baby's room became the back room again, and Milo's parents stopped exchanging the smallest of tender gestures. From the age of four, Milo never saw them sit in the same room at the same time, although they continued to share a bed, and argue. He'd block his ears with his teddy bears until Mrs. Cauldershot, with hands like sandpaper, yanked them away from him. 'Best to keep busy,' she told him. 'Sitting around never helped anybody.' Which is probably true. Milo has done more sitting around than keeping busy and look where it's got him, en route to becoming a fire hazard. But then wasn't Gustaw mercilessly busy? Isn't it possible he walked into the storm to *stop* being busy, to inhale the brisk air, to die?

The bubbly Canadian girl died of a heart attack at forty-two.

'Wakey, wakey,' Pablo says, 'you don't want the boss man on your back. We got fleas. He wants us to pull up the hall carpet.' Pablo tucks his track pants into his socks and starts ripping up broadloom with an X-acto knife. Just the mention of fleas starts Milo scratching. He too tucks his pants into his socks.

'We got to get poison to spray on these suckers,' Pablo says. 'If I bring bugs to my girlfriend's, she'll kill me.'

Pablo's girlfriend is always about to kill him. Milo has difficulty understanding what Pablo gets out of the relationship, but then who is Milo to judge, having blown each and every one of his relationships? 'I don't think she'll kill you, Pablo.'

'Are you fucking slackers getting a move on?' bellows Wallace. 'No fucking group therapy, you read me?'

Wallace doesn't like it when Pablo and Milo commune.

'She told me,' Pablo says, 'I'm not committed. She says I'm always doing stuff without her. What's she talking about, I gave her a ring.' He rips up more carpet. 'What's she want from me? I gave her a *ring*.'

Milo rolls up pieces of carpet and binds them with twine. 'Maybe she wants affection rather than material things. I mean, rings are just rings.' Although maybe if he'd given Zosia a ring, she wouldn't have dumped him. 'Where did you buy it?' he asks.

'Walmart. They got nice jewellery there.'

'Oh, so it wasn't like an engagement ring?'

'Shit, no. It was a honey-I-love-you ring. That's what guys do, they buy girls rings. You never done that?'

'No.' Zosia left a silk scarf behind. In moments of howling woefulness Milo lies with it draped over his face. What if he'd bought her a honey-I-love-you ring? 'How much did it cost?'

'What?'

'The ring.'

'Fifty bucks.'

'Maybe it was too cheap. Maybe she wanted an expensive ring.'

'Not Maria. She don't like extravagances.'

'How do you know? I mean, maybe she just says that.'

'*Qué?*'

'Maybe she just says she doesn't like extravagances. Maybe she's secretly hoping you'll splurge.'

'What do you know? You never bought a girl a ring.'

The sound of splintering wood interrupts them. 'I told you deadbeats to shut the fuck up.'

'*Come mierda*,' Pablo mutters, which Milo knows from previous translations means 'eat shit.'

At McDonald's, Pablo continues to work out the girlfriend thing. 'Sometimes, when she's shouting at me, I'm thinking she's trying to reach out. I saw that on *Oprah*. When people shout, they're just trying to reach out.'

Is that what Milo's parents were doing? Is that what Christopher and Robertson were doing?

'She's shouting because you're not fucking getting it, asshole,' Wallace says.

'You are a very negative person, Wallace. Always. You are just trying to protect yourself from being hurt.'

'By who, dickwad?'

'You never loved a girl, Wallace.'

'What the fuck do you know about it?'

'I know you never loved nobody. Not even your mother.'

'Fuck you, asshole, you fucking Mexican.'

'He's Cuban,' Milo says.

The afternoon shift involves spraying bug killer throughout the house. Pablo takes charge, even spraying himself.

'That's toxic,' Milo warns.

'If I bring fleas to Maria's she'll kill me.'

'It's getting hard to breathe, Pablo.' They remove more labelled garbage bags and broken exercise equipment. On good days Milo discovers books in the deserted homes but the only books here are *How to Eat What You Want and Stay Skinny* and *How to Get the Love You Want*, both of which Pablo intends to give Maria.

'You have to forgive people,' he says. 'That's what it's all about.'

'Forgive them for what?' Milo asks.

'What they did to you, forgive them. I saw this movie about this family who were all mad at each other. At the end they forgave each other, were all, like, hugging and kissing. It made me cry.'

'It's a fucking movie, butthead,' Wallace says, emptying a chest of drawers at their feet.

'Wallace, people do forgive each other. If you love somebody, you forgive them.'

Milo tries to forgive his father. Everyone has to move beyond blaming their parents, don't they? Particularly if their parents are dead, or presumed dead. Increasingly Milo feels a seeping regret for opportunities lost, distances maintained, intentions misunderstood. After all, as his father was so fond of telling him, he's had it easy. Milo was not a child in war-ravaged Poland, did not cower under a table while five drunken Russians raped his beloved sister. According to Gus, Poles were spineless, letting the Nazis, then the Russians, walk all over them. According to Gus, Poles turned on Poles so they could steal their pigs. Poles betrayed the Jewish boy who'd been buried under corpses and had run naked to Gus's father's barn. When the Nazis came for Jakob, he was in the woods searching for his cousin, even though it was assumed that the cousin was in a mass grave along with Jakob's parents and uncle. The Nazis lured the Jews to town squares by telling them they were taking them to Palestine. Then they'd march them to the graves, force them to strip and trample the recently murdered to make room for their own soon-to-be-dead bodies.

When Jakob returned from searching for his cousin, Gustaw's father told him he had to leave immediately or they would all be shot. Jakob had become like a brother to Gus; they'd shared a bed and talked about outer space and how one day Jakob would fly a rocket to the moon. Gustaw never forgave his father for ordering Jakob to leave. He watched his friend creep into the woods like an animal. Within days he was back, shivering and begging for food. Gus's mother packed him some bread and cheese. Gus's father told Jakob that if he returned again, he would shoot him.

Such grim reminiscences cause Milo tremors of compassion for his father, until he remembers Gustaw swatting his head after parent-teacher interviews. 'How can my son be such an *idiot?*' Milo knew that Gus was longing for his other sons who weren't idiots, the ones who died before they were born.

...

Robertson tosses the ball for the dog. Fortunately for Sal, Robertson, unlike normal children, is never bored by this activity. He can play fetch for hours.

'How goes it?' Milo asks, approaching slowly because sudden movements startle the boy. 'Any snails about?'

'Didn't look.'

'Did you go to school today?'

'Nope.' Robertson has difficulty interacting with people but not with animals. Dogs strain against their leashes to lick his palms. 'My dad left.'

'Did he say anything to you?'

'About what?'

'Why he was leaving?'

Robertson begins speaking in the rushed manner he adopts when he doesn't understand but wants to appear as though he does. 'He's tired. I don't know, maybe he's just tired of me, he works too hard, maybe he just needs a rest. Mummy says it's all right. It's just for now. I'm not easy to be around. I get mad and I don't know why. I'm going to finish the patio.' Since April Robertson has been laying patio stones on gravel in symmetrical patterns. Tanis said she knew he was different when he was three and lining up his toys. He would become extremely distressed if she tried to tidy up, thereby disturbing his order.

'It's looking good,' Milo says, offering Robertson some cashews. The boy takes a handful and scatters them around the garden for the squirrels. Sal, ball in mouth, pants at his feet. Robertson takes the ball and tosses it. Milo lies back in the grass, not wanting to crowd Robertson with conversation. It's hard to imagine the house without Christopher. Tanis will drink alone. Robertson will seek refuge in World of Warcraft without Christopher to stop him.

Scratching at flea bites, Milo sees Tanis preparing dinner. How strange to set places for only two. What can Christopher be doing? Watching TV in a Days Inn? Does he despise himself for hitting his son? It's not the first time he has had to be rough with him. When Robertson has episodes in stores, and onlookers stare disapprovingly – believing him to be a spoiled child in need of discipline – Christopher throws him over his shoulder and carries him out. He has no choice but to force him into the car and wait for the tantrum to pass. The car functions as a therapeutic quiet room, a term they learned after sending Robertson to the Child and Parent Resource Centre. Overall, it seems to Milo, Christopher has shown tremendous restraint. As much as he loves Robertson, there are times when Milo feels an urge to slap some sense into him.

Sal lies on her back with her paws in the air, waiting for Robertson to rub her belly.

'Robertson,' Milo says. 'Sal wants tummy rubbing.'

Robertson rubs her tummy but doesn't talk to her as he usually does.

'Have you ever tried pretending you're an alien?' Milo asks.

Robertson doesn't respond. Unlike normal people, he doesn't feel compelled to reply to mindless chatter.

'Because,' Milo continues, 'I've found that pretending to be an alien with the capacity to vaporize at any second helps me through difficult situations.'

'You mean like being beamed up on a transporter?' Robertson is a Trekkie, his favourite characters being the androids who, though emotionless, have great curiosity – and wistfulness – about being human.

'I prefer having the capacity to vaporize at any second,' Milo says. 'Who wants to wait around for a transporter?'

'So where do you vaporize to?'

'My planet, where everybody thinks like I do. We get along great, no wars. So I don't mind visiting Earth occasionally. I find it quite fascinating, actually. Studying humans.'

'As long as you can vaporize at any second.'

'That's right.'

Robertson faces Milo, which is a bit disconcerting. Generally he avoids eye contact and glances at people sideways. Under such scrutiny, Milo realizes the absurdity of his alien ploy. It works for him because he has never experienced the kind of suffering and isolation Robertson endures daily.

'Are you saying I should pretend I'm an alien at school?' Robertson asks.

'Anytime you feel like it. Generally I become an alien when people act like assholes. I also picture them naked and make mental notes for my report.'

'Who do you report to?'

'Other aliens. My comrades back home.'

Robertson considers this, blinking repeatedly as he does when he's working things out. '*You* can do that because you're an actor,' he says. '*I can't do that.*'

Tanis has told Milo that children with Autism Spectrum Disorders are very literal. They miss nuances, which is why socializing proves challenging for them. Social conventions and codes are beyond the comprehension of the autistic – they don't understand that people rarely say what they mean.

'I don't see why you can't vaporize,' Milo says. 'It's all in your head. How you look at things. If you can vaporize at any second, there's no point sweating over anything, just vanish.'

'You *can't* vaporize at any second. That's stupid.' He leaves abruptly, as he often does without so much as a 'see you later.' Social niceties never seemed important to Milo until he met Robertson. Sal glances briefly at Milo, who offers to toss the ball for her. She too turns away, trailing Robertson. Once in the kitchen, Robertson shuts the blinds.

3

*S*tanding or sitting naked in front of strangers in cold rooms pays thirty bucks an hour. Despite the space heater, Milo feels a chill, which adds to the thrill of being nude in front of strangers. They *must* look at him, have paid to look at him, he exists – even with the spreading gut and thinning hair – and can't be ignored. There is power in this, and in his ability to hold a pose for twenty minutes. A concentration is required that he is unable to muster outside the studio. Outside, his thoughts run on, split up, turn back, scrambling over one another. In the studio they sit quietly with their hands folded in their laps.

It is while he's standing with one arm overhead and the other resting on his uplifted forehead that his mission becomes clear. He must find Christopher. Without Christopher, Tanis and Robertson cannot mend. Tanis doesn't realize this; she will soldier on, clipping back her hair. Robertson will absorb the blame for the loss of his father just as Milo internalized the blame for the loss of Gus, despite searching for him long after the police called off the sniffer dogs. Clambering in the ravines, acting a grief he could not feel, he spoke to the homeless about the old man in the beige windbreaker, following their leads, imagining his father a King Lear under exploding skies. During his quest, Milo lost twenty-four pounds and developed a swarthy complexion. Wallace called him the Marlboro Man. Women looked at him differently but Milo did not return their glances, so intent was he on his task. When asked about Gus, he simulated anguish, hoping that by acting it he would feel it. As the weeks passed and he could no longer ignore the fact that money was not being withdrawn from Gus's account, and no credit card transactions were being reported, Milo continued to walk the city. If he stopped searching, it meant Gustaw Krupanski of Krupi and Son Ltd. was dead. The only interruptions Milo allowed were auditions during which he tried not to think; but thinking about not thinking destroyed his spontaneity, and he stood empty, unable to give or take. His agent told him the same thing happened to Olivier. 'Sir Larry couldn't look anybody in the eye,' Stu said, 'asked the other actors not to look at him because it would throw him. For a while he couldn't even be alone onstage. Seriously, chief, everybody goes through rough patches. Your dad died, give yourself time to grieve.' Milo waited to be struck and pitched into the throes of grief he'd acted when he still knew how to act. As though preparing for a part, he read about the stages of grief, assuming some common behaviours, all the while appalled at how badly he was acting.

'Did you tell Robertson to pretend to be an alien?' Tanis has been pounding on Milo's back door for several minutes.

'Yes.'

'What were you thinking? He feels like an alien *all the time*. Not a second goes by when he doesn't feel like a total freak.'

'Being an alien is quite different from being a total freak,' Milo says.

'Oh, really? How so?'

'Aliens belong on other planets. They aren't total freaks on their own planets.'

'He tried to strangle a boy today. He said he was pretending to be an alien when a human threatened him. He had no choice but to respond with his superior alien strength.'

The image of Robertson, nurturer of snails and small creatures, grabbing the throat of another human being, forces Milo to seek support from the fridge. He leans against it, sobered by its rumble. 'I'm sorry,' he says. 'It was supposed to stay inside his head.'

'What?'

'A different perspective.'

'What perspective?'

'Of being special. He *is* special, just not everybody can see it. I was trying to help him feel special regardless of what people say.'

'Well, it didn't work, Milo. The school's hysterical. They don't want him back.'

'They can't stop him.'

'Would you want to go where you're not wanted? Where you're *despised*?'

'What if I go with him?'

'What do you mean?'

'I could go with him and hang out in the yard, shoot some hoops.'

'They're not going to let some strange man into the schoolyard.'

'You could tell them I'm not strange.'

'Oh, okay, so I say, "This is my neighbour, an unemployed actor who's got nothing better to do than hang around my son". That would make him real popular.'

Robertson scrambles towards them holding two snails. 'These were under the steps. Don't know what they're doing there. I'm going to put them on the hostas.'

Tanis rubs her face. Milo knows she despairs over her son's concerns for pests that destroy her foliage. Robertson charges to the hosta bed and sets the snails carefully onto the leaves.

'Has he forgotten he tried to strangle somebody?' Milo whispers.

'Who knows. Who knows what's going on in his head.' She starts down the steps.

'Where is Christopher working these days?'

'Why do you ask?'

'I was just curious,' Milo says. 'He was downsized, wasn't he? Didn't he get some other job?'

'At Empire Financial, why?'

'Oh, well, someone I know is looking for work in the financial industry. I thought I'd mention that Christopher just got hired.'

'He was hired months ago. Get with the program, Milo, and please don't mess with my son's head. He's got enough problems.'

Robertson begins lining up patio stones. Afraid to mess with his head, Milo lies down on the grass on his side of the yard. Sal sniffs him briefly before wandering off. 'The patio's coming along great,' he offers. Robertson keeps working. If only life could be as simple as creating some small order amidst the chaos.

'He took the ball from *me*,' Robertson says after several minutes. 'I was playing by myself and he took the ball.'

'Whose ball was it?'

'The school's.'

'I guess you're probably supposed to share it then.'

'They don't share it. They *never* share it. I had it first. He wasn't even playing.'

'Who?'

'Billy.'

'Were there other kids around?'

'Just Billy. He wasn't even playing. He said I couldn't play but he wasn't even playing.'

'Billy the Bully,' Milo says. 'What an asshole.' Tanis would want him to remain objective. She invariably tries to view the altercation from the other kid's perspective to help explain the situation to Robertson. Her experience in human resources has led her to believe that problems can be solved. In Milo's experience, problems cling like barnacles. 'I would've kicked his ass,' he says.

'Strangling's probably not the best choice,' Robertson admits.

'Going for the throat usually scares people.'

'He was scared all right.'

'The hitch is you could kill a person by mistake, going for the throat.' Milo doesn't look at Robertson for fear of making him retreat. Instead he listens to the soft tapping of the bricks.

'He was scared all right,' Robertson repeats. Is this how delinquency begins? Will he crave the adrenalin buzz he felt with Billy the Bully's neck in his grip? Did he throttle the boy because his father hit him? Milo certainly did. Nothing relieved the sense of injustice like kicking around another, preferably smaller, boy. Little provocation was required. Although Milo had the sense to only beat up strangers who couldn't trace him. In the schoolyard he was just Milo the nose-picker.

'The principal says I can't go back unless I apologize.'

'That's rough.'

'Would *you* apologize?'

Milo has never been good at apologies. Generally he avoids confrontation, despite inner rumblings of rebellion. With his father he would feign obedience, until Gus, fed up with his diversion tactics, would fling whatever was on his plate – potatoes, beets, Brussels sprouts – at him. *How can my son be such an idiot?*

'Would *you* apologize?' Robertson repeats.

'Probably. To avoid further trouble.'

'Then they'll just hit me again and I won't be able to hit back.'

Tanis summons Robertson for dinner. 'Right now, please,' she adds. Before the vaporizing alien incident, she would allow him to dawdle. Does she no longer consider Milo a good influence?

He lies with Zosia's scarf over his face, picturing her smoky, weary eyes. She expects the worst, and when it happens only shrugs, trudging onward. She views Canadians as overindulged children to be tolerated but not taken seriously. She called Milo a *coaster*. 'You coast,' she said in her Latvian accent, heavy on the c's and slow on the s's. 'One morning you'll wake up and you'll be old and you'll have nothing.' Zosia studied electrical engineering in Russia, worked hard among misogynists to earn her degrees. In Canada the only work available to her, despite retraining, was waitressing, which is how she met Milo. Zosia was attracted to him because he wasn't an alcoholic. She said all Russian men are alcoholics. With such low expectations, Milo could not disappoint, or anyway that's what he thought, until she dumped him. He wishes he'd bought her a honey-I-love-you ring.

Wallace told Milo that Zosia was after Canadian citizenship. 'She wants your fucking wedding vows, butthead.'

This, of course, had not occurred to Milo. He'd thought she was after his body and his mind, not necessarily in that order. She certainly wasn't after his income. Should he have it out with her? Gus was a big believer in 'having it out' with people. Maybe Milo should show up at the Copper Pipe where Zosia slings designer pizzas and simply ask, 'What did I do?' He could even take a honey-I-love-you ring along as backup.

He lifts her scarf a few inches off his face then lets it drift back down as he hears Wallace returning from the airport. Milo agreed to board Wallace's mother for a sizeable cash sum. Normally Wallace's baritone carries upstairs easily but Milo hears only a chirpy British voice. He has never met Wallace's mother, even though they lived blocks away growing up, because she was always working two jobs. Someone knocks on his door.

'Who is it?'

'Can I talk to you for a sec?'

Behind the door stands a tremulous Wallace. 'What's the problem?'

'I fucking forgot to make up her bed. Do you have any, like, nice sheets and towels?'

'Whatever's in the closet.'

'They're fucking sad, man, they're, like, *totally* used.'

Milo hears clomping on the stairs. 'Did I hear you use that word again, Wally?'

'Sorry, Mum, I was just ...'

She appears, tiny, sparkly, with electric currents for eyes. 'Are you Milo?'

'Yes. You must be Mrs. ... ?'

'Call me Vera. What's all this fuss about then, Wally?'

'It's just,' Wallace murmurs, 'we don't have nice towels and stuff.'

'What's that got to do with the price of cheese?'

Wallace stares at his feet. 'It's just, I wanted you to have something pretty.'

'What codswallop. Let's have a cuppa.' She turns and climbs down the stairs with surprising speed. 'Will you join us, Milo?'

Wallace looks imploringly at Milo and mouths, 'Please!'

'Not tonight, thank you, Vera,' Milo says. 'There are some digestives in a tin beside the tea things.'

'Oh, how lovely,' Vera exudes. 'Just what the doctor ordered.'

Wallace pushes Milo into the bedroom. 'I'm not going to make it through this.'

'Sure you will.'

Wallace hasn't seen his mother since she returned to her native English burb years ago. He comes up with annual excuses not to visit her. She lives with her sisters who, according to Wallace, are all a hundred and never shut up.

'She wants to meet my girlfriend,' Wallace moans.

'You don't have one.'

'Like I don't know that.'

'Just be honest with her.'

'Are you fucking *nuts*? Can you set me up with somebody?'

'What?'

'You know people, like, actresses and stuff. I'll pay her. She just has to act nice and be polite.'

'Oh, come on, Wallace.'

'Waal-leee ... ? Your tea's getting cold. Shall I make us a sanny?'

Wallace presses his hands together in a pleading gesture. 'I'll pay you a bonus.'

'Waal-leee ... ?'

The bullish Wallace morphs into a small boy with downcast eyes and a timorous gait. 'Coming, Ma,' he calls back in a singsong voice Milo has never heard before.

In the morning, Milo, ducking behind parked cars, follows Tanis and Robertson to school. A year ago Robertson allowed Tanis to put two fingers on his shoulder as they crossed the street. Now, almost her height, he maintains a distance between them. He says he doesn't need her to walk him to school, but she insists because it is his last year at the neighbourhood school. Next year he will have to take a bus. She has admitted to Milo that she can't imagine putting Robertson on a bus, watching the doors close behind him, trying to see through the windows as he searches for a seat. 'It'll be rush hour,' she said. 'He's bound to freak.' They have even considered buying a used car, having sold the Subaru last year to pay off debts.

Mother and son part half a block from the school so the kids in the yard won't see her. Tanis keeps waving but Robertson doesn't look back. Milo hides behind some recycling bins as Tanis retraces her steps. She stares hard at the pavement as she walks. Once she has turned the corner, Milo ambles towards the school, pulling his baseball cap low over his forehead. Posses of children part as Robertson makes his way through the yard. Once his back is turned they make faces or pinch their noses. Robertson stops beside the basketball net. Boys ignore him, jumping up and around him. Robertson says something Milo can't hear above the racket in the yard. A boy in a hoodie shoves him and flips him the finger before resuming dribbling the ball. A stout man with wiry hair, presumably a teacher, approaches Robertson and leads him into the school. The bell rings and the kids begin to line up outside the doors. The boy in the hoodie continues to shoot hoops until the stout man returns. 'Billy,' he says sharply, 'now.' Billy misses one more shot before slouching towards the entrance. The man pulls off the boy's hood, revealing a shock of red hair.

Now Milo knows who Billy is.

•••

He puts on his suit, the one he wears for corporate-type auditions, hoping to blend in at reception. He carries a busted cell he used as a prop in *Waiting for Godot*. He received good notices for that performance, although he didn't really understand the play. The director told him he was an 'instinctive actor' and that he shouldn't get 'hung up on the words.' This made sense to Milo because, in university, he played George in *Who's Afraid of Virginia Woolf?* – another play he didn't really understand – and didn't get hung up on the words but channelled the rage he felt towards Gus into George and let it spew all over Martha. After the show he felt free, cleansed, ready to party. In the morning seething resentments returned, and he couldn't wait to get back on stage to spew all over Martha again.

He invited Gus to the opening night of *Waiting for Godot*, even though he knew his father would be bored out of his mind. The next day, when Milo showed the old man the good reviews, Gus shrugged and ate another sausage.

While waiting for the receptionist to notice him, Milo pretends to text on the busted cell. She takes five hundred more calls before looking at him. 'Are you waiting for someone?' she inquires. She must be in her forties but has a mouth full of braces.

'Christopher Wedderspoon, please.'

'Is he expecting you?'

'Actually, no, I'm just passing through. My plane was delayed and I thought I'd take the opportunity to go over a portfolio with him.' Milo holds up the briefcase he uses for corporate-type auditions.

'Your name, please?'

'Milo Krupi.'

She presses buttons and speaks into her headset. 'Milo Crappy's here to go over a portfolio. He doesn't have an appointment.' She pauses, squinting at Milo, then repeats, 'Milo Crappy.'

'Krupi,' Milo interjects. 'We used to be neighbours.'

'He says you used to be neighbours.' Because she's staring at him while speaking into the headset Milo assumes she's addressing him.

'That's right,' he says, 'we *were* neighbours. Actually, I still live beside his wife.'

'Mr. Wedderspoon will be with you shortly. Have a seat.'

'Thank you.' Does this mean he will he be forced to 'have it out' with Christopher right here, amidst the teal furnishings of the waiting room? Sitting on a stuffed chair, he can't help but notice the receptionist looking at his shoes. They're Gus's shoes, a little small and in need of polish. Gus took great pride in polishing his shoes. They are the wrong colour for the suit. He pretends to text again while rehearsing in his head the heart-rending speech that will convince Christopher to return home.

4

*C*hristopher slumps on a stool at the Quick Fixins counter with his head in his hands. It would have been preferable to have this heart-to-heart in a private office with a window overlooking the city. Milo could have paced as he explained the gravity of his mission, gazing sorrowfully out the window as he searched for the right words. But Christopher appears to have come down in the world and has only a cubicle. Milo isn't sure what his job is. Christopher used to manage other people's money, or lose it, which may be why he is now in a cubicle.

'I will always support them,' he says.

'No one doubts that.'

'You swear she doesn't know you're here?'

'Scout's honour.' Christopher was a scout leader so Milo feels this oath is appropriate. Scouts had been an escape for Christopher as a kid and he'd hoped it would be the same for Robertson. But Robertson never moved with the crowd, instead lingered over anything that caught his interest.

'She thinks he can be normal,' Christopher says. 'I know he can't.'

'Don't you think normal is overrated? I mean, who wants to be normal? Robertson has a concentration, an intensity of thought, a single-mindedness, a ... ' The words Milo so carefully chose to describe the wonder of Robertson escape him. He is *drying*, as they say in the theatre, and there is no prompter to feed him his line. 'What I mean is,' he stammers, 'he has a tenacity, a ... a direct-ness. He can't lie. How many people do you know who can't lie? He's incapable of dissembling.' *Dissembling* is a word he'd thought would impress, but Christopher remains inert. 'Robertson is unique,' Milo sums up. 'No one thinks like he does. I think he's quite noble.'

'He can't control himself. And he's getting bigger. I'm scared he's going to kill her.'

'Shouldn't you be there to prevent that from happening?'

'She won't let me. She thinks she can handle him. She thinks I put his back up.'

'Maybe you do. I find it's best to give him space when he fixates on something.'

'So he grows up expecting people to get out of the way when it suits him? What kind of an adult will that make? Nobody will be able to stand him.'

Milo shifts a stir stick on the counter. 'Maybe he'll find a niche. There's an autistic woman who designs machinery for slaughterhouses. She's number one in her field.'

'Yes, we've all heard about the ones who have "special gifts." Robertson has no special gifts. It's not like in the movies. Most of them aren't math geniuses, most of them stay angry in institutions, banging their heads into padded walls.' Christopher rubs his face in the same manner that Tanis does.

'*I* think he has special gifts,' Milo says.

'Like what?'

'His relationships with animals.'

'Try looking at his report card, Milo. He's a C average. This is no wonder kid here.'

'All I'm saying is, don't give up on him. You'll lose him and you'll lose yourself.' This sounds like something Pablo would say. 'Forgive him, Christopher. We all have to forgive.'

'Forgive him for what?'

Milo isn't sure. He is acting badly again. 'A friend of mine believes that life's challenges are lessons.'

'Really. Well, I'm tired of learning the same lessons.'

'My friend says that we learn the lessons more deeply the second time around.'

'Is your friend graduating any time soon?'

'Not in this life.'

'Ah.'

Christopher stares at the *Enjoy Our Comfort Food, You Know You Want To!!!* sign beside the coffee maker.

'They both need you,' Milo says, feeling the words clumsy on his tongue. 'I know it's easy for me to talk ...'

'Yes, it is easy for you to talk. You don't live with it every hour of every day.' He bunches up his napkin and pushes it into his empty cup, then sits motionless. 'I love those two more than my life. I would give my life for them, would gladly die for them. Unfortunately that wouldn't help.' He slides off the stool without looking at Milo. 'Thanks for dropping by. I appreciate your concern.' As he speeds past, he sniffles and wipes his eyes. Milo envies him for knowing how to cry.

'Maria threw me out,' Pablo says, beached on the couch.

'Why?'

'She wants me to be a Catholic.'

Vera mashes potatoes with verve. Milo hasn't seen the masher in years. Mrs. Cauldershot used it to pulverize potatoes, squash, turnips and parsnips. Milo's mouth would fill with the formless sludge and he would consider spitting it back at her but instead forced it down – it was easiest to just obey.

'Don't you look nice, Milo,' Vera says. 'All dressed up like a banker. What's the occasion?'

'Do you hear what I'm telling you?' Pablo wails. 'Maria wants me to believe in God Almighty.'

'That's just plain unreasonable,' Vera says. 'If she loves you, she must respect your beliefs.'

'Where's Wallace?' Milo asks.

'He just got in from the office and went to freshen up a bit.'

'The office?'

'She gave me back the ring,' Pablo whimpers, rubbing his knuckles into his eyes. 'Can you believe that? She gave me back the *ring*.'

'She'll come round,' Vera says, mashing. 'You wait and see. Fancy some bangers, Milo? We'll fry you up a couple. Wally adores bangers and mash.'

'What's she want from me?' Pablo cries. 'I *love* her.'

'Leave her alone for a bit,' Vera advises. 'Nothing makes a girl's heart grow fonder than a bit of rejection.'

Sprawled on Milo's bed, Wallace looks fearful.

'What are you doing in here, Wallace?'

'She won't look for me here.'

'You can't stay in my room. This is *my* room. You don't pay for this room.'

'She's frying, isn't she?'

'Yes. Bangers and mash. Your favourite.'

'That kind of food kills you. If you don't stop her she'll just ... she'll just ... you have no idea.'

'Wallace, you're a grown man, buck up.'

'She thinks I have a job.'

'You do have a job.'

'She thinks I have a respectable job.'

'Doing what?'

'Accounting.'

'What's wrong with junk removal?'

'Are you fucking *nuts*? Don't blow my cover. Pablo's in on it. I'm paying him a bonus to shut his trap. Same goes for you.'

'How many bonuses are you paying me? Are you keeping an account of my bonuses?'

'Very funny.'

'I need my room now, Wallace.'

'Waal-leee ...?'

Milo holds the door open. 'Out.'

Burping bangers and mash, he presses his ear against the wall. He knows they're home because the lights are on, but he hears nothing, not even the television.

'Have you got rats?' Vera asks.

'No.'

'What are you listening for then?'

'Oh. Just my neighbours.'

'Spying on them, are you?'

'I just want to make sure they're all right.'

'Might be better to pop round for a visit. Have you got a Hoover?'

'A what?'

'She wants to vacuum,' Wallace moans, climbing the stairs like a dying man.

'Oh, that's not necessary,' Milo says.

'It needs doing,' Vera says.

'I'll get to it.'

'That's what Wally's witless dingbat of a father used to say.'

'Ma, can you just leave it alone?'

'It's not good for your asthma, Wally.'

'You have asthma?' Milo asks.

'His father smoked,' Vera says.

Wallace drags the vacuum cleaner out of the hall closet. 'Here,' he grumbles. Milo marvels at his restraint regarding the F word.

'Jolly good. Now everyone clear out.'

The three of them seek refuge in the living room, sitting with bowls, spooning Vera's instant pudding into their mouths. Pablo repeatedly checks his cell for texts from Maria. 'Women,' he sighs.

Wallace whispers, 'So, Milo, when are you going to set me up with a girlfriend?'

'I'm not. That is so ...'

'Retarded,' Pablo offers.

'Look who's talking about retarded,' Wallace says.

'Get your own girlfriend,' Pablo says.

'Looks like you just lost a girlfriend, asswipe.'

The vacuum switches on again. They can hear her banging it into furniture.

'She'll want to do the windows next,' Wallace warns.

'You should be nicer to her, Wally,' Pablo says.

'Don't call me Wally.'

'You're lucky you have a nice mother. I saw this movie about a guy who hated his mother and then she died and he was really broke up about it, couldn't do nothing, eat, sleep, go to work, nothing. He had, like, a total nervous breakdown.'

Wallace turns on the TV and grimaces at players slamming a puck around.

'So then the mother comes back as a ghost,' Pablo continues. 'At first the guy's, like, totally freaked out and everything.'

The vacuum shuts off again and Milo thinks he can hear Robertson on the trampoline.

'But then the guy's like, *coño*, I can say things to my mother I never could when she was alive …'

'Like "get the fuck out of my face,"' Wallace says.

From the kitchen window, Milo sees Robertson jumping on the trampoline, flapping his arms. He can do this for hour-long stretches, going into a kind of trance. Tanis says it releases tension.

'After the guy gets used to his mother being a ghost,' Pablo elaborates, 'he asks her things he couldn't ask her when she was alive because he hated her so much.' He points his spoon at Wallace. 'Hate blinds you, Wallace. Don't hate your mother.' The vacuum starts up again.

'How does it end?' Milo asks.

'She explains everything. Like why she had to be so mean. She was trying to protect him. Your mother is just trying to protect you from the dust bunnies, Wally.'

'Don't fucking call me that.'

'Does the ghost just vanish again?' Milo asks.

'*Sí.* She has to go back to the other side. It's really sad because the son tries to hug her for the first time in his adult life but he can't because she's a ghost, right? So he tells her he loves her and they blow kisses. It made me cry.'

'Everything makes you fucking cry,' Wallace says.

The vacuum shuts off again. 'Waal-lee … ? Can you move the beds for me, love?'

The baby spider plants should catch Robertson's attention. Several have sprouted from the mama plant and require transplanting. With his fingers Milo digs a hole in the soil and carefully lays a baby spider plant in it. Before filling the pot to the rim, he waters the roots. Once he has patted down the soil he places the pot on the back steps and repeats the procedure with the next plant. He knows he has too many spider plants. Zosia referred to his house as 'the jungle.' Whenever possible, he gives plants away. He has never dared offer one to Tanis because the plants in her house are carefully selected for light conditions, and planted in glazed pots to complement their foliage.

Vera shakes a broom out the back door. 'All that bouncing is going to make that boy's brain leak out his ears. Have you seen Wally?'

'Try my room,' Milo says.

'What's he doing in your room?'

'He likes the view.'

The screen door slams behind her. The trampoline becomes silent. Milo doesn't look around for Robertson but tries to appear absorbed in his planting while contemplating the apparent non-existence of ghosts. If they don't exist why do they keep popping up in movies, books and memories? Two thousand years of civilization and we're still obsessed with spooks. Is it because death is the ultimate reproach, a constant reminder that you never resolved anything? You sat in your jungle and pretended it didn't matter, told yourself that once he was dead it would be over. Which of course it isn't. If a ghostly Gus showed up would he explain why he was such a prick? Would Milo attempt to hug him?

Robertson hands Milo the next baby spider plant. 'Can I put the earth in?'

'Of course.' Milo watches as the boy slowly, deliberately, pours the soil and hollows out a space for the roots. 'Did you go to school today?'

'Yup.'

'How was it?'

'Sucked.'

'Did you have to apologize?'

'Yup.'

'How was that?'

'Sucked.'

'Is Billy off your case?'

'They were passing around notes.' Robertson carefully tips the watering can over the plant. 'They're not supposed to. Mrs. Bulgobin told them not to but they do it anyway. They pass them when she isn't looking.'

'What's in the notes?'

'They say I'm a fag and that I blow Mr. Hilty.'

That eleven-year-olds are homophobic and know about blowing shocks Milo but he tries to appear unfazed. 'How ignorant,' he says finally.

'Don't tell Mum. She'll call the school and I'll get into more trouble.'

'How do you know what's in the notes if they don't pass them to you?'

Robertson digs in his pocket for a crumpled piece of paper and hands it to Milo. Scrawled on the paper in black marker is 'Robertson blows Mr. Hilty.'

'They always call me a fag but they haven't said I blow Mr. Hilty before.' Robertson speaks without malice, as though he's not hurt by the slander but understands that it's intended to humiliate.

'Whose handwriting is that?' Milo asks.

'Billy's. He can't write for shit. Mrs. Bulgobin has to get him to do his homework over so she can read it.'

'This is evidence,' Milo says, handing the note back to him. 'You could get Billy Butthead into serious trouble if you hand this over.'

'Can I give a spider plant to Mrs. Bulgobin?'

'Of course.'

'She doesn't like me.'

Robertson frequently declares that people don't like him. Milo has tried asking, 'What makes you think that?' but the alienation is firmly entrenched, and now he thinks his father doesn't like him either.

'Mrs. Bulgobin brought a hamster to school. She's leaving it in the classroom, which isn't right. Hamsters are nocturnal; they shouldn't be disturbed during the day. When I told her, she said Puffy would adapt. I said how would you like it if somebody put you in a cage and forced you to stay awake when you should be sleeping?'

'What did Mrs. Bulgobin say?'

'Nothing. She was handing out worksheets.'

'I think hamsters in classrooms are pretty common,' Milo says.

'That doesn't make it right.'

Milo approaches Tanis while she's hanging laundry. In the old days, before the increased debt load, she would use the dryer. He hasn't seen her hanging it in the evening before.

'They're talking about rain,' he says.

'It's May, monsoon season is supposed to be over.' She struggles with a sheet. He grabs one end and stretches it away from her. She tosses him a clothes peg. They work side by side hanging the remaining clothes. Tanis seems unconcerned that he is handling her undergarments. The simplicity of her panties moves him: no lace, no leopard spots or zebra stripes, just dove grey. He has admired them flapping on the line, but feeling them is a revelation. He shoves a pair in his pocket.

'Has he talked to you about the hamster?' she asks.

'Yes. That's unfortunate.'

'That's all he talks about, not what those little pricks did to him or about his dad leaving. It's all about Puffy.'

'Maybe he can't talk about the other things.' Milo knows he must remain silent re Billy's note and the alleged blowing of Mr. Hilty. 'Would it be possible to rescue Puffy?'

'What do you mean "rescue"? It's a classroom hamster.'

'What if we offered to buy it?'

'They're not going to sell the classroom hamster. And anyway, they'd just get another rodent, and Robertson would obsess over that one. It's hopeless.' She shakes the last towel hard before pegging it on the line. 'He's not supposed to feel hurt, but he does.'

'Have you tried calling Christopher?'

'Why would I do that?'

'Don't you have to sort out visitation rights? And you could tell him about the bullying.'

'There's always bullying. Billy's mother phoned and gave me an earful, threatened to press charges.'

'Did you tell her Billy hit Robertson in the head with a basketball?'

'Of course. "Not my Billy," she said. "He wouldn't do that. Sometimes them other boys get rough but not my Billy. Your son should be in a special school for boys like him."'

'Did you tell her there are no special schools?'

'Why bother?'

With the laundry basket empty there is nothing left for them to share. He hopes she'll offer him a glass of wine. They could sit at the kitchen table, conversing easily as the light fades.

'Good night, Milo.'

'Good night.'

5

*P*ablo is lying on the couch covered in a blanket.
  'What are you doing here?' Milo demands.
  'Sleeping over.'
  'You can't sleep over.'
  'Vera said it's okay. Just till things cool down with Maria.'
  'Did she call you?'
  'Not yet. Vera says give her couple of days.'
  'You can't sleep here for a couple of days.'
  'I've got cash. Wallace paid me a bonus.' Pablo hands Milo two twenties. 'Two nights. *Claro?*'
  'What happened to your pants? You spill something?'
  'What?'
  Pablo points to Milo's pocket. The moisture from Tanis's underpants is spreading to his crotch. 'What's in your pocket?'
  'Nothing.'
  'It's leaking, take it out.'
  Milo turns his back on Pablo as he removes the underpants but Pablo is off the couch and watching him. '*Coño*, you stole her panties.'
  'I didn't steal them. I was helping her hang laundry.'
  'They're nice, cotton. That's healthy. I don't like those nylon, shiny kind. The pussy's got to breathe, man. She's married though, right?'
  'Not exactly.'
  '*Qué?*'
  'He's left. The husband's left. It's none of your business.'
  'Don't get testy. I'm happy you're in love with a woman.'
  'I'm not in love with her.'
  'You stole her panties. Don't be afraid to love, Milo. It is the one true thing. People afraid to love are lonely, always.'
  'Would you mind? I just want to lie on *my* couch and watch TV.'

'*No hay problema.*' Pablo grabs his blanket and settles on the La-Z-Boy, Gus's La-Z-Boy on which Milo never sits. The chair groans as the Cuban pushes it into the reclining position. 'I love these chairs, man. I wanted to buy one for my mother but she died.'

'Maybe she'll come back as a ghost and you can get her one.'

The remote is not where Milo left it. He searches under newspapers, cushions and jackets.

'Looking for this?' Pablo waves the remote. Milo snatches it and surfs: reality shows, hospital shows, cop shows, all bilge in which he is not starring. How depressing to be facing the black hole at the end of the tunnel and realize that your father was right. Had Milo embraced Krupi and Son Ltd. he might have found a wife and they might have had children and a Labradoodle. He wouldn't be fingering another man's wife's panties.

'So, who you going to get to be Wallace's date?'

'No one.'

'Oh, come on, Milo, he said he'd pay a hundred bucks. You could probably get him up to a deuce, split it with the girl, one of those nudie *chicas* from your art class. I'd like to see one of them.'

'You won't be here.'

'Why, when's she coming? You asked her already?'

'Would you please just go to sleep?'

'No problem.' Pablo pulls the blanket under his chin and squeezes his eyes shut. A talk show is on. A starlet, throttled by cleavage, says she believes in reincarnation. The host compliments her on her breasts, how they're real, how when she lies down naked in movies her breasts flatten out. 'A lot of actresses,' he says, 'when they lie down they stick straight up.' The audience guffaws. The actress asks the host if *he* believes in reincarnation. 'Only if I get to come back with headlights like yours,' he replies. Milo turns off the television and listens for noises next door. Nothing. The panties, bunched in his grip, have lost their grace. He hangs them over the arm of the couch.

'Do *you* believe in reincarnation, Milo?'

'You're supposed to be sleeping.'

'I believe in energy impressions,' Pablo continues. 'All our life we put out energy and it leaves impressions.'

Milo dreads going upstairs where he will be surrounded by Wallace and Vera. This house, Gus's house, has always seemed cavernous. Now it feels like a crowded subway car moving in the wrong direction. If he didn't need the cash, he'd evict the lot of them.

'We leave energy impressions on each other,' Pablo explains. 'All over our hearts and minds and souls. That is why it is so important to forgive. You don't want to leave negative impressions for all time. Think about that, Milo, negative energy impressions for always.'

Is that what Gus left? Negative energy impressions for always all over? The fucker has dented Milo's molecules.

He arrives early, knowing that teacher supervision doesn't begin until eight-thirty, and pretends to be waiting for a bus, keeping his hand on the Spider-Man hood in his pocket. Vera's bacon butties congeal in his gut. At breakfast Wallace was wearing a blazer a size too small and a tie. He left for 'the office' in the Friendly Junk Removal truck. 'Where's your motor?' Vera asked.

'It's in the shop,' Wallace lied. 'A buddy's lending this to me.' He pressed a fifty into Milo's palm before leaving. 'More later,' he said. 'You know what to do.'

Billy the Bully slouches a hundred metres up the street. Milo feels a fury tunnelling through him. He looks around for possible witnesses: only a few stragglers in the yard. If he intercepts the little fucker and drags him behind the dumpster in the parking lot, no one will know. He pulls the Spider-Man hood over his head and strides towards the boy, who is fiddling with his personal listening device, and grabs him by the hoodie.

'What the fuck?' the boy gasps, swatting at Milo's hands as he hauls him off the sidewalk.

'You harass Robertson one more time and I'll cut your balls off and sling them over the hoop, got it?'

'Who the fuck are you?'

'That includes notes, online or off. You slander him again and you will enter a world of pain.'

Billy's squirming forces Milo to grab his orange hair. 'Tell me you understand, you little shit,' he says. 'Understand? Hands off Robertson.'

'I understand.'

Milo releases his grip, and Billy crumples to the tarmac. Fleeing, Milo feels euphoric, energized, like he did as a child after beating up smaller boys: like he can fly – up, up and away. Who says violence doesn't pay?

'We need you to take your shirt off,' the casting director says. His hair is swept up as though he has been licked by a large cow.

'Do you have a problem with that?' a short woman with sharply cornered glasses demands. 'We need to see you with your shirt off. If you have a problem with that, you can go.'

'I'm no James Bond,' Milo says.

'We don't want James Bond,' the woman quips.

Milo starts to remove his shirt, surprised by his bashfulness – he who stands naked in front of strangers. Cool air presses against his nipples.

'Good,' the woman says. 'Now run around, please.' She makes a circular motion with her hand, flashing scarlet fingernails.

'Run around?' Milo asks.

'Do you have a problem with that?'

'The room is small.'

'You can't run around in a small room?'

'Just run around,' the casting director urges, making shooing gestures. 'It'll just take a second.'

Milo begins to run. Commercial auditions have conditioned him to accept humiliation, to co-operate as though lobotomized, no acting required.

'That's great,' the casting director says. Milo feels his gut and breasts bouncing as he runs from one wall to the other.

'Run in circles,' the scarlet-nailed woman orders.

The circles are tiny, causing a mild dizziness, but Milo perseveres, dreaming of cheques.

'That's excellent,' the casting director says.

'Enough?' Milo asks.

'Keep going,' the woman orders, stepping behind the camera. The client and director will view the footage later, will discuss Milo's bouncing breasts and gut, his Everyman expression.

'That's excellent,' the casting director repeats. Panting, Milo feels a sudden urge to remove all his clothes, to wag his penis in the scarlet-nailed woman's face. His hand moves to his fly.

'That's enough,' she commands. 'You can put your shirt back on in the hall.'

'Thanks for coming in,' the casting director says, putting a firm hand on Milo's naked back and ushering him out.

In the corridor a young woman with pink streaks in her hair and an exposed midriff says, 'I know you. I so totally loved painting you. Your body is, like, so totally Everyman.'

Milo has never met one of the artists outside the studio. That this curvaceous young woman has traced his naked contours with a brush causes both mild arousal and embarrassment. He puts his shirt on. 'Do you work here?'

'I work for the caterer.' She points to food trays on a cart. Her toenails are painted rainbow colours. She smells of patchouli.

'Do you aspire to being a painter?' he asks.

'I *am* a painter. You're my favourite model, totally. I keep trying to get you back, but unfortunately most of them want this dancer who's, like, ripped.'

She has seen him naked and is still willing to talk to him. Astonishing. Freed from concerns that his physique will disappoint in the bedroom, he wants to take her right here on the linoleum. 'I didn't get your name,' he says.

'Fennel.'

'I'm Milo.'

'Nice to see you again, Milo.'

'What's that clinking sound?' he asks.

'Ankle bracelets.' She turns to the cart and he knows time is running out.

'Would you come to my house for dinner?' he asks.

'What?'

'There's money in it. A hundred bucks.'

She stares at him and the planet shudders. 'Go fuck yourself.'

'It's not like that,' he says. 'It's an acting job. My friend needs a date to impress his mother. She's visiting from England and thinks he's got a girlfriend. All you'd have to do is be nice and polite for a couple of hours. He might even pay two hundred bucks.' Milo is willing to sacrifice his bonus to prevent Fennel clinking away.

'Cash?'

'Of course. Here's a down payment.' He hands her Pablo's twenties and Wallace's fifty.

'I know karate,' she warns. 'I can inflict bodily harm.'

'I'm sure you can but that won't be necessary.' He pulls out his pen and feels around in his pockets for a scrap of paper.

She holds out her arm. 'Use my wrist.'

'Are you sure?'

She nods glumly. He recognizes the resignation, the need for cash. Art supplies don't come cheap. As he pens his address and phone number on her tender flesh, he senses that she is trying to avoid further bodily contact.

The door to the audition room swings open and the scarlet-nailed woman prods Milo. 'We told you to leave.'

'I *am* leaving.'

'Is this man bothering you?'

'Did he do something wrong?' Fennel asks.

'I didn't do anything.'

The scarlet-nailed woman points her cell at him. 'Leave immediately or I'm calling security.'

'What did he do?' Fennel asks, looking worried, and he feels his chances of recruiting her waning.

'He's unstable,' the scarlet-nailed woman says, grabbing a sandwich from the tray. Behind her back, Milo holds his thumb and pinky to his ear to indicate that Fennel should call him but she looks away. He suspects he is no longer her totally favourite model.

Playing the role of a dad picking up Junior after school, hoping to appear stable while gripping the busted cell, Milo walks purposefully through the heavy doors and scans classroom nameplates until he locates Mrs. Bulgobin's. She's still in there, helping a girl with math. Milo lingers in the corridor, leaning against the wall while pretending to be engrossed in texting. Bulgobin leads the girl out. 'We'll make a photocopy and you can practise at home,' she says. They walk past Milo without a glance. He darts into the classroom, spots the hamster cage and fits it into the garbage bag he has punctured with air holes. Back in the corridor he resumes a preoccupied manner with the cell in one hand and the garbage bag in the other. The wiry-haired, stout man who retrieved Robertson from the schoolyard approaches.

'That's a bit pricey,' Milo says to the cell, looking down at the floor in an attempt to hide his face. 'See if you can get him down a bit.' He pretends to be listening then says, 'I won't go any higher. Tell him he's dreaming.'

Once the wiry-haired man is out of sight, Mrs. Bulgobin waddles towards him.

'It's dropped in value by at least half,' Milo tells the cell as the hamster scurries around in the cage, causing it to shift. 'That's my final offer, tell him he's lucky to get one at all. If he gives you any grief, just pass.'

Mrs. Bulgobin disappears into her classroom and Milo makes haste before she has the opportunity to notice the missing cage.

To hone his acting skills, Milo has always sat in public places observing the ebb and flow of humanity, making note of character details: body language, gaits, clothing choices, mannerisms – all tools for his trade. Gus called him the World's Greatest Loiterer. So waiting outside the Empire Financial building, watching the gainfully employed rush home from the daily grind, feels quite natural to him. He prefers it to being in Gus's house with Vera and Pablo. How long before she discovers the rodent in the basement? Already she is spending an inordinate amount of time below deck, taking charge of Wallace's dirty laundry collection. How wonderful to have someone care enough to pick up your socks stiff with grime, and your skid-marked Jockeys. She's been 'mending' Wally's pants and shirts, sewing on buttons, stitching seams. With her every nurturing gesture, Wallace cringes like a man in torment.

Christopher appears outside Empire Financial looking as though he has forgotten something. He rubs his forehead, feels in his pockets and checks his cell. He begins walking in one direction then changes course, takes a few more steps then stops again, rubbing the back of his neck. The Christopher that Milo knows never hesitates in this manner. He moves with confidence and purpose, circumventing life's disappointments. This new uncertainty must be the result of having hit his son, who he would give his life for; unhinged by remorse, he no longer knows which direction to take.

Abruptly he crosses the street, not bothering to check for cars. Milo ducks into a Mr. Sub until Christopher passes, then begins tailing him. Christopher stares hard at the ground as he walks in the same manner Tanis does. He stops to buy a newspaper from a box, then stands stiffly for several minutes before heading into a Burger King. Milo slips into the Burger King while Christopher orders, sitting at a table covered in wrappings, hoping to appear as though he has just finished a meal. Christopher, order in hand, finds a cleared table by the window. He sets down his food and his paper but touches neither. He checks his cell again, slides it back in his pocket and sits with his head in his hands. Milo had hoped they could make casual contact, giving him a chance to hint at the growing distress on the home front. Minutes pass but Christopher does not touch his food or look at his paper. A squabbling, overfed family swarms the table beside him. The normal boys fling fries at each other. The father slaps their heads. This gets Christopher's attention. 'Eat!' the father orders. Christopher watches them shoving food into their mouths. The pregnant mother stares at the wall, sucking on a pop. 'Shut up,' the father commands when the boys try to speak between mouthfuls.

Christopher leaves the Burger King without his food or his paper. Milo follows with Pablo's words in his head: *Don't be afraid to love, Milo, it is the one true thing. People afraid to love are lonely, always.* Isn't Christopher lonely? What has love brought him but suffering? Milo can't think of one real-life lasting love story. The movie stars acting eternal love, between bouts in rehab, are always divorcing in real life. It's all illusion. So why bother with any of it? Except for Robertson. He must help Robertson.

'Christopher!' he calls.

Christopher, crossing the street without checking for cars, turns his head in Milo's direction just as a cab, pulling a U-turn, slams into his legs.

6

'What kind of name is Fennel?' Pablo asks, stretching out on the couch.

'It's a herb,' Milo says.

'Who the fuck names their kid after a herb?' Wallace mutters. 'Get her to change it, just for the night. Make her Debbie or something.'

'I'm not even sure she's coming.'

'Sabrina,' Pablo suggests. 'Or Margarita.'

'I'm not getting her to change her name. It'll just get confusing.'

'We could call her Fen,' Pablo suggests. 'Or Fenny. Fenny's nice.'

'Call her Fennel,' Milo says more loudly than he'd intended. Vera's frying animal parts.

'Anybody for calf livers?' she calls.

Wallace leans towards Milo and whispers, 'Did you see them in the fridge? She soaks the fucking things in milk then dunks them in flour and fries them.' He puts his finger in his mouth to suggest gagging.

'Have you got any cling film, Milo?' she asks.

'She means Saran Wrap,' Wallace explains.

'Sorry, must be out,' Milo says.

'Add that to the list, Wally.' Wallace begins to cough. He has been coughing regularly since the vacuuming and has even procured a puffer.

'Something's not right with your cooker, Milo,' Vera adds. 'The heat's a bit off.'

'Try putting your head in it,' Wallace grumbles.

'What's that, Wally?'

Milo hears banging on the back door. Suspecting it's Tanis, he considers running for cover. Christopher made him promise to tell her nothing. 'It'll kill her,' he wheezed while Milo covered him with his sweatshirt and shouted at the gawpers to back off. A man in a Detroit Red Wings jacket prodded Christopher. 'Are you a doctor?' Milo demanded. The Red Wings fan started to straighten one of Christopher's legs. 'Don't touch him!' Milo shrieked, shoving the man. 'Nobody touches him until Emergency Services gets here.' He stood over Christopher, waving his arms. When Christopher lost consciousness, word went around that he was dead, which caused gasping and hysteria. The cab driver sat on the curb shaking his head and praying.

'The lady from next door would like a word with you, Milo,' Vera says.

'Okay, tell her I'll be right out.'

Pablo winks at him. 'Don't be afraid to show your true feelings.'

'What true feelings?' Wallace asks.

'About the fence,' Milo says, kicking Pablo.

Vera picks up Tanis's underpants. 'Hel-lo, somebody forgot their knickers.'

All eyes fix on the underpants.

'They're Maria's,' Pablo blurts.

'Patched things up, have you?'

'Not totally,' Pablo says. 'I still have to stay here a couple of nights, if that's okay.'

'No way are you rutting on my couch,' Wallace says.

'It's *my* couch,' Milo intervenes.

Tanis appears with her hair sprung loose and takes her panties from Vera. 'Those are mine, thank you. Milo, can we speak privately for a moment?'

He sits on one of Gus's peeling Muskoka chairs, wishing Tanis would sit on the other one, but she remains standing with arms crossed, the panties scrunched into her fist.

'Remember,' she says, 'Robertson had a Halloween party a couple of years ago and nobody came but you?'

'Christopher's assistant came as Dorothy.'

'You came as Spider-Man.'

'Did I? Hunh. I'd forgotten. I wonder what happened to that costume.'

'Billy Kinney was assaulted by a man wearing a Spider-Man mask.'

'Billy who?' Milo knows exactly who Billy is.

'He woke up this morning with a headache but it got worse after the assault so his mother took him to emerg. Did *you* knock him down?' She stares unwaveringly into Milo's soul, leaving energy impressions.

'Of course not.' He did not knock him down. The boy collapsed before him. He can't say this, can't admit he was there and fled.

'Where were you this morning?'

'What? Here.'

'Vera says you left early.'

There's no question he's going to have to snuff the old crow. 'That's right. I had an audition. That was an experience and a half. I had to run around with my shirt off.'

'You had an audition at eight-fifteen this morning?'

'Correcto, you going to arrest me?' He tries to sit back casually, crossing one leg over the other. He tries to smile bemusedly or innocently – he's not sure which. His mouth freezes in the confusion. 'I'm sorry about the underpants,' he says. 'I don't know how I walked away with them.'

'I know you care deeply about Robertson. But this won't help him. Please don't do it again.' She walks out of his yard into her own, spared the knowledge that her husband is in the trauma centre fighting for his legs and maybe his life. Milo feels so ill suddenly he can't get off the chair.

'Are you asleep?' Robertson asks, squatting by the other Muskoka chair and picking at the paint.

'No.'

'You looked like you were sleeping.'

'I was just thinking.'

'About what?'

'Oh, ice cream. Do you want some?'

'What flavour?'

'Death by Chocolate.'

'Sweet.'

'I'll be right back.' He is afraid that Robertson will grill him as Tanis did and he will act equally badly.

Pablo, Wallace and Vera are watching a reality show featuring a born-again aging bombshell who insists she saves marriages by selling vibrators, fruit-flavoured condoms and lubricants. 'What about the whips and chains, ducky?' Vera demands.

'I can't believe we're watching this,' Wallace says but it is Vera who controls the remote.

'Shut up, Wally, you might learn something.'

Milo scoops massive amounts of ice cream into the bowls, hoping to console Robertson.

'Mum would never let me have that much,' he says.

'Is that right? Well, you're in my yard now.'

Robertson focuses intently on the ice cream, carving it delicately with his spoon. Milo sees Tanis on the deck, presumably looking for Robertson. 'We're having ice cream,' he calls out, attempting to sound cheery. 'Death by Chocolate. Want some?' Tanis doesn't smile.

'Fifteen minutes,' she calls back. Milo remembers too late that she never allows Robertson chocolate before bed because it makes him hyper.

'How was school?'

'Billy got beat up by a guy in a Spider-Man mask. Mum thinks it was you.'

'That's absurd.'

'That's what I said. I said Milo is way too chicken to do something like that.'

Way too chicken?

'Who do you think it was?' Milo asks.

'I don't know but I'm glad. Billy wasn't at school. I hope he never comes back. Probably will though.' Robertson makes little satisfied murmurs as he savours the ice cream. He is entirely in the moment. Milo sees this as one of his gifts. How many people actually live in the moment? Everybody's always thinking about what's happening later or yesterday or ten years ago, ten years from now. He hears his screen door open. 'Have you got any silver paper, Milo?' Vera asks.

'She means aluminum foil,' Wallace interprets.

'No, sorry,' Milo says.

'Add that to the list, Wally. Would you care to join us for a sherry and a spot of cheese, Milo?'

'No, thank you.'

'Add cream crackers to the list, Wally.' The screen door closes.

'Who's that old lady?' Robertson asks.

'Wallace's mother.'

'Is she a new boarder?'

'Short-term.'

'She's loud. Just like your dad. Except your dad swore. It upset *my* dad. My dad never swears.'

Milo searches for signs of damage in the abandoned son. Tanis sees it – wears her child's heart like her own – but to the untrained eye, Robertson just looks like a boy delighting in ice cream. Listening to his contented murmurs, Milo tries to push thoughts of Christopher's mangled legs from his mind.

The ten-block walk to the Copper Pipe takes longer than he'd imagined. He tires, leaning against a newspaper box, weighted with sin – why, when he has freed Robertson, however temporarily, from suffering? Did not Billy the Bully deserve a little scare? And didn't Milo do everything he could for Robertson's broken father? The firefighters told him he did the right thing, even the EMS team thanked him for not moving Christopher. So why does Milo feel that he has failed? Gus would say, 'It's not your concern.' Nothing was. Gus looked out for Gus and Milo. Everything he did was for Gus and Milo. Except it wasn't really Milo but Gus's fantasy of the strapping progeny Milo was destined to become, who would grab a mallet and chisel and emulate the master, carry on the grand tradition of Krupi and Son Ltd. When Gus's clients grew tired of arguing with him, and hired instead what he called ass-kissers to pour their sidewalks, Gus tried to expand his landscaping business. 'People with more money than brains' wanted stone driveways and steps, fences, flower boxes. But even people with more money than brains grew tired of arguing, which left Gus no one to kick around but his son. He picked fights about anything: stray socks, leftovers, TV shows, lawn mowing. Why? Did he feel guilty for surviving a horrific war? Did he abuse his son by way of penance? Milo can't remember him once demonstrating affection, although there is a photo of the two of them his mother must have taken. A very small Milo balances on Gus's knee, biting into a candied apple. Gus looks as though he's waiting for a bus. And yet Milo's mother, Annie, in a sober moment, whispered to him, 'Your dad would do anything to protect you. He'd pick a fight with God if he had to.' So why didn't Milo feel protected?

He sits next to a sickly weeping fig.

'Milo,' Zosia says, apparently not in the least surprised to see him. 'Are you ordering?'

'A Sleeman's, please.' She's put on weight; maybe she's overeating because she misses him. 'I just thought I'd drop by,' he calls after her, attracting the attention of pizza eaters. He leans back in an effort to appear relaxed.

Shrivelled weeping fig leaves fall into his lap. Zosia and the moustached bartender stand a little too close. The bartender puts his hand on the small of her back and says something that makes her snort. Zosia never laughs, only snorts. She returns with Milo's beer but doesn't linger.

'We splurged on a couple of things,' a woman in stripes at the next table announces. 'First we bought a house, then we bought a car, a *new* car, we didn't want a used car. We wanted something reliable, you know, we'll drive it for fifteen years, run it into the ground, that sort of thing. Anyway, now we're ready.'

For what? Milo would like to know. The man beside her looks as though he never sleeps.

'I'm doing Pilates,' the striped woman declares. 'It's supposed to help with stress but all that breathing makes me tense.'

Zosia swings by again and ruffles Milo's hair, which seems a friendly gesture if not fraught with desire. 'How's the acting business?' she asks, her s's sounding like z's.

'I had a commercial audition today,' he says.

'Good for you.' She says *good for you* to anyone. Pablo admired her for this, felt she was being positive, while Milo knew she was just bored, her engineer brain hungering for electronic circuits.

'Do you remember Christopher?' he asks. 'My neighbour?'

'The grass cutter.'

'He got hit by a car today.'

'Killed?'

'Don't know yet.'

'Poor little boy.' She used to construct tall towers with Robertson that would eventually tumble. 'You must build with him.'

The striped woman waves frantically at Zosia. 'Excuse me, miss, there is no eggplant on this pizza. We specifically requested eggplant.'

Zosia stares at what remains of the pizza.

'There was *no* eggplant,' the striped woman assures her.

'Why didn't you tell me that before you ate it?' Zosia inquires.

The sleep-deprived man says, 'You better not charge us for eggplant.'

'There was no eggplant,' the striped woman repeats.

'We're not paying for any eggplant,' the sleepless man insists.

'Whatever,' Zosia says, which was her fourth English word. She turns back to Milo. He considers ordering a pizza but he is cash-poor due to Fennel's advance. 'You don't have to order,' she says.

'Oh, okay, well, I was just wondering if you'd made any progress on the job front?'

'Zilch. You?'

'My agent says I'm experiencing a renaissance as Everyman.'

'Good for you.'

'We'd like our bill, please,' the striped woman says.

'Make sure you deduct the eggplant,' the sleepless man adds.

Milo forgot to buy a honey-I-love-you ring. How could he have come all this way and occupied a table for the price of one beer without a *ring*? Where words have failed, a gesture might have spoken volumes. He shakes a fig leaf out of his hair. 'You might want to water this tree,' he says but she is gone.

He knocks softly on the sliding doors. Tanis approaches, groggy, opening the doors only a crack. 'What is it?'

'Robertson wanted to give Mrs. Bulgobin a spider plant.' Milo holds the plant up to the light.

'Why?'

'He doesn't think she likes him.'

'She doesn't. Why would he give her a plant? Was this your idea?'

'Definitely not. He helped me plant the babies.'

'I see. Well, spider plant, Spider-Man. Don't you think she might connect the dots?'

'I hadn't thought of that.'

'That's your problem, Milo. You don't think. Good night.' She slides the doors closed. He wants to call after her but he is way too chicken.

'Thoughts are circular,' Pablo says. With the La-Z-Boy in full reclining mode he is able to trace large circles in the air with his arms. 'You ever noticed that?'

Milo, remote in hand, surfs.

'You wake up and you think it's a new day and what happens? Circles.'

An actress straddles an actor on a couch. He fondles her breasts. 'Which is not necessarily a negative thing,' Pablo adds. '*Life* is circular. Me and Wallace were doing demolition at the Centre of Circular Wisdom because Sarah Moon Dancer don't want no square walls there anymore, and she said ...'

Milo cranks the volume, amplifying the actress's orgasmic moans. Vera stamps on the floor above. 'Turn that bloody thing down,' she calls. He does to stop her stomping downstairs.

Pablo adjusts the La-Z-Boy to a sitting position. 'Sarah Moon Dancer says we have to accept life's circularity before we can begin our transformational healing.' The actor rolls the actress onto her back and thrusts into her. 'Your neighbour was mad about the panties, wasn't she? I wouldn't worry about it. Women like it when men steal their panties, they just don't show it.'

'Did Maria call?'

'I left another message.'

'You can't stay here.'

'You need a friend, Milo. I saw this movie about this guy who's, like, so bottled up inside, you know, like he can't talk to nobody, and then he meets this waitress who's, like, totally open. At first he's, like, "no way am I hanging out with a waitress," you know, but she's so totally open ...'

'They get naked,' Milo interjects.

'Not right away. It's a journey, right?'

'Circular.'

'Exactly.'

Milo retreats to a cot in the basement and watches the hamster cage, expecting Puffy to scurry about on the wheel experiencing his circularity, but no, in the dead of night, the nocturnal rodent is asleep. Hanging from hooks above Milo's head are Gus's implements for cutting, drilling, sawing, bashing and splitting rock. They have always frightened Milo with their sharp edges and blunt heads. One mistake and off goes a finger, oops, there goes a foot. His father took great care of his tools, sharpened and oiled them on his days off. Milo inhales the toxic stench of oily rags and Varsol in an attempt to get stoned, to forgive and be forgiven – to begin his transformational healing. Another fig leaf drops from his hair.

7

'They want to see you again,' his agent says. 'ASAP. These folks are serious.'

'They made me run around half-naked.'

'Whatever you did, chief, do it again. We're talking serious coin here. Three spots, *national*. We're talking serious residuals.' Stu runs his hand over his bald pate as though checking for growth. 'Your new look is working for you, seriously.'

'What new look?'

'Are you serious? You've filled out a bit, you're looking more mature.'

When Zosia dumped him, Milo stopped seeing a barber and shaving regularly. 'I've been thinking of getting a haircut.'

'Are you crazy? This look fits a demographic they're targeting. Go for it. Seriously. Can you sing?'

'No.'

'They just want you to be a regular guy singing while you sling back a few.'

'I can't sing.'

'Sure you can.' Stu rubs his thumb and index finger together to suggest the serious coin awaiting Milo. 'Three fifteen.'

'Today?'

'That's what I'm telling you, chief. They're hot to trot.' His phone rings again. 'I've got to take this one. Let me know how it goes. You look great, seriously.'

The black eyes and swelling make Christopher almost unrecognizable. His nose has been splinted and bandaged. A plastic tube, poking out from his ribs a few inches below his armpit, drains into a plastic container. His right lower leg is encircled in metal hoops. Wires attached to the hoops pierce his skin, presumably to hold the bone fragments in place. His left upper leg is splinted. A clear tube runs from under the blankets to a receptacle filled with urine, marked with gradations. Christopher doesn't seem to recognize Milo, or maybe doesn't want to recognize him. Hooked up to an IV, he is probably disoriented by morphine. The patient in the next bed has numerous visitors who bump against the dividing curtain, speaking loudly in what Milo thinks is Portuguese. He sits on the vinyl chair beside Christopher's bed, staring at the metal hoops on his leg, unable to imagine his pain. At least he still has both legs. Milo didn't ask the nurses for a prognosis because they knew he wasn't a relative. He did inquire if any relatives had been notified. The nurses remained poker-faced, just as they did when he was six and his mother was rushed to emergency. They wouldn't let him see her. Years later he assumed it was because Annie was already dead and they didn't want a six-year-old crawling over the corpse. His father even forbade him to go to the crematorium. Milo didn't know what a crematorium was but he wanted to go. At the funeral, falling temperatures had turned the melted snow to ice. The pallbearers repeatedly lost their footing, causing the coffin to tip and the white flowers to tumble to the ground. Milo wanted to put them back but his father restrained him. The pallbearers tried to retrieve them but each time they managed to put the flowers back another foot would slip, the coffin would tip and they'd have to begin the process all over again. Milo thought it was funny except that his mother was being slammed around in the box and he feared her bones would break. After they pushed her into the hearse, Milo scampered around collecting the remaining flowers, most of them trampled. He put them in a glass of water when he got home but they turned brown and died anyway. Mrs. Cauldershot threw them out. Milo wanted to visit his mother's grave, to take flowers and sit beside it and talk.

'There is no grave,' Gus said.

'How come?'

'Because I scattered her ashes at Grandma's farm, in the orchard. That's what she wanted.'

'Can I go to the orchard?' He knew his grandmother was very ill and found his visits tiresome.

'Eat your meat.'

Milo hated his father for burning his mother. Chewing on pork, he decided to make a grave for her in the backyard behind her lilac, where no one could see.

'Milo?' Christopher mumbles, sounding nasally. 'What did they do to my nose?'

'Splinted it.'

'I can hardly breathe.'

'There's probably swelling. Your face is pretty bruised.'

Christopher closes his eyes, clearly exhausted from being trapped inside a fractured body. The Portuguese behind the curtain chortle.

'Milo?'

'Yes?'

'Did you fuck my wife?'

'Of course not, how could you think that?'

'I have to piss,' Christopher says.

'You're hooked up to a catheter.'

Christopher grunts slightly. 'Is anything coming out?'

Milo looks at the tube. 'Nothing yet.'

Christopher winces.

Milo sees yellow. 'Bingo.'

A nurse with a limp shuffles in and examines the urine receptacle. 'Good output,' she says. 'Keep it up.' She pushes past the curtain and speaks loudly to the Portuguese crowd. 'This is trauma ICU. We have limited visits here. He needs to rest now.'

The Portuguese apologize. Milo hears kissing as they bid adieu to the patient.

'That goes for you too,' she says to Milo. One of her eyeballs doesn't move.

'I'll just say goodbye.'

She holds up two fingers. 'Two minutes.'

Christopher continues to stare at the hoops on his leg. Milo ponders the clumsiness of life and death, the endless stumbling and smashing into things. The circularity of it.

'I don't know what you're doing here, Milo, but whatever it is, you don't have to do it. Are they all right? You didn't tell them?'

'No.'

The limping nurse returns to check Christopher's chest tube.

'What's that for?' Milo asks.

'His lung collapsed. Broken rib. Off you go. You can see him tomorrow.'

'I'll bring you some fresh fruit,' Milo says but Christopher is once again freed of consciousness.

The agency people and the clients sit behind a table, sipping bottled water. Milo starts removing his shirt before he is asked. The casting director with the cowlicked hair and the scarlet-nailed woman with the sharply cornered glasses hover.

'What's shakin', Milo?' asks a fleshy-lipped man in a leather jacket who Milo assumes must be the director. 'So, what have you been up to?'

Milo loathes show-biz folks' uninterested, insincere questions. 'Well,' he begins, 'I got up this morning, ate some toast with marmalade, had a dump, got on the subway and visited a friend who got smashed by a car, then I scooted over to see you guys.'

'Super, do you think you can run around for us again?'

'Absolutely.' He starts to run, so fast he bashes into the wall. The people sitting at the table chuckle. Trained to respond to laughs, Milo runs faster and hits the wall harder.

'Whoa, boy,' the fleshy-lipped director says. 'Do you know the song "Ninety-nine Bottles of Beer on the Wall"?'

'One of my faves.'

'Do you think you can sing it while you're running?'

'No prob.' Milo resumes running, belting out, 'Ninety-nine bottles of beer on the wall, ninety-nine bottles of beer, take one down, pass it around, ninety-eight bottles of beer on the wall.'

The table-sitters respond favourably and he wishes they'd attended *Waiting for Godot.*

'Ninety-eight bottles of beer on the wall,' he hollers, 'ninety-eight bottles of beer, take one down, pass it around, ninety-seven bottles of beer on the wall.'

'Super,' the director says. 'Now take a swig for us.' He hands a beer bottle to Milo. 'Drink it like you've been in the desert for a week.'

Milo grabs the bottle and gulps so feverishly that the beer – actually ginger ale – spills onto his breasts and gut. His audience roars. Milo rubs the ginger ale over his breasts and gut, making primordial noises, further delighting the table-sitters.

'Super,' the director says. 'Do you lift weights?'

'Do I look like I lift weights?' More laughs. He can do no wrong.

'See those dumbbells over there?' the director says. 'Could you lie on the floor and lift them, do a kind of a bench-press thing, singing the beer song at the same time?'

It occurs to Milo that they might be hot to trot because no one else could withstand this degree of humiliation. But what does he care, the actor who can't act? It's all clumsy and relentless, this stumbling and smashing into things – a fucking obstacle course terminating in a crab walk to the crematorium. He drops to the floor and rolls onto his back, belting the tune while swinging the dumbbells. He tries swinging one leg up then the other. The table-sitters stand and he feels an ovation pending.

'Do you want me to jack off as well?' he yells. The laughter halts, replaced by a quick intake of breath. The table-sitters stand motionless before resuming their seats and sipping their bottled water.

'You are one wild and crazy guy,' the director says. 'Good to meet you. Thanks for coming in.'

The casting director snatches Milo's shirt off a chair. 'Upsy-daisy,' he says.

'You can dress in the hall,' the scarlet-nailed woman snipes before turning to the director and muttering, 'I told you he was unstable.'

And it's over. Milo's fifteen minutes of fame.

Pablo, bare-chested, a small mound of muscle, suns in one of the Muskoka chairs. Where there is sun there is the Cuban. In winter he chases the rectangles of sunlight spilling through windows.

'Why are you always here?' Milo demands. 'You don't live here. I said you could stay two nights.'

'Sorry, sir, but I don't got no place to go with Maria mad at me.' He only calls Milo *sir* when he's being obsequious. 'I got another twenty for you.' Milo snatches it from him.

Vera shakes a broom out the back door. 'What's that mouse doing in the cellar, Milo?'

'What mouse?'

'It got out of the cage and chewed up Wally's socks.'

'Where is it now?'

'You just said "what mouse" like you didn't know about no mouse,' Pablo says.

'It's a hamster. I'm taking care of it.'

'Well, you've done a bloody poor job of it,' Vera says. 'Lord only knows what it will get up to next. The wiring, I expect.'

'I'll find it.'

He digs around in the hall closet for Gus's fishing net, although he hasn't seen it for years and suspects it's behind all the other gadgets he can't bring himself to trash.

'Bit of a rat's nest, isn't it?' Vera observes. She's polishing his mother's silver candle holders. 'These are lovely. It's a shame you let them tarnish. I've never seen anything half so grand.'

'They were a wedding present for my mother.'

'She must have been a lovely bride. Have you any photos?'

'No.' He does but doesn't want to show them to her.

'It must have been heartbreaking for you, losing her so young. Wally says you know how to cook because you had no mum. His sweetheart's coming on Saturday.'

'She is?' Fennel called despite his instability? She must be cash-starved.

'She sounds darling. I thought you and I could put our heads together and come up with something top-drawer. Oh, and I darned these socks for you.' She hands him the socks. No one has ever darned his socks. 'Wally's the same way, always wearing through his heels. I hope you don't mind me doing a bit of your laundry, it just seems a bit rash running the washer just for Wally.' She sets the candle holders on the table. 'Won't Fennel be impressed? It's a nice name, Fennel. Very original. Have you met her?'

'No.' How did he become so mired in deceit? Soon he won't be able to speak for fear of uttering the truth.

'You can't go wrong with Yorkshire pud and a nice roast. What do you say, Milo?'

'Super.'

He lies prone on the basement floor searching for Puffy. Seeing the candle holders caused his heart to spasm. Annie polished them monthly. After she died they slowly tarnished until Mrs. Cauldershot shoved them in the closet.

'Where are Mummy's candlesticks?' Milo asked.

'What do you care?' Mrs. C. replied.

'They're Mummy's.'

'Well, Mummy's not here to polish them. Your father doesn't pay me to sit around polishing silver.'

What did he pay her for, Milo wanted to ask, because it seemed to him Mrs. C. spent a lot of time sitting around watching TV. When Annie stopped getting out of bed, Gus hired Mrs. Cauldershot to help. But Mrs. C. scared Annie and 'made no bones about the fact' that she thought Annie was 'spoiled' and 'lazy' and should 'pull herself together.' Annie and Milo huddled together while Mrs. C. slammed around the house, cursing at the world's injustices. She softened when Gus was around and always made sure dinner was ready when he came home. Milo found her niceness as she served his father even scarier than her meanness. With Mrs. Cauldershot in the house, Milo knew his mother would never come out of her room. So he brought the candle holders and polish to Annie and helped her rub them till they sparkled. When his mother didn't seem to care about the candle holders anymore, he buffed them himself, hoping to impress her, but she didn't seem to notice. 'Look, Mummy,' he'd say, waving them in front of her uninhabited eyes. Why does he care so much about Annie when he hardly knew her? Is he mourning for what might have been, drowning in fantasies of devoted mother love when, doubtless, her only devotion would have been to the bottle? And can he hold this against her when he, after returning home with what Gus referred to as a 'bullshit of arts degree,' began drinking on the side? Just beers, then more beers. It gave him the courage to utter the occasional profanity at the old man, even though he understood that Gustaw had once been a boy who lost everything, who got off a boat – or was it a plane – in a strange country with little more than the clothes on his back and a sack of tools. Why can't Milo forgive? What right has he to judge? He who runs around half-naked in front of strangers?

If his father were here, Milo would say he is sorry – for what exactly he isn't sure, but there it is, a sticky guilt that no amount of rubbing will remove.

He places Puffy's cage on the floor and shakes more hamster food into the bowl, then grabs the empty laundry basket and collects sawed-off ends of wood from his father's projects. It's eerie touching them, knowing that his father's hands held, measured, sawed and discarded them. Gus spent most of his retirement down here. His old cassette player, coated in dust, perches high on a shelf. Milo presses *play* and hears what he thinks must be Polish folk songs. Gus refused to speak Polish, why would he listen to it? What memories and longings did he allow out of the box during his subterranean hours? One photograph of him as a child in pre-war Poland survived. In what must have been his best clothes, he stands holding hands with a girl in a gingham dress. Milo once asked who the girl was. 'Can't remember,' Gus said.

'You're holding her hand,' Milo, who was only seven, pointed out. 'You must remember her if you held her hand.' He, personally, had never held a girl's hand, although he'd thought about it. The girl in the picture had dark eyes and braids and was slightly taller than Gustaw. In her other hand she gripped a daisy. 'Did you give her that flower?' Milo asked.

'Can't remember.'

'What was her name?'

'Go help Mrs. Cauldershot with the dishes.'

Milo hasn't seen the photo since, but he suspects the dark-eyed girl ended up naked in a mass grave.

'What are you doing?' Robertson asks.

'Building.'

'You never build.'

'I thought I'd try. I have all these bits of wood and I thought maybe I'd make a sculpture.'

'What kind?'

'I don't know. Do you have any ideas?' Milo's been in the yard for forty-five minutes pretending to be interested in wood scraps while Robertson has been on the trampoline.

'You could make a tower,' Robertson suggests.

'Do you think that's possible? They're all different shapes.'

Robertson takes the scrap from him and finds another piece that fits perfectly. He picks up the hammer and digs around in the tin for the right nail. This could take hours, which was what Milo intended.

'Somebody stole Mrs. Bulgobin's hamster,' Robertson says. 'Mum thinks it was you.'

'How outrageous.'

'That's what I said. I said, "Milo is way too chicken."' Anyway, Mrs. Bulgobin thinks I did it. I'm just worried about Puffy. I hope the kidnapper is taking care of her.'

How easy it would be to reveal the truth, but then Robertson would feel obliged to tell his mother. And Tanis would be very angry, even angrier, with Milo, and order the hamster back to school, which would distress Robertson even more.

'I hope they didn't feed her to lizards,' Robertson says, hammering another block of wood onto the tower.

The four of them eat cream crackers with processed cheese while watching a reality show featuring foodaholics. Pablo isn't using a plate. Cracker crumbs fly in all directions.

They hear banging on the back door again.

'Must be your lady friend from next door,' Vera says.

With her hair unbound, Tanis looks mildly deranged. 'Did you go into the school yesterday?'

'The school?' Milo leans against the door frame in an effort to appear nonchalant. 'Why would I do that?'

'The hamster is missing.'

'What hamster?'

'The hamster Robertson was worried about. Someone *stole* the hamster.'

'Who would steal the hamster?'

'Someone who doesn't want Robertson to be extremely worried.'

'Well, that would be very considerate of them.'

'No, it would not. Because Mrs. Bulgobin thinks Robertson took the hamster and is lying about it. I was called into the principal's office again today. They believe my child is evil. They don't admit this, of course, because it wouldn't be politically correct to condemn a mentally challenged child.'

'I took the hamster.'

'I know you did.'

He could kiss her at this moment because she doesn't accuse, doesn't shout. She just knows. 'What do you want me to do about it?'

'Take it back and explain.'

'It's escaped.'

'How?'

'I guess the cage wasn't closed properly. It's on the lam in the basement.'

'Does Robertson know?'

'No.'

'Let's find it.'

They crawl around on the basement floor with flashlights. He would like to reach out and touch her, console her, make it all better.

Pablo's workboots, unlaced as always, appear before him. 'Fennel's on the phone.'

'Who's Fennel?' Tanis asks.

'Some nudie *chica* from Milo's art class. She's coming for dinner Saturday.'

'She's not a model, she's a painter.' With Tanis's eyes on him, he tries to appear laid-back, as though having a *chica* dinner guest is not out of the ordinary.

'I asked if she likes strawberries,' Pablo says, 'because me and Vera are making trifle and Vera says lots of people are allergic to strawberries. She knows a lady who breaks out all in hives.'

'Go for it, Milo,' Tanis says. 'I'll keep up the hunt.'

'You want me to help?' Pablo asks. Leaving Pablo in the basement, bare-chested and familiar with Tanis's underpants, causes Milo unease.

He checks the kitchen to make sure Vera is out of earshot before picking up the phone. 'So I hear you're coming Saturday,' he whispers. 'Thank you.'

'Yeah, but now I'm scared I'm going to screw up, like, I mean, I'm a lousy liar.'

'I'll do the lying, just be nice and polite.'

'I'm not giving back the cash if I screw up.'

'You won't screw up. Just show up. Please.'

'I can't promise how I'll act. I'm pretty spontaneous. I mean, sometimes I say the wrong thing and I don't even realize it. What's my boyfriend's name again?'

'Wallace, or Wally.'

'How will I recognize him?'

'He's bigger than everybody else.'

'Tell him if he touches me I'll kick his nads in. And I don't eat mammals.'

'Does that mean you won't eat roast beef and Yorkshire pud?'

'Last I heard a cow is a mammal.'

'Couldn't you just have a bit of meat, just for show?'

'Not negotiable.'

'Okay, well, I'll sit beside you and when Vera's not looking you can slip me your mammal.'

Back below ground, Milo finds Pablo lifting Tanis, clutching her around the hips as she checks around ceiling beams. Her naked thighs below her cut-offs and Pablo's naked chest are pressed together. Milo restrains a strong impulse to swing one of Gus's mallets at his head.

'Nothing here,' Tanis says.

'Put her down,' Milo orders, more gruffly than he'd intended.

She puts her hands on Pablo's naked shoulders as he sets her down.

'Would you mind putting a shirt on?' Milo almost shouts. 'This isn't fucking Cuba.'

'*Sí, señor.*'

Immediately regretting having revealed his lurid jealousy, Milo practises damage control. 'I just don't understand why you can't wear a shirt. This is Canada. It's polite.'

'Don't shirt up on my account,' Tanis says and Milo suspects she enjoyed rubbing against Pablo's smooth brown muscles. How disgusting: in the midst of the hamster crisis she is feeling up a Cuban. He would like to scream that her husband may be dying.

'I'm going outside,' he says.

He sits by his mother's grave even though her body was burned. The lilac has tripled in size since the day Milo taped two sticks together and stuck them in the ground.

These feelings he has for Tanis are completely inappropriate. These feelings must stop.

'Are you all right?' she asks.

'Quite. Did you catch it?'

'No. Why are you hiding in the bushes?'

'I'm resting.'

She sits beside him. He wants to slide his tongue over her legs.

'Pablo was just trying to help,' she says.

'I know what Pablo was doing.'

'You didn't tell me he worked on a mushroom farm. It's criminal how they exploit those workers. It's good of you to take him in.'

Oh, so Milo has done something right for a change, except he hasn't done it.

'You have to speak to the principal, Milo.'

'I know.'

'Thank you for building with Robertson.'

'Is he in bed?'

She nods. 'He's been walking in circles again.'

'Maybe the hamster would help. If he had it to care for.'

'Stealing is wrong.'

How can she believe in right and wrong? It's never that simple. 'I'm the one who stole it. *I'm* the sinner. Robertson could be the hamster handler.'

She stares at her house as though waiting for someone to come out of it. 'Billy Kinney's in a coma. It was an aneurysm. I hope, for your sake, you didn't cause it.' She starts to get up but he grabs her hand.

Robertson appears in his pyjamas with the dog in tow. 'What are you guys doing?'

'What are you doing out of bed?' Tanis asks, snatching her hand away.

'I'm worried about Puffy. Maybe we should call the police.'

'Possum, you have to stop worrying about the hamster. Whoever took it must have really wanted it and will take care of it.'

'Unless they feed her to their lizards. People buy boxes of mice to feed their lizards.'

'The hamster is in my basement,' Milo declares, without looking at Tanis who will despise him for his weakness in the face of righteousness. Robertson blinks repeatedly as he computes this new information.

'I took Puffy,' Milo explains, 'because I wanted you to stop worrying about him.'

'Her.'

'Her. But she has escaped and you are the only man who can rescue her.'

Robertson and Sal charge to Milo's. Tanis remains disconcertingly still.

'You shouldn't have done that,' she says and walks away. He listens to the soft flapping of her flip-flops before hurrying to his computer to find out exactly what an aneurysm is, and if he could have caused it. *An aneurysm is a pre-existing defect in an arterial wall that, over time, balloons and thins out. Eventually the ballooned vessel can burst, causing bleeding in the brain and loss of consciousness.*

A pre-existing defect causing loss of conciousness. Does that mean the aneurysm made Billy crumple, not Milo? *There can be a genetic link. Family members are often screened after a case is found. Triggers for the rupture can be random. Stress and raised blood pressure may contribute. An aneurysm is usually but not always lethal, depending on its location, the extent of the bleeding and how quickly care can be delivered.*

Stress and raised blood pressure may contribute. Like being grabbed by a man in a Spider-Man mask and hauled behind a dumpster? Or not.

8

*m*ilo sits on the bench and waits alongside the other naughty boys who pick their noses and swing their legs. The principal's secretary is on the phone enthusing about her slow cooker. 'I just put a bunch of stuff in the pot and go to work and when I come back it's cooked. I'm not kidding. You have to fry the meat a bit first though, right, but then my neighbour told me to just add the flour, like, just dump it on top.'

Milo stands again, hoping to get her attention.

'That's what *I* thought,' the secretary says, 'but my neighbour said just dump it on top. I'm not kidding. She just throws stuff in and comes back eight hours later.'

'Excuse me,' Milo interjects. 'Do you have any idea when Mr. Gedge will be in?'

'Do you have an appointment?'

'No.'

'Well, then I can't help you, sir.'

'But these boys are waiting for him. How long do they usually have to wait?'

'We don't mind waiting,' one of the boys offers.

'It's way better than being in class,' adds the other. They're both wearing T-shirts emblazoned with superheroes.

'May I ask what this is regarding?' the secretary inquires.

'It's about the missing hamster.'

'What about it?'

'I know where it is.'

'Did you bring it with you?'

'No.'

She narrows her eyes for several seconds while flicking her pen. 'One moment.' She dials what Milo suspects is Gedge's cell. 'Your name, please?'

'Milo Krupi.'

'A Mr. Crappy's here,' she says. 'He says he knows where the hamster is.' She pauses, still eyeing Milo. 'No, he did not bring it with him. He's waiting to see you.' She removes one of her shoes and shakes something out of it. 'Very good, sir.' She hangs up. 'Mr. Gedge will be here shortly. Take a seat.'

How absurd that Milo, a grown man, should feel his bowels loosening while waiting for the principal. Mr. Grocholsky, in this very same office, unjustly reprimanded him for talking in class. It wasn't Milo's fault that Dean Blinky and Horace Blunt, gabbing on either side of him, were exchanging hockey cards. Just as it's not his fault that Billy the Bully had a ballooning vessel in his head that burst. Tanis is unjustly reprimanding Milo. He tries hard to believe this as he stares at dirty linoleum between his feet.

The stout, wiry-haired man who retrieved Robertson from the yard appears and speaks gruffly to the naughty boys, concluding with, 'I don't want to see you here again.' Off they schlump to be enlightened. 'Mr. Crappy?'

'Yes. Actually, it's Krupi.'

'Come into my office.'

The decor has changed. Pictures of sailboats adorn the walls.

'What's this about the hamster?' Gedge asks, hands on hips, clearly not a man to mince words.

'I took it.'

'Or did your child take it? It's perfectly natural to want to protect your child.'

'I don't have a child. I took it.'

Gedge, no doubt accustomed to listening to excuses, waits for one.

'I took it because hamsters are nocturnal. It's very stressful for them to be exposed to daylight when they should be sleeping. On Google it says the rate of hamster death is higher in classrooms because the hamsters are constantly exposed to noise, artificial light and handling.'

Gedge sits at his desk, taking a deep breath. While waiting for his exhalation, Milo has visions of last night's carnage. When Tanis insisted the hamster had to be returned, it was as though she'd plunged a knife into Robertson.

'If you're not a parent,' Gedge says, 'how did you know about the hamster?'

'A friend of mine is in the class.'

'And who might that be?'

'I'd rather not say.' He must protect Robertson from further persecution. The head-banging did not stop until four a.m.

'It wouldn't be Robertson Wedderspoon by any chance?'

'Robertson who?'

Gedge takes another deep breath. 'Did it occur to you, Mr. Krupi, that in rescuing the hamster for your friend, you caused the other children considerable distress?'

'That did occur to me, yes. For this reason I was hoping you might allow me the opportunity to explain my actions to them. And, of course, I'd like to reimburse the school for the price of the cage and Puffy.'

'I take it you don't intend to return the hamster?'

'I'd rather not. My friend is very attached to it. I was hoping that, when I tell the children about the trauma and shortened life spans of hamsters in classrooms, they might not want Puffy.'

Gedge places his elbows on the desk, clasping his hands under his chin. 'In all my years, Mr. Krupi, I have never encountered such a situation.'

'It is unusual.'

'I have half a mind to report you to the police.'

'I completely understand that, sir, and if, after I have spoken with the children, you still wish to press charges I will not resist arrest.'

These are not the upturned faces of the innocent. With brand names stretched across their apparel they are the pawns of the consumer age. Already the judgmental expressions of their parents shadow their faces. These are Robertson's foes, and Milo has no choice but to plead for mercy. 'They get tumours,' he explains, 'from the stress caused by lack of sleep and handling.'

'You mean they get cancer?' a boy in a Roots Athletics hoodie asks.

'That is correct. And the tumours grow and make it difficult for them to swallow. They stop eating and eventually die.'

A girl in an American Apparel tank top says, 'Mine got tumours on his testicles. They got so big he couldn't walk.' The other consumer pawns titter.

'It wasn't in a classroom though,' the boy in the hoodie, a future litigator, points out. 'Which means they die anyway, even if they're not in a classroom. You've got no proof they die sooner in a classroom.'

'As I said, it's all online.'

'Don't believe everything you read online,' the litigator scoffs.

'Try to imagine,' Milo says, 'living in a small cage with nothing but wood shavings and dried seeds for company. Imagine it's bedtime and you're exhausted but you can't turn the light out and you hear loud voices and chairs scraping and doors slamming. Imagine you're finally about to doze off when a *giant hand* opens the cage and grabs you.' Milo raises his hands, spreading his fingers to make them giant-like. 'Suddenly you're hoisted into the air and being passed around. Each time you try to escape, the *giant hands* grip you tighter,' he tightens his fists, 'so hard you can't breathe and you feel your life being squeezed out of you.' Some of the children's mouths gape. 'Imagine you're blindfolded, because hamsters can't see in daylight due to their large pupils. So there you are, a blinded hostage, suffocating, lost in space with no knowledge of when this torture will end. You wait for the giants to kill you, to squash you between their massive palms ...'

'I think you've made your point, Mr. Krupi,' Mrs. Bulgobin interjects.

'And then what happens?' Milo persists. 'You get dropped back in the cage with nothing but wood shavings and dried seeds for company. And as much as you hate the loud, bright, noisy cage, you prefer it to being in the giants' grip. You live in fear of the giant hands reaching in and grabbing you again and again, squeezing the breath out of you ...'

'That's enough, Mr. Krupi.'

'And they do,' Milo says, 'day in and day out, they *snatch* you from the cage.'

'I'm calling Mr. Gedge,' Bulgobin says.

'Let's take a vote,' Milo says. 'Who thinks Puffy should be forced to live caged in the classroom forever?'

The litigator raises his hand.

'That's one vote for jailing Puffy for life,' Milo says. 'Hands up for those who think Puffy should be free?'

Many hands shoot up.

'Case closed,' Milo says. 'I've made a donation to your school so you can either buy a snake or a lizard, or think of something fun to do like have a pizza lunch. Thank you so much for your time and co-operation.' He thinks he smiles warmly but respectfully at Mrs. Bulgobin before hastily bowing out.

...

'We want raw emotion onstage,' Geon Van Der Wyst advises Milo. 'Don't think *stage*.' He makes air quotes with his fingers when he says *stage*. 'Forget *stage*. There is no fourth wall. You and the audience are symbiotic. Your emotional reality and their emotional reality are one.'

Milo avoided this kind of touchy-feely bilge when he knew how to act, but now he is desperate for a job and Geon Van Der Wyst is famous for acquiring grant funding for multimedia projects no one ever sees.

'It's about trust,' Geon emphasizes. 'No trust, no raw emotion. Remove the barriers and it will come.'

'Is there a script?' Milo asks.

Geon Van Der Wyst looks wearily at his assistant, an emaciated woman named Hunter.

'No script,' Hunter says. Her eyes are heavily lined with black pencil.

'I saw you in *Godot*,' Geon says. 'I felt you pulling at the restraints.' He mimes pulling at restraints. 'I believe you have immense power. But you have to trust it.'

Eleven other actors file into the room. Geon claps his hands twice. 'Friends, we are going to perform a trust exercise, although it is not only about trust, but underlying currents. We must sense these currents, anticipate them as we learn from one another. You follow?' The actors nod, some of them looking malnourished and unwashed. 'Stand in a circle,' Geon orders.

Milo looks for familiar faces, or at least cute girls.

'Place your palms together,' Geon orders. 'Now listen carefully to my instructions. When I say "Begin," Milo will say "Zip." As he says "Zip," he will direct one hand to snap out in the direction of another person. That person will then take Milo's energy and immediately say "Zap." He or she will then slide their palms together and send the energy in the direction of someone else by snapping out their hand and saying "Zoop." This requires extreme concentration, trust and focus. You must listen intently to the word because the group must retain the sequence, "Zip Zap Zoop." You will be disqualified if you say "Zap" or "Zip" when you should be saying "Zoop," or "Zip" when you should be saying "Zap" or "Zoop." You must *listen*.' Geon points to his ears. 'Listen, trust and focus.' He claps his hands twice. 'Milo, begin.'

Milo, with his palms pressed together, aims his hands towards a girl with cornrows. 'Zip,' he says. Startled, the girl quickly points her hands at a man in a sailor's cap. 'Zap,' she says.

'Zoop,' the sailor says, pointing at a youth dressed in black who blurts, 'Zap.'
'Wrong,' Geon shouts. 'You are disqualified! You should be saying "Zip."
You weren't listening. You must *listen*.' Geon points to his ears again. Hunter
escorts the disqualified youth out. Geon claps his hands. 'Focus, everyone.
Start again. Etienne, what do you say?'
    'Zap?'
    'Precisely. Begin.'
    And on it goes for two hours until only six actors remain. Milo's feet
ache from standing, and he pines for an honest day of junk removal. Geon
directs them to sit in a circle on the floor. Etienne, in the sailor's cap, mutters,
'*Quelle blague.*'
    Geon claps his hands. 'You who remain are the guardians of trust.' Hunter
serves them grape Kool-Aid and chocolate chip cookies, which the guardians
consume with gusto. Geon claps his hands again. 'What have we learned from
this exercise?' The actors, exhausted, their mouths full of cookie, look appre-
hensively at one another.
    'It's all circular,' Milo says.
    'Precisely.'

He places the plums and grapes on Christopher's bed table. The food tray has
not been removed. Milo lifts the lid and is disturbed to see that the food is
untouched. Christopher appears to be sleeping, the air moving through his
nostrils causing a faint whistle. They have bandaged his head. What can this
mean? Milo sits and waits, worriedly eating grapes. The Portuguese man on
the other side of the curtain has developed a hacking cough.
    'Milo?'
    'Yes?'
    'Are you fucking my wife?'
    'You already asked me that.'
    'I'm asking you again.'
    'No.'
    'Are they okay?'
    'They're fine.' More lies.
    'You didn't tell them anything?' Christopher sounds winded.

'No, but I think I should. I think they should know.'

'If you tell them, I'll kill you. One more disaster and she'll crack.'

'Why did they bandage your head?'

'They drilled a burr hole in it to let the blood out. Subdural bleeding.'

A ponytailed nurse appears with a needle. 'I need more blood samples, Mr. Wedderspoon.'

Christopher remains listless as she taps his arm, searching for a vein. She seems very young to Milo, fresh out of nursing school.

'He's having trouble breathing with that splint,' Milo says. 'I don't think they put it on right. His nose looks crooked.'

'Yeah, he'll have to get it fixed later by a plastic surgeon.' She pokes the needle into Christopher's arm.

'What do you mean *later*? Why can't they fix it now?'

'That would be an elective procedure. There's big waiting lists for OR time.' Blood spurts into the syringe.

'So you mean he has to walk around with a nose that makes it hard to breathe for months? Couldn't they see it was crooked in the operating room?'

'Milo, we've already been through this,' Christopher says. 'They're waiting to see if I die.'

'Given the extent of his other injuries,' the nurse explains, 'the nose isn't a priority.' She sashays away with Christopher's blood.

'The worst part,' Christopher says, 'is I have to breathe through my mouth, which dries it. So I drink water, which bloats my bladder.'

Milo tries to think of something constructive to say.

'What are you doing here, Milo?'

'You already asked me that.'

'No, I said whatever you're doing here, you don't have to do it.'

Milo has been waiting for Christopher to remember that he was at the scene of the accident, *caused* the accident by calling his name, forcing Christopher to turn his head away from the cab. Maybe he does remember.

'Does your head hurt?'

'Not anymore.' Christopher closes his eyes. 'Please go away.'

...

He tries the sliding glass doors but they're locked. He knocks on the glass. Usually, after episodes, she keeps Robertson home, even lets him sit by the dryer, which she normally avoids running due to the cost of hydro. The rhythm of the drum rotating soothes him. Milo knocks again, holding his face close to the glass to peer in. He hears pop music. Tanis never plays pop because it makes Robertson hyper. An intruder must be in the house. Milo pounds on the door. 'Open up, I know you're in there.'

Pablo, shirtless, slides open the doors. 'Hello, sir, *qué pasa?*'

'What are you doing here?'

'Cleaning windows.'

Milo doesn't believe this for a second. 'Where's your bucket?'

'In the living room.'

'Where's Tanis?'

'She took him to the doctor.'

Milo pushes past Pablo into the living room. Sure enough, there is a bucket and a squeegee. 'Why are you washing her windows?'

'She asked me to. She said if I need cash there's stuff that needs doing that her husband used to do.'

'I can't believe you're taking her money.'

'Why? Is she broke?'

'That's not the point.'

'The point is you're the one who took her panties. Me and Tanis are just friends. She needs a friend right now.'

'*I'm* her friend.'

'That's not what she says.'

'What did she say?'

'Take a chill pill, man. This lady's got you real wound up.'

He drinks beer on the deck with the Cuban because he doesn't want to go home to Vera.

'I think Robertson feels too much,' Pablo says. 'Tanis says people don't think he feels but I think he over-feels and that's why he freaks out.'

'Suddenly you're an expert.' Milo eats more pretzels.

'Most of us can, like, stop freaking out, you know. But he's feeling so much all the time, like, maybe screaming is his way of shutting out feelings. How do *you* shut out feelings, Milo?'

'I don't have feelings.'

'You love Tanis. You're shutting out those feelings.'

'I don't love her.'

'We all shut out feelings, and it makes us sick, keeping all those feelings locked out. I saw this movie about this guy who didn't believe he deserved to be loved. The whole movie, people were, like, trying to love him but he pushed them away and he got sicker and sicker. So finally all the people who love him show up at the hospital and, like, hug and kiss him and tell him how much he means to them, and he's so sick he's too weak to push them away anymore. He's, like, dying and he's just figured out how to love. It was so sad. It made me cry.'

'Aren't you supposed to be cleaning windows?'

'You know what Robertson was doing when I came over?'

'What?'

'Moving pots and pans around. She lets him take stuff out of the cupboards and move it around. She says it helps him decompress.'

'What are you lot up to?' Vera calls from Milo's back porch. 'We've been looking all over for you two. Wait till you see the goodies we bought for supper tomorrow. We even found some lime cordial and Scotch eggs!'

With a Scotch egg lodged in his intestines, he checks his email. His agent, Stu, expresses dismay over Milo's *unprofessional behaviour* at the beer ad callback. 'We need to talk,' he says. More importantly, Geon Van Der Wyst wants Milo to participate in phase two of the audition for the show without a script. The group will meet in a rural setting. A van will pick Milo up at three p.m. on Sunday, a welcome diversion. A day in the country, free from domestic turmoil, might speed his transformational healing. Geon advises him to bring a sleeping bag, which suggests an overnighter.

'Milo!' Pablo and Vera call from downstairs. He holds pillows over his ears but Pablo flings open his door. 'Milo, come quick, your dad's on T V! You got to come right now, man.'

'Buzz off. My father's dead.'

'Wally says they never found no body. He says he's even got the Nazi scar.' Pablo grabs his arm and hauls him downstairs where Wallace and Vera, gin and tonics in hand, crowd the couch.

'What kind of sick joke is this, Wallace?' Milo demands.

'No joke. The fucker was there.'

'Don't use that word,' Vera says.

'What am I supposed to say? He was a mean fucker. Everybody hated him.'

'Wally!'

Wallace swills more G&T. 'I'm telling you, the fucker was there.'

'Where?'

'It's a show about people who think they're on reality shows,' Pablo explains. 'Like, in real life, they think there's hidden cameras everywhere.'

'My father thought he was on a reality show?'

'Shit, no, he was in the home for crazies.'

'A retirement home,' Vera clarifies. 'It was another gentleman in the home who thought he was on a reality show.'

'So what was my father doing there?'

'He was a client.'

'Just sitting there,' Wallace says, 'like the fucker he was, just sitting there passing judgment.' Wallace played street hockey in the neighbourhood. Whenever he hit a ball or a puck onto Gus's property, Gus would keep it.

'My father wouldn't be caught dead in a retirement home.'

'It's a miracle,' Pablo says. 'You've been given a second chance, Milo. If I saw *mi padre* again I would tell him I forgive him for screwing my cousin.'

'You saw some guy in the background of a shot,' Milo says, 'who resembled Gus. Hallelujah.'

They hear pounding on the back door.

'Must be your lady friend,' Vera says.

Tanis's hair reaches out in angry tentacles. 'I need to speak with you privately.'

He sits on a Muskoka chair. She stands with arms crossed. Before she can accuse him of further misdeeds, he tells her about liberating Puffy.

'So where is it now?'

'Still in the basement. I'd like Robertson to have it, if that's all right with you.'

She drops into the other chair and deflates. This is not the reaction he'd expected.

'Is Robertson all right?' he asks. 'What did the doctor say?'

'Nothing new. He's on a mild sedative which he hates because it disorients him.'

'Well, as I say, the kids don't want the hamster back so there's no reason Robertson can't keep it. I think caring for another living being might help him through all this.'

'You don't get through it. It goes on and on.'

'If you'd prefer, I can keep it here and he can visit it.'

'Billy Kinney is dead. They couldn't stop the bleeding. Even after they opened his skull to put a clip over the aneurysm.' Tanis tilts her head back and stares at stars shrouded in smog.

'I'm sorry to hear that,' Milo says quietly, except it feels as though he's shouting because *not always fatal* should mean the little fucker's still breathing at least.

'They took him off the ventilator this afternoon,' she says.

'How do you know all this?'

'I called his mother.'

'Why?'

'Because I care. Unlike yourself.'

'But she threatened to press charges against Robertson.'

'So?'

'So, she denies that her son bounces basketballs off Robertson's head.'

'Her son is dead.'

This isn't really happening. In seconds the lights will fade to black and Milo will step out the stage door and feel cool air on his face.

'I haven't told Robertson,' she says. 'I have no idea how he'll react.'

'Is he going to school tomorrow?'

'Tomorrow is Saturday.'

Milo is no longer inside his body but above in a hot air balloon looking down at the accidental killer, the paunchy Everyman who can do nothing but blunder. Whoever was in that body has vacated, never to return. Hot air swirling in and around him makes him feel about to pass out. 'At least ... ' he murmurs, 'at least he can go to school on Monday without being bullied.'

'How can you even say that? A child has died.'

'He tormented Robertson,' he pleads. 'That's over at least.'

'It's never over. There are always more bullies. Life is a war.'

She retreats in her flip-flops. The doors slide shut and he hears the click of the lock.

9

'Sarah Moon Dancer told me,' Pablo says, 'it's time for reflection.'
Milo stares grimly at a romantic comedy. The sultry schoolteacher has discovered that her cowboy lover is an outlaw. She throws her honey-I-love-you ring at him.

'Sarah,' Pablo continues, 'says we've been spending way too much time buying stuff to impress people who don't matter. Greed is over, Milo. And hobris.'

'Hubris.'

'Hubris? What's hubris?'

'Arrogance, pride. Too much of it.'

'Sarah says hubris makes us self-destruct.'

In constant replay in Milo's mind is the image of the boy prostrate on the sidewalk. Had he run for help, would the little shit still be alive? Even more shameful, Milo's main concern is that he doesn't get implicated in the death. True, he did not *intend* to kill, and a murder conviction requires proof of intent. Reverberating from the consequences of his violent behaviour, in a clammy sweat, he squeezes some solace out of the fact that Robertson won't be shoved, slandered, fingered and humiliated at school. But Billy was only a child. Does Billy being a bully make it okay that he's dead? Absolutely not, Milo tells himself. Then why isn't he soaked in remorse? Has he, like the Michigan boy who shot his beloved grandfather in the head, been desensitized by the human slaughter, real and unreal, he sees flashed on screens daily? The Michigan boy said he felt like he was watching a movie about himself and he understood why people murder because 'you feel like nothing could ever hurt you just for that split second.' Isn't that how Milo felt when he fled the scene of the crime? The boy who shot his grandfather said he guessed he did it because of 'sadness and pent-up anger.' Is that why Milo did it, because of the sadness and pent-up anger he feels towards his father who may or may not be dead? The Michigan boy is in prison for life.

The cowboy outlaw shoots the lawman who has been tailing him and slings back whisky in the saloon.

'Did Maria call here?' Pablo asks.

'Why would Maria call here?'

'My cell died. I don't think she wants to see me again, ever. She works hard at her jobs, you know, and she wants a big wedding with a priest and everything. She deserves that. She deserves better than me.'

Anxiety expanding within causes Milo to tremble. 'How 'bout a whisky?' he asks, the bad actor seeking refuge in the bottle, appalled that his meagre existence can go on despite his atrocious act. He digs around in the sideboard for a bottle but instead grips something soft. He pulls out his father's wallet, which he'd assumed Gus had taken with him. The familiarity of its worn leather causes momentary paralysis. Gus could stride in at any second and demand, 'What do you think you're doing with my wallet?' It was strictly off limits. If Milo needed money, he had to ask, and even then there were no guarantees. If at all, the cash was withdrawn slowly and kept in hand until Milo feebly reached for it, avoiding Gus's laser stare.

'No whisky?' Pablo asks.

Milo pulls out a bottle of brandy. By the time the outlaw has shot six more lawmen and resumed copulating with the sultry blonde, Pablo and Milo have consumed several brandies. A haze settles over them. Only now does Milo have the courage to open the wallet. He finds two twenties, some bus tickets, Home Depot receipts, credit cards and a photo-booth shot of himself as a child. Milo can't remember the shot or the photo booth. His teeth protrude and he looks as though he's trying to force a crap. Why would Gus keep this photo in his wallet? Did he show it to his concrete associates and share a good laugh? Did he look at it wistfully, remembering better days? *Were* there better days? Has Milo forgotten something, so pent-up is he with sadness and anger?

Pablo peers over his shoulder. 'Is that you?' He starts to giggle. 'You look like a beaver.'

Milo shoves the photo back into the wallet.

'*Coño*,' Pablo says. 'That's him!' He pulls out Gus's driver's licence. 'That's the old guy on the show.' He holds the licence inches from his nose. 'He's even got the Nazi scar.'

It was Russians who split open Gus's face. They left him for dead, after raping his sister and stealing what remained of his family's food and livestock. When Gus's mother and father returned, Gus's mother cried for thirty-six days. His father stopped speaking.

If he is alive, why hasn't he come home? Milo checked the TV guide. He could contact the show's producers. Or forget about it. Wallace, sauced, was not of sound mind. The scar is the problem. Milo used to invent stories about his father fighting off the Nazis. Usually, he equipped Gus with a variety of farm implements, but sometimes his dad swung at the Krauts with bare fists. If it is the old man, what if he doesn't want to be found? What if he ran away and is not waiting to be forgiven or understood, or to justify his paternal cruelty by explaining that he'd wanted to protect Milo? The father who kept an ugly photo of his son close to him at all times is in hiding.

Best forgotten, denied. All of it.

Vera has them 'tidying up a bit.' 'We want to impress Fennel now, don't we?'

Pablo flops on the couch again.

'Get off your arse,' Milo says. 'Help me out here.'

'With what?'

'Vera wants you to do the windows.'

'I don't do windows.'

'You just did Tanis's.'

'That's because she paid me.'

'Is that the only reason?'

'You have a dirty mind, Milo.'

Milo has been keeping an eye out for Robertson, hoping that the news of a liberated Puffy will brighten the boy's face and free Milo, however briefly, from his brewing guilt and fear of going to prison for life.

'I don't know about you lot,' Vera calls from the kitchen, 'but I like to see a vase of flowers on a table, something cheery.'

'I'll go,' Milo says, seizing the opportunity to escape.

'I've got to go to Tanis's,' Pablo says.

'What do you mean you've got to go to Tanis's?' Milo demands.

'She wants me to check her eavestroughs. She says rain's been spilling over.'

That this musclehead has easy access to next door infuriates Milo. He snatches Gus's twenties and strides to the only florist in the neighbourhood. He chooses what he hopes will be a suitably cheery bouquet and decides to stroll by the Copper Pipe, giving Zosia the opportunity to see the bouquet and wonder whom it's for. But police tape cordons off his ex-lover's place of employment. One of the plate-glass windows has been shattered and replaced with plywood. Panic propels Milo to the neighbouring used bookstore, where a pile of Danielle Steel affronts him.

'Are you looking for anything in particular?' a hunched man on a stool inquires.

'No, ah, yes, actually, do you know what happened next door?'

'A shooting.' The man studies Milo over his reading glasses.

'Was anybody hurt?'

'Several people.'

'Do you know who?'

'Didn't frequent the place.'

'Do you know if they were customers or employees?'

'Couldn't say.'

'Did anybody die?'

'A couple were critical.'

Even the phone booth fights him, its cracked doors jutting like teeth. Milo bashes through them. Zosia's number is out of service. He phones the police and is put on hold for twenty minutes until finally a PC comes on the line to tell him only the victims' relatives have been notified. Milo calls hospitals until he runs out of change. He has lost her, imagines her bloodied against terracotta tiles. Gunned down in the land of opportunity.

'Answer it,' Wallace hisses. He is wearing his one-size-too-small blazer-and-tie combo.

'You answer it, man,' Pablo says. 'She's *your* girlfriend.'

'You watch it, dickbag.'

'Was that the bell?' Vera calls from the kitchen.

Milo opens the door. Fennel, looking prettier than he remembers in a floral skirt and blouse, makes a peace sign with her fingers.

'Is that Fennel?' Vera scuttles towards them, wiping her hands on her apron. 'Aren't you lovely. Wally, you didn't tell me she was such a looker. Come in, love.'

Milo steps behind Vera, trying to make eye contact with Fennel while pointing repeatedly at Wallace. Fennel barely perceptibly nods.

'What will you have?' Vera asks. 'A G&T, a sherry?'

'Gin's fine, thanks,' Fennel says.

'Off you go, Wally, work your magic.' Vera winks at Fennel. 'He's always been good at a cocktail.'

The Cuban, topless of course, offers Fennel a spot on the couch then spreads himself inches from her.

'Are you dressing for dinner, Pablo?' Milo demands.

'It's so hot, man, with the cooking and everything.'

'Why don't we all get naked?' Milo suggests. Fennel fidgets, looking at Pablo. She probably wants to paint him, probably wants to trace his greasy contours with her brush. Disgusting.

'Go put a jumper on, Pablo, there's a love,' Vera says, sitting next to Fennel and patting her knee. 'Wally hasn't told me much about you. I think he wanted to surprise me.'

'Are you surprised?'

'Well, I must admit, I did imagine someone a bit older.'

'I'm better breeding material,' Fennel says.

'Wal-lee, you didn't tell me you've been thinking about little ones.'

Wallace, G&T in hand, falters. 'Just thinking about it, Mother.' His hand grazes Fennel's as he offers her the glass. Fennel drinks deeply while Wallace watches, apparently mesmerized. He sucks on his puffer.

'Oh, wouldn't that be a lark,' Vera says, 'a bonny grandkiddy. Might be a bit big, though, for a little thing like yourself.'

'I'll stretch.'

Wallace reddens. Pablo returns in a muscle shirt. '*Mi madre* was four-foot-eight and had seven nine-pound bambinos.'

'Your father should've been arrested,' Fennel says.

Over dinner, the alcohol softens edges. Fennel's admission that she is a painter enables her to hold forth. 'Van Gogh, totally. I mean, *nobody* was doing what he was doing. He was, like, *living* the paint. He ate paint.'

'Ate it?' Pablo asks, leaning towards her.

Fennel nods. 'Sucked on the tubes.'

'*Coño.*'

'Who's for more mash?' Vera calls from the kitchen.

'I thought he cut his ear off,' Milo says, slipping Fennel's mammal onto plate.

'That's bullshit,' Fennel says. 'Gauguin cut it off. He was, like, this awesome swordsman and Van Gogh was, like, nuts, so Gauguin had to fight him off.'

'Why was he nuts?' Wallace asks, softly. He has been uncharacteristically quiet.

'He was depressed.'

'Why?'

Fennel appears nonplussed, as though she can't believe she has to explain it to him.

'Maybe nobody loved him,' Pablo offers. 'And he loved nobody.'

'His brother loved him,' Milo says.

'That's bullshit,' Fennel says. 'If he loved him, no way would he have left him to rot in the Yellow House.'

Vera spoons overcooked Brussels sprouts onto their plates. 'Would you care for more roast, Fennel?'

'No thank you.'

'Are you sure? Don't be shy. I like a girl who enjoys her meat.'

'*I'll* have more,' Milo says, even though, after Fennel's serving, he feels as though he has swallowed a cow.

'I like a man with an appetite.'

'Maybe his brother loved him,' Pablo suggests, 'but he couldn't express it. Sarah Moon Dancer says we have to re-establish boundaries and communication pathways with our families.'

'Were you over at that crazy bitch's again?' Wallace says.

'I had to help her with her wind chimes.'

'No way do you go over there, you read me? She owes me three hundred bucks.'

'Who's Sarah Moon Dancer?' Fennel asks.

'Some psycho bitch.'

'She has a healing circle,' Pablo says. 'You don't know how to heal, Wallace, that's why you're so angry all the time. Maybe if you let Sarah help you on your Earthwalk you would learn to embrace other people's gifts.'

'Who's for more pud?' Vera dumps shrivelled Yorkshire puddings onto plates. 'I do so enjoy a party. What about dancing? Pablo was playing something Latino earlier. I like a bit of rumba.'

Milo has never really understood drunkenness because at the end you're back where you started, only it's worse. The three of them mambo and samba and God knows what. Milo repeatedly turns the music down so as not to disturb Tanis and Robertson. Wallace, in another gin-induced stupor, has been relegated to kitchen clean-up. With dishrag in hand he watches forlornly as Fennel, Vera and Pablo gyrate and shake. Milo, his cold-sober assistant, pulls him back into the kitchen.

'What is it with Pablo and women?' Wallace asks.

'Muscles.'

'Besides that.'

'No brains.'

'Nah, he's got some fucking animal thing going. Women are always looking at him.' He scrubs ferociously at the roasting pan. 'She hasn't even looked at me once, did you notice that? She's supposed to be *my* girlfriend and she hasn't even fucking looked at me once.'

'Lots of girlfriends don't look at their boyfriends.'

'Yeah, but we're supposed to be acting. I'm *paying* her to be my girlfriend.'

'Maybe avoiding eye contact is part of the act. We didn't give her specific instructions.'

'Don't bullshit me. She wants to fuck that sleazy Mexican.'

Milo scrapes leftovers into the compost bin. 'I don't think Vera's noticed.'

Wallace pours himself a sherry.

'Maybe you should lay off the hooch,' Milo suggests.

Vera pops her head in. 'How's everything? A bit of a drudge, isn't it? Sorry about that. Don't worry about the tins, I'll do them in the morning. I think I need a bit of air, actually, not feeling quite myself.' She stumbles slightly. Milo grabs her elbow and escorts her to a Muskoka chair where she passes out.

'Wallace?' Milo shouts, fearing another dead body. 'Wallace, come here, quick!' He grabs Vera's bony wrist, feeling for a pulse. Wallace teeters on the porch.

'What's the problem?'

'I think she might need medical attention.'

'Nah, don't sweat it. She always nods off. That's why she loses her glasses. They slide off.'

'I can't feel a pulse.'

'Forget about it.' Wallace returns to kitchen duty. Milo pats Vera's face. She swats at his hands without opening her eyes.

Robertson emerges from the darkness, barefoot in his pyjamas. 'She looks dead.'

'She isn't.'

'How do you know?'

'She just slapped me.'

'That was before. Maybe she's dead now.'

'I don't think so. She's just sleeping. Where's your mum?'

'In bed. She took one of my pills to help her sleep. She pretends they're for me but really they're for her.'

'You took one though, too, didn't you?'

'I spit it out. Why are you people making so much noise? If my father was here he'd be steamed.'

'It's almost over. It was a dinner party for Wallace.'

'Is it his birthday?'

'No. Listen, I've still got the hamster. I talked to your class about how Puffy needs sleep and quiet during the day. They agreed to let me keep him.'

'Her.'

'Her. If your mum doesn't want you to have it, I could keep her and you could visit her.'

Even in the poor light Milo can see that relief is not brightening Robertson's face. He is blinking repeatedly and swaying slightly. 'Do they still think I took her?' he asks.

'Not at all, I told them I took her. They don't even know you're involved, which you aren't. You had nothing to do with it. So you can go to school tomorrow like it's any other day.'

'Tomorrow's Sunday.'

'Right. Monday then, you can go to school without worrying about the hamster or what anybody thinks.'

'Billy Kinney is dead.'

'I heard.'

'Did you push him?' Robertson asks.

'No.'

'Mum thinks you pushed him.'

'She's mistaken.'

Robertson begins to walk in circles. Milo would like to take his hand and lead him to Puffy but knows he can't touch him. Only Tanis can touch Robertson when he's awake and even then with only two fingers, and he makes sure there is a two-foot gap between them.

'Do you want to see Puffy?' Milo asks, heading towards the house, hoping Robertson will follow.

Vera wakens abruptly. 'What's all this then?' she blurts before losing consciousness again.

'Robertson?' The boy has faded into the darkness. Milo listens for the sliding doors but can hear nothing but Latino trumpets and Wallace yelling, 'You fucking Mexican!' The sound of bodies crashing into furniture and Fennel's screams cause Milo to run to the living room where the two meatheads are locked in a violent embrace. He turns off the stereo and shouts, 'Party's over! Everybody out!' He grabs Fennel's arm. 'You too.'

'Where's my money?'

'Where's her money, Wallace?'

'You think I'm going to pay that slut?'

'A deal's a deal,' Milo says.

'She should pay me, I fucking pimped her to that Mexican.'

Milo pulls out Gus's remaining twenty and hands it to her. 'You got any money, Pablo?'

'No, sir.'

'You just got paid for doing Tanis's windows and eavestroughs. Hand it over.'

Pablo disengages from Wallace and feels around in his jeans before pulling out crumpled bills. 'Me and Fenny can't help what we feel for each other, Wallace.'

'You say another word and I'll fucking kill you, you read me? You fucking sex addict.'

'He's not a sex addict,' Fennel says.

'Oh no? He's a fucking pussy junkie. Try talking to his ex, she got sick of putting out for him.'

'That's a lie,' Pablo gasps.

'Enough!' Milo shouts. 'Out, everybody.' He tries to shove them towards the door.

'I live here,' Wallace points out.

'Me too,' Pablo says.

'What's all this brouhaha?' Vera demands. 'Has anybody seen my glasses?' The four stand motionless while she looks behind sofa cushions. 'I had them when we mamboed but then I think I took them off during the samba.'

'They're probably in the grass by the chair,' Wallace says. 'They probably slipped off while you were sleeping.'

'We'll find them in the morning,' Milo says. 'It's late, you should go to bed, Vera.'

'What about you lot?'

'We're all going to bed.'

'Fennel's kipping here, is she?'

'No!' they all say.

Vera winks. 'Don't be chaste on my account.'

'Up you go, Mother. You get first dibs on the bathroom.'

'Yes, thank you, good idea.' She takes the stairs slowly, reminding Milo that soon she will slow to a stop and die, leaving behind many negative energy impressions. The front door slams. Nothing remains of Fennel but a whiff of patchouli. Milo finds a flashlight and searches behind the bushes, on and under the trampoline, but sees no trace of Robertson. The sliding doors are locked. The boy must have gone inside.

Back in the Muskoka chair he tries to make sense of the senseless: Billy dead, Zosia possibly in critical condition, Christopher possibly dying from complications, Gus possibly alive. But there is no sense to be made, only the pounding awareness that he has caused damage that he is powerless to mend.

10

The only remaining seat in the minivan is between a large black man named Franklin and a small Chinese man named Sungwon. Milo squeezes between them. Aruthy, the girl in cornrows, sits in front with Hunter, who informs them that Geon Van Der Wyst has requested that they not speak until they arrive at their destination and receive further instructions. When Hunter isn't swearing at drivers, she talks on her cell, with her left hand draped over the wheel. Bertie, the Australian, and Etienne in the sailor hat occupy the middle seats. Milo suspects he is in the company of non-union performers, possibly illegals. Geon is known for combining cultures. His most acclaimed production, for which he won an award, involved 'movement performers' from every continent who spoke only their native tongues and were therefore forced to improvise bodily communication.

As they transcend industrial parkland and track housing and begin to see trees and fields, the tension that has been grappling Milo lessens slightly. Being relegated to silence as they escape civilization allows him to doze, lulled by the movement of the van, until it comes to an abrupt halt on a dirt road behind several other vehicles.

'What's going on?' Milo asks before remembering he is forbidden to speak. Already he is blowing the audition.

Hunter climbs out, still on her cell, and pushes her way into a group of agitated drivers. Milo looks at his companions. 'Did you see anything?'

Sungwon holds his finger against his lips.

'I think we can talk now,' Milo says. 'This might be an emergency.'

His collaborators stare at him as though he has suggested mutiny. Hunter yanks open the door and clambers back in. 'Roadkill.'

'Can't we move it?'

'It's not totally dead. They're waiting for a forestry guy.' She calls Geon to give him the news.

Milo taps her shoulder. 'Can you ask him if it's all right for us to talk under these exceptional circumstances?'

'Milo wants to know if they can talk,' Hunter says. She flips down the sun visor and checks her eyeliner in the mirror. 'Gotcha,' she says, pocketing the phone.

'What did he say?'

'He says you can't talk.'

'That's absurd.'

'He says "use it."'

What can this possibly mean? Is Geon Van Der Wyst insane? Has Milo put his life at risk travelling north to nowhere with strangers? Is a group sacrifice pending? No one will be able to trace the illegals. And, of course, Milo revealed his plans to no one. He hid in his room while the hungover stumbled about and fried animal parts below.

Use it. Is this part of the audition? Maybe there is no roadkill. This is Geon's way of testing to see who will challenge the status quo. No way will Milo sit unquestioningly in the overheated van. The irritated drivers, in Firestone caps and fishing hats, do not welcome a stranger.

'Where'd *you* come from?' a goat-faced man inquires.

'Toronto. We're trying to get through here.'

'We're all trying to get through here, mister, you just wait your turn.'

Milo sees the deer sprawled on the road, its rear legs twisted at awkward angles like Christopher's.

'We could cut us some good steaks out of that one,' a man in a fishing hat comments.

'Shit like this happens all the time in Newfoundland,' a man in a Firestone cap says. 'They got moose runnin' all over the place. My brother-in-law got killed instantly hitting a moose.'

'What happened to the moose?' Milo asks, approaching the doe carefully, not wanting to add to her terror.

'Who is this guy?' the man in the Firestone cap demands.

'From Toronto,' the man in the fishing hat says.

Blood leaks from the doe's nostrils as she tries to pull herself onto her front legs, but her battered hind legs betray her. Milo speaks softly to her as he pulls off his sweatshirt and lays it over her shoulders. 'You'll be fine,' he murmurs, knowing that she is beyond help, that the forestry guy will inject her with lethal chemicals. No more will headlights stun her. He wants to apologize for cars, roads, the human race.

'Is he nuts or what?' the goat-faced man demands.

Milo strokes the doe as he has seen cowboys stroke skittish horses in movies. If he can offer some comfort in her last moments, maybe she will not feel that she is dying alone. It's when he removes his T-shirt to blot the blood on her haunches that she swings a front leg at him. At first the impact seems tolerable – she is frightened, of course she must strike out. But the pain, rather than subsiding, increases. It's as though his ribs have been crushed and, with every inhalation, his shattered bones puncture his lungs. The goat-faced man slams a spade into the doe's head, not once but three times. Her blood spatters Milo's face and torso while he wheezes, 'Stop!' at the goat-faced man. The doe falls back, and Milo, breathless, feels as though he is being slashed from within.

'A fractured rib,' the doctor says. Very tall, she looms over the examining table.

'Just one? It feels like more.'

'X-rays don't lie. We'll wrap you to stabilize it. And give you some more pain medication. Just be glad it wasn't a horse. A kick from a horse can kill you. The doe was half-dead from the sounds of it, didn't have much strength left. Count yourself lucky.'

'What's happened to her?' Milo asks, feeling the drugs beginning to work, causing the present moment to matter intensely as he can't rush to the next. Stalled by opioids, he fixates on the deer's fate. 'Is she dead?'

'You rest now,' the giantess says. 'I'll let your friends take you home once you're good and calm.'

'What happened to the deer?' He pictures the men in fishing hats carving steaks out of her flanks.

'What's done is done,' the giantess says. 'No point fretting about it. Rest now.' She exits, closing the door behind her. Milo stares at the doe's blood speckling his arms. *What's done is done.* Does that mean *he's* responsible? Did he cause her death as well? Had he not interfered, would the forestry guy have found a way to save her? Has he caused the demise of yet another living being? What right has he to live with the blood of innocents on his hands? Although Billy wasn't innocent. Or was he? What if he wasn't a sociopath, just misunderstood and mistreated? What if he began his short life full of light and love only to be rebuffed at every turn, despised for shows of weakness, applauded for displays of aggression? What if he, like Gus, survived hardship only to become hardened as he trudged onward in the only manner known to him?

Hunter leans over him. 'Ready to roll? Geon wants to talk to you.' She hands him the phone.

'Milo? Milo, are you there?'

'Yes.'

'Bad accident.'

'Worse for the deer.'

'Do you think you can work or do you want to go home?'

The thought of returning to Gus's house induces a deadening sensation. 'Of course.'

'Of course nothing, Milo. Does it hurt?'

'Not really.'

'Can you run?'

'Sure.' He can't possibly run but actors always lie about their capabilities.

'Use it. Give me back to Hunter.'

Milo passes her the phone. She says 'gotcha' several times then pockets the phone.

'Time to hit the road,' she says.

'We need to fill my prescription.' He waves it at her.

'We'll get it when we stop for water.'

There's no water where they're going?

Franklin and Sungwon prop him up in the van. After another dose of painkillers, an intoxicating sense of well-being permeates Milo, a feeling that he wishes to share. 'Aren't we lucky to be here?' he says. 'Breathing this air and communing with nature? I can't remember the last time I was in the wilderness. Seriously, I mean, I just never go. We have lost touch with the earth, with the pulse of living things. How can we expect to live in this world without a connection to nature? No wonder we think we can control it, we're never in it.'

'Is he allowed to talk?' Franklin asks Hunter, whose cell is no longer working due to the remoteness of their location. As they turn up yet another dirt road, there is only forest.

'We're here,' Hunter says.

They all look at the trees.

'There's a path,' Hunter explains, climbing out of the van.

They follow her, swatting at bugs. Branches snap in their faces, long grass and weeds snag their ankles until they arrive at a small clearing.

'Teepees,' Milo exclaims. 'How wonderful. Are they real? I mean, made by Indians?'

'First Nations people,' Hunter corrects.

'Right. Did they make them?'

'This is part of a reservation.'

'Do they know we're here?'

A gaunt First Nations person in a Chicago Fire Department T-shirt steps out of one of the teepees. 'Want some Kool-Aid?' he inquires.

'Gary's going to look after you,' Hunter explains, turning back down the path.

'You're leaving us?' Aruthy asks.

'I'll pick you up tomorrow. Give me your watches and cells.'

'Are you crazy?' Etienne says.

'Geon wants you to forget your urban existence for twenty-four hours.'

'Where is the little fucker?' Bertie demands.

'Toronto.'

'What?' Franklin says, looking smaller surrounded by trees.

With night closing in, Milo becomes giddy from the woodsy smells, the silence, the inky darkness. He has always wanted to sleep in a teepee. 'It's going to be great, guys. Just us in the wilderness with Gary as our guide.'

'I'm no guide,' Gary says.

'Hand over your watches and cells,' Hunter repeats, hardly visible in the darkness. 'Gary's got hotdogs. He'll tell you what to do.'

Bertie stands firm with arms crossed. 'How are you and Geon going to bloody know what we're up to if you're not here?'

'We'll know.' She vanishes before they can stop her.

'It'll be fun, guys,' Milo says.

Gary builds the campfire with ease.

'Are you going to burn ceremonial grasses?' Milo asks.

'Marshmallows,' Gary says.

'Marshmallows. How marvellous.' Milo spears a hotdog with a twig. 'Isn't there a marshmallow plant? Didn't you use to make something medicinal from its root? Or maybe its bark? Medicine men were always boiling bark.'

Gary hands him a hotdog bun.

'Please tell me there are no snakes here,' Aruthy says.

'They don't bite,' Gary responds.

'What about bears?' Etienne inquires.

'Don't carry food around. They smell food.'

'What about wolves and wildcats?' Bertie adds.

'They don't bother you. But there is water.'

'That's good, isn't it?' Milo asks.

'If you can swim.' Gary squirts ketchup on a hotdog.

They offer Aruthy a teepee to herself but she insists she'll be too scared on her own. 'It's not like we're getting naked,' she says. Bedding down in the teepees creates a camaraderie, or at least Milo – on pill number six – thinks so. They have been well-chosen; he sees that now in his altered state. Maybe Geon *is* a genius. After smearing themselves with bug repellant, they lie listening to croaking frogs, the utterances and foraging of nocturnal animals, and the wind rustling in the trees.

'Can somebody tell me a bedtime story?' Aruthy asks.

Bertie doesn't volunteer so Milo begins. 'There was once a young Polish boy who lived on a farm. He helped his father tend the animals, and seed and harvest the crops. The boy trusted and loved the animals and always, when it was time to slaughter the pig, he would run into the woods, away from its squeals.'

Bertie snaps open a plastic container and pulls out what looks like tissues, which he uses to wipe his armpits.

'What are you doing?' Aruthy asks.

'Baby wipes. Brad Pitt uses them.'

'But then a war starts,' Milo continues, 'and soldiers invade the village. They steal food, and rape women and girls. They march Jews out of their homes into the fields. When some of them resist, they are shot. A terrified boy runs for the woods but the Germans send the dogs after him. As the canines tear into the boy's flesh the mother's screams are muffled by a Nazi's gloved hand. The boy's father breaks away and tries to pull the dogs off his son but he is shot instantly. The other sobbing children cling to their mothers while their fathers stand powerless, staring at the soldiers. And then the order is given. Soldiers line up in front of them, take aim and fire.'

'I think I saw this movie,' Aruthy says.

'It better have a bloody happy ending,' Bertie says.

'Fortunately, the farm boy and his family are safe in a neighbouring village. They give the Germans whatever they demand. This leaves them starving but they manage to survive on three potatoes a day. They didn't have internet back then, so when the Russian invasion happens, nobody in the village knows about it. The farmer and his wife leave to attend to a sick relative. When they return they find their son under a table with a gash in his face and their daughter unconscious on the floor, her skirt pulled above her waist, her blouse and underwear ripped and blood leaking from her vagina.'

'I don't like this story,' Aruthy says.

'Here's the happy part,' Milo says. 'The boy becomes a teenager and crosses the ocean to begin a new life.'

'What happens to his sis?' Bertie asks.

'She drowns.'

'On purpose?' Aruthy asks.

'Nobody knows. The boy finds her body caught in the rocks. It's possible that she slipped. That's what the farmer tells everyone. He says it was an accident.'

'What does the boy think?'

'He doesn't say, and rarely talks about the war in his new life in the new land. He's too busy building a business and a family. Unfortunately, his wife gives him only one son. She tries and tries but fails to produce a live birth until finally she has a heart attack, leaving the boy, who is now a man, with a small son. Now there are two lost boys.'

'That better not be the bloody happy ending.'

'Years pass. The son grows up and the father grows old. They rarely speak due to the weight of the tragedy between them. The father despises the son for his weakness, his easy life; "You never had to work for anything," he tells him. "It's all been handed to you." Tensions grow, they hurl accusations, until one night the old man walks into a storm and does not return. The son searches for him for months without success. Then one day – you'll never guess – the old man shows up on a *reality show*. He isn't dead! The son, overcome with joy, reunites with his father, who has been hiding in shame, believing that he failed not only the sister he let drown, or the parents he deserted, or the wife he fucked to death, but his *son*. He believes he has failed his only son and cannot face him. But his son, now a mature man able to recognize life's complexities, forgives his father. Tears gush down their cheeks as they embrace.'

'Curtain,' Bertie says.

Gary wakes them in the dead of night and tells them to look for notes tagged to trees lit by candlelight. Aruthy spots the first note, which reads: *Our insignificance is often the cause of our safety.* Below this in big block letters it says, *GALLOP.*

'He wants us to bloody gallop?' Bertie demands but Gary has disappeared into the darkness.

'I'm not used to this kind of dark,' Sungwon admits. 'This is, like, really dark.' Unless they stand by the candle, they can't even see each other.

'*Quelle blague,*' Etienne mutters, squinting at the note. He is not wearing his sailor cap and his stringy hair hangs over his face.

'I don't mind galloping,' Milo says. 'Maybe it's a kind of warm-up.' He tries to gallop but even the opioids can't block the pain. 'At least, if we keep moving, the bugs can't catch us.' He shuffles into the inky woods in search of another note.

'We should stick together, mate,' Bertie calls after him.

The next note reads: *Man's feet have grown so big that he forgets his littleness.* The block letters say, *SKIP.* Milo skips, completely ignorant of what is underfoot. Heading full tilt into the unknown heightens his already drug-induced hyper-awareness. He is one with the darkness, the woodsy sounds and smells. The others stumble behind him, cursing and swatting at bugs. The next note reads: *Strange how few, after all is said and done, the things that are of moment.* 'Of moment,' Milo enthuses, 'of course!' *RUN.*

'Milo ... ?' they all call after him.

A man can look upon his life and accept it as good or evil. Good or evil, accept it. So what if you murder a defenceless boy. *HOP.* Adrenalin fuels Milo's wounded body as he hops to the next note.

It is far, far harder for him to confess that it has been unimportant in the sum of things.

Unimportant in the sum of things, of course! *CARTWHEEL*. It is during the cartwheel that he jams his hands into nettles and lands on his head. The others, hopping and running and galloping, catch up with him. 'You all right, mate?'

'What's that one say?' Milo asks, pointing to the next note.

Aruthy reads: *'Trifles make the sum of human things, and half our misery from our foibles springs.'*

'Oh, that is so true,' Milo howls. 'It's all *so* true!'

'It says *STRIP*,' Aruthy adds. 'That's not going to happen.'

'Can you get up, mate?'

Milo's hands throb, as do his ribs, but up above the clouds have parted and the stars are singing to him.

'I hear water,' Etienne says. They all listen.

'Let's go,' Milo commands, astonished by his new role as leader. He doesn't even have to act it, he *is* the leader.

Closer to the river, another note shimmers against a tree. *The displacement of a little sand can change occasionally the course of deep rivers. SWIM.*

'Someone's blowing out the candles,' Aruthy observes. 'How are we supposed to find our way back?'

'We're not,' Milo explains. 'Isn't it great?'

'Merde,' Etienne mutters.

Milo starts to remove his clothes, believing this to be his chance for absolution. 'I'm going in.'

'You can't see the edge,' Sungwon warns. 'Like, how are you supposed to know where to climb in?'

'Do we always have to see the edge before we move forward?' Milo asks, certain that he and Geon are of like minds. The man is a *genius*! Milo has no doubt that working with Geon will help him reconnect with his inner actor. Finally someone understands his talent. He *was* pulling at invisible restraints in *Godot*. He sees that now. He was afraid because he didn't really understand the play. Must we always really understand? Must we always fear what we can't really understand?

'Milo?' they call after him.

Let them remain onshore, timid and afraid. Naked, exposed to nature, without thinking – *of moment* – he clambers over rocks and pebbles that pinch his feet. The sound of rushing water beckons and the stars sing.

11

'You all right, worm turd?' Gary and two identical First Nations persons, wearing Fidel Castro hats, sit in lawn chairs. Kerosene lamps illuminate their faces. The river rushes metres away.

'You swallowed enough of that river to kill you,' Gary says.

'It's polluted,' one of the twins explains.

'Want a Hostess cupcake?' the other asks through missing teeth.

After the initial fight for life, Milo surrendered to the currents. This felt right and true. The stars told him so.

'Why'd you jump in the river?' the toothless twin inquires.

'I was told to.'

'You always do what you're told?' Gary throws the clothes Milo left behind in the woods at him.

'Why are you wearing a girdle?' the other twin asks.

'It's a chest wrap. I got kicked by a deer.'

'Cool story, bro,' the toothless twin says. 'You'd better get up before a snake bites your balls.'

'Brush the sand out of your crack or you'll be sorry,' the other advises.

The stars are no longer singing but pressing down on Milo. Pain ricochets inside his ribs. 'I need my drugs,' he says.

Gary tosses them at him. 'Give him some Mountain Dew.'

The toothless twin hands Milo a can of pop. 'I'm Elvis and this is my brother, Elton.'

Milo swallows pills and pulls on his clothes. 'Don't you have native names?'

'Oh, you mean like Little Red Cedar Canoe Man?'

'Or Little Eat Shit Suck Dick Man?' adds Elton.

'You don't get to call us "native,"' Gary says. 'We get to call each other native but to you white-asses we're the People of the First Nations.'

'Because we were here first,' Elvis says. 'You play poker?'

'Not for a long time.'

'Ever play for money?'

'I don't have my wallet on me.'

Gary tosses it to him.

'I've only got twenty bucks or something.'

'If you got a bank account,' Elton says, 'you got money.' He unfolds a card table.

'I should probably get back to camp.'

'Good luck finding it,' Gary says.

'Can't you take me?'

'I'm not saving your life again, worm turd. Play cards.'

Elton pulls up a lawn chair for Milo. Elvis hands him a cupcake and deals.

As dawn creeps above the pines, Milo is down one hundred and fifty bucks and has eaten six Hostess cupcakes, mainly to delay card plays. 'I really should get back to camp.'

In a crate of an SUV blaring country music they drive to an isolated convenience store/gas station that has an ATM. The First Nations people surround Milo as he withdraws the cash. When he hands it over, they pat his shoulders. 'Good job, bro.'

'Now can you take me back to the camp? I should probably put something on my hands. They've been stung by nettles.'

'What're you going to put on them?' Elvis asks.

'I thought maybe you could suggest something.'

'Marshmallow root tonic,' Gary mutters.

'Compress of deer shit works good,' Elton adds.

'Bear piss lotion,' Elvis says.

In the SUV nothing can be heard above the yowling of country singers. Gary is not going back the way they came and Milo comes to the numbing realization that he is a hostage. Even if he made a run for it he wouldn't get far with the cracked rib. He doesn't even know where he is.

'You ever go to the casino?' Elvis shouts over the racket.

'No.'

'Last city dude we had up here, he lost bad.'

'Blew his head off,' Elton adds.

'Is that where we're going?' Milo asks, but both brothers start wailing along with the radio. Will the First Nations people force him to gamble and steal his winnings until the ATM runs dry? Will they offer him a gun with which to blow his head off? At the junction of two highways, the SUV pulls into a Tim Hortons. Elvis opens the car door for him. 'Double double?'

'I'll wait in the car.'

'No you won't,' Garry says, grabbing him by his collar and pulling him out of the car.

'You want some Timbits?' Elvis asks.

'I don't want anything.'

'You on a diet?'

While they order, Milo heads towards the washroom then walks briskly out the glass doors. Hitchhiking is the only option. An overcast sky offers no indication as to which highway heads south. He plods on, waving his thumb at the occasional vehicle, the pain returning despite the pills. The SUV, blaring about cheatin' hearts, pulls up alongside him. 'Where d'you think you're going?'

'Home.'

'You live in Timmins?'

'We got Timbits,' Elvis says.

'He's on a diet,' Elton advises.

The SUV pulls ahead, cutting Milo off. 'Get in the car, worm turd. I'll take you back to camp.'

'How do I know you're not lying?'

'You don't,' Gary says. 'Get him in the truck.'

Within seconds Elvis has him in a neck lock and pushes him into the truck. At the camp Milo receives a hero's welcome. 'I bet Geon's impressed,' Aruthy says. 'I bet he's going to give you the lead.'

The People of the First Nations climb back into the SUV and screech off. A white-ass squats in the clearing with a stick the length of his arm and some twine, a spindle and a board for the spindle to grind into.

'What's going on?' Milo asks.

'He's making fire,' Aruthy explains. 'He's a survivalist.'

The survivalist wears a Tilley hat and has three different knives hanging from a belt slung around his torso. A paunch bulging over his khakis makes him look more like a golfer than a survivalist. He continues to drill the stick into the board. In minutes they can smell scorched wood and a tiny ember lights up the grass. 'Now you try it,' Reggie instructs. They take turns, struggling to get even the smallest spark. The procedure takes two hours, during which Reggie describes in detail his year living alone in a remote northern cabin a ten-day canoe trip from civilization. He learned about wild edible plants and tanning animal hides. Milo, sweaty and exhausted, is the only one to fail to create some kind of flame.

Next they are to build debris huts for shelter.

'But we have teepees,' Milo protests.

'You won't have teepees come the Apocalypse,' Reggie points out. 'I slept in a debris hut for three months one winter.' Milo would like to ask why but feels this might diminish his chances for the lead. He swallows more pills and joins the others in the woods hunting for fallen tree limbs. Finding a location for his debris hut proves challenging. He clambers farther into the woods until he spots a perfect Y-shaped nook in a tree for a ridgepole. Finding a suitable ridgepole takes time as most of the fallen branches aren't long or thick enough to support much weight. Finally he uncovers a fallen aspen bough, which fits perfectly into the nook. Next he sets out to gather more branches to rest against it. Losing all sense of time and his associates, without thinking or acting badly, he moves farther into the woods to gather smaller branches and armloads of dead leaves for insulation. Endorphins produced by these exertions flood his system, blocking any sensation of pain. A clear-headedness, a sense of purpose, a euphoria engulf him.

Rain patters relentlessly on his debris shelter. A series of tiny black worms crawl along the ridgepole that sits inches above Milo's face. Leeches? Maggots? Will they slither up his nostrils and into his ears? Mrs. Cauldershot always told him not to lie on the grass because ants would crawl into his ears and tunnel through the wax into his brain. Occasionally he would disobey her and lie on the grass, waiting for the ant invasion, for certain death – a freedom of sorts. But then a tickle would begin on an arm or a leg and he'd jump up, shaking imagined ants out of his ears. Milo cannot jump up and escape the leeches and maggots. If he tries to sit up or roll over, twigs prod him from all sides. He hears pawing outside. Do coyotes eat humans? His feet extend beyond the entry to the hut. He waits for the clamping of a canine jaw while he fumbles for his painkillers. He is able to pull the plastic container from his pocket but removing the childproof lid without extending his elbows to the side proves a struggle. After several tries, twisting his body for leverage, he is able to pop open the lid and chew several tablets. Exhausted, he flops back and stares at the leeches or maggots.

Reggie lived alone in the woods for an entire year and advised them that the most important quality in a survival situation is feeling that you *deserve* to survive. 'Survivors,' he said, 'never give up. It's well-documented that the quitters fail.' Gus repeatedly called Milo a quitter. In retaliation Milo started a Quitters Only club when he was getting his bullshit of arts degree. While the achievers developed ulcers and migraines, the quitters read Camus and smoked doobies.

What made Gus think *he* deserved to survive when his wife, sister, parents, Jakob and millions of other people did not? Milo has never felt that he deserves to survive. As associates have succumbed to fatal illness, demanding of fate *why me?* Milo has wondered *why not me?* Marlene Temple, who played his mother in *Death of a Salesman*, died after 'a long battle with cancer.' Marlene had seemed indomitable. While her co-star, a veteran of American eighties sitcoms, hammed his way through the role of Willy Loman, Marlene remained unfazed. Night after night Milo fumed about the complete lack of professionalism of the American sitcom star. Marlene calmly played solitaire on her laptop. Now she's dead. Didn't she feel she deserved to survive? And what about Tanis's nephew, studying IT at community college? He killed himself with a sleeping pill/narcotic/vodka cocktail. Did he give up and consequently fail?

What's giving up anyway? Isn't one man's failure another man's great achievement? The pilot who couldn't drop the bomb, the soldier who couldn't shoot the child, the president who refused to go to war? The bad actor who accidentally killed the bully? Was Annie a quitter because she self-medicated with Bailey's Irish Cream?

She always told Milo to colour inside the lines. 'Why?' he'd ask.

'Because you're supposed to.'

'Who says?'

'Don't let your dad see you're not inside the lines.'

He'd slap the colouring book shut when he heard Gus's key in the lock. He only coloured because Annie allowed him to sit with her if he appeared to be *doing* something. She didn't like it when he *mooned*. 'Don't moon,' she'd say. 'Go play.'

The pawing outside stops. Only the rustling of leaves and woodland critters remains. The opiate blanket delays Milo's reaction time as he comes to the alarming conclusion that he is, in fact, alone and abandoned. Increasingly his survivalist heroics seem meaningless. A suffocating despondency confines him even more than the twigs and leaves. Quitter thoughts descend upon him; he doesn't *deserve* to escape the mud and leeches and maggots. Who gives a shit about his debris-hut building skills anyway? Something cackles in the trees above. Even the animals scorn him. Except he has survived, has he not? Faced with a coyote and God knows what poisonous crawly creatures and plants and snakes and rivers, he has not given up.

Suddenly the narcotic shifts gears, elevating Milo above the debris hut, among the stars looking down upon his human toil, and he says loudly into the darkness, 'Wait a minute, now just wait *one* minute. I do! Yes, damn it, *I* give a shit!' All of them, all of them want him to stay *inside the lines*. The People of the First Nations, Geon Van Der Wyst, his fellow thespians, his fucking useless agent, the dead or alive Gus, Zosia, even Tanis who he'd thought was a kindred spirit, a free-thinker, a fence-opposer. Even Tanis has rules by which he must play. Fuck her, fuck all of them. Bunch of fucking caged thinkers. He's in the wild now, free in body and soul. He needs nothing and no one. He will make fire, dig up wild edible plants and tan animal hides. He will *survive!*

12

He wakes in unimaginable darkness. Despite repeated blinking, the dense and sooty blackness remains. He tries to sit up, slamming his head into the ridgepole. He rolls onto his stomach, dragging himself out ass-first. Remembering the leeches and maggots, he shakes himself and ruffles his hair, shedding twigs and leaves and creepy-crawlies. He digs his fingers into his nose and ears then shouts, 'Get me out of here!' into the thick silence. His mouth is so dry his lips stick to his teeth. What was he *thinking*? Gus used to say this and Milo tried to appear as though he had been thinking when in truth he had no idea what he'd been thinking. *You weren't thinking*, Gus would conclude. *You don't think.* Tanis also said this. Thinking has only meant trouble for Milo. All those gnawed thoughts rattling around inside his skull. Who needs that shit? He should be home in bed, thoughtless, preparing for another day of junk removal. Why must he always chase the dream, the big break, the ticket to a life free of cash woes? Although it's not really about cash, is it? It's about recognition, approval. *You did a good job there, son.* Why couldn't he have said that? Just once. When Milo painted the entire house barf beige as instructed, all his father saw was the drips. 'Fuck you, old man!' Milo shouts. Then 'Get over it!' to himself. He begins to dance what he imagines to be a First Nation peoples' dance, hopping on one leg while lifting the opposite knee to his chest. He begins to chant, periodically pounding his chest and uttering war cries. Or just cries. Because he is so utterly and irrefutably alone. 'Fuck you!' Milo shouts at the invisible forces pitted against him. His screams comet through the woods, burning themselves out until there is nothing left but the ricocheting pain, which in itself has become company of sorts – a reminder that he is alive, not a quitter, still a fighter, deserving of survival. For what? To do what? Watch TV, eat, shit and Facebook? The stars told him he could pack it in – where are they now, the fuckers? The chickenshit stars are hiding behind clouds. 'Come out and twinkle fucking twinkle!' he shouts.

'Stop making so much noise.'

Milo stumbles. 'Who's that?'

'Tawny Farmer. Who are you?' The voice sounds young.

'I can't see you.'

'Stop jumping around and shouting.'

Is she a teenager? What's she doing in the woods at this hour? 'Sorry,' he says, 'I didn't think anyone could hear me.'

'The animals hear you. They need sleep.'

'Of course. Sorry. Where are you?'

'Right in front of you.'

Milo stares in front of him for several seconds before he can see the outline of a small person.

'What're you doing here?' Tawny asks.

'Umm, well, I'm part of a theatre group.'

'Where's the other part?'

'I don't know. I'm lost, actually.'

'That's too bad.'

'Yeah, well I was trying to make the best of it. I built a debris hut.'

'A what?'

'A shelter.'

Conversing with a faceless voice makes him gesture as though talking with the deaf. Never before has he understood the need to read facial expressions. Is this girl in cahoots with Gary and company? Is this some kind of prank? Are they about to descend upon the worm turd and steal what is left of his cash?

'What are *you* doing here?' he asks.

'Getting you to stop making noise. Are you okay? You seem pretty freaked.'

'I'm fine.'

'If you say so.'

Twigs crunch as she starts to walk away, leaving him desolate in the maw of the muddy, buggy night. 'Wait,' he yelps. 'Where are you going?'

'To my trailer.'

'Can I come?'

'To my trailer?'

'Yes. I won't be any bother. I'm just ... I'm just ... ' He feels sobs of humiliation pending. He *is* a quitter. He doesn't deserve to survive. He sucks in air to prevent an avalanche of dejectedness. At least she can't see him.

'Come on.' He feels her hand in his, firm and warm, taking charge. He follows like a child.

Kerosene lamps illuminate the small trailer. Stuffed animals occupy the pullout bed. Spread across the table are books: *Relationships for Dummies*, *Dating for Dummies* and *Why He Isn't Calling You Back*. Dressed in sweatpants and a sweatshirt, Tawny looks overweight and homely, despite her long, shiny black hair. Milo would like to shield her from the books, assure her that males are taken in by the packaging and that the how-to pulp won't help her, that one day the right guy will come along and see beyond the packaging. Milo can't say this because he doesn't believe it. She will go on blaming herself for being unable to become something she is not. She will endure endless diets, bad jokes and fucks in her search for love and approval.

'Is this part of the reservation?' he asks.

'Yeah. It was my dad's workshop. He carved stuff for the cottagers. Stuff to put in their gardens. And driveways. They like having their names carved on signs.'

'Is he no longer with us?'

'Snowmobile accident.'

'I'm so sorry. Is your mother alive?'

'I guess you could call it that. What about your parents?'

'My mother's dead and I thought my father was, but now some people think they saw him on a reality show. I suspect they're mistaken.'

'You don't want him to be alive?'

'Not really.'

'Why not?'

'He's an asshole.'

Tawny sits on the pullout bed. 'I thought my dad was an asshole but then he died and all I could remember were the nice things about him.'

'I don't have that problem.'

'You just aren't remembering hard enough. Stop thinking about all the bad things all the time. I'm trying to do that with my mom before she's dead. Like, not see all the bad things all the time.'

'Is she ill?'

'No, but everybody dies. That's what's so dumb about humans. We pretend we're not going to die. Animals don't do that. If people told me *my* dad was on a reality show I'd go looking for him so I wouldn't spend all day wondering if he was dead or not. I'd sleep better.'

'I sleep better thinking he's dead.'

'Not me, I miss my dad. He used to take me on his snowmobile. I'd hold on tight and feel totally safe. I never feel that anymore.'

Milo tries to remember if he ever felt totally safe with his father. Maybe in the truck while Gus focused on the road, both hands firmly on the wheel. 'I've been feeling guilty about hating him,' he admits.

Tawny passes him a bag of Oreos. 'Maybe unconsciously you knew he wasn't dead. Like, you could feel him around you. I don't feel my dad. He's definitely dead. You're lucky.' She bites an Oreo. 'Do you have a girlfriend?'

'No.'

'Why not?'

'Just hasn't worked out.'

'What do the girlfriends say when they ditch you?'

'The last one said I coast.'

'Is that bad?'

'I think she just got tired of me. I think she wanted someone with ambition.'

'You don't have ambition?'

'Why should I when we're all dying anyway?'

'To make things better for future generations.'

He has read that the People of the First Nations look out for future generations. Unlike the white-asses who only look out for Number One. 'Do you go to school?' he asks.

'I'm going to be a lawyer. I'm going to fight for Native rights. What's it like in Toronto?'

'Busy. Polluted. It's nicer up here.'

'Guess that's why you were screaming to get out.' She picks up a newspaper. 'What sign are you?'

'Virgo.'

'*Something about you is commanding attention these days. You have what is called presence. When you walk into a room, heads will turn. You can join any conversation effortlessly and quickly lead the discussion. Be prepared to be the life of the party.*'

'Can't wait.'

'Do you want to sleep?'

'Where?'

'Here.' She pats the bed. 'I have to study anyway.' She pulls a backpack from under the bed and starts spreading textbooks out on the table. 'I need the chair,' she says.

The prospect of horizontal dozing on a soft, dry surface entices him. He rolls onto the bed trying to think of something he can offer in return for her kindness. 'Tawny?'

Already she has the books open, pen ready, revealing the lawyer in her.

'Don't try too hard with the guys,' he says. 'They don't like it when you try too hard. They're turned on when you don't seem to care.'

'That's twisted.'

'It is.'

She looks back at her books while he coasts into oblivion.

Banging on the trailer wakes him. 'Worm turd, you in there?'

Tawny pushes the door open. 'Stop making so much noise.'

'Is he in there?'

'Who?'

'The actor.'

'What actor?'

Milo drops to the floor by the bed.

'I seen him!' Elvis squeals, rapping his knuckles on the window. 'What you hiding him for, Tawny? Did you get lucky?'

'Get out here, boy,' Gary orders. 'You've got people looking for you.'

'What people?' Tawny demands.

'It's all right, Tawny,' Milo says, realizing this could be the moment he has been waiting for. Is it not possible that his infernal night has been a trial by fire? That once again he will receive a hero's welcome? Geon will ask to speak to him personally on his cell, commend him on his innovation and fortitude and award him the lead. Milo scribbles his address and phone number on a slip of paper and hands it to Tawny. 'If you ever make it to the Big Smoke, give me a call.'

The SUV jerks up a dirt road. Elvis puts his arm around him. 'Did you get any pussy?'

'Are you crazy? She's just a child.'

'Elvis has dirty dreams about her,' Elton says.

'Where are we going?' Milo asks.

'Wouldn't you like to know,' Gary replies.

'So no petting or nothing?' Elvis asks.

'Nothing. Leave her alone. She's a nice girl.'

'Her dad was a prick,' Elvis says.

'Used to throw beer bottles at her,' Elton adds. 'So Elvis wants to save her but she's not too interested.'

'She just doesn't know me good enough yet.'

'Where are we going?' Milo repeats. 'Where are the other actors?'

'They left,' Elvis says.

'Left? Where did they go?'

Elvis shrugs.

'Gary,' Milo persists, 'you must know where they went.'

'I just follow orders.'

Is it possible that, by pure chance, Milo has so far escaped being *disappeared*? Who are these mad men anyway? 'I demand to know where we're going. I want to talk to Geon Van Der Wyst.' Gary cranks the volume on the radio.

They pull up outside a vinyl-sided prefabricated house. A balding dog yaps at their heels. Elton kicks it. Elvis puts his arm around Milo's shoulders. 'Could you say some nice things about me to Tawny? Like, she don't even know about my model-airplane collection yet.'

Inside several sombre First Nations people sit on plastic chairs apparently waiting for something.

'Sit down,' Gary orders. Elvis and Elton take the chairs on either side of Milo. A wizened, white-haired man shuffles to the front of the room. The other People of the First Nations watch him with great interest and Milo concludes that he must be the leader and has, no doubt, experienced much abuse at the hands of white-asses. Is that what this is all about then? As the only white-ass present, is Milo expected to justify the raping and pillaging, the introduction of firewater, the spreading of disease and the appropriation of land, the kidnapping and abuse of Native children, the merciless enforcement of Christianity? How can he possibly excuse white man's greed and hubris? Is this the condition for his release? Will failure to adequately justify the heinous acts of his pale-face brethren condemn him? Or is this another Geon Van Der Wyst scheme? Milo looks around for hidden cameras. Is this part of the show? A white man cut adrift in Indian territory, his only weapon his wits?

'My name is Al,' the old man says, 'and I'm an alcoholic.'

Everyone else says, 'Welcome, Al.'

'Last week,' Al continues, 'my son Joe asked me to go over to his place to watch hockey on his big television.' Al speaks slowly, each word weighted. 'He has asked me many times to go over to his place to watch hockey on his big television and I have always said no because they drink beers. I know it hurts my son's feelings when I say no. He is a good boy. He is off the reservation and working at Mr. Lube. He has his own place. I am very proud of Joe but when he is watching hockey with his friends, he drinks beers.' The other alcoholics murmur ominously. 'But last week I decided that I could not say no to Joe again. I decided I would go to his place and watch hockey on his big television.' Al pauses, looking studiously at the floor then up at the ceiling. The other alcoholics wait expectantly. Outside, the balding dog yaps. 'Last week I sat with my son Joe and watched hockey on his big television. I did not drink one beer. Not one.' The alcoholics jump up and applaud, offering 'thank you for sharing' and 'good job' and 'way to go, man.' Al wipes his eyes as he shuffles back to his seat.

Elvis, still applauding, nudges Milo. 'Don't it make you proud to be human?'

Al and Joe watching hockey. A longing clutches at Milo. He *must* see his father again. Must sit together watching hockey. Milo stopped watching hockey with Gus during Gus's fat period, after Annie died, because Gus would rail at the players, even Guy Lafleur who could do no wrong in Milo's eyes. Gus's bitterness consumed massive amounts of Doritos, Pringles and sour cream 'n' onion potato chips. Milo stayed in his room listening to the game on the radio. But now things will be different. Look at Tawny, longing for the father who thwacked her with beer bottles. Had she not been blinded by resentment they might have had a proper conversation; an understanding might have formed. Now he's dead. But Gus is not. Gus is waiting to be found. Milo has failed miserably; he can see that now. Too much time spent picking at self-inflicted wounds. And what about Robertson and Tanis? And Christopher stranded in the hospital? They need Milo. *Stop thinking about the bad things all the time*, Tawny said. What did the horoscope say? *You are commanding attention these days. You have what is called presence. When you walk into a room, heads will turn.*

As more alcoholics humbly confess to staying on the wagon, Milo applauds so hard his hands burn.

13

*H*ow can Gus's house be empty? Where are the gin-swilling barbarians? Are there no innards to fry, no mambo to grind? Milo feels as though he is still on the Greyhound bus, lurching and rumbling, each bump on the road jabbing his rib, forcing him to grunt.

Immediately he turns on his computer and searches for *Reality Check*, the reality show about people who think they're on reality shows. He leaves a lengthy message in their viewer response mailbox explaining his quest to the show's producers, Birgit Kaiser and Sammy Sanjari. Next he emails Geon Van Der Wyst demanding an explanation for why he was left behind in the woods. The only message in Milo's inbox is from his agent, who wants to have a chat to make sure 'we're still on the same page.'

After taping a plastic garbage bag over his chest wrap, Milo showers for twenty minutes, exalting in running water. Next he intends to eat real food. Fed and shaved, he will be ready to face Tanis, to come clean about Christopher, because this can't go on. Just like a fever must be allowed to reach its peak to cure sickness, so must the incendiary truth about Christopher be allowed to burn. Milo is prepared to receive angry words from both Tanis and Christopher. The important one is Robertson. He must learn about his dad's plight. And that his dad would give his life for him.

It's while Milo's sitting at the kitchen table, savouring a cheese and pickle sandwich, that the three musketeers barge in.

'Where's Robertson?' Pablo demands.

'How should I know? I just got here.'

'So you didn't take him on a little jaunt?' Vera queries.

'Why would I take him on a little jaunt?'

'He's missing,' Wallace clarifies.

'Tanis will know where he is,' Milo says.

'Not this time.'

'Robertson's *disappeared*,' Pablo wails. 'Tanis thought maybe *you* took him. We've been looking all over for him. Me and Vera in the woods and Wallace in the truck.'

'I've cruised the entire fucking neighbourhood ten times.' Wallace sticks his fingers in the pickle jar and fishes one out.

'Did she call the police?'

'Not right away,' Pablo says. 'She don't like cops. She says if they find him they'll scare him.'

'They won't understand his handicap,' Vera clarifies.

'But she did call them? Have they started a search?'

'I saw a couple of cops down the street going door to door,' Wallace says. 'Next they'll get the dogs out.'

Pablo sticks his fingers in the pickle jar. 'That would, like, totally freak out Robertson. Hope they don't taser him.'

'I'd better go over there,' Milo says.

'That might not be such a great idea,' Pablo says. 'She's totally flipped out – like, she's not talking to nobody. She was screaming at the cops.'

'That's after she was screaming for the kid,' Wallace says. 'She was running all over the place screaming for him. Busted her ankle.'

'What?'

'She was in the ravine looking for him and tripped. She's on crutches.'

He knocks on the sliding doors and presses his ear against the glass. 'Tanis?' All the lights are on, which is unusual because of her concern about the hydro bill. But this evening the house is ablaze, as though Tanis is trying to transform it into a beacon for her son.

Then suddenly she's behind the glass, almost unrecognizable, her hair wild and her eyes frantic. She doesn't open the door. 'Do you have him?' she demands.

'Of course not. I would never take him anywhere without your consent.' Hunched over the crutches she seems smaller, frailer. 'Please, can we talk?'

She opens the door but turns her back on him as she hobbles to a chair.

'Tell me what happened,' he pleads.

'If I knew, would I be here?' Her voice sounds hoarse, probably from all that screaming.

'When did you last see him?'

'Last night,' she says. 'In bed. Safe in bed.'

'Did you tell him about Billy?'

'Why would I do that? Sleep tight, baby, and by the way Billy's dead.' She starts rubbing her face as though she's trying to rub it off. 'The dog's gone. He either took her or went looking for her.'

'Where would Sal go?'

'The ravine.'

'Did you call for her there?'

'Of course,' she shouts. 'What do you think I've been doing? Sitting around waiting? My boy is gone. *Gone!*' She starts to moan, swaying back and forth on the chair.

'He was outside in his pyjamas the night of the party,' Milo says. 'Has he been doing that lately? Getting out of bed and walking around outside while you're sleeping?'

'How am I supposed to know what he's doing while I'm sleeping? I shouldn't sleep. I was wrong to sleep. Mothers of autistic children should never sleep. I should know that. He was in *bed.*'

'So you woke up this morning and he was gone?'

'How stupid are you? I want you to go now.' She stands on one leg with difficulty and starts hobbling towards him. 'Go.'

'I want to help.'

'You can't help. You kill little boys. Out.' She lifts a crutch and jabs it at his chest. 'Out. Go.' She starts to swing the crutch at his face. 'Get out!'

The three amigos are eating liverwurst sannies. 'Where did you look for him?' Milo demands.

'All over,' Pablo says.

'Be more specific.'

'We had a look in the woods,' Vera says. 'A bit tricky with all that shrubbery. My stockings are in tatters.'

'Did you go north or south?' Milo asks.

Pablo pushes a pickled egg into his mouth. 'Which way is north?'

'Did you go right or left when you entered the ravine?'

Pablo stands and re-enacts their entrance to the ravine. 'Right.'

'Are you sure, love? Seems to me we went straight down the middle.'

'Did you follow the path?'

'Sure, because it was hard for Vera to walk in the forest.'

'How far did you go?'

'You mean, like, how many miles?'

Vera offers Milo a pickled egg. 'We were only gone an hour or so.'

'Leave the ravine to the cops,' Wallace advises. 'Only nutcases go in there at night.'

Milo swallows more codeine and grabs his flashlight. 'Robertson will hide from the cops.'

At the base of the street the ravine fans out. Its steep slopes make the land unattractive to developers, allowing it to become a sanctuary for the homeless and a haven for druggies. Blanket tents dot the wilderness, as does litter, cigarette butts, used syringes and condoms.

Sodden from the rain, the undergrowth offers little traction, and Milo repeatedly loses his footing. When he looked for his father he was not methodical about it. He did not comb the woods but followed what he thought were leads: a broken branch here, a used tissue there. He worried that he would get lost if he strayed too far from the path. This time he will traverse the terrain beyond the path. 'Robertson!' he shouts every few steps, stopping to listen for a response. If the child is injured or traumatized he may be unable to respond. 'Sal!' Milo also calls. He is wearing his four-hundred-dollar glasses, which he rarely does because he's afraid of losing them. He needs them only for driving and auditions that require him to look intelligent. In the woods they enable him to see more clearly into the brush. After an hour of traversing, he squats on a fallen trunk. The spill from city lights filters the darkness while distant traffic drones. 'Robertson,' he calls for possibly the three hundredth time. He too is growing hoarse while trying not to think about what might be happening, or might have happened to Robertson. On the opposite slope he sees the flicker of a lighter, then the glow of cigarettes or spliffs. This sign of human life offers no comfort because humans offer Robertson no comfort. Milo resumes traversing, watching the glowing dots dance as the smokers move the butts to and from their mouths. It makes perfect sense that Robertson ran away, given the circumstances. After Annie died, Milo ran away on a regular basis. Despite his stash of Pop-Tarts, after several hours his stomach would rumble and he would return to Mrs. Cauldershot, who would say, 'Oh, it's you. Did you run away again?'

Robertson ran away because his father left him and because he is despised at school. Many with Autism Spectrum Disorders are not supposed to be able to interpret emotions in others. But Robertson must see his mother becoming unwound, must see her taking pills, see her hair spiralling out of control, see her hanging laundry in the rain. It must frighten him.

The glowing dots bounce and move across the slope. The beam on Milo's flashlight weakens.

The impact from being tackled and slammed into the ground leaves him winded. In the darkness a boot pushed against his throat makes him choke. Hands roughly search his pockets. 'Take my money,' Milo manages to utter before remembering he left without his wallet.

'Where is it?' a faceless figure demands.

'I forgot it.'

The boot pushes harder into his neck. 'Do you want to fuckin' die?'

'It's true. I'm looking for a boy. I left it at home.'

'He's a fuckin' faggot lookin' for some crackhead to blow.'

'We'll get you a boy. Where's your fuckin' money?'

Milo doesn't resist but holds his four-hundred-dollar glasses away from his assaulted body in an effort to protect them.

The faceless figure pulls out Milo's keys. 'You got a car?'

'No.'

'Don't bullshit me.' The boot pushes harder.

'He's right, there's no fuckin' car key here.'

'What are these pills?'

'Painkillers.'

'Take the fuckin' narcotics.'

'*Where's* your fuckin' money?' The hands search Milo's back pockets. 'This guy's a fuckin' joke.'

'A fuckin' faggot. Take his flashlight.'

'Fuckin' waste of time.' While Milo holds his glasses at arm's length the faceless figure kicks his legs. The boot kicks his head.

•••

'What're you doing here?'

'What?'

A flashlight shines in his face. 'What're you doing here?'

'Robertson?' Relief at seeing the boy surges through Milo.

'You got beat up,' Robertson says.

'Did you see anything?'

'Nope. But nobody lies in the dirt.' Sal sniffs Milo.

'Where are my glasses? Give me your flashlight.' Sure enough the glasses are intact inches away. Milo puts them on.

'You don't wear glasses,' Robertson says.

'I do sometimes. What are you ... why did you run away?'

'I didn't run away. I left and you better not tell anybody where I am.'

'Your mom is really worried about you. She called the police, they're looking for you.'

'She wouldn't do that. She thinks cops are fascists.'

'Well, she was frightened and didn't know what else to do so she called them. You just disappeared. Why didn't you leave a note?'

'Too complicated.' Robertson says this when he is about to shut down. Milo wants to throw his arms around the child and hold him close but knows this would cause a full freak-out and retreat. Changing tactics, Milo inhales deeply and produces what he hopes will pass for a contented sigh.

'What a beautiful night,' he says. 'You can even see stars.'

Robertson rubs Sal's tummy.

'I was out in the country last night,' Milo adds. 'With real Indians.'

'Why?'

'I was auditioning for a show.'

'What kind of show?'

'I don't actually know.'

'So why did you audition for it?'

'I wanted a job.'

'Did you get it?'

'Don't know yet. I learned how to build a debris hut.'

'What's that?'

'A shelter made from dead branches and leaves and stuff.'

'Could we make one now?'

Sleep-deprived, with pulsating pain in his head, neck, ribs and legs, the last thing Milo wants to do is build another debris hut. If Robertson were a normal child, Milo could coax him home with offers of pizza and ice cream and mother love. 'It's pretty dark,' he says, feeling for his opioids before remembering that the muggers took them.

'No it's not. The moon's almost full. You can see fine when you get used to it.' Robertson starts digging around in the brush. 'How big do the branches have to be?'

When Milo was earning his bullshit of arts degree, he became infatuated with a coltish runner who dreamed of making the Olympic team. He never got to sleep with her but watched her race many times and was always astonished at how ready to expire she looked after passing the finish line. She told him the pain got so bad in the last laps that it was as if she were being stabbed. In the final lap even her eyeballs started to burn, but she'd say in her head to her body, 'This is it, no second chances. Show me what you've got.' Milo is having a similar conversation in his head with his tortured body as he searches for deadfall. Miraculously they spotted a tree in the moonlight with a Y-shaped nook at a good height. Robertson, full of vim and vigour, thanks to his steady diet of granola bars and juice boxes, searched tirelessly until he found what he considered to be the perfect ridgepole. Now, in his last lap, Milo's body must show him what it's got, because collapsing at Robertson's feet will only frighten him. Milo must appear in command of the situation. If Robertson has confidence in him, he may be able to convince him to return home. If Milo comes off as anything less than Mountain Man, Robertson will lose interest and vanish again. So despite the stabbing pain, Milo bends down repeatedly to fill his arms with branches and leaves. He had hoped that hunger would draw Robertson back to civilization, but the granola bars have eliminated this option, although Milo has tried muttering that a cup of hot chocolate would 'go down real nice about now.' He doesn't know why he's talking as though he is in a Western. Robertson pays him no heed anyway, so focused is he on the task at hand. His face is filthy as are his clothes, a little wild boy.

'Did the Indians teach you this?' Robertson asks.

'No. It was a survivalist.'

'What's that?'

'A man determined to survive come the Apocalypse.'

'Does he know when it's coming?'

'No, but when it does, he'll be ready.'

'That's smart,' Robertson says, stuffing more mud into the crevices of the hut.

'Is it? I mean, would you want to go on living when human life on the planet has ended?'

'Definitely. It would be totally boss.'

Milo imagines the autistic emerging from the detritus, freed from society's nagging demands, rebuilding the world their way.

Robertson stands back and appraises their work. 'This is epic.'

'I'm glad you like it but you might want to go home and get a sleeping bag if you plan to camp out here.'

'Sleeping bags are for wussies.' He scrambles into the hut. Sal scurries after him.

Now what? Should Milo make a run for it? Get Tanis? How could she manage the terrain on crutches? And what if Robertson isn't here when they get back? And where is *here*, exactly? Without a flashlight how effective will Milo's return journey be? What if he can't find the hut?

'Epic,' Robertson says again. Milo has never seen him so exhilarated. Turning him in, sending him back to the jail of home and school, would be a betrayal. But what about mother love? Unconditional love? Acceptance? Does Robertson not need this? Although Tanis doesn't really accept him, does she? She wants him to be normal. That's it then. She has lost him by trying to make him into something he is not. How many parents lose their children by trying to make them into something they are not? The coltish runner's parents were unable to hide their disappointment when she failed to make the Olympic team. She became a real estate agent, grew hips and children. Milo sees her ads on benches at bus stops. All that suffering just so people can sit on her face.

'Milo?'

'Yes?'

'Are you coming in?'

The hut is small; it will be hard to keep his distance.

'Actually, pardner, I was kinda pinin' for some viddles and a comfy bed.'
Why is he talking cowboy again? Robertson doesn't respond, has probably
shut down. A siren wails beyond the woods in the urban jungle and suddenly
Milo would much rather be here than there. He hears a click and sees the glow
of Robertson's flashlight through the debris hut.

'Milo?'

'Yes?'

'Do you want a granola bar and an apple juice?'

'Sure.' He crawls inside the hut until he is a foot from Robertson, who has
laid out two bars and two juice boxes and three dog biscuits for Sal.

'We have to ration,' the wild boy explains. They chew and swallow slowly.
Periodically Robertson caresses the sides of the hut. 'Epic,' he says.

14

Something raps against the ridgepole. 'Anybody in there?'

'Shhh,' Milo hisses, scrambling out.

'What's going on here?' a bodybuilder cop demands.

'Nothing, just *please* be quiet. He freaks out so easily.'

'You got the kid in there?'

'Robertson Wedderspoon? Yes. Do you have a cell, can you call his mother?'

'We have to see the boy first.'

A sumo wrestler cop and a dog circle the debris hut as though checking for bombs.

'It's just,' Milo tries to explain, 'sudden moves startle him. He's autistic.'

'We heard. What's your name?'

'Milo Krupi. I'm his neighbour.'

'You stayed here all night with him?'

'No. I was out looking for him and got mugged. He found *me*, actually.'

'Why didn't you take him home?'

'Because he didn't want to go home.'

'He's a kid. He has to go home.'

'I know, but I was trying to do it gradually, in daylight, so we wouldn't get lost.'

'Why doesn't he want to go home?'

'Oh, domestic trouble. His parents broke up. And school, he's bullied at school.'

The cop taps the hut with his baton. 'You built this?'

'We both did. It's a debris shelter. Robertson was very happy making it. I didn't want to ruin it for him by forcing him to go home.'

'Is that right? Well, how 'bout you let him talk for himself?'

'Actually, I'd prefer it if you'd let me wake him.'

'Mr. Crappy, you're under suspicion for kidnapping. We don't want you talking to him.'

'That's absurd. He's my friend.'

'Let's see what *he* has to say about it.'

The sumo wrestler grips Milo's arm. 'Stand over here, please.'

'Could you take your hat off?' Milo asks the bodybuilder.

'What?'

'You'll look less threatening if you take your hat off. Plus I don't think you'll fit through with the hat on. It's pretty snug in there.'

The sumo wrestler continues to grip Milo's arm while the bodybuilder kneels in front of the debris hut. 'Robertson?' he inquires.

'He's asleep,' Milo explains.

'Shut up,' the sumo wrestler advises.

'Robertson,' the bodybuilder repeats, 'it's all right. You're safe now. You can come out.' Sal, turned feral by her taste of the wild, charges at the cop, barking excitedly. The police dog, still on a leash, lunges towards her, also barking.

'Milo?' Robertson cries, sounding terrified.

'I'm right here, buddy. It's the police. They've come to find you.'

'Shut up,' the wrestler repeats.

'Milo, you promised you wouldn't tell anybody. Did you tell them?'

'I didn't, buddy. Honest.' The wrestler tightens his grip.

'You told them, you told them, you told them!' Robertson shrieks.

The bodybuilder pushes Sal aside, takes off his hat and crawls into the debris hut, club, gun and all. Within seconds Robertson is shrieking and kicking, causing branches and leaves to pop off the hut.

'It's okay, son,' the bodybuilder says, 'we're not going to hurt you. Your mom's really worried about you and she wants you home.'

'My mom says police are *fascists!*' Robertson yells. 'I'm never going home ever, ever, ever, ever, ever!'

'Let me talk to him,' Milo persists.

'Shut up.'

Robertson's high-tops poke through the hut as he kicks. 'I'm never going home ever, ever, ever, ever, ever!' The hut vibrates as he bangs his head against it. Within seconds the bodybuilder drags him out, kicking and screaming.

'Call his mother,' he says to the wrestler. 'Tell her the fascists are on their way.' The bodybuilder strides through the woods with the wailing, flailing boy in his grasp.

...

'Do you know this man?' the bodybuilder asks Tanis.

'He's my neighbour.'

'We found him with your son.'

'*I* found him,' Milo interjects. 'Actually, he found me.'

'Shut up,' the wrestler says.

'He built some kind of wigwam with your son last night and slept in it.'

Tanis, who has been looking and acting like a madwoman, opens and closes her mouth several times. Already she has further alienated the police by accusing them of mistreating her son. 'Get away from him,' she kept yelling at them. Milo had to restrain Robertson while she strapped on the protective helmet. They can hear him thumping as they stand in the front hall.

Tanis looks at Milo with eyes completely unfamiliar to him. 'You knew where he was?'

'Not until the early hours of this morning,' Milo explains. 'He didn't want to come back and I didn't want to force him. I mean, it was dark. We could have gotten lost.'

'So how long were you planning to stay in the wigwam?' the bodybuilder inquires.

'Hopefully not long. I was hoping he'd get hungry and I could interest him in some pancakes or something.'

Tanis sits and stares at nothing. 'Why didn't he want to come home?'

'He didn't want to go to school,' Milo says, which is easier than explaining that the pressure to be normal has overwhelmed Robertson.

'Well, ma'am, if you're satisfied that your son's safe, we'll be on our way.'

'What do you mean "safe"? He's never safe.' She starts getting loud again. 'He's bullied in the schoolyard every single day. What kind of sick world allows a boy to be bullied *every single day*? What kind of sick, perverted world?' Both cops edge towards the door.

'So you want no charges laid?' the bodybuilder asks.

'Charges?'

'Against your neighbour here.'

'For what?'

'He kept the boy in the wigwam, ma'am.'

'It was a debris shelter,' Milo interjects.

'Get out,' Tanis orders.

Milo and the cops look at each other because they're not sure whom she's talking to.

'All of you. Get out. Now.' She starts swinging her crutch. The cops hurry out but Milo lingers. The wrestler reaches back for him. 'You too, asshole.'

Vera's frying bangers again, and bread in the banger grease. 'Off with the muddy shoes,' she commands.

'I found him,' Milo says.

'We know,' Wallace says. 'We can hear him trying to split his head open.'

'Poor little tyke,' Vera says.

'Where was he?' Pablo asks.

'In the ravine. He didn't want to come home so we built a shelter.'

Wallace bites a piece of toast. 'With what?'

'Debris. It's called a debris shelter. Robertson loved it.'

Vera pats Milo's shoulder. 'Go wash up, then come have some brekkie.'

He eats the fried pig and bread because he doesn't know what else to do.

'So you're a hero, Milo,' Pablo says. 'Did Tanis go crazy when she saw him? I saw this movie about this stripper whose son got kidnapped and she was, like, totally freaked out, and when the cops found him she was, like, totally hysterical, hugging him so hard. She was crying and everything and even the CIA agent got emotional. It made me cry.'

'Tanis can't hug Robertson.' Milo eats another sausage even though he doesn't want it. They couldn't hold Robertson still enough to wash him. He is up there, thrashing, covered in filth.

'You look knackered,' Vera says. 'I'd say a good rest is in order.'

'I need painkillers. I cracked a rib.' He lifts up his T-shirt, revealing the chest wrap.

'Goodness gracious, how did you do that?'

'A deer kicked me.'

Vera and Pablo exchange dubious looks. Wallace, engrossed in the personals, isn't even listening. Vera digs in her purse. 'Take some of my back pills.'

'What's in them?'

'Haven't the foggiest.'

Milo swallows four.

He wakens to T V noise and Vera slamming things around in the kitchen, but no head-banging. Robertson has probably fallen asleep on the floor. How will Tanis lift him by herself? He presses his ear against the wall.

'Milo?'

'What?'

Wallace beckons him from his bedroom. 'Can you come here for a sec?' This is the new Wallace who asks rather than commands. Milo walks into his room and watches him hurriedly close the door. 'She's been out of control since you left,' Wallace says. 'It's like she owns the place.'

'I've noticed.'

'It's *your* house. You can stop her.'

'No I can't. You know I can't.'

Wallace sits on the bed and starts coughing. 'I wish she'd croak.'

'Why? She seems pleasant enough. She's doing your laundry and mending your clothes, feeding you ...'

'Call that food? I've put on four pounds already. I'll pay you a hundred bucks if you make the kitchen off limits.'

'I have no energy to fight her, Wallace. You may have noticed that I am injured.'

'So tell her that's why. Say you're injured and you can't eat fried food, just raw juices and shit.'

'Wallace, what is the problem? Why can't you just *talk* to your mother?'

'Oh, like you could talk with your father. When are you picking him up?'

'What?'

'You can't just leave him there.'

'Are you telling me if your mother was being cared for in an institution, at no cost to you, you would go get her?' This gives Wallace pause. 'And anyway, we don't know if it's him. I haven't seen this famous footage.'

'It's him.'

'So you keep saying.'

'Do you have Fennel's number?'

'Of course not.'

'Pablo won't give it to me.'

'Did you offer him a hundred bucks for it?'

'Very funny.'

'Why does Pablo have it?'

'Are you kidding me? He's been all over her.'

'What about Maria?'

'Yesterday's news.' Wallace starts coughing again.

'So you're saying he took Fennel out?'

'They went to some art opening then came back and made out on the couch.'

'You watched?'

'I was getting a beer, okay?'

'Where was Vera?'

'Asleep in the chair.'

'You mean they were getting it on while she was asleep in the chair?'

'You got it. Depraved, I'm telling you, that Mexican's got to go.'

'What'll you pay me to get rid of him?'

'Are you serious?'

Milo has no idea how to accomplish this but he could use the cash. 'Three hundred.'

'Two.'

'Two-fifty.'

'Deal.'

'Wal-leee? I've made steak and kidney pud. See if Milo wants to join us.' Milo shakes his head, making throat-cutting gestures. Wallace sucks on his puffer. Within seconds Vera's on her way up. 'Oh, there you are. What are you lot up to? You look better, Milo, have a bit more colour.'

'He's all better, he's going to have supper with us.' Wallace slaps Milo's back, igniting sparks of pain.

'Do you have any more of those back pills?'

'Where's Pablo?'

Vera hacks away at the pud with a serving spoon. 'He's at Tanis's.'

'Why?'

'She wants bolts on the doors. Up high where the boy can't reach them.'

'That's insane.'

'What's insane about it?' Wallace says. 'It'll keep him safe.'

'That's not safe. That's prison.'

'Better than getting molested in the ravine.'

'Is that the bell?' Vera wipes her hands on her apron and heads for the door.

'It's probably some assfuck selling something,' Wallace mutters.

'Fennel!' Vera exclaims. 'How lovely, we were just sitting down to supper.'

'I've eaten, thanks. Is Pablo here?'

'Fucking hell,' Wallace grumbles.

'He's over at the neighbour's doing a bit of handiwork. He'll be back in a tic. Why don't you join us for a sherry?' She pulls Fennel into the kitchen.

'Hey, Milo,' Fennel says, ignoring Wallace.

'Are you sure you won't have a bite?' Vera pours her a sherry.

'No, thanks. I'm supposed to paint Pablo.'

'Unfucking believable,' Wallace mutters.

'Pardon me with knobs on,' Vera says.

Fennel takes several gulps of sherry. 'The light is totally Vermeer right now. I love early summer evenings.'

'Who doesn't?' Wallace mumbles.

'Now what's going on between you two?' Vera demands. 'Some kind of lovers' spat?'

Fennel eyeballs Milo. 'How long do we have to keep this up?'

'What up?' Vera asks.

'Everything's fine, Mother,' Wallace interjects. 'Can I have some more pud?'

It is a testament to Wallace's desperation that he requests seconds. Immediately Vera springs from her chair to spoon more horror. 'I had a frightful time finding kidneys. I haven't found a proper butcher.'

'We don't have proper butchers here,' Fennel says. 'Just superstores full of drugged meat.'

'It's a shame. There's nothing like a good butcher. We have one gives us bones for stock. Ettie makes the most marvellous soups. And, of course, we let the doggies chew on the bones. Do you remember that song, Wally, about the fox catching the chickens and the little ones chewing on the bones?' She sings, '*And the little ones chewed on the bones-oh-bones-oh-bones-oh and the little ones chewed on the bones.* He loved that one, couldn't stop singing it. Do you remember it, Wally?'

There is no place to hide but the basement. To block out the pandemonium above, Milo plays Gus's Polish folk music. Pablo clambers downstairs with Gus's hammer and screwdriver. *'Qué pasa?'*

'I can't believe you put locks on his doors.'

'Only the ones that go outside.'

'He'll have to ask permission to go out his back door into his yard, does that seem right to you?'

'It's not about right, Milo. It's about safe.'

'How is it safe to lock him inside? He'll go nuts.'

'He's already a little nuts.'

'He is not. You're nuts. You're all nuts.'

Pablo drops the hammer and screwdriver on Gus's workbench.

'Put them back where you found them,' Milo says.

Pablo looks around. 'I can't remember where I found them.'

'*Always* put things back where you found them.' Gus used to say this. Milo grabs the hammer and screwdriver and hangs them carefully on Gus's tool rack.

'He's like a feather,' Pablo says. 'Skin and bone.'

'You lifted him?'

'She asked me to.'

'You put him to bed?'

'Of course.'

This is too much. The Cuban has to go.

'Milo, you're not mad about me dating Fenny, are you?'

'Why would I be mad?'

'You met her first. Wallace is mad about it. He don't even let me do junk removal. He's using Jorge.'

'Well, now that you're Tanis's handyman, you have another source of income.'

'I'm sorry things didn't work out between you two.'

'To what would you be referring? Unlike yourself, I don't throw myself at every woman who happens to be in the neighbourhood.'

'Me and Tanis are just friends. I know you love her, Milo. She's just not receptive right now, you have to let her process her life changes. Sarah Moon

Dancer says we have to watch and listen, not always *do*. You're kind of Action Man right now, Milo. Maybe you should just chill for a while.'

'Maybe you should just mind your own fucking business.'

'Who's for a bit of lime sorbet?' Vera calls.

The hamster spins on its wheel. 'Christ,' Milo mutters, 'I forgot about Puffy.' Looking after Puffy is way beyond his current capabilities. Already the cage stinks and needs cleaning. 'Can you take the hamster to Robertson?'

'*Qué?*'

Booting Pablo out and scoring the two fifty loses importance in the face of this latest crisis. Milo needs a go-between. He lifts the cage. 'Please, can you take it over there? She'll take it from you. It'll help Robertson, I'm sure of it.'

Fennel flounces downstairs and drapes herself over the blockhead. 'Oh, that is so cute. I totally love hamsters.'

'Please, Pablo?' Milo asks, wishing he had cash to offer as a bonus.

'Please what?' Fennel inquires.

'I've got to take the mouse over to Tanis's,' Pablo says, and in that instant Milo trusts him more than anybody. How frightening.

Not a word from the *Reality Check* people nor Geon Van Der Wyst. Nothing to do but scrape the chipped paint off the Muskoka chairs. Pablo poses against a tree – topless, of course, with his jeans rolled up and his fly slightly unzipped – while Fennel, glugging sherry, smears paint on a canvas.

'Shouldn't he be naked?' Milo asks. They don't bother to respond, so rapt are they in each other's drunken gaze. Disgusting. Her masterpiece doesn't even remotely resemble Pablo. Wallace has seized the opportunity to mow the lawn, which he never does. Not only that, he gets out the Whipper-snipper and buzzes the edges. 'Mind the lilac bush,' Milo shouts over the racket. He keeps checking Tanis's windows to see if the noise will prompt either her or Robertson to look out.

Action Man. For the first time in his life he has taken charge, and look where it's got him. At least she accepted the hamster. Maybe, while watching Puffy languishing in a cage, she will twig to the fact that she has caged her son. Tomorrow Milo will linger in the yard before they head to school and pretend to be weeding, then casually say, 'Hey.' Tomorrow he will watch and listen.

15

*S*ammy Sanjari has replied, suggesting they get together for lunch and a chat, when would be a good time? Suspicion heats Milo's face. Why doesn't Sammy just come out and tell him where the Gus look-alike is? Is he expecting a bonus? Lunch costs money. Milo emails that lunch won't be necessary; all he requires is the address of the retirement home. *We'd love to meet you*, Sammy replies. *Please, lunch is on us.* By 'us' does he mean Sammy and Birgit Kaiser? The photo of Birgit on the *Reality Check* website suggests that she is mostly teeth, hair and breasts. Why is there no photo of Sammy?

And who says this is the right thing to do anyway? What's Milo supposed to do with his father – if it is his father – once he's put him in a cab and brought him home? Isn't life chaotic enough with the barbarians and Fenny and God knows what else? Then, in his inbox, appears a message from Geon Van Der Wyst. *We are so glad to hear you made it back, Milo, we were somewhat concerned but Gary assured us that all went well.* 'Somewhat concerned?' 'All went well?' *As you may imagine, Hunter did not intend to leave you behind but, as you separated from the group and night was falling, it became necessary, for the sake of the others, to return to the city. We greatly appreciate your efforts on our project and it is with regret that we must inform you that we have decided to go another way with it.* 'Another way'? What way? What's 'it'? Does anybody have a fucking clue what 'it' is? *We wish you every success in your future endeavours. Best, Geon Van Der Wyst.* WHERE'S MY FUCKING WATCH? Milo replies. Gus gave it to him for his twenty-first birthday. It even has *for Milo from Dad* inscribed on the back of it.

He searches the *Reality Check* website and looks at Birgit's breasts again. Nobody else wants to buy him lunch. He wouldn't actually have to *do* anything, would he? He could just watch and listen and eat something besides animal parts.

...

Once Vera has gone to bed he creeps downstairs hoping for some distraction from the idiot box, but Wallace is slinging back vodka coolers and studying the personals again.

'*Good-looking male with Portuguese background,*' he reads, '*extremely active, looking for Asian-slash-Filipino woman for long-term relationship.* Like, what's that supposed to mean?'

'He prefers Asians.' Milo searches for the remote.

'But, like, I mean how can you know you only want a long-term relationship with an Asian-slash-Filipino woman?'

'Maybe they're more submissive than North Americans.'

'I'd say that's one sick fuck.'

Out his bedroom window, less than an hour ago, Milo watched Pablo making out with Fennel. It began against the tree then concluded beneath the lilac bush.

'*Tall, slim, very friendly, clean, handsome gent, 60, seeks adventure with younger woman.* How much younger do you figure?'

'Sixteen.'

'Sick fucker.'

'At least he's very friendly and clean. Where's the remote?'

'Fuck, Milo, look at this. *Lost Relative: Anyone knowing the woman B. W. Neblett, nee Burgess, about 84, please call Victoria Nikolas, nee Neblett.* She married a fucking Greek and now she's looking for her mother. She's even advertising for her and here you are acting like your dad's dead.'

'Where's the remote?'

'Do you know what those places are like? They stink like sewers and the staff abuse the old folks. Or drug them stupid so all they do is watch TV and shit their nappies. No way would I leave my mother in one.'

'Strong words from a man who just told me he wishes his mother would croak. Where's the remote?' The ugly, irrevocable truth is that Milo masturbated while watching Pablo getting it on with Fennel. 'Why do you read the ads, Wallace? Have you ever actually tried calling one of those numbers?'

'Fuck no.'

Milo gives up searching for the remote, treads into the kitchen to look in the fridge, sees a bowl of milk with animal organs in it and immediately closes the fridge door.

'I can't figure out why Fennel doesn't like me,' Wallace whines. 'What did I do? I was nice to her, wasn't I nice?'

Milo tears open a bag of chips, or *crisps* as Vera calls them.

'It's that fucking Mexican,' Wallace concludes.

And there he is, at the back door, the cat who ate the cream. 'Man, am I starved,' he says.

'Has he contributed to groceries?' Wallace demands, still on the couch. 'I haven't seen him *once* contribute to groceries.'

Pablo reaches into Milo's bag of chips. 'Zosia says hi.'

'What?'

'Zosia, your ex, she says hi.'

'She's not wounded?'

'You mean, like, wounded in love? Are you worried you broke her heart, Milo? That's a good one.' He chortles and shoves chips into his mouth. 'She's fatter though.'

'Did she ask about me?' Milo has been in denial, not wanting to imagine the possibilities. Now that she is unharmed, all he wants is to rest his head on her shoulder.

'I said you were between jobs.'

'What did she say?'

'"Very good." She's moved on, Milo. She's a very forward-thinking person, you need her kind of energy in your life. Too bad you blew it.'

'What the fuck do you know about it?' Wallace grumbles.

'There you go with that anger wall again, Wally.'

'Don't call me Wally.'

'I'm telling you, that bitterness will consume you, man. You'll end up this burnt-up carcass. I seen it happen.'

'Where's Fennel?' Wallace grabs the chips from Milo.

'She went home.'

'What, she didn't want to dry-hump on the couch?'

'Fenny's not too comfortable here.'

'Her name is Fennel.'

'She feels your hostility, Wally, but she totally loves Vera.'

'Is somebody calling?' Vera queries from the top of the stairs.

'Nothing. Everything's fine, Mother. Go back to bed.'

'I could have sworn I heard my name.'

'I was just saying Fenny loves you,' Pablo explains.

'Does she now? How darling. Is she kipping over?'

'No, she has class early.'

'Well, tell her she's welcome anytime she feels a bit peckish.'

'Mother, would you please just go to bed.'

'Keep your wig on, Wally.'

'It's just you need sleep. You can't keep falling asleep in chairs. It's embarrassing.'

'For who?' she asks.

'Oh, for fuck's sake.'

'Has anybody seen my glasses?'

'Sarah Moon Dancer has a Congo African Grey parrot,' Pablo says, pushing the La-Z-Boy into the reclining position. 'She got him from a rescue centre. His previous owners were Iranians.'

Zosia has moved on and Milo continues to coast, his wounded heart barely beating.

'The Iranians locked the parrot in a closet,' Pablo says. 'When he's stressed out he speaks Farsi. He reminds me of Wally.'

'Wallace doesn't speak Farsi.' Milo grabs the remote and stops at a tennis tournament, although he has no interest in tennis.

'The parrot's name is Fuego. Do you know what *fuego* means, Milo? Fire.' Pablo pulls the blanket up to his chin. 'Sarah said she called him fire because he was so angry all the time. Just like Wally, he was burning up with anger. She says when she got Fuego, he was so lonely he was plucking his own feathers. That's what parrots do when they're stressed out, and sometimes the feathers don't grow back. There's a whole bunch of bald parrots at the rescue. They have to keep them in specially heated rooms. That's what Wallace is doing. He's so lonely he's plucking his own feathers.'

A tennis player misses a ball and strides around the court, shaking his racquet.

'Fuego says "yubba dubba doo" a lot, and tells Sarah to clean up his poop. "Fuego did a poopoo, Mommy, pick up my poopoo." He's really smart. He likes to sing "Jingle Bells" and when Sarah gets takeout, Fuego says, "What'd you get me?" He loves lemon grass.'

'Wallace hates Thai food. And he doesn't sing "Jingle Bells."'

'I wish he would let Sarah help him with his transformational healing.'

'All Wallace wants is to fuck Fennel. If you want to heal him, let him at her.'

'I can't believe you said that, Milo.'

'I can't believe a lot of things. You living in my house, for example. What else did Zosia say?'

'About what?'

'There was a shooting at her restaurant, for fuck's sake, didn't she mention it?'

'No, she said her mother's sick. She's really worried about her but she's scared if she goes home they won't let her back into Canada.'

Zosia scared? Unimaginable. If he'd married her, this wouldn't be happening. But she never asked him to marry her. Should he have asked *her*, with a honey-I-love-you ring in hand? Why is it the guy who has to bring this stuff up?

'Does she have a boyfriend?'

'*No sé*. You don't still love her, do you, Milo? Now that you love Tanis?'

'I don't love Tanis.' The losing tennis player starts berating a judge.

'Sometimes I think I still love Maria, but then I think of Fennel and it's like, it's like she's all the stars in my firmament. My father always said he couldn't love only one woman but I'm a one-woman man.'

'You said that about Maria.'

'It was different with Maria.'

'Where did you see her?'

'Who?'

'Zosia.'

'College and Spadina. Me and Fenny were getting art supplies.'

The loser tennis player misses another ball and starts to cry in the rain. Umbrellas pop up in the stands as the crowd disperses.

'Order what you want,' Sammy says. 'The rib steak is bootiful.'

'Goes great with sweet potato fries,' Birgit offers. She looks older than on the website. Grey roots show beneath her voluminous blond hair.

'I think I'll have the salmon,' Milo says.

'Bootiful.' Sammy waves the menu at the waitress. Milo drinks more beer.

'We're so glad you watched our show,' Birgit says.

'Actually, I didn't. Some friends did.'

'So *you* didn't see your father?'

'My friends did. He has a Nazi scar. Actually, it's Russian.' Tanis and Robertson did not leave the house this morning. Milo loitered in the yard from seven a.m.

'You must be overjoyed to discover that your father is still alive,' Birgit says.

'Overjoyed.'

'Bootiful,' Sammy says, tucking into the breadbasket. Milo marvels that Sammy's hair doesn't move, although it's combed straight back from his forehead. Milo tried this style once in an effort to look like a young William Hurt. But the hair just flopped over his face.

'Why won't you tell me where he is?' he asks.

'Aha,' Sammy says, pointing a mini baguette at him, 'because we have to be sure you're not an imposter.'

'Who would I be pretending to be?'

'Yourself.'

'People try all kinds of stuff,' Birgit clarifies.

'Why would I pretend to be myself? I mean, who wants to be me?'

'You'd be surprised,' Sammy says.

'There's a lot of sickos out there,' Birgit adds.

'So, how do we know you are, in fact, you?' Sammy inquires.

'Driver's licence? Although I guess that's not much use since you don't even know my father's name. What about my father's driver's licence?' He pulls out Gus's wallet and shows them his picture. 'Is that him?'

'Could be,' Sammy says. He and Birgit study Gus's and Milo's driver's licences.

'They've got the same last name,' Birgit says. 'Is Krupi Italian?'

'Actually, it was originally Krupanski. Polish. Gus changed it when he came to Canada. His real name is Gustav, but spelled with a w.'

'So you're first generation,' Birgit concludes. 'That sells.'

The food arrives and Milo tries to enjoy his salmon but they keep staring at him.

'Your father was beat up by Nazis?' Sammy inquires.

'Russians. Well, first Germans, then Russians.'

'Your father escaped?' Birgit asks.

'Eventually.'

'Bootiful.'

They drive in Sammy's Mercedes to the *Reality Check* headquarters to show Milo the footage. When he sees Gus limp in the vinyl chair, it's as though someone is bouncing a basketball off his head. Gus never sat limp. Gus was chronically energized. Even in the La-Z-Boy he caused friction. 'Can I see it again?' Milo pulls his chair closer to the screen. They play it for him six times.

'I take it that's him,' Birgit says.

'It is.'

'Bootiful.' Only now does Milo notice the cameraman hidden behind the plastic palms. 'So now we talk business. We tell you where he is if you let us put you on the show.'

'I don't want to be on the show, this is private.'

'How much do you want?' Birgit demands.

'It's not about money.'

'Of course it is.'

'We'll pay you a thousand dollars,' Sammy offers. Even Milo knows this is low. He tries to guess how high they will go, what it's worth to them. A few thousand would temporarily free him of junk removal and auditions for Everyman commercials and shows going different ways.

'Two thousand,' Sammy says.

'I'm not sure I'm ready for this,' Milo says.

'You said you wanted to see him,' Birgit says, pulling a chair next to him and sitting with her breasts within groping distance. '*You* contacted *us*.'

'Yes, but now that I've seen him, I'm not so sure.'

'What's not to be sure about?' Sammy cries. 'He's your father. You love him, he loves you.'

'Turn the camera off,' Milo commands.

'Certainly,' Sammy says, gesturing to the cameraman.

'I'll have to think about it.'

'Three thousand.'

'What's the institution like?' Milo asks.

'Is that what concerns you?' Sammy asks. 'No worries. We can make it nice.'

'Which means it's not nice.'

'What do you want for free?' Birgit says. Her perfume is becoming pungent as she becomes agitated. 'We'll get you a new wardrobe and clean you up a bit, clean your dad up.'

'It will be bootiful.' Sammy spreads his hands, suggesting headlines. '*The Reunion of a Lifetime.*'

'Twenty thousand,' Milo says.

'Ten,' Birgit replies.

'Fifteen.'

'Eleven. That's my final offer. Take it or leave it, now or never.'

If he walks away from this, he will lose Gus. Again. And eleven G's.

'Deal.'

Stu, the agent, is flattering a client who works regularly. 'Seriously, chief, you were awesome.'

'I wasn't sure, dude.' Dino Maffucci works regularly because he is cast whenever an Italian thug is required.

'It was Actors Studio stuff, chief, seriously. You were right there. It was like ... you didn't want to kill him but you had to kill him.'

'I'm always worried I play stereotypes.'

'Absolutely not. Seriously.'

Dino notices Milo. 'Whassup, dude?'

'Not much.'

'Did you audition for that concentration-camp flick?'

'No.'

'You're lucky, dude, a bunch of queens running the show. They made me take my shirt off.'

Milo doesn't admit that he took his shirt off for a beer commercial and that he strips naked for thirty bucks an hour.

'Is that a problem, chief?' Stu asks. 'You work out. You might as well flaunt it.'

'Not in front of a pack of queens. Save it for the chicks, dude.'

'I hear ya,' Stuart concedes. It baffles Milo that Dino hasn't figured out Stuart is gay. Dino's cell blares Beatles music. He checks caller ID. 'It's my mom.' He starts speaking Italian into the phone.

'Are you busy, Stuart?' Milo asks. 'You said you wanted to talk.'

'Just let me finish up with Dino.' He fawns over the knucklehead for another twenty minutes before ushering Milo into his inner office.

'The agency people were not happy with your attitude,' Stu says.

'Really? I can't imagine why.'

'Where is your professionalism, Milo? Seriously, I have a reputation here. If I can't send you to auditions 100 percent certain that you will behave in a professional manner, I have no business sending you at all. Do you think those agency people will ever trust me again? Absolutely not. My professional affiliations are at stake here.'

Milo would like to walk out, or fart loudly, but who else would have him as a client? He tries to look pensive because he can't bring himself to apologize.

'Do you have anything to say for yourself?' Stu demands.

'What's the concentration-camp flick?'

'I am not sending you on one more audition until you give me your word that you will behave professionally.'

'You have my word.'

Stu takes a call about shooting days for some actor Milo's never heard of. There are always more of them, fresh out of acting school, pumped for stardom. Milo surreptitiously glances at the papers on Stu's desk, looking for signs of potential jobs. He sees several contracts. Somebody's working.

Stu hangs up. 'So, where were we?'

'Concentration-camp flick. What is it?'

'It's HBO. They need a guard.'

Sounds like an excellent opportunity for a bad actor. 'Count me in.'

'Only if you swear on your mother's grave that you will behave in a *professional* manner.'

Milo doesn't tell him that his mother doesn't have a grave. 'I swear.'

Because Stuart's office is near College and Spadina, Milo wanders the neigbourhood on the off chance that he might run into Zosia. He's concerned about the fat development; surely it's a symptom of something else: diabetes, elephantiasis, depression. He knows from watching his mother swell up that antidepressants cause bloating. If the weight gain is depression- or stress-related it will only increase as a result of her anxiety regarding her mother. Zosia admired her mother, who kicked Soviet ass –

she said she learned about endurance from her mother. During rare moments of vulnerability, Zosia admitted to missing her mother. And now the old woman is sick in a poor country receiving God only knows what kind of medical care.

'Yo, dude,' Dino Maffucci says. 'Twice in one day, buddy. Must be kismet, you want to grab a java? I'll buy.'

Why not? If he sits by a window he can keep an eye on the street.

'You been busy?' Dino asks, setting espressos on the table.

'What do you know about the concentration-camp flick?'

'It's a love story. I read for the good Nazi.'

'How'd it go?'

Dino shakes his head several times, indicating it didn't go well. 'Don't you hate it when the director's, like, sarcastic if you show any pride or positivity? You're, like, sitting there, with no idea how you're coming across, and these queens are acting like you're boastful or something when all you're trying to do is look confident. I hate it when that happens – it's, like, *I'm* the guy auditioning, cut me some slack, dude. Plus they wanted me to cry. I can't just, like, start bawling on cue. I mean, who does that?'

'Was this before or after you took your shirt off?'

'That's the worst part, right, like, I'm standing there and I know I've blown it and I just want to get the fuck out of there and they ask me to strip.'

'Does the good Nazi have nude scenes?'

'Not total, it's TV, right. But yeah, there's love scenes. There's this, like, totally erotic scene where he's feeding the Jewish girl potato pancakes. She's, like, starving, right?' Dino stirs more sugar into his coffee. 'Anyway, why're you interested? Stu set you up?'

'Just for a guard.'

'I heard if you fit the uniform, you get the gig. They got all this Nazi garb from some other Nazi flick. And tell them you love dogs.' His phone blares the Beatles again.

The queens sit behind a table littered with the compulsory bottles of Evian. They do not ask Milo to take his shirt off. A harried woman fits him into a Nazi guard jacket. 'Eureka,' she says, glumly. No one has provided pages to prepare.

Milo hesitates to raise the question of lines now that the suit fits. The queens pass his resumé around while cracking open pistachio shells.

'I speak some German,' Milo offers.

'Oh, really?' a heavy-lidded one responds.

'*Meine luft kissenfahrzeug ist voll mit aulen.*'

'Impressive.'

Milo doesn't tell them this means *my hovercraft is full of eels*, and is the only German he knows.

'We don't actually need you to speak German,' another queen says, chewing a pistachio.

'He looks good,' a third comments. They seem to be looking at Milo's body and not his head.

'Interesting about Hitler and all that strychnine,' he says in an effort to draw attention to his head.

'Pardon?'

'Oh, well, Hitler had digestive problems and took strychnine to stop farting. People thought he was a vegetarian because he loved animals, but really he quit meat because it made him rip.'

'You don't say,' the heavy-lidded queen says.

'On newsreels,' Milo adds, 'you can tell he's doing major sphincter tightening to stop gas emissions.' This gets a laugh from the queens. The suit fits *and* he got a laugh. The entertainer in Milo takes over and he snaps his heels together, thrusting his arm skyward, '*Heil Hitler.*' The queens titter as he marches about the room, swinging his arms and legs. '*Achtung!*' he commands.

'Good, okay, now the Russians are shooting at you,' the heavy-lidded queen directs. Milo ducks bullets, scampering from one end of the room to the other. '*Scheisse,*' he says, which means *shit*.

'Okay,' the queen says. 'Bang, they got you.'

'They did?' Must he die so soon?

'Yes. You're shot in the chest.'

Milo grabs his chest and stumbles backwards. He looks at the blood on his hands and says '*Scheisse*' again.

'Okay, now you fall down and die.'

Falling down without padding isn't recommended but the show must go on. Milo stumbles into a wall, then slowly, hands over chest, slides down it, gasping until he collapses on his side. After some laboured breathing and shuddering, he lies inert.

'Good,' the heavy-lidded queen says and looks at his pistachio-eating associates. 'Anything else you'd like him to do?' Milo waits for them to ask him to take his shirt off.

'How do you feel about dogs?' a tight-lipped queen inquires.

'I love dogs, totally. Canines rule.'

'We'll be in touch,' the heavy-lidded queen says.

The harried woman removes the Nazi jacket and hustles the headless body out of the room. Stick *that* professionalism up your arse and smoke it.

16

The lovebirds sprawl, intertwined, on the couch, sharing a container of Häagen-Dazs. Pablo waves his spoon at Milo. 'Java Chip, want some?'

'Where's Wallace?'

'He had to take Vera to get her hair done.'

'And drive her to a bridge party,' Fennel adds.

Milo digs in the fridge for the mayo and opens a can of tuna. 'Have you seen Robertson?'

'No. I went over to find out when Tanis wants me to stain the deck.'

'Was she all right?'

'Pretty quiet. I told her about Sarah Moon Dancer's Family Healing Circle.'

'And?'

'She said she'd Google it. She don't realize how hurt she is.'

'Who does?' Fennel says.

'It's so sad,' Pablo continues, 'because Sarah empowers families to embrace their gifts and abilities. She believes that every soul and every body bring with them divine wisdom on their Earthwalk. Where's Robertson's dad, Milo?'

'How should I know?'

'Weren't you friends?'

'Far from it.' Milo mashes mayo into the tuna.

'Does he know you're in love with Tanis?'

'I am not in love with Tanis.'

'He stole her panties,' Pablo informs Fennel.

'No way,' she says. 'That is, like, so totally romantic.' They stop talking and start necking. Milo takes his tuna outside and sits in one of the Muskoka chairs. Sammy didn't give a date. Apparently in the world of *Reality Check*, Sammy and Birgit go where the action is. If something more exciting than *The Reunion of a Lifetime* comes up, Gus will be bumped. They paid Milo only a thousand down.

The silence next door verges on haunting. Usually, on warm nights, Robertson and Sal are out playing fetch. The drawn blinds darken the yard normally illuminated by the light spilling through the sliding doors. Milo knows that no amount of knocking and pleading will cause Tanis to yield. He considers throwing a rock at Robertson's window but fears he might break it. Besides, the noise would frighten the child. No, Milo must watch and listen and try not to think.

'You fucking Mexican!' Wallace bellows.

'We can't help our feelings, Wally. You're not the boss of me.'

'You call me that again and I'll fucking kill you!'

How insane with jealousy will Wallace have to get before he strangles Pablo? Does he have one true feeling for Fennel or is it all a pissing contest? Does Milo have one true feeling for Zosia, or Tanis for that matter? What is a true feeling? Sammy and Birgit advised him to show his true feelings on the show. 'Don't hold back when you see your father,' they said, 'cry if you want to.' Pablo urged Milo to show his true feelings to Tanis. Sitting very still in the Muskoka chair, Milo tries to feel his true feelings about anything: the newly risen Gus, Zosia, Tanis. Killing a child.

In college, a Buddhist harmonica player told him all that mattered was what he was doing in the moment. 'All the other stuff is meaningless,' he said. 'Don't believe your thoughts, your thoughts aren't real. Just because you *think* it, doesn't mean it's real.' So how do you recognize a true feeling if you can't trust your thoughts? Do you trust a hard-on? The hockey player who dated the coltish runner told Milo, 'When she stops giving me a boner, I'm gone.' A boner is an undeniable feeling, yet men are frequently criticized for thinking with their dicks. Why, when it's a true feeling? More true than Milo's relentless, untrustworthy thoughts chattering, contradicting, accusing. 'Don't label yourself,' the Buddhist harmonica player cautioned. 'The more you label yourself, the more you limit yourself.' Milo's only label was president of the Quitters Only Club. The students with more ambitious labels went on to ambitious jobs with labels. They clung to their labels like bits of wreckage in a tumultuous sea. What is Milo supposed to cling to? Pablo says Tanis doesn't realize how hurt she is. How can she realize it if she can't trust her thoughts?

He climbs onto the trampoline and bends his knees, springing upwards, expecting to land on his feet, but the tramp jumps up at him, knocking him on his ass and bouncing him perilously close to the edge. He crawls to the centre of the tramp, stands and bends his knees only slightly to propel himself skyward. Again the tramp slams back at him, pitching him onto his belly. It looks so easy when Robertson does it. Several more tries toss Milo to all corners of the trampoline, alerting his cracked rib despite Vera's pills.

'You have to keep bouncing,' Robertson coaches from his window. 'Pretend you're on a drum.'

Is the thrill Milo experiences when he sees the boy a true feeling?

'Flap your arms,' Robertson instructs.

Milo flaps his arms. 'Ask your mum if you can come out and play,'

The lovebirds, chased out of the house by Wallace, climb onto the tramp.

'What are you doing?' Milo demands.

'We just want to try it,' Pablo says, jumping in time with Milo.

'I won a bronze medal for tramp,' Fennel informs them, also joining the beat. If they break the rhythm, Milo will be jettisoned. 'I can do somersaults,' Fennel offers.

'Oh, this I gotta see,' Pablo says.

'No,' Milo protests, feeling as though he is on a runaway train. Fennel spreads her legs and touches her toes in the air, displaying her thong. Next she hugs her knees to her chest mid-jump. Pablo, leaping in sync, applauds. Milo looks up mid-bounce and sees that Robertson is gone from the window. Perfect. He will join them. Tanis won't object to him playing with Pablo, her trusted handyman. The lovebirds bounce holding hands. Milo, for Robertson's sake, keeps jumping, although his legs are starting to burn.

The sliding doors open and the madwoman hobbles out on her crutches. 'What do you think you're doing? This is private property.'

'We thought Robertson could join us,' Milo says, spotting the boy behind the doors.

'This is private property,' she repeats. She has never referred to boundaries before.

'Slow down, guys,' Pablo orders. 'We all have to slow down together or we go flying.'

'Get off the trampoline!' Tanis shouts, waving a crutch. If she had both legs she would be hauling them off it.

'It's okay, Tanny,' Pablo says. 'We just thought we'd try it.'

'Get off it.'

'I want to play!' the boy screams from behind the door. 'Why can't I play?' With the bouncing subdued, Milo is able to sit on the tramp. 'We'll keep an eye on him.'

'You must be joking,' she says. 'Get off my property.' The boy howls, banging his head into the doors. 'Stop that,' she orders. She never speaks to Robertson this way.

'You can't lock him up,' Milo pleads.

'Don't tell me how to look after my child. Get off my property or I'll call the police.'

'Police are *fascists!*' the boy shrieks as sobs tear his throat.

Pablo takes Milo's arm and helps him off the tramp. Fennel jumps down in one swift movement. 'We're sorry, Tanis. We had no idea.'

'Well, you do now. Keep out.'

'You can't do this,' Milo protests. 'He needs to be outside.'

'What he needs are people capable of taking responsibility for him.'

'I will do that. You know I will do that.'

'I know you build wigwams, steal hamsters and kill children.' She hobbles through the doors and wedges her body between Robertson's head and the glass. The boy's cries are only slightly muted as she slides the doors closed.

'It's like she's possessed,' Fennel says, swilling a G&T.

'What's she mean about you killing children, Milo?'

'I have no idea.'

'She's totally changed,' Pablo observes. 'She don't even look like Tanis.'

'It's really sad,' Fennel concludes.

'She loves him more than breathing,' Milo says. 'She told me that once.' He tried to imagine what loving someone more than breathing would feel like. He wasn't aware that he loved breathing, although he understood that if he stopped he would be dead.

He tried calling Christopher but the hospital switchboard claimed he has no phone.

Pablo massages Fennel's feet. 'Sarah says special-needs kids carry a powerful medicine with them.'

'Totally,' Fennel agrees.

'She says you have to honour the dance of the physical, mental, emotional and spiritual aspects of a kid with special needs.'

'The problem with the politically correct term "special needs,"' Milo says, 'is that we don't know what those special needs are.'

'Maybe they should be called unknown-needs kids,' Fennel suggests.

'If we knew what their special needs were,' Milo continues, 'we wouldn't have to torture them day in and day out. We could set them up with what they specially needed and let them be.'

Stu phones in a panic because the queens want Milo to be Nazi set dressing tomorrow. Milo hadn't realized they'd started shooting. 'Do I have any lines?'

'Not at the moment. You're replacing Guard Number Twelve and might get upgraded. Seriously, they liked your energy. Why didn't you tell me you speak German?' Stu hangs up before Milo can ask what happened to Guard Number Twelve.

Pablo rests his head in Fennel's lap. 'Maybe we should get Sarah over here. She only charges, like, a hundred an hour or something.'

The door swings open and in stomps the carnivore. 'What are you lot up to?'

'Who won?' Pablo asks.

'We did, of course.' She has only been here a week and has already found a bridge partner. Within minutes she's munching crackers and cheese. 'Where's Wally?'

'Upstairs,' Pablo says.

Vera thrusts crackers and cheese at the horizontal Pablo. 'You'll get indigestion eating at that angle.'

Pablo sits up. 'Vera, Fenny and me have something to tell you.'

'You're having it off.'

'We couldn't help it,' Pablo admits. 'We love each other.'

'She's all the stars in his firmament,' Milo adds.

'I thought as much. What's to be done? Just make sure you don't hurt my Wally.'

'He's pretty worked up about it,' Fennel says. 'The truth is I never was his girlfriend. Milo hired me to act like his girlfriend so you'd be happy. That he had a girlfriend, I mean.'

'He's not a pansy, is he?'

'Definitely not,' Milo hurries to assure her, then wonders if, in fact, Wallace is a repressed pansy, which would explain his overcharged bullish nature.

'I had a cousin went that way and nobody down the pub would talk to him.'

'There's nothing wrong with homosexuals,' Fennel says.

'Didn't say there was, ducks, just nobody down the pub wants to talk to them.'

Nazi Guard Number One is a marketing consultant.

'Then why are you doing this?' Milo asks.

'I've always wanted to step on the boards,' Number One says. 'A childhood dream. You know what they say, better late than never.'

'So you can just take time off market-consulting to be a Nazi?' The boots feel tight but Milo doesn't admit this, fearing that the harried wardrobe woman will alert the queens, who will send him back to junk removal.

'The fact of the matter is,' Number One says, 'I pick and choose my clients, make my own sched. Are you an actor full-time?'

'Yes,' Milo asserts while recognizing the absurdity of such a statement. Does being an unemployed bad actor full-time qualify as being an actor full-time?

'Have I seen you in anything?'

Milo takes a handful of Smarties from the catering table. 'I did a Canadian Tire ad a while back.'

'Cool. My agent's setting me up with some ad agency contacts.'

'Very good,' Milo says, which makes him think of Zosia and her positivity. She wore an amber ring from the Baltic Sea her mother gave her. When she missed her mother she turned the ring inward and held the amber against her cheek. Now her mother is 'really sick.' What can this possibly mean: cancer, a stroke, heart failure?

'The fact of the matter is,' Number One says, 'I've got the acting bug bad. I'd like to do some theatre. The real stuff. I'm taking acting workshops. Pretty intense.'

Number One's costume and helmet fit perfectly. On first meeting, he made it clear that he'd been on set the longest of the guards. He warned Milo to watch out for Guard Number Eight who, according to Number One, made a pass at him.

Milo's helmet fits loosely. A glum wardrobe assistant lined the rim with felt but still the helmet slides down his forehead. Even in tight boots and a loose Nazi helmet, the sight of himself in a full-length mirror startled Milo. They'd buzzed off most of his hair. In uniform he looked like just another Nazi out to torch homes and murder women and children. He saw himself riding a tank into Gus's village, rounding up the Jews, marching them to the pit and ordering them to remove their clothes. When the prop master put a rifle into Milo's hands, he levelled it at his reflection and had to say, 'You talking to me?'

Prisoner Number Ten, in tattered stripes, grabs a handful of mixed nuts. 'Does anybody have the time? They made me take off my watch.'

'They made everybody take off their watch,' Number One says. 'It's a period picture.'

'Does anyone know what happened to Guard Number Twelve?' Milo asks.

'They didn't tell you?' the Prisoner asks.

'What?'

'Heart attack,' Number One says. 'Keeled over right in the middle of a march.'

'A nice guy too,' the Prisoner says. 'He kept asking if he was hurting me.'

'Did they try to revive him?' Milo asks.

'Oh yeah, all that jazz.'

'You saw it?'

'We all saw it. It held up shooting.'

Milo tries to visualize Number Twelve dying of a heart attack but all he can picture are actors dying in movies. 'What was it like seeing somebody really ... die like that?'

The Prisoner chews nuts. 'Depressing.'

'I thought he was faking it,' Number One says. 'Trying to get upgraded. Only three of us have lines.'

'Are these his boots?'

The Prisoner looks closely at the boots. 'What size are they?'

'Ten.'

'Possibly. He wasn't particularly large.'

How apt. Milo had an English prof who frequently said *how apt* when Milo did poorly on assignments. How apt that the headless body is walking around in a dead man's boots.

He calls Tanis during lunch. When he phoned from home she didn't answer, thanks, no doubt, to caller ID. 'It's me,' he says, expecting her to hang up. A gaping wound of a pause festers between them. 'I am so very sorry about everything,' he says. 'I was just trying to help him. He was so happy in the debris hut. You should have seen him, he was ecstatic building that thing and I knew if I forced him to go home he would start screaming or bolt or something.'

Why won't she speak?

'And I ... you see ... well, I keep thinking about that orca at Sea World killing his trainer. He's going crazy in the tank. I mean, imagine being a whale in a tank. That would be like us being trapped in a bathtub. I mean, whales don't normally kill humans, but there he is, banging around in the tank, turning psycho. Do you know what Jacques Cousteau said about dolphins in tanks? He said watching dolphins in tanks is like watching humans in solitary confinement.'

'What's your point?'

'I'm scared that, locked up, Robertson might turn violent and hurt you.' He can't say that, in solitary confinement, the boy is bound to go insane.

'He would never hurt me. Please don't interfere.' She hangs up. Once again Milo is suspended in time and space, unable to touch what matters to him most. In a dead man's boots.

During his first big scene, he takes his frustration out on Prisoner Number Six with the butt of his rifle. 'That hurts,' the fallen man in stripes protests. The fight coordinator demonstrates again how Milo is supposed to fake the blows, allowing the prisoner to react. 'He *acts* the hurt, get it?' the coordinator demands. 'You *act* the blow, can you do that? Act?' His disdain for Milo causes his jowls to twitch. 'Got it?'

'I thought I might whistle in this scene.'

'What?'

'Whistle. You know, it's just another day's work for a Nazi, all this killing and torturing. I thought my character might whistle while he works. Could you ask the director if he thinks that's a good idea?' Milo is hoping to attract the director's attention, get upgraded and therefore move up the pay scale. He hasn't met the director, has only seen him in the distance making theatrical gestures and kissing the dogs.

'It might be an interesting juxtaposition,' Milo elaborates, 'a Nazi guard whistling a happy tune while he's sending people to their deaths. It's just a thought.'

'No thoughts,' the fight coordinator says.

Christopher is no longer in Trauma ICU. After chasing several nurses and waiting patiently until one of them finally agreed to look up Mr. Wedderspoon on the computer, Milo located him on the geriatric floor. Apparently there are no beds available on the orthopedic floor. He is in a ward with the demented and incontinent. 'Doesn't his insurance cover a semi-private room?' Milo asked yet another uninterested nurse staring at a monitor.

'He's on the waiting list,' she said.

The moist old men have their TVs on but don't appear to be watching them. A frighteningly thin patient in a plaid bathrobe curses his bowel as he repeatedly shuffles to and from the toilet. Christopher seems unconscious, although not comfortably sleeping. Beneath his newly crooked nose is an unfamiliar scowl. The splint and the external fixator are still on his legs, the catheter continues to leak fluid, but the chest tube has been removed. Milo sets a carton of frozen yogourt on the table and checks the phone. He dials his home number and immediately hangs up when Vera answers. He pulls a chair close to the bed and waits.

'You again,' Christopher murmurs. This is what Mrs. Cauldershot used to say.

'How are you?'

'Never been better.'

'I had your phone hooked up.'

'Why?'

'In case you want to call somebody. And somebody might want to call you.'

'Ah.'

'So you still can't get out of bed?'

'I ran a couple of Ks this morning.'

'Have they given you a prognosis?'

'Minimum of eight weeks before I can bear weight.'

'Jesus Christ.'

'*He* doesn't care.'

'I brought some frozen yogourt. I'm afraid it's melting.' He removes the lid and hands the carton and a plastic spoon to Christopher. To his surprise, Christopher begins to eat the yogourt, slowly, delicately, like Robertson.

'How's my family?' he asks.

Milo intended to confess his crime and despicable lack of remorse, and inform Christopher of Tanis's bizarre behaviour and imprisonment of Robertson. But seeing Christopher, increasingly frail, has stalled him.

'That's what gets me through,' Christopher says, 'knowing they're going about their days, ignorant of this hell. I see them eating dinner, playing cards. She always lets him win, he's a lousy loser.'

'How long since you've talked to her?'

'Since I left. Ten fun-filled days. She doesn't return my calls.'

'If you call from here, she won't know who it is.'

Christopher puts the frozen yogourt back on the table.

'They miss you,' Milo says, 'and you miss them.'

'She doesn't miss me.'

'She does.'

'Did she say that?' For the first time he stares directly at Milo, his blue eyes looking surreal against his bruised skin. 'Look, Milo, I know you mean well, even though you want to fuck my wife. But I'm so tired. Indescribably tired. I don't want to do this anymore. I'm only keeping it up so my employer's insurer deposits disability cheques into the bank account that supports my family. Otherwise, this learning-to-walk again business, who needs it? What happened to your hair?'

'I got a part in a Nazi concentration-camp flick.'

'How thrilling.'

'Robertson needs you.'

'I hit him, and I'll hit him again. He doesn't need that.' Christopher covers his face with his hands the way Tanis does.

'My father used to hit *me*. It's not the end of the world.'

'Isn't it?'

'I survived.'

'I don't know who I am around him anymore. I can't trust myself. Or him.'

'He's only eleven.'

'Then he's twelve, thirteen, eighteen. It doesn't get easier. Most parents end up doing more not less. The kids have no friends, don't go to college.'

'I don't have friends,' Milo offers. 'And I barely made it through college.'

'Don't expect him to be something he's not. Try imagining being overwhelmed by sensory data, unable to prioritize or edit sounds, textures, visual details.'

'But Robertson's calm a lot of the time.'

'When he's able to create a local coherence. That's what his patterned behaviours are all about.'

'Well, whatever he's doing works for him, doesn't it? Most of the time he's fine.'

Christopher drops his head back on the pillow and stares at the ceiling while Milo sits in squirmy silence wanting to plead Robertson's case but not knowing how.

'All he can manage,' Christopher says, as though by rote, 'are simple and immediate tasks. He needs sameness and predictability. We can't offer that his whole life. I can't.'

'So you'd put him in an institution?'

'I didn't say that.'

'You just said you can't look after him his whole life.'

'His life may be short. It happens.'

Is that why he left, because he was afraid he might put a pillow over the child's face? Is this what he means when he says he doesn't know himself around Robertson, can't trust himself?

Christopher closes his eyes again. 'I don't know who he is anymore. He scares me. When he loses it, I can barely restrain him. And the social workers are useless. Did you ever meet the last one?'

'With the dead flowers in her vw bug?'

Christopher nods. 'She used jargon like "benefit finding" and "meaning-based coping processes" and told us to seek "positive-toned emotions" so we could "positively evaluate" our circumstances, "thus minimizing or mitigating the negative implications." Tanis beat herself up trying to make sense of this psycho-babble. I wanted the woman out of the house. We always had to leave her alone with Robertson and he'd be wrecked after the therapy or whatever it was.'

'Was she the one who was supposed to help you discover hope?'

'She didn't call it hope. It was "a cognitive set based on a reciprocally derived sense of successful agency." I wrote it all down, showed it to Tanis, told her we were wasting our money. You know what Tanis said? "It's essential to set goals and work towards achieving them." It was like she'd been body-snatched. I put up with it until Robertson came out crying because he didn't know what was going to happen to him after we die. "What happens to me when you die?" he kept asking. Apparently pointing out that he would be left all alone in the world was part of his therapy. I told the stupid bitch to get out. Tanis was furious with me. She can't see what's happening to him. She's too close.' He stares at the contraptions on his legs. 'When she was pregnant she made all kinds of plans. I felt lucky to have married someone so together. After Robertson was diagnosed, she kept making plans. When the plans failed she'd make more plans. I don't fit into her plans anymore. Can't.'

'A Buddhist harmonica player once told me,' Milo says, acting badly because he doesn't know how to act, 'to cease hoping. He said ceasing to hope frees you to live in the moment.'

'Is this the same guy who told you life's challenges are lessons?'

'Different guy.'

'Ah.'

Christopher squeezes his eyes shut, forcing tears to snake down his cheeks. 'I'd like you to go now, Milo. Thanks for the yogourt, but you better take it or it'll melt.'

He bangs for several minutes on the door of Geon Van Der Wyst's headquarters. Hunter eventually opens it while talking on her cell. She holds up a finger to suggest that she won't be long. But Milo is forced to wait twenty minutes, surrounded by posters of Geon Van Der Wyst's shows without scripts going in different directions. When she takes yet another call on her desk phone he shouts, 'Where's my watch, bitch?' He has never called a woman a bitch to her face before and consequently feels himself vibrating.

Apparently unperturbed, still on both phones, she pulls open a drawer and tosses the watch at him. Not quick enough to catch it, Milo watches it crash to the floor. 'You stupid cunt,' he says, astonished at how good it feels to fling abuse, even though Hunter seems oblivious and keeps talking on her phones. He picks up the watch and sees that the crystal isn't cracked and the second hand continues to tick. Gus told him it would last a lifetime. 'Forget that Jap trash,' Gus said, 'you want Swiss.'

Still on the phone, Hunter nudges him out of the office. 'Fuck off, bitch,' he says but already she has the door bolted behind him. He hurls Christopher's carton of yogourt at it. Back on the street, he glances at a newspaper box. A front-page shot of the orca halts him. Sea World has announced that it has no intention of putting the violent whale down because he is a popular attraction, good for business, particularly now that he has killed three humans.

How apt.

17

*W*hen he was small Milo found solace in his collections of marbles, matchbooks, condiment packets, stir sticks, plastic cutlery, mini soaps and shampoos. All went into shoeboxes under his bed that Mrs. Cauldershot had to remove when vacuuming. 'What in God's name have you got in those boxes?'

'Treasure,' he replied. The boxes were carefully bound with elastic bands. He knew Mrs. C. didn't have the patience to open them. When he was supposed to be sleeping he'd take out his flashlight and examine his acquisitions, wishing he could share them with the baby he imagined would have grown into an adoring little brother. His mother assured Milo that he didn't kill the baby, that it was already dead when he flushed and that she left it in the toilet because she wanted the doctor to see it. Milo hadn't looked in the bowl, only noticed the curled-up, watery and bloody fetus swirling around after he'd pressed the lever and his mother shrieked, 'Don't flush!'

From then on, when he heard his mother making terrible sounds in the bathroom, he held his teddy bears against his ears. Once he peed himself rather than look in the toilet. He only went into the bathroom in the morning, after his father had shaved.

Pushing open the door to Gus's house, he longs for shoeboxes full of treasure.

'You better watch out,' Pablo warns. 'Vera threw a spoon at Wally.'

'What tosh,' Vera scolds from the kitchen. 'All your namby-pamby ways, I should have known.'

'I'm no fairy.'

'I don't care what you are, but don't lie about it. That's just like your father. I heard nothing but lies from that witless dingbat.'

'Maybe he was scared to tell you the truth.'

'What in God's name is that supposed to mean?'

'You've got fixed ideas about things. You get miffed when they don't turn out the way you want.'

'I get miffed when I get lied to. You can rub noses with boys if you like, but don't skulk about while you're doing it. Brace up. You're thirty-six years old, Wally, it's time to get on.' She marches into the living room and sees Pablo and Milo. 'What are you lot up to?'

'We live here,' Milo says.

'Right.' She sits rigidly on the couch but, after a moment, begins to sag. Pablo takes her hand.

'It's okay, Vera, we don't think he's a fag.' He signals to Milo that he should second him on this, but now that he has been forced to ponder Wallace's sexual orientation – the fact that he has never been seen with a girlfriend and only makes references to nights of debauchery – Milo feels uncomfortable attesting to his heterosexuality.

'It's not important anyway,' he says. 'He's still Wallace, whatever his preference.'

'All I ever wanted was a grandkiddy,' Vera whimpers. 'A bonny grandkiddy I could call my own. All my sisters have them, scores of them, dashing about.'

Wallace cowers. 'Ma, I just haven't found the right girl yet.'

'You don't find them without looking.'

'I haven't found one either,' Milo offers, 'and I'm thirty-seven.'

'And I only just found Fenny,' Pablo says. 'It's hard to meet the right girl, Vera.'

'It is,' Wallace and Milo chime.

'Milo found the right girl,' Pablo says, 'but then he lost her.'

'What are you talking about?'

'Zosia was the right girl, Milo.'

'What do you know about it, you little spic?'

'She was after his fucking passport, butthead.'

'She loved you, Milo.'

'Bullshit.'

'You're just too afraid to love anybody because of what your father did to your mother. You're not your father, Milo.'

'What is this? Did I ask for a fucking therapy session?'

'Stop using that word,' Vera shouts. She never shouts.

'Sorry,' Milo says.

'I'm going to bed.' She climbs the stairs slowly, like an old woman.

Pablo kicks off his workboots and tosses his socks on the floor. 'Everybody's afraid of turning into their fathers, Milo. I see my father in my hands. Every day that *hijo de puta* is in my hands. You look like your dad.'

'How would you know, dickbag?' Wallace twists open a vodka cooler.

'Same eyes, same chin. The nose must be your mom's. I've got my mama's lips.' He purses his lips and makes kissing sounds. Wallace groans. Milo surfs. Pablo pushes the La-Z-Boy into reclining mode. 'Do you guys ever think about who you were before you were born?'

'A serial killer,' Wallace says.

'I think I was a girl in China,' Pablo says. 'With bound feet.'

Milo turns up the volume on *Canada's Next Top Model*. Pole-thin girls strut about in tiny dresses.

'Sarah asked me, "What is your original face, Pablo?" And I couldn't think of it, like, what my original face is – you know, you spend your whole life showing different faces to please different people, it's hard to know what your original face is. What do you guys think your original faces look like? I think Milo's is the face on that little boy in his dad's wallet. He looks so scared, like he thinks he's done something wrong but he doesn't know what it is.'

This is the story of Milo's life, thinking he's done something wrong but not knowing what it is. Everybody else seems to know: Tanis, Zosia, Gus, Mrs. Cauldershot.

'Sarah says if you hold your hands lightly over your face and focus on breathing deeply, you will discover your original face.'

'Would you shut the fuck up about that crazy bitch?' Wallace says.

'Sarah says it's not who you are with other people that counts, it's who you are when you're alone. What goes through your mind in those moments of aloneness.'

'I wouldn't know,' Milo says. 'I'm never alone. I have squatters living in my house.'

'I'm moving out soon, Milo. Me and Fenny are moving in together.'

'No way,' Wallace says.

'Yes way. We just need to find a place.'

'You fucking Mexican.'

'He's Cuban,' Milo says.

En route to brushing his teeth, he hears Robertson shouting on the other side of the wall. 'I'll eat you for fucking breakfast!' It sounds as though he's throwing things. 'I hate you, I hate you, I hate you.'

Vera stops on her return trip from the toilet. 'He needs a good hiding, that one.'

'Will you be able to get to sleep?' Milo asks.

'Don't worry about me. You look knackered though. How 'bout a nice rum toddy?'

'No thank you.' He fetches a pillow and lies on the floor beside the wall. He can hear Robertson pacing and knows he will do this for hours in his big slippers. Milo puts his hands lightly over his face and focuses on breathing deeply.

Wallace's snores wake him. He presses his ear against the wall. Robertson is still pacing, although with less energy. Milo gently knocks on the wall, waiting a few minutes before knocking again, a little harder. The pacing stops. Milo knocks again, three times. After several seconds, he hears Robertson knocking back three times. Milo tries knocking four times. Robertson knocks back four times. Rejuvenated by this breakthrough in communication, possibly wearing his original face, Milo knocks back and forth with his comrade in unknown needs.

Guard Number Eight does not make a pass at Milo but joins him again for lunch. Yesterday he spoke heatedly about Holocaust deniers and worldwide growing anti-Semitism, but today he seems intent on recruiting Milo as an ally in what he refers to as a testosterone minefield. 'They're all homophobic,' he says.

'Not the director and the producers.'

'No, which is why they've hired beefcakes. I only got the job because of Inga. It's so predictable that they would hire homophobes.'

'I think the Nazis *were* homophobes.'

'Only on the surface.' Number Eight pulls apart a chicken wing. 'Half of them were flaming queers – all that showering with Hitler youth. They had to kill their empathetic, female sides to survive.'

'I'm trying to figure out if a friend of mine is gay.'

'Why?'

'His mother's very upset and I'd like to assure her that he isn't gay, if he isn't gay.'

'If she's very upset, he's probably gay.'

'But he's always talking about wanting a girlfriend, and reading the personals.'

'Does he ever answer them?'

'No.'

'Then he's definitely gay.'

Guard Number One and Prisoner Number Ten sit at the next table gripping chocolate brownies. 'The fact of the matter is,' Number One says, 'I'm old enough to be her father.'

'Whose father?' Number Eight inquires.

The Prisoner licks icing off his fingers. 'His father is marrying a girl who could be his daughter.'

'Whose daughter?'

'Mine,' Number One says.

'So what's the prob?' Number Eight asks. 'Are you jealous?'

'Were we talking to you? I don't believe we were including you in this conversation.' He turns his back on Number Eight. 'The fact of the matter is, he didn't give me any warning, just showed me the ring and announced he was marrying the gold digger.'

'It's *his* life,' Number Eight says, which is what everybody says, as though a life can exist free of the constraints imposed by other lives. As though we're all planets in our own orbits, revolving around one another without ever intersecting. As though Christopher can walk away from his lost son, or Milo can walk away from his lost father.

His cigarette acting attracts the director's attention. Milo hasn't smoked for years and feels his lungs convulsing.

'Oh, I adore the ciggy butt,' the director says while stroking one of the dogs. 'He should put it out on a prisoner. Can we do that?' He looks at the fight coordinator who looks at the special effects director. Neither of them appears enthusiastic. Milo inhales deeply and blows smoke rings in Prisoner Number Four's face. The prisoner starts to cough. 'Oh, I *love* that,' the director says. 'Is he the only smoking guard?'

'As far as I know, sir.'

'We definitely need more smoking guards. I completely forgot about cigarettes. I mean, *nobody* smokes anymore, you just never think of it. Back then girls were exchanging fucks for ciggies. What's your name?'

'Milo Krupi.'

'Inspired work, Mr. Crappy.'

'I was wondering if I might whistle.'

'Whistle?'

The fight coordinator groans.

'Yes,' Milo says. 'While I commit genocide, I thought I might whistle.'

'That's brilliant.'

'He's an extra, sir,' the assistant director points out. 'He can't make any sound.'

'So, give him a line. Can you think of a line, Mr. Crappy?'

Aware that this is his big chance, Milo puts on his sadistic Nazi face and growls, 'You Jews are *vermin*.'

'Oh, I love that. Have him say that. And smoke and whistle.'

How marvellous to stub out a cigarette on a prosthetic cheek – the magic of movies. 'Brilliant,' the director said. Guard Number One and Prisoner Number Ten congratulated him – although Number One made it clear that he still has more lines – and invited him to a sports bar.

'This knob one of my exes picked up,' Number One says, 'we're talking a total loser. He's not even good-looking *and* he's overweight. You know what she says about him?'

'What?' the prisoner asks.

'She says, "Something shines through him." What a crock.'

'Maybe something does,' Milo says.

'Like what?'

'I know this short, nondescript Cuban. Girls are crazy about him.'

'Yeah, well, *he's* got the Latino thing going, this guy is total white bread.'

'Women never want what they say they want,' the Prisoner advises. '*My* ex always said she wanted a kind and sensitive guy but then she went for the exact opposite.'

'It was interesting what Guard Number Eight said about our feminine sides,' Milo comments.

'That fag said something interesting?' Number One says.

'What did he say?' the Prisoner asks.

'Oh, something about how we're always beating up on our feminine sides. Maybe that's what's wrong with the world. If our feminine sides were allowed to flourish, there would be no wars.'

'I doubt that, buddy boy. Try dating one of my exes.'

When Gus beat up on Annie was he beating up on his feminine side? Kick the shit out of your wife and you'll be a man? He didn't actually kick her – it was all verbal abuse except when he threw food. Once he hit her in the face with a meatball. It was almost funny.

'My exes,' Number One says, 'given the opportunity, would cut off my balls and shove them down my throat.'

'I felt that way about *my* ex,' the Prisoner admits, 'until we met at our high school reunion and she asked me to dance. It was a tender moment. I was her first. She said she'd always cherish that.'

'Then she went off to ball a rock star,' Number One says.

'Actually, a forklift driver.'

'Can I get you boys anything else?' a chesty waitress in a tank top asks.

'Another round,' Number One says.

'Do you think we're scared to tell the truth?' Milo asks.

'What truth?' Number One wipes sweat off his forehead.

'Do you think men are more scared to tell the truth than women?'

'Truth is subjective,' the Prisoner points out.

'Okay, so are men more scared to reveal their subjective truths than women?'

The Prisoner munches peanuts and Number One drains his beer.

'I have a friend,' Milo says, 'who doesn't tell his mother stuff because he's afraid she'll get miffed.'

'Makes sense,' Number One concedes.

'But that means he's lying.'

'So?'

'Lying is wrong.'

'Are you one of those numbnuts who want honest relationships?'

'Of course.'

Number One snorts and the Prisoner snickers.

'I don't want to lie to loved ones,' Milo insists. 'That's insane.'

'At least that way you don't hurt anybody,' the Prisoner points out.

'I think you're wrong. I think by lying, we hurt our loved ones more.' The beer and the euphoria generated by today's movie magic have led Milo to believe he might be thinking profound thoughts. Can he trust them when his thoughts aren't real?

Number One yawns. 'I lie to my mother constantly.'

'Me too,' the Prisoner admits. 'Keeps her happy.'

'But that's outrageous, that's ... that's so counterproductive.'

'You don't lie to your mother?' Number One asks.

'My mother's dead.'

'Oops.'

'I'm so sorry,' the Prisoner says.

'That's why you're thinking about women all the time,' Number One concludes.

'Is it?'

'No doubt about it. I knew a guy, his mom died in a car accident when he was ten and he spent the rest of his life sanctifying her, and let me tell you, no woman could live up to her image.'

'I don't think that's the case with me. I mean, my mother was an alcoholic.'

'No shit? So what kind of chicks do you go for?'

'All kinds. Whoever'll have me.'

Number One nods sagely. 'That's because you had no mother. Mothers make you feel special.'

'Which is why you lie to them,' the Prisoner adds.

'Yeah, you don't want to disappoint them. What you need is a woman who makes you feel special.'

'So I can lie to her.'

'Exactly.'

···

No stench of boiled or burnt animal entrails assaults him, no lusty lovers or closet homosexuals crowd his living room. Only Vera sags on the couch gripping an empty wineglass and a photograph.

'Hey, Vera. Where is everybody?'

'Wally had to work late at the office and then he had a date. I think it's good he's dating again, don't you?' The alcohol has allowed uncertainty to creep into her usually stalwart expression.

'Sure.' More lies.

'He says he isn't a pansy.'

Milo busies himself making a peanut butter sandwich. 'Has there been any action next door?'

'She took the boy away in a taxi this morning. He says the most terrible things to her. I wouldn't stand for it.'

'Did they come back?'

'I haven't a clue. Pablo was sanding the deck.' She shuffles into the kitchen. 'An Indian gentleman phoned for you. He said it was urgent, said he'd call again.'

'When was this?'

'Around tea time.'

If it's Sammy Sanjari, what could possibly be urgent? Has Gus had another stroke? The one three years ago disoriented him for weeks. When Milo tried to help, Gus shouted, 'Leave me alone!'

Vera pours herself more sherry. 'It's a busy time of year in accounting, Wally says. That's why he always has to get back to the office.'

Milo feels peanut butter sticking to the roof of his mouth.

'I don't think he likes me very much,' Vera says. 'I don't know why. I loved him so much. He was such a bonny big boy. So different from his father.' Unsteady on her feet, she grips the counter. 'I tried so hard to do the right thing.'

'I think it's tough for a lot of parents when their kids grow up,' Milo says. Gus repeatedly demanded, 'I did all this for *you*?' as though hoping the real Milo would stand up.

'I wanted more kiddies,' Vera says, 'but they made a hash of things when they opened me up. Wally'll be such a marvellous father, don't you think so, Milo?'

'Sure.'

'And now he has his business sorted, the timing couldn't be better. It's a dependable business, accounting, isn't it?'

'Definitely.'

'Very respectable. I knew Wally would make something of himself in the end. He's always been good at numbers.' She toddles back to the couch and picks up the photograph. 'Isn't he a looker?' It's a school portrait of Wallace looking suspicious. Is this his original face? 'I made him wear that shirt,' Vera says. 'I said, "Wear something smart, show your respect."' She tucks the photo carefully in her handbag before adjusting a cushion behind her head. 'I told him, once he's settled, I'll move back here and look after the kiddies. Nobody can afford good help these days.'

Wouldn't it be better for all concerned if Milo tells her the truth so she can cease to hope and be freed from her fixed ideas about things? It can't go on, this deception. With her delusions shattered she'll be able to live in the moment. 'It's ironic, isn't it,' Milo begins, 'that Vera means truth. Vera?' Her head slumps forward and her glasses slide to the floor. Milo places them on the end table.

Gus bought him a Polaroid camera for his twelfth birthday. The gift astounded Milo not only because of its cost but because it meant Gus was entrusting him with something valuable. A peroxide widow who hoped to snare Gus had insisted they drive to Niagara Falls. Milo, eager to test his camera, expressed enthusiasm. Gus, who preferred to tinker in his basement, agreed on the condition that Milo photograph the sights. Walking down Lundy's Lane, Milo took pictures of cars. Never before had he seen so many sparkling automobiles, many of them sports models. His father and the widow had to wait while he took the shots. She repeatedly put her arm around Gus while he grew impatient with Milo. 'What are you taking pictures of that for? You're wasting film. Take pictures of the *sights*.' Milo wanted to shout, 'Why give me a camera if you're not going to let me take my own pictures?' but he didn't. He took many shots of the falls, and of his father and the grasping widow. Where are those photos now? The camera disappeared over time. Gus resented the cost of the film and Milo resented not being able to take pictures of cars or bugs or Mrs. Cauldershot's spider veins when she nodded off after lunch.

He picks up on the first ring.

'Good evening, is that Milo?'

'It is.'

'Bootiful, you ready for *The Reunion of a Lifetime?*'

'Not really.' Poor reception makes Milo suspect Sammy's calling from his car.

'No worries. We'll make it easy for you, treat you like a king. You'll love it. Somebody will pick you up at eight.'

'What? Tomorrow?'

'We've had some difficulties but now we're ready to roll. Are you excited?'

'Not really.'

'No worries. Everybody's a little shy at first but when those cameras start rolling, it's showtime. You'll love it. Tomorrow, first thing.' Milo listens to the dial tone briefly before trying Tanis's number. Her voice-mail message still includes Christopher.

Kneeling, he knocks twice gently and waits, pressing his ear against the wall. He knocks twice again, listens, then knocks four more times and waits. He knocks until his knuckles throb.

18

The management of the institution housing Gus has allowed the *Reality Check* crew to occupy several rooms. Sammy and Birgit greet him in the corridor. 'What did you do to your hair?' Sammy gasps.

'I had it cut for a movie. I'm an actor.'

'An actor?' Sammy looks at Birgit. 'He's an actor.'

'I heard.'

'Have we seen you in anything?' Sammy asks.

'I did a Canadian Tire ad a while back.'

'Bootiful,' Sammy says, although he doesn't look pleased. He and Birgit huddle briefly before turning back to Milo. 'What about a wig?' Sammy asks.

'A wig? Why?'

'To make you look handsome. Don't you want to look handsome?'

'No. I want to see my father.' He's still not sure this is true but tries to appear resolute.

'What's the movie?' Birgit demands while checking her cell.

'*Love, the Final Solution.* I'm off today, they're doing interior love scenes.'

'A good part?' Sammy asks.

'I play a Nazi guard.'

The hair-and-makeup/wardrobe woman has been staring at Milo steadily. 'What about a hat?'

'I don't wear hats.'

'Brad Pitt wears hats,' Sammy says.

'I'm not Brad Pitt.'

'No duh,' the hair-and-make-up/wardrobe woman says. Her excessive eye makeup makes her resemble a raccoon.

Sammy rubs his hands together. 'Val is going to make you look the *best* you can be. Still you, but better.' He winks at Milo and nudges him into a small room with Val. Two inmates with failing hearts and minds attempt to join them. 'Nice to see you too, Gramps,' Val says, kicking the door closed in their faces. Smoking a cigarette, she thrusts some garments at Milo.

'I don't think you're allowed to smoke in here,' he says. The facility's stench of pureed food, shit, piss and disinfectant is nauseating him.

'Try them on.' She points to a foldout screen. Milo takes the clothes behind it to change.

'You look like your father,' she says.

'You've seen my father?'

'I had to fix him up. He looked pretty rough. They don't hose 'em down too regularly in this dive.'

'Did you talk to him?'

'I don't speak Polish.'

'He speaks English.'

'Not to me he didn't.'

Gus never speaks Polish.

'Anyway,' Val says, 'he's got good bones. You've got his eyes and chin. We're dressing you guys to accentuate the similarities.'

Milo zips up the casual cream trousers. 'I never wear light pants, they stain too easily.' He pulls the golf shirt over his head. 'I never wear golf shirts.' He steps out from behind the screen.

'What's your shoe size?'

'Eleven.'

She digs around in a box of shoes and pulls out some loafers. 'Try these.'

'I never wear loafers.'

'You're an actor, you wear anything.'

'I'm not acting now. This is supposed to be me meeting my father for real.'

'Nothing's real.' Val pulls a sports jacket from a rack. 'Let me guess, you never wear sports jackets.'

'Never.'

She helps him put it on then turns him towards the mirror. 'You look hot.'

He has to admit, out of his crumpled jeans and T-shirt combo, into apparel with shape, he does look hot, or anyway, warm.

'What's on your neck?' she asks.

'My neck?'

'You've got a rash.'

'Really?' He steps closer to the mirror and sees red blotches on his chest and neck.

'Are you allergic to anything? Synthetic blends?'

'Not that I know of.'

'What did you eat for breakfast?'

'What I always eat.'

'Okay, so it's nerves. Relax, it's spreading.'

So distracted has Milo been by the activity around him that he hasn't considered what effect the pending meeting might have on his physical and emotional health. Now, with redness consuming his body, he realizes it could kill him.

'Sit here,' Val commands. In the mirror he's alarmed by the splotches on his face. 'Breathe deeply,' she says. Milo tries but the air stops at his neck.

'I can't breathe,' he wheezes.

'Sure you can.' She drapes a scarf around his neck to hide the rash.

'That makes me look like a pansy,' he says, struggling to remove the scarf, which seems to be strangling him.

Val slaps the back of his head. 'Get a grip.'

'I'm not wearing this. Brad Pitt doesn't wear scarves.'

'Johnny Depp does.' She tries again to wind it around him but he pushes her away.

'I'm getting Sammy.' She leaves the door ajar, enabling a codger in a golf hat to wander in. He points at Milo.

'Tell my lawyers to sue them,' he commands.

'Right away, sir.' Milo starts removing the clothes.

'Keep your pants on,' the old man orders, grabbing Milo's arm with surprising strength. 'What do you think you're doing?'

'Leaving.'

'Nobody leaves. It's locked up. They catch you, they'll put you in the hole.'

Shaking him off, with only one leg in his jeans, Milo makes a break for the corridor.

'Man overboard!' the codger yells. 'Man overboard!'

On hearing Sammy's voice, Milo runs in the opposite direction, stumbling over walkers and wheelchairs. Two Jamaican orderlies block him. 'I'm not a patient,' Milo explains, 'I'm with the show.' They grab his arms.

'Take it easy, mon,' one of them says. 'No runnin' in here.' His breath smells of Juicy Fruit gum. 'Why don't you put your pants on?'

'Sure, yes, of course.' Milo pushes his other leg into his jeans as Sammy and Birgit approach.

'What seems to be the problem?' Sammy asks.

'I've changed my mind.'

'You signed a contract,' Birgit says.

'You can have your money back. I made a mistake.'

'We all make mistakes, Milo,' Sammy says, taking his arm from the orderly and digging his fingers into Milo's bicep. 'The important thing is to learn from them. The biggest mistake is to make the same mistake twice. Remember how you made a mistake when you thought your father was dead? All that time he was still alive. You walked away from him when he was *still alive*. Now he is still alive and you are walking away from him again. That would be a big mistake *twice*.'

'I don't owe him anything. He sucked as a father.'

'My father sucked too,' Sammy says. 'He hit me with sticks when I did badly at lessons. And you know why he did that, Milo?'

Shoeless, Milo slumps against the wall.

'He hit me when I did badly at lessons because he didn't want me to be like him. He wanted a better life for me.'

'Bring on the violins,' Milo mutters.

'He hit me because he loved me. And here I am today in a new country with a new life. Bootiful.' Sammy starts leading him back to Val's lair. 'All fathers love their sons, my friend. All fathers want a better life for their sons.'

'He's even redder,' Val observes. 'I can't cover that.'

'No worries,' Sammy says. 'He's going to calm down now.'

Behind the folding screen, before Milo changes into the cream trousers, Birgit hands him an orange pill. 'Let it dissolve under your tongue. It'll help you relax and stop the rash.'

'Is it an antihistamine?'

'Same family.' As the pill dissolves under his tongue, she strokes his hair. His mother used to do this. 'You'll be fine,' Birgit says. Nobody has touched him for months. Tanis won't even let him hold her hand. Still stroking, Birgit murmurs in a throaty voice, 'You'll be awesome.' He wants to bury his face in her bosom but she starts talking sharply to a crew member on her walkie-talkie.

Garbed in the sports jacket and slacks, Milo emerges from behind the screen.

'Bootiful. Very handsome. Have a seat.' Sammy pats the chair beside him. 'Your father loves you, my friend.'

'He said that?'

'He didn't have to say it.'

'What have you told him?'

'About what?'

'*The Reunion of a Lifetime.*'

'Nothing. We want it to be a surprise.'

'So how did you explain putting makeup on him? And changing his clothes?'

'He didn't ask. He's very quiet.'

Gus isn't very quiet. 'He must have said something.'

'About what?'

'Anything.'

'Did he say anything to you, Val?'

'Not in English. He enjoyed the shave.'

'He's so happy to have visitors,' Sammy says. 'They say he never gets any.'

Birgit, still on the walkie-talkie, looks at her watch then at Milo. 'Feeling any better? A little more relaxed?'

'A little.'

'He's less red,' Val observes and starts sponging foundation onto his face. Due no doubt to the orange pill, a filmy sensation is spreading over Milo, a Teflon feeling.

'My father,' Sammy says, 'was the only schoolteacher in our village and very strict. He would beat my brother and me more than the other boys. He was a very proud man. After he hit us, my brother and I did much better at our lessons.'

'I know a man who's left his son because he hit him.'

'You mean the son left the father because he hit him.'

'No, the father left the son.'

'How does the son feel about this?'

'Terrible.'

Sammy nods knowingly. 'You see, it is better to hit your son than to desert him.'

'How hard did your father hit you?'

Sammy lifts the hair at the back of his head, revealing a three-inch scar. 'Hard.'

Gus only hit Milo hard on the head once, when he took the truck without permission and skidded on black ice into a mailbox. After the hefty blow Gus looked as shocked as Milo felt. 'You could have been killed,' was all he said before descending to the basement.

If hitting equals love and a desire for a better life for your son, maybe it is possible that all that abuse was a manifestation of deep caring. The Polish refugee didn't want his son to be like him, a common labourer at the mercy of fascists and communists and people with more money than brains. The father tried to beat his likeness out of his son. And when he couldn't, he ran away. When Christopher couldn't change Robertson, he ran away. Why do we have to change each other? Why can't we leave each other alone? Milo isn't sure if these thoughts are real.

'Your father loves you, my friend. And you love him. It's time to heal.'

Val powders Milo's face. 'That's the best I can do,' she says.

'Bootiful.'

The man in the armchair appears to be Gus but has the slack expression of the Botoxed. Is this his original face?

Cleared of other inmates, a corner of the lounge has been staged with paisley curtains, a flower arrangement, a coffee table, a pastoral painting and two easy chairs that do not match the worn vinyl chairs scattered throughout the retirement home. Sammy nudges Milo, urging him towards Gus. 'Go get 'em, tiger,' he whispers.

'Hi, Dad,' Milo says. Gus looks at him quizzically and shakes his hand when Milo offers it. 'How are you?'

'*Cześć*,' Gus says. Milo has never seen him in beige casual slacks, a golf shirt and a sports jacket. Val has combed his hair to one side, creating a part. Gus never parted his hair, always wore a brush cut.

'I'm really sorry it took me so long to find you,' Milo says. 'There was this crazy misunderstanding. The police thought you were dead. I searched for you for months.'

'*Mówię po polsku.*'

'I don't speak Polish, Dad.'

'*Skąd jesteś?*'

'I don't speak Polish.'

Gus shakes his head. '*Nie rozumiem.*'

Milo turns to Sammy. 'Why isn't he speaking English?'

'You don't speak Polish?'

'Of course not.'

'Why "of course not"? Your father's Polish.'

'That doesn't mean I speak Polish.'

'*Cicho,*' Gus says.

'Dad, speak English.' Even the orange pill can't dull the panic erupting inside him as he realizes his co-star has forgotten his lines. Milo sits back in his chair and crosses his arms in an effort to appear unperturbed. 'So, what have you been up to since you took off?'

'*Nie rozumiem. Mówię po polsku.*'

'The house is as you left it. I haven't changed a thing.'

Gus shakes his head. '*Nie rozumiem.*' There's something about his jaw, a looseness Milo doesn't recognize. Gus grinds his teeth in his sleep and clenches them all day long.

Intensely aware of the cameras, Milo tries to don an acceptable face, certainly not his original one. 'Okay,' he says, smiling slack-jawed back. Two can play this game. 'Have it your way.'

'*Skąd jesteś?*'

'Fine, thanks, and yourself?'

'*Gdzie mieszkasz?*'

'Oh, the usual, a little this and that.'

'*Rozumiesz?*'

'She's fabulous. She sends her love. They all do. The 'hood just hasn't been the same since you took off. Folks stop me in the street and say, "Boy, do we ever miss Gus, he was such a people person."'

Gus shakes his head. '*Nie rozumiem.*'

'Him too. He says, "Gus was a lot of fun at a party."'

Gus looks at Sammy. *'Proszę przetłumaczyć?'*

'Milo,' Sammy says, 'what's going on here?'

'What's going on is this asshole is trying to humiliate me as he has humiliated me my entire life. Well, you know what?' Milo stands, emboldened by the orange pill and his structured clothes. 'I don't give a shit, play the Polish ignoramus if you want, you fucking sadist.'

'Nie podniecaj się.'

'Same to you, old man. I felt sorry for you living in this shithole but, frankly, you seem pretty happy so why don't we just leave you here. Maybe they'll let you keep the outfit. Nice haircut, by the way, makes you look like a pansy.'

Gus waves his hands and shakes his head. *'Nie chcę z Tobą rozmawiać.'*

'Yeah, fuck you too, asshole.' All his life Milo has been afraid to say 'fuck you' to his father. 'Fuck you!' he repeats, feeling liberated, in command, totally Teflon.

'Jesteś wariat!' Gus looks frightened as he tries to scurry out of the room.

'You're upsetting him, Milo.'

'Good, because he's upset me my entire fucking life!'

'Nie rozumiem. Nie chcę z Tobą rozmawiać.'

'Speak English, motherfucker!'

'Skurwysyn.'

'Cut,' Birgit says.

Like two boxers in a ring, they are kept at opposite sides of the room. Val and Birgit fuss over Gus while Sammy looks deeply into Milo's eyes. 'Is that any way to talk to your father?'

'He's fucking with my head. I don't need this shit. It's over.'

'It's not over, my friend. Long after he's dead you will regret this moment, you will say to yourself, "Why couldn't I have been more understanding? He was an old man and I called him terrible things."'

'I won't regret it.'

'When I left India I told my father I was never coming back. The look on his face will stay with me forever.'

'I don't give a fuck about you or your father.'

'You know what my father said? He said, "Son, do what you must." He understood that I needed to be completely free of him to succeed. Well, you know something, not a day goes by when I don't wish I'd held him to my breast and said thank you.'

'What's stopping you? You should do a reality show.'

'He has passed. I missed my chance but you, my friend, you can set things right.'

'I am not your friend.'

'I have someone here who would like to talk to you.'

An unnaturally small woman, maybe a dwarf, sits beside Milo. Her feet don't touch the floor. 'I'm Dr. Dingle.' She folds her tiny hands in her lap. 'I've been observing your father. I was hoping your meeting would answer a few questions for me. Your father is suffering from an acquired brain injury.'

'Where did he acquire it?'

'That's the piece of the puzzle I was hoping you could help me with. Has he had a stroke in the past?'

'Yes.'

'That suggests he may have had another one. Or he may have experienced head trauma.'

'You mean someone hit him?'

'Or he had a fall. There are many ways to injure the brain. Whatever the cause, the result in his case is amnesia. Having watched your exchange, I believe he has forgotten how to speak English. I had hoped, on seeing you, it would come back at least partially, but alas, that is not the case.'

Alas? Milo watches Gus offer a brain-damaged grin to Birgit who strokes his hair as she stroked Milo's. Will Gus bury his face in her bosom?

'A CT scan,' Dr. Dingle says, 'showed damage to his hippocampus and medial temporal lobe. The common assumption following a stroke or a brain injury is that no further recovery is possible after twelve to eighteen months. However, while this may be the norm, I've seen this generalization proved false in individual patients.'

'Which means?' Milo asks.

She shrugs and holds up her tiny hands. 'His amnesia may or may not diminish. Try jogging his memory. Take him home and show him family photos and familiar places, cook him his favourite meals.'

What a repugnant thought. 'What if he doesn't want to remember?'

'He can't know what he doesn't want to remember.'

'How do you know? Maybe he wants to forget me and my mother and his shitty life. Maybe he wants to live a happy dumbfuck Pollack life.'

'Milo,' Sammy says, 'think about what you're saying.'

'No, you think about what *you're* saying. He's happy here, look at him, he's happy.'

'He has terrible nightmares,' Dr. Dingle says.

'How do you know?'

'The staff have to sedate him quite frequently. Otherwise he's fully functional and fit as a fiddle. He doesn't belong here, Mr. Krupi. He should go home.'

'What if I don't want him home?'

'Then you'll have to make other arrangements. We accepted him on a temporary basis because he had no identification and no known relatives. Now, as next of kin, you must take responsibility for him.' She hops off the chair. 'Fear not. The brain has great powers of repair and regeneration. Undamaged areas can take over some of the functions of damaged ones. I will give you medication should he have difficulty sleeping. Otherwise, as I say, he is in good health. He is very fond of apples.' The dwarf scoots past the crew members.

'Bootiful. So you see, my friend, he's not fucking with your head. You just have to be patient, take him home, show him some pictures.'

'I don't have any pictures.'

'Everybody has pictures. Have a look around, it will be good for the show, the before and after.'

'Forget the show, all right, forget it.'

The old codger in the golf cap who foiled Milo's escape shuffles into the room and points at him. 'Tell my lawyers to sue them.'

Only after Sammy has bought him several beers and Birgit has stroked his hair does Milo realize there is no way out. He is condemned to a life of shovelling his father's shit. How absurd to have imagined he could be free of him. Like a benign growth, Gus will live in Milo's brain – inoperable – slowly taking up space, decreasing blood flow until Milo's grey matter succumbs, leaving only the tumour throbbing inside his skull.

Sammy, of course, is still reminiscing about India. 'My brother and I sold goods at the market. We had to keep strict accounts. If we came up short, my father would beat us with a stick. Always he was saving for our education. My mother made the best chapatis and dahl in the village and people would bring bowls and we would fill them for a few rupees.'

Birgit looks at her watch. Milo resists an impulse to rest his head on her shoulder.

'Everything was for our education. His sons meant everything to him.'

'What's your brother do?'

'I am proud to say he was recently chosen Salesman of the Month at Scarborough Nissan.' Sammy puts his arm around Milo. 'Today is a day for forgiveness, my friend. How 'bout we go back in there and free your father from this prison?'

'Alas,' Milo says, taking the plunge and resting his head on Birgit's shoulder. Amazingly, she doesn't push him away. Is it possible she likes him? He has never slept with an older woman. Could she be the mother figure he has been missing? Will she make him feel so special it will become necessary to lie to her so as not to disappoint? Will she perform deviant sexual acts because she will be grateful to have a younger man? Are these thoughts real? Nothing's real, Val said. She is outside the bar sucking hard on cigarettes. Periodically she looks in on Milo, Sammy and Birgit and shakes her head.

'I'm just a child,' Milo mutters.

'Everybody is just a child, my friend. That is what is so bootiful about human beings. We are all children. Your father is a child searching for his home. A lost child. You cannot desert him, my friend, you will never forgive yourself. It's time to take you father home.'

'What? Now?'

'Yes, now.'

'Forget it.'

'There's no time like the present.'

Milo sits inert in the back of Sammy's BMW, no longer Teflon but bludgeoned by the combination of the orange pill and beers. Beside him, Gus stares eagerly out the window like a child on an outing. When they arrive at the house, with the crew in tow, Milo shows him the living room and the kitchen. Gus doesn't appear to recognize any of it. Milo leads him upstairs and shows him the back room that was formerly the baby's room. 'This is where you sleep,' he says. When Annie died, Gus vacated the master bedroom and inhabited the back room, which had become a depot for junk he retrieved from other people's garbage. He made early-morning rounds on garbage day, collecting broken gadgets that he insisted were perfectly good, merely in need of 'a little fixing,' and stored them in the back room. After Gus's disappearance, Milo took the liberty of removing some of the junk to make room for a stationary bike he'd intended to ride on a regular basis. Gus sits on the bike, now coated with dust, and begins to pedal. The camera crew moves in for the shot.

'*Ale maszyna!*' Gus says, smiling his unfamiliar simpleton smile.

Milo points to the narrow bed. 'I hope you still find the bed comfortable.' The old Gus preferred firm mattresses. After Annie died he said he never again wanted to sleep on that marshmallow.

Vera pokes her head in the room. 'He looks just like you, Milo. Same eyes and chin.'

Pablo squeezes in beside her. 'Milo must have his mama's nose.'

The small space is becoming overheated with bodies. Sammy nudges Milo again, signalling him to speak. 'After Mother died,' Milo says, 'you couldn't sleep in the big bed, remember?'

'How touching,' Vera says.

'After *my* mother died,' Pablo says, 'my father humped my cousin.'

'Cut,' Birgit says.

Vera serves potato cakes with lamb chops. Gus digs in. '*Jestem głodny,*' he says.

'I like a man with an appetite,' Vera says.

'*Dobra kolacja.*'

Sammy nudges Milo. 'You used to love lamb chops, Dad, do you remember? Mrs. Cauldershot was always frying them up, with mashed potatoes and sprouts. You used to say, "What's wrong with a simple boiled potato? Why do the English have to mash everything?"'

'Easier on digestion,' Vera says.

'It's like with refried beans,' Pablo says. 'If you cook the shit out of the beans they don't make you fart.'

Gus grabs another chop and two potato cakes.

'He's half-starved,' Vera says. 'When my cousin Alfie went into a home he lost forty pounds. Starving, he was, thinner than when he came back from the Jap camp.'

'*Chce mi się sikać,*' Gus says.

'What's he on about?' Vera asks.

'I don't speak Polish.'

'He looks a bit peaky.'

Sammy nudges Milo again. 'Are you all right, Dad?'

'*Chce mi się sikać,*' Gus repeats and stands up, revealing a wet patch on the crotch of his beige slacks.

'Cut,' Birgit says.

After Val has found his father some dry slacks, Milo leads Gus and the crew to the basement, hoping that the sight of his beloved tools will jog his memory. Gus touches the mallets and chisels carefully then looks at Milo. '*Jakie masz hobby?*'

'No,' Milo says. 'It's *your* hobby. You're a stonemason.'

Gus runs his hands lightly over some blades. '*Bardzo nieźle.*'

Milo presses the start button on the cassette player. As soon as he hears the Polish folk music, Gus smiles his dopey smile. '*Lubię muzykę.*'

'You used to love moo-zi-kah.'

Gus begins to sing and dance, which he never does. '*Lubię tańczy.*'

Pablo starts to clap in time with the music. Sammy signals Milo to start clapping. Gus begins a geriatric jig and Pablo joins in, linking arms with the old man.

'*Cudo,*' Gus says and begins to chuckle, which he never does.

19

Sammy, Birgit and the crew leave with assurances that they will be in touch. No mention is made of Milo's remaining ten Gs. He doesn't inquire about the balance owing because he hopes never to see Sammy and Birgit again. He puts Gus to bed and collapses on the couch. Pablo is already in position on the La-Z-Boy. 'Your old man seems nice,' he says. 'Maybe you just didn't know the whole person. It's hard to know a whole person. Sarah says we must not fear mystery in our relationships.'

'What happened with Robertson? You were sanding the deck when she took him in a taxi.'

Pablo tosses a sock on the floor. 'She asked me not to tell anybody.'

'Why?'

'She don't want people to know.' He tosses his other sock.

'You can tell *me*, I know about all the weirdness over there.'

'This is weirder. She don't want people to know.'

'I'm not "people."'

'Sorry, but I'm a man of my word.' Pablo tucks his blanket around him.

'Can you at least tell me where she took him?'

'To that centre where they take the kids when they freak out.'

'Did she leave him there?'

'She was planning to. They've got this room the kid can go crazy in.'

'The quiet room.'

'He can't hurt nobody in there.'

'Did he hurt her?'

'I'm not telling you, Milo.'

'Vera said he was saying terrible things to her.'

Pablo pretends to be sleeping. Milo throws a cushion at him. 'What are Sarah Moon Dancer's views on Autism Spectrum Disorders?'

'I told you already, she says they have special gifts.'

'Has she ever tried living with one?'

Pablo unwraps a stick of Trident and starts chewing. 'Do you think they'll let me be on your reality show?'

'It'll be hard to keep you out of it.'

'I've never been on TV. I wish Maria could see it.'

'I thought you were over Maria.'

'I am, I am,' Pablo says, a little too forcefully.

'Where's Fennel?'

'She had a late class. She's always going to class.'

'Yeah, well, some people have ambition and actually want to do something with their lives.'

'What do *you* want to do with your life, Milo?'

He had an answer for this once. He was going to be a star of stage and screen. He picks up the remote and sees earthquake victims scrambling in rubble. The door swings open and in ambles Wallace with a woman. 'Hey, boys,' he says. 'Meet Lorraine.'

'Hi, Lorraine,' Pablo says.

'Aren't you cute,' Lorraine says. Her lips seem overly large and overly red.

Wallace heads for the kitchen. 'I bought more vodka coolers, did the Mexican drink them already?'

'I didn't drink no vodka coolers, Wallace.'

'Fucking wetback.'

'Is that nice?' Lorraine says. Wallace returns with two vodka coolers and begins to fondle Lorraine, who seems not to notice. 'Is this your house?'

'It's *my* house,' Milo says.

'Actually, it's his dad's house,' Pablo clarifies. 'Only his dad don't know it because he got hit on the head or something and can't remember nothing but Polish.'

'How'd that go?' Wallace asks.

'He's upstairs, don't wake him, apparently he has nightmares.'

'Who doesn't?' Lorraine says. 'Last night I was stuck in an elevator shaft and any second the elevator was going to whoosh down and cut off my legs.'

Wallace sits in the armchair and pulls her onto his lap but seems uncertain of his next move. Lorraine puts her arm around him and he resumes groping her breasts, awkwardly, as though he feels he should. An earthquake survivor holds her dead child in her arms and wails. Milo turns off the TV and heads for the Muskoka chairs. The moon, although no longer completely full, provides enough light to reveal the outlines of things. He stares at the trampoline and tries to imagine Robertson on it, life as it was before Christopher left. *It's not who you are with other people that counts,* Sarah Moon Dancer said, *it's who you are when you're alone. What goes through your mind in those moments of aloneness.*

What goes through Milo's mind in his moments of aloneness are concerns about what's going through other people's minds: Tanis, Christopher, Robertson, Gus.

Alas.

Then he sees her, on her newly sanded deck, sitting very still with her back to him. No light shines from the kitchen or Robertson's window. He approaches slowly, stopping several feet from her. 'Did you leave him at the centre?'

'Who told you he was at the centre?'

'Pablo.'

'What else did he tell you?'

'Nothing.'

'Good.' She drinks from a wine bottle that must have been intended for the couple to share. 'There was this mother there,' she says, her speech slightly slowed by the alcohol. 'Her son is sixteen, low-functioning ASD, like really out of it, and he's been bullied for years. It never stops, she says, no matter where she takes him he's called a retard and tormented. Anyway, they pulled his pants down and got their cells out and broadcast his penis worldwide. He kept trying to pull up his underwear but they just yanked it down again. Apparently it went on for fifteen minutes before they heard a teacher coming and took off. All the teacher saw was the violated boy throwing chairs. She sent him to the office. He told the principal nothing. The mother only found out because the sociopaths sent the link to her son and she knows his password. So there she was crying and telling me all this while her boy was trying to destroy himself in the quiet room.' She drinks more wine. 'On my good days, I believe my son has a future.'

'He does.'

'No, he doesn't.'

'He does. The bullies are the problem. He's not the problem.'

'There is no life without bullies. Bullies rule.'

Milo would like to disagree but must admit that much of his life has consisted of submission to bullies in and out of uniform. 'Isn't there some way to avoid them, take him somewhere safe?'

'Like where?'

'He was so happy in the ravine.'

'He can't live in the ravine, Milo, get real, please.'

'What did he do to you?'

She drinks more then swishes the wine around in the bottle.

'Please tell me what he did to you.'

'It's not important.'

'It is to me.'

'Why?'

'Because I love him.' He has never said this before, never thought it before. Is it real? He fears she will think him insincere, or say he has no right to love Robertson or that he has no idea what love is. All of which might be true.

'He tried to strangle me.' Her voice becomes so thin and shaky he has to step onto the deck to hear. 'When he was a baby he'd push his forehead into my neck so hard it left bruises. It was like he was trying to push through me to something. It was like I was in the way. I'm in the way.'

'No, you're not.'

'He never looked for me when I picked him up from daycare. Other kids, they'd *look* for their parents, and get excited when they saw them. I could've been anybody. I just wanted him to reach for me once. Just once.'

'He doesn't express himself that way.'

'How does he express himself, Milo? Since you're the expert.' Her venom shocks him. She's in pain and wants to kick the shit out of her female side.

'You mean more to him than anybody,' Milo says.

'Only because I feed and shelter him and put up with his abuse. I could be anybody. Christopher's right.'

'No he isn't, I'm sure he isn't.'

'What makes you so sure? You're projecting *your* needs onto my son. You don't know my son. Nobody knows my son. My son doesn't even know my son.'

'I think he does. I think he knows himself better than most of us know ourselves. He sees what's in front of him. The rest of us are running around trying to see something else, be something else. He just is.'

The screams from the house cause them both to freeze. 'It's my father,' he says.

'Your father's dead.'

'No, he's not.'

Gus takes the blue pill supplied by the dwarf without hesitation. '*Jezu Chryste*,' he mutters.

'He doesn't care,' Milo says.

'*Przepraszam.*'

'Are you okay?' Milo can see that Gus isn't. Sweating and shaking, he can barely hold the glass steady.

'*Gówno*,' Gus says.

'I think you had a nightmare.'

'Of course he had a nightmare,' Vera says. 'My cousin Alfie had terrible nightmares after the Jap camp. Even after he went dotty he kept having nightmares about the Japs.'

'If he was dotty,' Milo says, 'how could you know what his nightmares were about?'

'Because he sounded like he was being tortured, just like Gus.'

'Gus wasn't in a camp, he was a boy.'

'Boys were in camps.'

'He wasn't in a camp. We're not Jewish.'

'You think they only put Jews in camps? What do you think they did with the DPs?'

'What's a DP?' Pablo asks.

'A displaced person,' Vera says. 'Eastern Europe was crawling with them, refugees escaping the Russians.'

Pablo scratches his armpit. 'So, were they, like, put in concentration camps?'

'Converted army barracks,' Milo interjects. 'They had food from the Red Cross.'

'Not enough. The soldiers kept them on restricted rations and imposed curfews. My sister Vicki married a Czech DP. The poor sods were already starved from being on the run, had lice and countless other illnesses, not to mention psychological problems. Zikmund was always terribly jumpy. Vicki had to be careful not to touch him when he was sleeping because he'd lash out at her. Once he gave her a black eye. That's when he explained to her about the camp, what the older boys did to the littler ones.'

'Gus never said anything about camps,' Milo says.

'Why would he? Not exactly something to be proud of.'

'He would have told me.'

'Alfie never talked about it. Neither did Zikie, except when he gave Vicki the black eye.'

'*Nie podniecaj się.*'

'We don't understand you, love,' Vera says. 'Speak English.'

'*Nie mogę tego zrobić.*'

'It's okay,' Milo says, 'don't worry about it.' He strokes Gus's hair the way Birgit did. Touching his father has always felt prohibited. His hair feels surprisingly soft. The stroking seems to calm Gus. He lies back on the narrow bed. 'Is the bed okay?' Milo asks.

'Okay,' Gus replies.

'He spoke English,' Pablo squeals.

'Okay?' Milo says again.

'Okay,' Gus replies, closing his eyes.

In his room, Milo goes online to search DP camps and learns that Poles were sheltered in Wehrmacht barracks in northern Bavaria. After fleeing from the advancing Soviets in eastern Poland, they were stranded in Czechoslovakia. Conditions were harsh in the camps; DPs lacked necessities and bartered their remaining belongings for milk or meat. Those who tried to return were met with hostility, their houses, possessions and jobs taken over by the communists. Many remained in the camps. In 1947 the United Nations Relief and Rehabilitation Administration closed the camps to new refugees. They were told to survive as 'free livers.' Countries were unwilling to accept them unless close relatives sponsored them. DPs were screened and questioned, and forced to undergo medical and skill testing. Up until 1951, Canada accepted qualified labourers. Gus. He must have lied about his age.

Vera knocks on his door. 'There's a woman in the loo, Milo.'

'Is there?'

'A strange woman. It's not Fennel.'

'I wouldn't worry about it.'

'Do you think she's Wally's date?'

The bathroom door opens and out swaggers Lorraine, fully clothed, her large lips newly reddened. 'Good evening, folks,' she says.

'Are you with Wallace?' Vera asks, looking minute beside the woman in stilettos.

'I was. But now I'm outta here.'

'No rush. I don't mind if you sleep over.'

'Who are you?'

'Wally's mum.'

'Oh.' Lorraine looks at Milo over Vera's shoulder. He holds his finger against his lips.

'Why don't you get back under the covers,' Vera says. 'We'll all have a nice brekkie in the morning. I'm not in the least old-fashioned. You needn't hide anything from me.'

'That's really nice of you, but I don't want to be any trouble.'

'No trouble. I love a crowd at breakfast. There were nine of us in my family and we made quite a stir in the mornings, I can tell you.'

'I don't eat breakfast,' Lorraine says, squeezing around Vera. 'I've got to watch my figure.'

'Oh, you must never miss breakfast, it's the most important meal of the day.' Wallace opens his door. 'Let her go, Mother.'

'I've only just met her. I'm so happy you had a date, Wally. She's lovely.'

'It wasn't a date, Mother.'

'I've really got to go,' Lorraine says.

'At this time of night? Surely not, it can't be safe for a girl on the streets.'

'She's not a girl, Mother, she's a hooker, all right, she's a *whore*. I paid her to fuck me.'

Vera, speechless for once, sways slightly. Milo quickly steadies her. 'Men do that,' he explains. 'Hire prostitutes. It's quite common.'

'It's a living,' Lorraine says. 'Nice meeting you folks.' Her stilettos click on the stairs. They all listen to the front door close.

'Go to bed, Mother.' Wallace shuts his bedroom door. Vera, leaning on Milo, stares at it.

'How 'bout a rum toddy?' he asks.

'I think I'll just go to bed, thank you. I'm feeling a bit knackered.'

'Okay, well, we'll see you bright and early for brekkie.' She continues to lean on him as he walks her to her room, Milo's parents' room with the marshmallow bed. 'Do we have any bangers?' Milo asks, even though the thought of ground pig stuffed in pigs' guts makes him heave.

'I'm not sure. You'll have to check.'

'Righteo, I'll do that.'

'Yes,' she says as though she has no idea what he's talking about. 'You do that.'

Tanis is no longer on the deck and their lights are out. She must have taken one of Robertson's tranks, otherwise how could she slumber with her boy locked in a padded room? Although maybe there is comfort to be found in a room in which you can scream your guts out and flail and kick. Milo could use such a room. More than anything he would like to kick in Tanis's door, charge upstairs and grab her, let her scream her guts out and flail and kick until there is no fight left and she lies limp in his arms. Christopher used to do this with Robertson when he was smaller. It could take an hour for the boy to surrender. Christopher would rock the exhausted child gently in his arms, and kiss his forehead.

Padded rooms. Annie sometimes stayed in one at the hospital, which meant she couldn't have visitors. When she was free to roam the floor, Gus took Milo for visits because he said it was important for mother and son to see each other. 'If it's important for us to see each other,' Milo argued, 'why can't she stay home?'

'She's sick. She needs help.'

'She's not sick, she's just tired. And she doesn't need help. You said Mrs. C. would help and she doesn't help at all. She scares Mummy.'

'Don't be ridiculous. You couldn't find a better woman than Mrs. Cauldershot. We're lucky to have her.'

Milo wanted to say, 'You love Mrs. Cauldershot more than Mummy.' But he feared a swat on the head. Also, he was scared if he blew Mrs. C.'s and his father's cover they would be even meaner to Annie. Already they teamed up whenever Annie had what Gus called *crazy ideas*, like sewing new curtains.

'Why won't you let Mummy sew?' Milo asked over pork chops.

'For what? Who needs new curtains around here, you? Besides, she never finishes anything.'

'She does too,' Milo argued. 'When she isn't sad.'

'She started in on those cushion covers,' Mrs. C. said, 'and look what happened. All that silk wasted.' She tenderly dolloped mashed turnips onto Gus's plate. 'She's not a finisher, that one.'

Milo couldn't believe his father was allowing Mrs. C. to speak so disrespectfully of Annie.

'Just let her be, son. Let her rest.'

It seemed to Milo that resting was killing his mother. At the hospital she rested in an armchair by the ping-pong table, watching the balls pinging back and forth. Milo thought it was great that hospitals had ping-pong tables, although he didn't understand why the table had no net or why none of the patients were bleeding or bandaged, on crutches or in wheelchairs. A teenager with a swollen nose and stiff hair kept praying. A bug-eyed girl beat her head against the wall. A hunched man paced and talked furiously to himself. The almost bald woman who shared Annie's room lay under blankets and never moved. Annie didn't look physically injured either, just numb and bloated. Milo would climb onto her lap and hope she'd stroke his hair while Gus ranted about the idiots he was working for and the idiots who worked for him. Annie rarely spoke but once she said, 'You think everyone is an idiot.'

Gus immediately argued that he didn't think everyone was an idiot.

'Name one person you don't think is an idiot,' she said.

'Don't be ridiculous,' Gus said.

'Name one.'

Gus looked around the recreation room as though hoping to spot a person who wasn't an idiot, but Milo knew his father thought all the doctors and nurses were idiots. The only person he didn't think was an idiot was Mrs. Cauldershot but Milo couldn't say this because it would upset Annie.

Gus patted her hand. 'You,' he said finally. 'You're not an idiot.'

'Sure,' Annie said, pulling her hand from his and rubbing it as though it hurt. When they were leaving, Milo asked the bug-eyed girl why she was banging her head.

'To get the poison out.'

Maybe that's what Robertson tries to do, get the poison out. Milo wouldn't mind cracking his own skull open, trashing those untrustworthy, destructive, remorseless, circular thoughts.

One morning you'll wake up and you'll be old and you'll have nothing, Zosia said.

Cloud cover has muzzled the moon. Pablo plops into the other Muskoka chair. 'Can't you sleep?'

Milo can't see him but hears him chewing gum.

'You know what Mother Teresa says, Milo? She says, "Either all life matters or no life matters."'

'I have no idea what that means.'

'Sarah told me she knew this guy who was a Tutsi in Rwanda when all the Hutus were hacking them with machetes. He saw chopped-up bodies all over the place. He saw a baby alive in its dead mama's arms. The baby kept reaching for its mother's breast because it didn't know she was dead. The Tutsi left the baby there. He could have tried to save it but he knew it would cry and the Hutus would find them and cut them to bits. He said all his life he remembers that baby.'

'Your point is.'

'He said he envied bugs. He'd be lying in dirt someplace, hiding from Hutus, and he'd look at a bug and wish he was it, just some bug that nobody wanted to murder. Just some bug living a bug life.'

'Your point is.'

'The bug's life matters too, Milo. All life matters or no life matters. You have to decide.'

'Why do *I* have to decide?'

'Everybody has to decide.'

'What did you decide?'

'All life matters.'

'Is that why you sprayed poison on those fleas? Don't the fleas matter?'

'Fleas cause harm.'

'And humans don't?'

'Okay, so maybe I shouldn't have killed the fleas. I'll have to ask Sarah.' Pablo chews. 'Do you think your father was in a camp?'

'No.'

'It would be hard to talk about though, wouldn't it? I mean, who wants to tell their son what big boys did to him in a camp.'

'Nobody did anything to anybody. He got on a boat and came to Canada.'

'When? How old was he? I mean, they wouldn't let some little kid on a boat. Maybe he was in a camp before he got on the boat. And maybe he got beat up, which is why he's so mean. Sarah says people who persecute most likely grew up with abuse or neglect.'

Gus's only comment about the war was, *It destroyed the killers and the killed, and the rest paid the price. End of story.* What price? Milo never asked for fear of being scolded, and now his father only speaks Polish.

'Sarah thinks Wallace is a super achiever because he's so driven and walks all over people. She says he was called on in childhood to make up for some family shame or tragedy. She thinks Vera married the witless dingbat because she got pregnant. Wally was expected to be the little man, you know, like, dependable, totally different from his dad.'

'What's Sarah say about you?'

'I'm a martyr. I go around doing everybody else's work, trying to keep everybody happy. She says my parents gave up on their dreams for me so I gave up on myself. She says I have to work on believing in myself.'

'I've never seen you going around doing everybody else's work.'

'Not now. But, like, before. In my family.'

'If you did some work around here, I'd believe in you.'

'You don't take none of this seriously, Milo, because you're an avoider. Avoiders are aware of problems but don't talk about them. Avoiders grow up in judgmental families with weak emotional ties. That's you all over.'

'I'm going to bed. If you disturb me, you will be on the street tomorrow.'

But of course he can't sleep. He pounds his pillow and wrestles his blanket, wishing he could be a bug living a bug life.

Sarah Moon Dancer said people who persecute grew up with abuse or neglect. Gus. But didn't Milo attack smaller, weaker boys? Didn't he just kill a child? What's wrong with *him*? He rolls over again.

How does it feel when your son, who you love more than breathing, tries to strangle you? Knocked unconscious by pharmaceuticals, how do you get up in the morning, knowing that he is locked up, far from you, alone, screaming at deaf walls? Knowing that when you arrive to pick him up, he won't look for you, won't reach for you, you could be anybody.

Not so different, really, from Annie. Milo wanted her to reach for him once, just once. It didn't seem to matter if he clung to her or watched TV or smashed his *Star Wars* figures. She wasn't really there. Sometimes she'd move her mouth into a tremulous smile but Milo didn't know what it meant. It didn't mean *I love you more than breathing*. It didn't mean *come and let me hold you* or *we're in this together*. That's what he wanted, an ally, but she couldn't commit. Gus was in the room even when he wasn't, watching them, judging them.

Was it in the void of his mother's love and the chill of his father's scorn that Milo developed the practice of avoidance that has served him so well on his Earthwalk, being aware of problems but not talking about them? Avoiders grow up in judgmental families with weak emotional ties. That's him all over. End of story.

20

'I've never in my whole life eaten an artichoke,' Guard Number One says. 'I don't know why.' He digs around on his plate for low carbs. 'I used to weigh one-fifty-eight, waist thirty-four.'

'Try power yoga,' Guard Number Eight suggests. He is gleeful because his earring has gone undetected by wardrobe.

'I strained a groin muscle doing Pilates,' the Prisoner says. 'My ex made me go.'

'You've got to quit doing what your ex tells you,' Number One says. 'That's why she's your ex, got it?'

The Prisoner receives regular text messages from his ex. They meet for brunch on Sundays, even though she's balling the forklift driver.

'Guys don't twig to the fact they can't eat like they did when they were twenty,' Number Eight says. 'Result: flab fest. Start running, do some core strengthening.'

'What are you, a fucking personal trainer?'

'Power yoga instructor.' Number Eight lifts his leg and pushes his foot behind his head.

'That's disgusting,' Number One says. 'We're trying to eat here.'

Why all this hostility? Milo can't understand the neuro-typicals, full of bluster and bile, insincerity and lies. Tanis wants Robertson to be normal. Must those with ASD mimic the neuro-typicals – keeping in check their appreciation of detail and patterns – and adopt the mindless behaviour of the majority?

He showed Gus the photo from his wallet this morning. The old man held the picture of the small boy looking like a beaver, nodded politely and handed the shot back. It's as though it never happened. Milo never sat on his knee with a candied apple while Gus appeared to be waiting for a bus. Gus didn't argue himself out of a business and a wife. He is a Polish farm boy in a new land, dancing jigs and discovering new words like *okay*. He said it several times this morning while Vera made him oatmeal. She said she didn't have the strength for a fry-up. She washed the dishes and went back to bed, leaving Gus and Pablo exchanging *okays*.

Number Eight has taken his foot from behind his head to study a newspaper. '"International experts,"' he reads, '"were asked to characterize the traits of intelligence, wisdom and spirituality." What do you think they said?'

'Like I give a fuck,' Number One says.

'Here's a hint,' Number Eight says. 'What did the wise men have?'

'Wisdom?' the Prisoner guesses.

'No shit, Sherlock,' Number One says.

Number Eight assumes the Lotus position. 'They say wisdom can be learned, increases with age and can be measured.'

'How do they measure it?' the Prisoner asks.

'They say it is a form of advanced cognitive and emotional development that is experience-driven.'

'So I guess what they mean is,' the Prisoner says, 'live and learn.'

'A friend of mine,' Milo offers, 'believes that life's challenges are lessons and sometimes we have to learn the same lessons over and over.'

'Sounds like a major sad-ass.' Number One chews on a carrot stick.

'He isn't, actually. He is pathologically positive.'

'Must be retarded.'

Milo finds a phone and calls home. Pablo answers.

'Is my father okay?'

'More than okay, Milo, he's helping me with the deck. He's fixing it in places I never even noticed.'

'Are you going to pay him?'

'Sure.' He doesn't sound sure.

'If you don't pay him, that's exploitation.'

'Of course I'll pay him, when Tanis pays me.'

'Is she around?'

'She went to the centre.'

'Is she going to bring Robertson home?'

'She didn't say.'

'Did she say anything?'

'About what?'

Milo would like to say 'me' but knows this would sound absurd. 'How's Vera?'

'I don't know. She's in her room.'

'She hasn't come out?'

'Not since breakfast. She says she's feeling under the weather. An Indian came by looking for you. A girl, like, a real Indian. Long shiny black hair, like Pocahontas.'

'What did she say?'

'She said, "Is Milo home?"'

The second assistant director signals that it's time to march prisoners. 'Chop, chop,' he says.

Christopher is no longer on the geriatric floor. Milo tracks him down on the orthopedic floor in a semi-private room.

'You again,' Christopher says.

'It's nice you have a window.'

Christopher's purple bruises have turned ochre. 'How's my family?'

'I was hoping you'd call Robertson.'

'I can't call Robertson without calling Tanis and she doesn't want to talk to me.'

'Actually, you can. Because he's not at home, he's at the Child and Parent Resource Centre.'

'Why?'

'They had a fight.'

'What do you mean "a fight"?'

'It got physical.'

Christopher tries to sit up but can't. 'What did he do to her?'

'She's fine but she needed a break.'

'What did he do to her? Milo, don't fuck with me.'

'He tried to strangle her. Because she locked him up and put bolts on the doors. He was going nuts.'

'Why did she lock him up?'

'To keep him from running away. He ran away.' And out the sad story tumbles: Billy bouncing the basketball off Robertson's head, Mrs. Bulgobin and the hamster, the Robertson-blows-Mr. Hilty note, the ravine, the debris hut, the cops. Christopher doesn't move while Milo paces and gesticulates. He omits telling him about Billy's death because he fears Christopher won't let him near Robertson if he finds out about his child-killing capabilities. 'I really think it would help if you call him. He needs to know you care.'

'No, Milo, *you* need to know I care. Robertson needs anti-psychotic medication. He's in good hands there.'

'But they don't love him. We all need people who love us. Antonio Banderas said that Melanie Griffith made it through rehab because of the power of the heart.' Milo can't believe he is quoting a Spanish movie star. 'Antonio said there is nothing in the world that cannot be cured by love.'

'Or plastic surgery,' Christopher says. 'Have you seen Miss Melanie lately?'

'Anyway, it's not just him. Everybody knows that love is the most important thing.' And everybody knows nobody loves Milo. Which must be why he thinks he *needs* someone to love him – that without strong personal attachments human existence is a dry bone waiting to be buried. But experience has taught him that relationships complicate, are messy – you get hurt. No relationships equals no complications, no mess, no hurt. Caring about Robertson has only caused Milo grief. He stands unwanted in a hospital room, or on a deck, when he should be out playing the field. Enough of this trying to heal other people's wounds, the world's greatest loiterer and avoider has had it. He's outta here.

'Do you have the number?' Christopher asks.

'What number?'

'For the centre.'

He knows it by heart, has been dialling and hanging up before anyone answers, fearing they will inquire about his relationship to Robertson, and he knows he can't lie. Or more to the point, Robertson can't lie. When told Uncle Milo is coming to see him, he'll say in that too-loud voice of his, 'Who's Uncle Milo? I don't have an Uncle Milo.'

'416-778-4923.'

Christopher dials and waits. 'Yes, good evening, I'm wondering if you can help me, I'm trying to talk to my son, Robertson Wedderspoon. Is he still in isolation? ... I see ... Well, visiting is a problem for me because I'm in the hospital myself, bedridden, in fact ... Yes, well, she didn't mention it because she doesn't know yet, we're separated, didn't she tell you? ... Yes, I understand that but policies waste time and I'm short of it. Can I speak with your supervisor?'

It takes ten minutes for Christopher to convince the staff at the centre to put Robertson on the line. 'Hey, buddy, how are you?'

Milo lingers by the curtain, waving vaguely at the neighbouring patient who is watching hockey and calling players cocksuckers. 'Their goalie's fucking killing us,' the patient exclaims, possibly to Milo. 'That guy's a fucking god. A fucking *god*!'

'Robby,' Christopher says, 'listen to me, I'm not angry with you ... no, I'm not, I'm angry with myself. Robby, I need you to listen to me ... Please, buddy, calm down ... None of this is your fault ... Okay, yes, well, that was your fault. What happened to stopping and thinking before you hurt somebody? Remember we talked about how you're getting bigger and you can hurt somebody by mistake? ... I know ... I know ... I understand that.'

'He's fucking *superhuman*,' the sports fan cries.

'I'm sorry too,' Christopher says. 'Yeah, well, Mum and I have stuff to work out ... Yes, we're going to try but you have to stop attacking her, bud ... I know you don't mean to ... Robby, you have to calm down, bud. You're freaking yourself out, stop and think, take a breath.' Christopher holds the receiver away from his ear and Milo can hear Robertson, in his too-loud voice, struggling to explain himself, talking too fast and stumbling over words. 'Buddy, listen to me. It's not your fault ... Can *I* talk for a minute? ... Will you let me talk? ... I know, bud, I'm sorry, but listen to me ... I can't talk to you when you're excited. Please take a breath and listen ... I know all that, Milo told me ... He's here, he told me everything, so you don't need to worry.'

'Cocksuckers,' the sports fan scoffs.

'Robby? Robby, are you there? Bud? Who is this? ... I was talking to my son. ... Yes, I understand that, but I am not ambulatory at the moment. ... Is she there? ... When do you expect her? ... Is she taking him home tonight? ... All right, well, have her call me, please. I'm at a new number, 416-668-4267, extension 209 ... I understand that, just please, let her know.' Christopher hangs up and folds his hands on his stomach. 'That went well.'

'He needed to hear from you.'

'She won't call.'

'She will.'

'He sounds terrible. That's why she's leaving him there. She's scared.' He covers his face with his hands. 'I don't know what I'm doing.'

'You're doing just fine.'

Christopher watches the phone and Milo digs around in his bad acting box for something encouraging to say. 'It said in the paper that wisdom is a form of advanced cognitive and emotional development that is experience-driven.' He can't believe he is repeating this drivel when he knows that experience burns you, covers you in scars so thick you can hardly move. You're too scared to move anyway because you know it will hurt. 'When do they expect Tanis to be back?'

'They don't. She's been in and out. She wanted to take him home yesterday but they discouraged her. Sometimes there are other ASD kids there. I think he feels less like a freak around them.'

'He's not a freak. *We're* the freaks.'

'Oh, shut up, Milo. Listen I ... I don't know what she'll say, if she does call, or if she'll even let me see him. But legally she can't stop me. The thing is, I can't move. Could you bring him here? If I give you cab fare and a letter, and whatever they need to grant permission, will you pick him up? I'm only asking because you keep hanging around.'

As a coaster and avoider, Milo's first instinct is to bolt. 'Shouldn't we wait and see if she calls?'

Christopher looks at him with the same how-could-I-possibly-have-thought-you-were-anything-but-a-piece-of-shit expression so commonly used by Gus. 'I forgot. You want to fuck my wife.'

'Unreal,' the sports fan says.

'Vera?' He knocks again. 'Vera, Pablo says you haven't eaten since breakfast. How about a spot of cheese with some sherry?' Pablo and Gus are below stuffing tacos with whatever they can scrounge in the fridge. Gus became very excited when he discovered a cabbage, '*Kapusta!*' he said and began slicing it thin and tossing it into the tacos along with leftover animal parts and grated cheese. Milo has never seen Gus eat a taco. Gus distrusts foreign food.

When Vera doesn't answer, Milo gently pushes the door open. A pile of darned socks, some of them Milo's, sits on the dresser. She has fallen asleep in the chair, Annie's chair, by the window. At Vera's feet lie her glasses and the wedding photo of Milo's parents. He sets both back on the dresser. He has avoided this room because the decor that Gus described as candy dish is oppressive. Did the floral wallpaper offer Annie solace or amplify her loneliness? The rest of the house, ruled by Gus, remained beige and brown, although he allowed her to paint the bathroom Citrus Zest Yellow. Milo remembers his mother's excitement as she dipped her brush and began transforming the dull walls that had stood passively while she hemorrhaged babies. All would be better from now on, Milo felt. She died three weeks later, without finishing the baseboards. Gus painted them in the same demented yellow.

What were her true feelings as she lay day in and day out on the marshmallow bed? When the ambulance and fire trucks arrived it was all very thrilling until they took her away on a stretcher and Mrs. C. started mashing parsnips. When she let Milo stay up to watch TV, he knew something was wrong. Halfway through *Hill Street Blues*, Gus came home, turned off the TV and sat Milo down at the dining room table. 'I'm very sorry, son,' he said. 'Your mother has passed.'

'Passed where?'

'She is no longer with us.'

'Where did she go?'

'She's dead, son. She had a heart attack.'

Milo knew about heart attacks, had seen them on TV. Men clutched their chests and fell to their knees. Women didn't have heart attacks. And anyway, his mother was sleeping.

'Are you sure?' he asked.

'I'm sure.'

'Because she could just be sleeping. She sleeps a lot. You don't know because you're at work.' He wanted his father to say, 'You're right, son, she's probably just sleeping.' He wanted today to be like yesterday and the day before that.

'She's dead, son, and I need you to be a big boy about it.' He patted Milo's shoulder.

Vera wakes abruptly. 'What's all this then?'

'Hi, Vera, I just wanted to make sure you're all right.'

'Why wouldn't I be?'

'Well, you've stayed in your room all day.'

'Have I? Heavens.'

'Why don't you come downstairs and have a bite with us?'

'Is Wally back from the office?'

'Not yet.'

'Awfully busy, that accounting business, isn't it? Have you seen my cardy?'

'You're sitting on it.'

'So I am.' She pulls the cardigan from under her. Milo helps her put it on.

'Would you like me to bring you up a tray?' he asks. 'Pablo and Gus are making tacos.'

'You have to be patient with him, Milo. Alfie and Zikie would get into the blackest of moods. Lost in their own worlds, they were.'

'Fortunately I don't think Gus remembers anything about the war. He seems pretty happy, all things considered.'

'He's just not letting on, just like Zikie.'

He hands her her glasses. 'Thank you for darning my socks.'

'It's no trouble, I enjoy it.' She takes the wedding picture from the dresser. 'Did you forget about this? You told me you didn't have any photos.'

'Yeah, well, I never come in here.' He can't admit he didn't show it to her because having his mother judged, alive or dead, by strangers has always made him flinch and, occasionally, punch walls.

'What a looker she was,' Vera says. 'And what a kind, intelligent face. Thoughtful. Do you miss her?'

'I didn't really know her. I was only six.'

'She'd be very proud of you.'

'Why?'

'You're an actor, acting in a movie. Very impressive.'

Vera picks up her mending and starts checking a pair of Wallace's socks. 'Have *you* ever hired a prostitute?'

'No, but people do it all the time.'

'Where's your girlfriend that Pablo mentioned?'

'I don't know. She's changed her number.'

'You could find her, if you set your mind to it. Youngsters give up so easily these days. If we lot had quit at the first sign of trouble, where would you be?'

Milo picks up Annie's burgundy and gold hand mirror. When she wasn't sad she would hold it at the back of her head to check her hair in the dresser mirror. Milo loved lying on the marshmallow bed and watching her do her hair and makeup. If he stayed very still she would forget about him and not tell him to stop mooning and go play.

'What do you think of my mother's decor?'

'A bit of a chocolate box, isn't it?' She's fastened the cardigan's buttons off-centre but he doesn't have the heart to tell her.

'Wouldn't it be great,' he says, 'if someone was proud of us for who we are, not what we do?'

'Actions speak louder than words, Milo. My nephew, Gilly, was always trying to impress his mum, talking about the poor Africans and how he wanted to dig them wells. He was always down the pub fundraising for his wells, and she always believed him because she loved him. The poor sod was living off the well money. Broke her heart when Ettie found out.'

Maybe now is the time to come clean about Wallace's line of work. Maybe it's none of the avoider's business.

'But Gilly wouldn't have made up all that stuff about wells in Africa,' Milo says, 'if his mother had been proud of him for who he was.'

'What's to be proud of? A grown boy sitting around watching telly?'

'He wasn't always a grown boy watching telly. Once he was a little boy doing little-boy things. Did Ettie love him for who he was then?'

Vera fingers her cardy buttons. 'He was an odd little boy, always wore his knickers under his pyjamas. Drove Ettie round the bend because then he'd forget to put clean ones on in the morning.'

'Why was he wearing his knickers under his pyjamas?'

'He said if he was kidnapped, he wanted to have his knickers on.'

'Why did he think he might be kidnapped?'

'Haven't the foggiest.'

Would it be hard to be proud of a son who wore his knickers under his pyjamas for fear of being kidnapped? Or who coloured outside the lines, or who pissed himself rather than brave the bathroom where he might find a bloodied fetus in the toilet bowl?

Maybe it's better that Gus has forgotten about the boy who looks like a beaver.

Pablo holds up an apple. 'You know what this is, Milo? Yaboowco.'

Gus nods, smiling his doltish smile. *'Jabłko.'*

'In English,' Pablo says. 'Come on, Gussy, say it in English.'

'Ap-pehl.'

'See, he's totally learning English.'

'Two words don't equal totally.' Milo shoves a taco in his mouth even though he isn't hungry.

'He's trying though, Milo, that's the important thing.'

'Is it? I thought love was the important thing.' Grated cheese falls from his taco onto the floor. Gus grabs the dishrag and wipes it up.

'He really likes apples. He's eaten, like, four. We've got to get some more.'

'We?'

Gus starts doing dishes, a task he always left to Milo once Mrs. Cauldershot was no longer on the scene. During a garbage run, he found an old dishwasher that he insisted he would fix but never did.

'You should see what Gussy did to the deck, you wouldn't believe it. It's like he's a carpenter or something.'

Milo taps Gus's shoulder, startling him. 'You don't need to do those. Pablo can do them.'

'No prah-blum,' Gus says.

'See, I taught him that too. Way to go, Gussy, no problem.'

Milo takes the dishrag from Gus and hands it to Pablo.

'Why do *I* have to do them?'

'Because you're the martyr.'

'But he likes doing them.'

'How do you know, do you speak Polish?'

Gus, backing away from Milo, fills the kettle and puts it on the stove. *'Nie przejmuj się,napij się kawy.'*

'Would you quit that?' Milo says, more loudly than he'd intended. 'Nobody speaks Polski around here.'

'He's just trying to communicate, Milo.'

'Oh, so he can't figure out that none of us know what the fuck he's talking about? How stupid are you, old man?'

'*Nie rozumiem.*'

'Here we go again. Fucking mind games. Shut up, all right, just shut up.'

Gus cowers by the stove. Milo has never seen him cower. Terrorizing his father sparks electricity in Milo's fibres. Pablo pushes him into the living room. 'Are you crazy, man? What do you think you're doing? You're scaring him. He don't know what you're saying.'

'How do you know? How do you know he isn't stringing us along so he doesn't have to take responsibility for his shit-can life? Why do you think he took off in the first place?'

'He didn't take off, Milo. He got hit on the head or had a stroke or something.'

'So he says.'

'He don't say nothing. He don't speak English.'

Admittedly there is the so-called proof in the CT scan, but scientists are the first to admit that we know very little about the brain and understand a fraction of its capacity. So what if his hippocampus and medial temporal lobe look a bit funny?

'You don't know my father. This is bullshit, total bullshit.' Milo storms out as his father used to do, leaving Milo alone in the creaking house. Gus wouldn't return for hours and Milo, fearing that something had happened to him, would become increasingly agitated and convinced that his father had been hit by a truck and that he, consequently, would have to go into foster care. He knew a boy called Ernie Batty in foster care who loathed his foster mother but would stop at nothing to please her, so fearful was he of being sent to yet another foster home. Ernie massaged Mrs. Vanelli's fat shoulders and scaly feet and acted happy when she gave him a used train set for his birthday.

When Gus returned, Milo would act suitably repentant, although he'd have forgotten what he was supposed to be repentant for. Father and son would go to bed wordlessly and in the morning Milo would rush off to school, practising avoidance. In the evening he would try even harder to be helpful and respectful.

'Fuck that noise,' Milo says to the night air. He hears footsteps behind him and whirls around expecting to see Pablo, but it's Tawny.

'You told me to drop by if I came to the Big Smoke.'

'Did I?'

'Did you find your father?'

'I did, and he's still an asshole.' He walks fast, forcing Tawny to trot beside him. He stops and faces her. 'What can I do you for?'

'Why are you angry at *me*?'

'Am I?'

'You shouldn't answer questions with questions.'

'Why not?'

'It means you're hollow, like a dead tree.'

'Maybe I am,' Milo says. 'What's that got to do with the price of cheese?' He shouldn't be venting at this poor child.

'Elvis says you spend too much time being angry.'

'He does, does he?'

'A lot of white-asses are like that.'

'Has he shown you his model airplane collection yet?'

She starts to walk away.

'Sorry, Tawny, I'm sorry. It's been a bad day.'

'That's what my father always said. It makes no sense. I didn't make his day bad so why did he hit *me*?'

'Because you were there. And because you would take it.'

'That's no reason to hit somebody.'

'I agree.'

'I think it was because he was really sad underneath.'

'Lots of people are really sad underneath and don't go around hitting people.' Or roughing up little boys.

'Yeah, but he was put in a res school and all that. All kinds of weird shit happened there, like they buried babies in tunnels. He hardly ever talked about it. Sometimes at dinner, to make us appreciate our food, he'd tell us about how the teachers got good meals while the students ate crap. His brother talked about it more, like when he was drunk, but my dad didn't want us to know what went on there. He was trying to shield us from it. One time he went back to look for a girl's grave, some girl he knew there who died.'

'Did he find it?'

'I don't know. He was drunk when he got home and then it was like he forgot he even went. Anyway, maybe your father is trying to shield you from shit that happened and that's why he acts like an asshole.'

By forgetting Milo's *entire* existence?

'If my father was still alive,' Tawny says, 'I'd make him tell me about it.'

Why bother when you're hollow, like a dead tree?

He gives Tawny his room and takes the couch, knowing he won't sleep because he hasn't slept properly since he killed the boy.

'She's cute,' Pablo says from the La-Z-Boy. 'I never seen a real Pocahontas up close. Nice hair.'

'She's a child, lay off her.'

'Take it easy, Milo. You act like I'm a sex addict or something.' He unwraps a stick of gum and pops it in his mouth. 'Tanis was looking for you.'

'When?'

'When you were out.'

'Does she want me to go over?'

'It's a little late. Call her in the morning.'

'How did she look?'

'Tired. She don't sleep even with the pills. She paid me so I gave some cash to Gussy. We're going shopping tomorrow to get some more yaboowcos and some kleb rah-zoh-vyh. He likes dark bread. And he wants some mas-woh.'

'Which is?'

'Butter.'

'How do you know all this?'

'You people who only speak one language don't get it. You figure it out, you keep trying and pretty soon you're talking. You don't talk, period, Milo. If you talked more, you'd figure stuff out.'

'Would you shut up for *one minute*? Where's the remote?'

Pablo points to the armrest beside Milo's head. He grabs it and presses the power button. The earthquake victims are old news. An oil spill steals the headlines. Pelicans, coated in crude sludge, struggle to fly.

Why does Tanis want to talk to him? Did she call Christopher? Is she furious with Milo for keeping the accident a secret? Will she forbid him from seeing Robertson, who has become the only light in Milo's darkening sky, in fact, all the stars in his firmament?

She bangs on the back door with her crutch. 'You told me you wouldn't do anything without my consent.' She leans on her crutches, looking, in the half-light, like some strange three-legged creature.

'What am I doing without your consent?' He honestly can't remember, so entangled is he in the lives of others.

'Taking Robertson to see him.'

'Oh.' Milo still hasn't made up his mind about this. He has Christopher's authorization and cab fare in his pocket, but as far as he can remember, he made no promises. 'Why wouldn't you give me your consent?'

'Because it will destroy him.'

'Who?'

'Robertson.'

'Interesting you should say that because Christopher thought learning about the accident would destroy you and here you are, swinging crutches around. When did you talk to him? Did you call him?'

'It's over, Milo. I'm not going to be forced back into a destructive marriage because my husband got hit by a cab. I'm sorry it happened and I'm glad he's receiving medical care but that's it, I'm done. I have a son who requires my full attention.'

'Does he? Couldn't you hire a guard so you, personally, wouldn't have to keep him locked up 24/7? How 'bout paying Pablo on an hourly basis to check the bolts? Although physical activity could be a problem. You might want to get an indoor mini tramp so the kid's muscles don't atrophy. And, of course, make sure he takes lots of vitamin D, you don't want his bones going soft, or do you? An invalid would be a lot easier to control, heck, just don't build ramps. He'd be trapped on the ground floor at all times so you could really give him your full attention.' Reading her expression in the poor light is impossible. He waits for a tirade, or a blow from a crutch.

'There was a mother there,' she says, sounding only weary, 'whose son punches her, kicks her, knocks her down and pulls out her hair. She's so desperate she contacted her MP to protest funding cuts for the autistic. You know what he said? He said her son would get better treatment in jail. Her *Member of Parliament* said she should charge her son with assault so a judge could order treatment, or sign custody over to Children's Aid. So you tell me, Milo, you tell me who will take care of my son when he is the size of a man.' She's getting loud again. 'The reality is no one gives a fuck. Her son has been on a waiting list for a group home for nine months. *Nine months*. He's on antipsychotics that make him clumsy. He slams into things. He's stopped speaking. She's terrified all the time. No one gives a *fuck*!'

He has never heard her say *fuck*. It scares him.

'If I told Christopher about this boy, you know what he'd say? He'd say, "It's only a matter of time." He's given up. He can rot in the hospital, for all I care. It's over.' She starts to hobble to her deck.

'Did you bring Robertson home?'

'That's no concern of yours. And don't say you love him. You don't even know him.'

He climbs his stairs and knocks on the wall, pressing his ear against it, listening for the shuffle of big slippers. He knocks again, harder, and waits. Until his father screams.

21

*P*ablo pushes the La-Z-Boy into reclining mode. 'It's getting hard to sleep around here.'

'I thought you were getting a place with Fennel.'

'We're looking. She don't want no dark place. The light has to be right. And she's so busy right now with her new teacher, Vitorio. He's always making them paint. Vitorio says a true painter either paints or dies. Fenny don't want to die.'

Gus took the blue pill from Milo without hesitation or recognition. The old man has come to expect the pill when he wakens from his private hell. Maybe Milo shouldn't give it to him and just let the old man scream his guts out. What will remain? Will the Polish farmer scram, chased out of consciousness by Gus's demons, his true inner ugly self?

'Vera don't look too good,' Pablo says.

'She wants grandkiddies and Wallace is not delivering.'

'Sarah says we have to stop *wants*. Wants are soul-destroying. I was depressed about Fenny being so busy with Vitorio and everything ... '

'Is she screwing him?'

'What kind of question is that?'

'Why else would you be depressed about her being "busy" with him?'

'He talks to her about art. I don't know nothing about art. Anyway, I was feeling sad about it, lonely and everything, and Sarah said, "It's not up to anybody else to make you happy, Pablo. It's not up to Fenny. It's up to you and you alone. Accept and celebrate that you are in charge of your own happiness."'

References to happiness make Milo uncomfortable. *Happy* is one of those battered words people use casually, frequently, but he's never sure what they really mean by it. The pursuit of happiness, what does that actually *mean?*

'So that's what you're doing here,' he asks, 'lying around taking up space, celebrating being in charge of your own happiness?'

'When did you get so mean, Milo? You used to be nice.'

Four times tonight Milo has been abrasive and callous: to Tawny, Tanis, his father and now Pablo. It's much easier than being nice.

Guard Number Eight is reading an article about laughing yoga and tries to get Milo, Guard Number One and the Prisoner to laugh big hahaha laughs with him. When they refuse, he dials up Laughter Yoga on the Phone and laughs with a man who lives alone in his dead mother's house in North Carolina. They share big hahaha laughs for five minutes. After he hangs up, Number Eight looks invigorated.

Dog treats are attached to a trainer dressed in prison garb to induce the dog to jump on him and appear to maul him. Milo has been instructed to crack his whip at the marching prisoners but to not actually hit them. A whipping scene does occur in the movie, according to Number One, who claims to have read the entire script. Milo is hoping that if he does good whip-cracking during the dog-mauling scene, he may be chosen to do the actual whipping, which would mean an extra day's work. But the whip proves awkward to handle, heavy, and it winds around his feet, tripping him. When he whips a prisoner by mistake, the fight coordinator snatches the whip and hands it to Number Eight, who is still wearing an earring. Number Eight cracks the whip perfectly and winks at Milo. The extras in soiled prison garb, covered in fake blood and bruises, feigning fear and suffering, force Milo to revisit the possible content of Gus's nightmares. The father he remembers was afraid of nothing, was beyond intimidation. What happens in Gus's dreams that leaves him trembling?

'What's the deal with your boots?' the fight coordinator demands with jowls twitching.

'My boots?' Milo asks.

'Something's making noise. I think it's your boots. Walk.'

Milo walks and, sure enough, one of his too-small boots has begun to squeak.

'Go to wardrobe and get new boots.'

'There are no more boots.'

'Then get them fixed, oiled, whatever.'

'But I'm needed in this scene.'

'Not in those boots.' And just like that, Milo is dismissed and replaced by the earring-wearing Number Eight.

The wardrobe trailer is not its usual hive of activity. Amy, the sullen assistant who lined Milo's helmet with felt, whimpers into her cell. 'I thought he loved me,' she sniffles. Milo stands unnoticed in the doorway. 'Because he *told me* he loved me ... he did, that's what he said, he told me he loved me more than he'd loved any of his other girlfriends ... he *did*, that's what he said ... ' She sees Milo. 'What do you want?'

'Umm, my boot is squeaking. They want me to wear different boots.'

'There are no more boots.'

'I told them that and they said to get you to oil it or something. They need me in the next scene. It's kind of urgent.'

'I've gotta go,' Amy says, pocketing the cell and wiping her nose. 'Give it to me.' Her eyes are very red.

'I'm sorry to bother you.'

'Just give me the boot.'

He'd prefer not to as, no doubt, it reeks from his sweaty foot. 'I thought we could try oiling it on the outside.'

'What kind of squeak is it?'

He walks back and forth a few feet.

'They look too small,' she says.

'No, they're fine, just a little snug.'

'Give me the boot.'

It takes him several minutes to unlace the boot, during which he can hear her gulping convulsive sobs. Were he not anxious to get back on set before Number Eight completely usurps his role, he would suggest he come back later. Instead he says, 'I'm confused about love as well. The use of the word, I mean. People use it a lot. I think it's probably overused, actually. I don't think people really know what they mean when they say it. I think some people say it just to make the other person feel better.'

'Oh, so now *you're* saying he doesn't love me either. You don't even *know* him. Give me the fucking boot.'

'Actually, I wasn't saying that, it's just it's become such a commonplace word. I said it recently, just out of the blue I said I loved somebody and it felt inadequate, like I wasn't sure it was the right word to describe my feelings for this person.' He hands her the boot. 'His mother doesn't think it's the right word either. On the other hand, the word *feelings* makes me uncomfortable as well.'

'What's his mother got to do with it?' Amy flexes the boot repeatedly, listening for the squeak.

'Pardon?'

'What business is it of his mother's to tell you *love* isn't the right word for your feelings? You should tell her to fuck right off.'

'Well, the problem is, I think I might love her too. I'm confused about my feelings for her as well.'

'You love the son *and* the mother?' She rips the insole out of his boot.

'I'm not sure. You see, most people seem to get by with the *love* word and the *feelings* word. They seem to understand them in an acceptable sense, but I find them hard to use seriously. I mean, they're so ... imprecise.'

'Try it now.' She hands him the boot. 'Don't lace it up, just see if it still squeaks.'

'It's pretty uncomfortable without the insole.'

'Walk.'

He does. No squeak.

'See, it was the insole.'

'But there are nails or something sticking up without the insole.'

'They're not nails, just nubby things, stitches or something.'

'Well, they hurt.'

'I thought you said they needed you on set. Suffer for your art.' She turns her back on him and starts smearing blood and dirt on prisoners' stripes. Milo returns to the set and reports to the second assistant director who tells him, 'Not now.' Gus would say this when Milo had a question or a suggestion. *Not now.* Milo knew damn well *not now* meant *never. Not now* meant *get out of my face.* Milo will not tolerate being told *not now* by the second assistant director. The director himself has shown Milo respect, he is not just another guard.

'Excuse me,' he says, 'but I am in this scene. The fight coordinator sent me to get my boot fixed.'

'Are you limping?'

'No.' The nubby things have been boring into Milo's foot for twenty minutes.

'Walk.'

'You've seen me march. I'm Guard Number Twelve.'

'I don't care what you are, walk.'

Milo takes a few steps, trying not to favour the sore foot.

'You're definitely limping. Are you injured?'

Milo can't admit that the boots are too small and the only remaining boots. 'No, it must be a cramp.' He shakes out his leg.

'Sit this one out,' the second assistant director says, turning to the continuity girl. And just like that, Milo is made redundant. Bodies move around him with purpose. 'Move over, Jack,' a crew member says. Shoulders nudge him, elbows shove him. He hears the crack of the whip as Number Eight herds the prisoners into the gas chambers. 'Out of the way, asshole,' another crew member says. Milo limps to the house block, now emptied of prisoners. Coke cans and Styrofoam cups litter the mud where, only days ago, Milo wowed the director with his smoking and whistling skills. How small, how trivial, how unimportant all this is, he is. Still in his helmet, he smacks his head into the side of the building, seeking the relief that Robertson must find when smashing his skull into hard surfaces. A girl prisoner, who'd said hi to Milo earlier, whose soft sandy hair reminded him of Zosia, sees him as she rushes back to the set from a Porta Potty but quickly averts her eyes. Zosia never averted her eyes; she'd stare into him, trying to understand. 'Explain it to me,' she'd say. But how could he explain feelings he couldn't understand? He bangs his head again. It only hurts, offers no respite. He matters to no one.

He rips babies off the mother spider plant and throws them in the trash. Why bother planting them when no one cares, when his jungle has been invaded by strangers. Two of them burst in giggling and flop down on the couch.

'Gussy's only got one pair of underwear, Milo. He's been wearing the same pair for three days, right, Gussy?' Gus nods, causing a fresh fit of giggles.

'Maybe he's afraid of being kidnapped,' Milo says.

'We've got to get him some undies.' Pablo digs around in his jeans and pulls out a crumpled twenty. 'Let's go to Zellers. Maria always buys Fruit of the Loom for her brothers there.'

'Not now,' Milo says.

'He's got no clean shorts.'

'*Bielizna*,' Gus nods. 'On-deh-vare.'

'Awesome, Gussy, that's it, underwear.'

'Vont kofee?'

'Totally, let's get us some kah-vah.' They charge into the kitchen. Milo flings himself on the couch and gropes around for the remote. It's as though he has swallowed hundreds of cotton balls, cramming his lungs, his guts. Stifled by fluff, his frustration at being inconsequential robs him of breath. He thrashes about like the asphyxiated until a hand smacks his face.

'Are you having a seizure?' Tawny asks. 'When my cousin has fits, we slap him and he gets better.' She slaps Milo again.

He pushes her away and sits up, feeling a small air passage opening. Why does he care about all this anyway? What's it matter to him if he matters to these idiots? 'Who gives a fuck?' he says out loud.

'About what?' Tawny asks.

'Any of it. What's going on around here.'

'What's going on around here?'

'Collusion and deceit. Who gives a shit? It's not my prah-blum.'

'Who said it was?'

'I'm a hollow tree, remember? Dead, dead, dead. I'd like to sleep now and this couch is the only vacancy. Good night.'

'It's only six o'clock.'

Pablo returns. 'Where's Vera?'

'I haven't seen her,' Tawny says.

'Vera?' The Cuban bounds upstairs. Where does all that energy come from? Are only the truly ignorant able to thrive in the bog of human existence?

'Do you have a headache?' Tawny asks. 'I've got some Tylenol.'

What business is it of his mother's to tell you love *isn't the right word for your feelings? You should tell her to fuck right off.*

'She's right,' Milo declares.

'Who?'

'That bitch has no right to tell me *love* isn't the right word.'

···

'I am here to see Robertson Wedderspoon. I have a letter from his father who is in the hospital and therefore unable to come himself. In the letter Mr. Wedderspoon explains that I am to take Robertson to visit him this evening. It will only be a short visit and I shall return with him forthwith.' Milo said *forthwith* in a commercial in which he played a servant to a lord in need of speedy muffler replacement.

Several staff members huddle over the letter. Christopher studied law before he became a financial advisor. Even Milo was intimidated by the legal-speak in the letter. 'Just a moment,' a woman in Birkenstocks tells him. Two others, in yoga pants, watch him. He remains standing, even though his foot is still tender from the Nazi boot. Sitting would suggest he is prepared to wait. A small autistic boy wanders into the waiting area, repeatedly patting the wall as though feeling for a secret passage. 'What are you doing out here, Curly?' one of the yoga-panted women asks. 'Come back to the playroom.' Curly doesn't hear or isn't listening. He stops in front of Milo, who is blocking his path. Milo steps aside and Curly resumes feeling for the escape hatch. 'Curly, let's go back to the playroom.' The yoga-panted woman makes sweeping gestures with her arms. 'Let's go back to the playroom. There are no toys out here.'

Curly makes it to the front door and begins pushing on it. 'No, Curly, you have to wait for your mum, she'll be here soon. Let's go back to the playroom.' She tries to take his hand but he pulls away from her. Both yoga ladies corner the boy in what looks like an effort to corral him into the playroom. Curly begins to yelp and slam his hands into the wall. The Birkenstocked woman appears with Robertson who, when he sees Milo, jumps up and down, shouting, 'It's Milo, it's Milo, it's Milo, it's Milo, it's Milo, it's Milo!' Curly yelps louder, engaging the Birkenstocked woman. With the jailers distracted, Milo makes a run for it, signalling for Robertson to follow. Giggling uncontrollably, he seems about to hyperventilate. Milo has never seen the boy so red-faced and tries to calm him but Robertson buckles over and collapses on the sidewalk, still gasping hysterically until he notices worms on the rain-soaked concrete. He begins to rescue the worms, picking them up with great care and setting them in the dirt beside the pavement. This could take hours. Milo spots a Baskins-Robbins and tries diversion tactics. 'How 'bout some ice cream?'

Robertson moves deliberately up and down the counter, scrutinizing the tubs.

'You go ahead,' Milo says to a busload of Chinese tourists waiting their turn. Twenty minutes later the boy has chosen one scoop of Mango Tango and one scoop of Jamoca Almond Fudge.

Having blown Christopher's cash on ice cream, Milo must take the child on the bus and walks with dread towards the stop. Robertson follows unquestioningly, intently licking his cone, and sits on the bench. Ice cream dribbles down his wrist.

'This is fun,' he says and Milo realizes that yes, it *is* fun. Could this be happiness? This tiny blip, this pause between one thing and another, when nothing can be done but wait for a bus? Sparrows crowd into a puddle, flapping their wings, splashing one another, puffing out their feathers and dipping their breasts into the water. Happiness.

But as the bus pulls in, Milo feels himself quivering, so fearful is he that Robertson will refuse to get on the bus. Milo's plan is to proceed without discussion, to just climb on board and hope that Robertson will follow.

'A bus. Awesome,' Robertson says, clambering up the steps.

Milo leads him to the back and offers him a window seat. Robertson bounces in the seat. An old woman in a rain bonnet watches him warily.

'This is epic,' Robertson says.

An unshaven middle-aged man, off-gassing beer, eyes a young woman fidgeting with her personal listening device. 'Do you play golf?' he asks her. When she doesn't respond he asks again, louder.

'She can't hear you,' Robertson says in his too-loud voice. 'She's got earbuds in.'

'She can hear me,' the drunk says, leaning over the girl. 'Do you play golf?'

'I don't think she does,' Robertson says.

'Who the fuck are you?'

The girl pulls out her earbuds and says, 'I don't play golf.'

'Oh, that's too bad,' the drunk says. 'I can't marry you then.'

'She doesn't want to marry you,' Robertson clarifies.

'It's a joke, you little fuck.'

'Settle down,' a bearded man in shorts says. Milo has noticed Robertson staring at the bearded man's prosthetic leg.

'Your fake leg looks cool,' the boy says.

'Thank you,' the bearded man replies. 'Want to see my stump?'

'Totally,' Robertson says. The old woman in the rain bonnet scowls. The girl fits her earbuds back in while the drunk slumps into a vacated seat.

The bearded man unfastens clasps, removes his prosthesis and his stump sock.

'Fuck me,' the drunk protests, 'I don't want to see this.'

'Don't look then,' Robertson says. The bearded man waves his stump at him. 'Awesome,' the boy says. 'Does it hurt?'

'The skin toughens up after a while.'

'Can I hold it?' He reaches for the prosthesis and the man hands it to him with the tennis shoe still on. The old woman gasps and scuttles to the front of the bus. The girl stares at the leg, apparently unimpressed. 'Fuck me,' the drunk says again, covering his eyes. Robertson runs his hand over the prosthesis's metallic surfaces and grips the shoe, flexing the foot. 'Epic,' he says.

'You should probably give it back,' Milo suggests.

'No rush,' the man says, scratching his stump.

'What happened to your real leg?' Robertson asks without looking directly at the man.

'Motorcycle accident. Never be in a hurry, nothing good ever happens in a hurry.'

Robertson holds the leg up like a telescope and peers into it. 'This is totally boss. You don't have to cut your toenails.'

'That's true.'

'I always forget to cut my toenails and they rip my socks.'

'Can you give him his leg back now?' Milo asks. 'We're getting off at the next stop.'

'Do you wear it all the time or do you hop around?'

'I do a fair bit of hopping,' the man admits.

'That is so totally badass. You must have amazing balance. I can't hop on one leg for long.'

'It just takes practice. I still use crutches around the house.'

'This is our stop,' Milo says, unsure if he should try to take the leg from Robertson, worrying that if he does it will cause an episode.

'Thanks for showing it to me,' the boy says, handing back the leg.

'Anytime.'

On the sidewalk, Robertson practises hopping on one leg. Not once has he asked where they are going, so engaged is he in the moment. Milo has never met anyone who doesn't want to know what's happening next. Rain splatters them again, soaking Robertson's T-shirt, but he continues to hop until they reach the hospital doors. 'I'm not sick,' he says.

'I know.'

'I mean, I'm not hitting or shouting.'

'I know that. We're not here because of you.'

'Are *you* sick?'

'No.'

'Then why are we here? I don't want to go in, I'm not going in.' He starts running, leaping off the sidewalk to make room for a wheelchair. A car honks and a driver shouts, 'Get off the fucking road!' Milo, with his foot still sore from the Nazi boot, chases after Robertson but the boy, fit from hours on the trampoline, moves at high speed. Pedestrians dodge him and turn around to watch the fleeing child, creating further obstacles for Milo who mutters, 'Excuse me,' as he stumbles around them, only to discover the boy has disappeared from sight. 'Has anybody seen a blond boy, eleven years old?' he asks as his feet slip in his rain-soaked sandals. 'A boy,' he shouts. 'Please, have you seen him? He was running.' No one cares. They keep their heads down in the rain, rushing for shelter. The sky darkens and rumbles and Milo remembers that Robertson is afraid of thunder. During storms he seeks out Tanis and stays close to her. She looks forward to bad weather for this reason. Where is she now as the storm rumbles? Is she imagining her son safe in isolation in a soundproof room? Milo has stolen her boy from her. The child she tried to keep safe, that she loves more than breathing – Milo has lost him. A feeling of defeat so massive, so crippling, descends upon him, forcing him to his knees as he calls the boy's name over and over. He looks in all directions but rain and nightfall make it impossible to see any distance. With each clash of thunder he imagines Robertson cringing, drenched, walking in circles. With no phone booth in sight, Milo shouts, 'Police, would someone *please* call the police?' But there is no one; all have run from the relentless downpour. Milo removes his slippery sandals and scrambles barefoot first one way and then another, calling, until his feet and throat are raw. It's over, he can't do this anymore. No matter how good his intentions, he causes harm. Mrs. Cauldershot told him he was nothing but trouble. 'Nothing but trouble,' he mutters.

'What is?' Robertson asks.

'Why did you take off?'

'Why did you take your sandals off?'

'My feet slip in them when they're wet.'

'I don't like thunder.'

'I know.' Again he resists the urge to grab the shivering child. 'Where did you go?'

'I'm not going to the hospital.'

'I was taking you to the hospital to see your dad.'

'My dad?'

'Yes, he was in a car accident. He asked me to take you to see him. In the hospital.'

Robertson puts his hands on his hips. 'Well, why didn't you say so?' Right away he is on the march, as though the world didn't almost come to an end.

22

A formidable woman in plum occupies the chair beside Christopher's roommate's bed. 'Your mother knows you're going to call her,' she says.

'I didn't say I'd call her,' the sports fan replies. His TV blares some game or other.

'She knows you will,' the woman in plum says.

'I didn't say I would.'

'She's waiting for you to call.'

'I'm not calling her.'

Contrary to expectation, Robertson doesn't appear to be destroyed by the sight of his father, unconscious and in ruins. The boy doesn't try to wake him but examines the tubes leading in and out of him, and the contraptions on his legs. He draws the curtain the full length of the rod and says to the sports fan and his companion, 'Can you please be quiet.' The woman in plum looks around the curtain at Milo.

'Is he talking to us?'

'He is. He's very sensitive to noise.'

'My father's sleeping. Please turn off your television.'

'Oh, come on, kid,' the sports fan says. 'It's the finals.'

'If you could just turn it down a bit,' Milo says.

'It's too loud,' Robertson insists. 'Do you have hearing problems?'

'Do you have manners?' the woman in plum demands.

'He's sincerely asking,' Milo explains. 'He's very literal.'

'He's very rude is what he is,' the woman says, jerking the curtain back. 'Turn it down, Travis.'

'It's the finals.'

'Turn it down and call your mother.'

'Robby,' Christopher murmurs. 'Buddy, I'm so happy to see you.'

'I'm happy to see you too,' Robertson says sombrely. 'You've got a lot of things attached to you.'

'Yes, quite a web, isn't it? That's why I got Milo to bring you here. Why are you all wet?'

'It's raining.'

The woman in plum pushes her face around the curtain again. 'Does he have to talk that loud?'

'He does,' Christopher says, and then starts to laugh or cry, Milo isn't sure which. 'It's so great to see you, Robby. I've missed you so much.'

'I've missed you too,' Robertson says flatly, fondling the external fixator.

'Be careful with that,' Milo cautions.

'You're shivering,' Christopher says. 'I have a jacket here somewhere, can you find it? They put my stuff that wasn't wrecked in a plastic bag and stuck it in the locker.'

Milo finds the bag and the jacket and fits it around Robertson who, it seems to him, has not once made eye contact with his father. 'What were you doing in a car?' he asks. 'We don't have a car anymore.'

'I wasn't in a car,' Christopher says. 'I was crossing the street. I got hit.'

'Did you look before you crossed?'

'No.'

'That's bad.'

'Yes.'

'How long before you get better?'

'Well, they say eight weeks before I can bear weight.' Christopher seems even frailer than he did yesterday and Milo can't imagine him finding the strength for rehab.

'Travis, call your mother,' the woman in plum commands.

'I'm not calling her. She *expects* me to call her. And anyway, I don't want to worry her. Did he score? Fuck, I missed it, he *scored*, shit. Fuck.'

'It's rude to swear,' Robertson says.

'If that kid doesn't shut the fuck up, I'm going to kill him.'

'So are you coming home when you get better?' Robertson asks.

'I have to see how it goes.'

'Mum didn't tell me you were in the hospital.'

'She didn't know,' Christopher says. 'I didn't want her to worry. She knows now but you don't need to tell her you visited me. Let's make it our secret, then Milo can bring you another time.'

'She won't let me go out with Milo. She thinks he's irresponsible and that he killed Billy.'

'That he what?'

'Killed Billy.'

'The kid who body-slams you?'

Robertson nods. 'She thinks Milo killed him wearing his Spider-Man mask but I know he's way too chicken.' Christopher stares questioningly at Milo, who attempts to shrug dismissively to suggest that he couldn't possibly have killed Billy.

'How did he die?' Christopher asks.

'He got in a fight with somebody in a Spider-Man mask and something in his brain exploded.'

'Well,' Christopher says. 'That's very disturbing.'

Still feeling Christopher staring at him, Milo tries to look preoccupied adjusting the blinds.

'On the other hand, Robby, this might mean you can start carrying a cell again if Billy's not around to steal it. I miss being able to call you, bud.'

'Somebody else will steal it.'

'I didn't know Billy stole your cell,' Milo says.

'Don't tell Mum. She thinks I lost it.'

'We didn't tell Tanis,' Christopher explains, 'because she'd expect justice in what would be a long-drawn-out affair, the only evidence being Robby's testimony, his word against Billy's. Hard to prove beyond a reasonable doubt.'

On the bus, the knowledge that Billy body-slammed Robertson and stole his cell reignites a fury in Milo that he must not reveal to the boy. He folds his arms tightly, restraining himself, while trying to think about other things like why sons avoid their mothers, lie to their mothers, for fear of worrying or disappointing them. Aren't their mothers disappointed and worried anyway? Isn't Tanis going out of her mind with worry despite her ignorance of the body-slamming and cellphone theft? Will the sports fan's lies stop his mother from fretting about him? Is not Vera starving herself with disappointment and worry despite her son's collusion and deceit? If Annie had lived, what lies would Milo have told her? He often lied to Gus to forestall interrogation. One lie would make another necessary and soon he would lose track of the falsehoods. Inevitably Gus would note the discrepancies and display the anticipated disappointment and worry. Now he has no idea who Milo is and therefore no expectations of him. Milo cannot disappoint or worry. This should be liberating.

'Is my dad going to die?'

'Absolutely not,' Milo says, far from certain that this is true. He knew an actor called Naylor Wiens who fell off a horse while shooting a commercial for breath mints. Naylor had lied about being able to ride. He and an actress, wearing fur hats, galloped towards each other on white horses. When Naylor fell off, he broke many bones and was strung up in a web similar to Christopher's. Naylor caught pneumonia and died.

'Maybe he'll get a badass fake leg like that guy's,' Robertson says. 'That would be cool.'

'No, he's going to keep both legs. So let's not tell your mum about the hospital visit, okay?'

'He didn't look too good,' Robertson says.

'I think that's inevitable, after a big accident like that. He'll get better.'

Only after they've been off the bus for ten minutes does Robertson ask where they are going.

'To the centre. Remember, I got permission to take you to visit your dad on the condition that I bring you back.'

'I'm not going back.'

Milo can see the boy bracing for a fight. 'You have to. That was part of the deal. Otherwise your mum will find out and she won't let you see your dad.'

'She can't stop me.'

'Robertson, you have to go back or they'll report you missing. Just tonight, okay? Can you do this for me? Please?'

At first the boy only hastens his pace but, as Milo matches his stride, he begins to run. 'You can't keep running away,' Milo calls after him, already short of breath and favouring his sore foot. 'Stop!' he shouts, fearing he won't be able to keep up. 'Please stop!' Robertson sprints onward and Milo, suddenly flushed with the adrenalin spawned by his terror of losing the boy again, races after him, tackling him. As they tumble to the sidewalk Milo uses his body to block Robertson's fall. Once safely on the ground his first instinct is to release the child to make sure he isn't hurt. But he knows if he loosens his grip he may be unable to restrain him. Instead he hangs on as the boy fights and squirms despite his arms being pinned to his sides. Milo endures kicks and head-butts but he will not let go. A man smoking a cigar, walking what looks like an oversized rat, stares at them. 'Everything cool here?'

'Totally cool,' Milo says. 'It's just seizures.'

'I hate you, I hate you, I hate you,' Robertson shouts.

Milo, still maintaining a vise grip, pulls them into a sitting position and leans against a fire hydrant. What a relief to be holding him finally, feeling the intractable life of him. He has only held Robertson when Tanis has asked him to lift the sleeping boy upstairs. Unconscious, the child feels soft and pliable. Conscious and infuriated, he feels wiry, a small mass of taut muscle.

'I hate you, I hate you, I hate you,' Robertson shouts again but with less force.

A stooped woman, dragging a shopping buggy, eyes him and shakes her head.

And then it is just the two of them, the captor and the captured, testing each other's strength and will, waiting it out. Milo's arms burn and his legs cramp but when the boy, exhausted, tips his head back and rests it against his shoulder, Milo presses his cheek against his silky hair and rocks him gently. An unfamiliar feeling spreads through him; he can't find words to describe it, he who is uncomfortable talking about feelings. What he knows is that for once he is in the right place at the right time. He will stay here, holding firm, for as long as it takes.

'Where have you been?' Pablo demands.

'What's it to you where I've been?'

'The TV people keep calling. And Wallace has gone AWOL and Vera won't come out of her room. She's starving herself, Milo. I tried cheese and crackers, a liverwurst sanny. Gussy and me even made cabbage rolls.'

'So that's what stinks,' Milo says. His house no longer smells like his house, or Gus's, for that matter. 'Where is he?'

'In the basement. He likes it down there. Please, can you talk to Vera? I seen an old lady starve herself before. *Mi abuela* when she found out my father was screwing my cousin, and that my niece was a *puta*. She didn't even drink water. She got dehydrated and went into a coma. It don't take long, Milo.'

'So let her die if she wants to. Why do we all have to *live*? I'm sick of this life-at-any-cost bullshit. If she wants to die, let her die.' Why he is presenting his callous face when moments ago, carrying the boy to safety, feeling his warm surrender, his trust, laying him gently on the bed while the yoga-panted women watched admiringly, he felt, well, happy.

'She don't really want to die. It's just she's upset about Wallace.'

'And Wallace is upset about Vera. Why can't everybody just *move on*?'

'Are you shouting again?' Tawny asks, nibbling on a cabbage roll.

'I wasn't shouting.'

'Yes you were. Why don't *you* move on?'

Milo feels his jaw flapping but no words come out.

'He used to be nicer,' Pablo says, putting his arm protectively around her.

'Hands off her!' Milo snaps as he climbs the stairs to his parents' room. 'Vera?' He knocks several times. When she doesn't respond he nudges the door open. She's asleep in the armchair. He picks her glasses up off the floor, sets them on the dresser and lies on the marshmallow bed. No one will bother him in here. His muscles tense, resisting the cushy mattress. It's as though if he lets go, he will fall. What really happened in this chocolate box of a room anyway? What could it have been like for Annie to endure the sexual advances of her husband knowing that any resulting pregnancy would likely fail? Why didn't the doctors tell her to stop? Maybe they did and Gus kept at, as he has always done. After the funeral, when Milo couldn't sleep because Annie wasn't there to kiss him good night, Gus took him for rides in his truck. This was the height of decadence to Milo, to be out in the world at night in his pyjamas in his father's truck. His mother wouldn't have liked it. His father didn't say much, driving with both hands on the wheel, but it was the two of them together in the world, against the world. In that truck, in his pyjamas, with the city lights flickering, Milo felt that only good things could happen. Eventually he'd fall asleep and Gus would carry him to bed. After several weeks Gus stopped the ritual, insisting it was a waste of gas and it was time for Milo to be a big boy and go to sleep by himself. Milo didn't question or plead, he obeyed and lay stiff with apprehension contemplating the endless nights ahead, filled with fitful sleep and nightmares in which his mother would die many deaths. Often he'd waken thinking he'd dreamed that she'd died, that she was downstairs pouring orange juice and shaking out his Froot Loops.

'Milo?'

'Yes, Vera.'

'What are you doing here?'

'Rumour has it you're starving yourself.'

'What tosh.'

'When did you last eat?'

'I can't remember. Breakfast.'

'Well,' Milo looks at his watch, 'that was sixteen hours ago.'

'Was it? Heavens.'

'Can I bring you up a tray?'

'I might be able to manage a cup of tea and a biscuit.'

'You're on.'

'Has Wally come back yet?'

'I'll check.'

Pablo's digging a spoon into a tub of ice cream. 'How's she doing?'

Milo fills the kettle and sets it on the stove. 'I'm making her tea and biscuits.'

'*Bueno*. You have to be quiet though. Fenny's painting Tawny.'

'What?'

'Fenny's never painted a real Indian before. I told her about Tawny and she came right over. Fenny loves that French guy who painted naked native girls.'

'You used Tawny as *bait*?'

'You can't go in there.'

Sure enough, Tawny, semi-nude, draped in a sheet, lies on the couch. On seeing Milo she quickly covers up.

'Pablo,' Fennel says, 'I told you not to let anybody in here.'

'It's *my* house,' Milo protests. 'And Tawny is my guest. You have no right to take advantage of her.'

'She's paying me,' Tawny says. 'I need the money.'

'I see. Great, okay, what else will you do for cash because this is the place for it – we've got hookers, gigolos, queers, coming and going at all hours.'

Fennel struts towards him and punches his shoulder. 'How is this different from you stripping for my art class?'

There has to be a difference, he just can't think of one.

'If there was a private room available,' Fennel says, 'we'd use it. Even the basement's booked.'

'Is he still down there?' Milo asks.

'He's fixing the kitchen chairs,' Pablo says. 'They're wobbly.'

Milo descends the stairs two at a time. 'Would you stop fixing things? Why do you have to *fix* things all the time?'

Gus, screwdriver in hand, nods and smiles. '*Cześć.*'

'This is nuts. You're supposed to have forgotten all this shit.'

'Milo,' Pablo calls, 'Tanis wants to talk to you.'

He expects her to hurl accusations or crutches. Regardless, he intends, as lovesick Amy advised, to tell her to fuck right off. But she sits demurely on his steps.

'I've been thinking about it,' she says. 'Maybe you should take Robertson to see Christopher. It's not for me to decide. They have to make their own decisions about their relationship. I'll call the centre tomorrow and tell them you're going to take him.'

Great, so what is he supposed to do now? How can he possibly explain? Why did he rush it? Nothing good ever happens in a hurry.

'Sal misses him badly,' she says. 'She's always looking for him. Robertson talks to her. I try but she's not interested. I don't speak her language.' She absently jabs the end of a crutch into the dirt. 'I'm so lonely. I had no idea I could be this lonely.'

He sits beside her, wanting to prolong this intimacy, her vulnerability. Is lying an option? Would the yoga-panted women join him in collusion and deceit?

'I've been trying to imagine my life without him. Parents do that, I'm told, when their kids turn into teenagers. They can see it coming: university, lovers, spouses. They have to let go. But I've never even considered that, I mean, that's always been so out of the question with Robertson, I just can't ... ' Her voice wavers and he fears she's repressing tears. He has never seen her cry.

'I mean,' she continues, 'it's impossible to imagine him being on his own so I don't. I just assume we'll always be together. Maybe that's wrong.'

Milo doesn't know if it is. He just wants to hold her tight, like he held Robertson.

'I mean, who am I to say what's right for him? I don't know, I just don't know anymore. It was simpler before. I saw a mother in a garden with her three-year-old. He wanted to help her, was busy digging in the dirt. Robertson used to do that.' She covers her eyes with her hand. 'I miss him so much. But when he screams at me, it's like … I don't know who is he or what he's capable of. I thought I did but I don't. Maybe somebody else can see it more clearly.'

'I took him to see Christopher this evening,' Milo confesses. 'They were great together, no problems.'

Immediately the bite is back in her voice and she's pulling away from him. 'What do you mean you took him to see him? They let you take him out without notifying me?'

'I had a letter from Christopher.'

She covers her face with her hands and remains scarily still. Somewhere a dog barks, a car door slams, a child's toy squeaks, but Tanis doesn't move.

'Robertson was really happy to see me.' There's that imprecise word again. 'I mean, he didn't hesitate to come with me. We had ice cream, and even rode on a bus. We met an amputee who showed Robertson his leg, the false one and the stump. Robertson thought it was totally badass. I think he had a good time. I mean, I think he was glad to get out.' He doesn't mention almost losing him twice.

She reaches for her crutches and stands awkwardly, without looking at him. 'That's the problem, Milo. As much as I want to, I can't trust you. Please keep me informed about your plans for my son.' She hobbles to her deck.

'Of course. Are you picking him up tomorrow?'

'I will seek the counsel of the professionals caring for him and will make a decision based on their feedback. Good night.' The doors slide shut behind her.

Vera's asleep in the chair again. He pats her hand. 'Vera, I brought your tea and bickies. Drink it while it's hot.'

'What? Oh yes. Thank you, Milo.'

How cruel the aging process is, he thinks, making us grow to look the same despite life experience making us distinctly different. In every white-haired, wrinkled and shapeless body is an individual screaming to get out.

'Is Wally back from the office?'

'I forgot to check.'

'He's all I've got, Milo.'

'What about your sisters?'

'Oh, they have their own troubles. They never forgave me for marrying Wally's father and moving here in the first place.'

'Why did you marry him?'

'Seemed like a good idea at the time. England was a mess for years after the war. Did you know he had Parkinson's disease?'

'Who?'

'Wally's dad. Wally doesn't like to talk about it, I think because he's afraid he might get it. We didn't know about it till long after I'd left the witless dingbat. He was living in a trailer up north. Wally went to see him. Of course the old man didn't recognize him and was half bats already. He chased Wally out with a fork. Next thing we heard he'd stopped eating and died. It's a good way to go, Milo, if people will only leave you alone.'

'Yes, but he had a progressive illness. He had a good reason to kill himself.'

'What's a good reason? I think people drag it out terribly.'

'A debilitating illness is a good reason.' He offers her a biscuit. She takes one but doesn't bite it.

'We all have our reasons. Everybody else should just sod off.'

He finds Wallace in an Irish bar he frequents after junk removal. A portly man saws at a fiddle while another, resembling a leprechaun, blows on a pipe. Wallace stares at the musicians but doesn't seem to be listening. Milo taps his shoulder.

'What are you doing here?' Wallace demands. 'No way am I buying you a beer.'

'We're all worried about Vera. We think she might be starving herself to death.'

'No such luck.'

'You can't really want your mother to die?'

'I don't see you too excited about your dad moving in.'

'I wouldn't want him dead, though.' Or would he?

'Could've fooled me.'

'Why don't you just talk to her?'

'About what?'

'Anything. All she wants is to be part of your life.'

'What if I don't want her to be part of my life? What's *my* say in all this?' He muzzles himself with his beer mug, taking several gulps, before slamming the empty mug on the bar. 'I don't get how we get stuck with these parents. We didn't ask to be born. They screwed and out we popped. Now they're dotty and we're supposed to look after them till they shit themselves to death. It makes no sense.'

'They looked after *us.*'

'Yeah, but we didn't ask them to, did we? It's not like we got to choose. We got stuck with them, broke loose and now that their party's over, we get stuck with them again. It makes no sense.'

Milo could talk about duty and responsibility but he doesn't really believe in these abstractions. He tries to think of what Pablo would say. 'She loves you, Wallace.'

'She loves her idea of me, dickwad, the little boy in that picture she carries around. She doesn't even fucking know me.'

'So, let her get to know you.'

'"Hi, Mom, I'm a sexually disoriented junk remover who suffers from erectile dysfunction and hasn't fucked a woman in years. Sorry about those grandkiddies you've been counting on. Guess you'll have to get some kittens you can kick around." I'm tired of this game, seriously.'

A tanked man and woman get up to dance but stumble into one another.

'She told me your dad had Parkinson's.'

'Yeah, now there's a gift you want to pass on to future generations.'

'He didn't know he had Parkinson's when you were born.'

'He didn't know much. That's the problem. People breed like rabbits and don't know shit. And somehow we're supposed to grow up and forgive them.'

'What do any of us know?'

'I know I'm carrying around a gaga gene. I know I'm totally fucked up and would totally fuck up Junior. You don't breed for the sake of breeding. We're not animals. It's not like the planet needs more humans. What's the total now, seven billion? We're worse than fucking locusts.'

Wallace has never spoken so freely or frankly to Milo. He can't think of a good argument. If Pablo were here he would tell Wallace about a movie with a happy ending.

•••

He checks his email. *Love, the Final Solution* has not contacted him regarding a call time for tomorrow. Doubtless, Guard Number Eight, in squeak-free boots and an earring, will be doing the whipping scene. Does this mean Milo won't get to die? Guard Number Twelve is supposed to be shot by the Russians. Milo died so well in his audition; surely the heavy-lidded queen will remember and request his participation in the Red invasion.

There is, however, a message from his agent regarding a commercial for cell-phones. And Sammy Sanjari is asking how Milo and his dad are 'getting along' and if they can arrange a time to 'wrap things up.' Milo doesn't reply. He phones Tanis even though he knows she won't pick up. He phones Christopher even though he knows the hospital blocks incoming calls after nine.

The casting director, whose hair looks as though it has been licked by a large cow, greets him effusively at the door. Milo would like to ask him why he has called him in when he behaved so *unprofessionally* in the audition for the beer ad, but the casting director immediately pulls him aside. 'Go wild with this one,' he urges. 'He wants crazy. You'd be perfect. Just don't hold back.' He pushes him into the audition room where a paunchy man in a leather jacket sits behind a table.

'How's it wagging?' the man asks. 'You're surprised to see me, right?' He has a puff of youthful hair that contradicts the many lines on his face. 'You're thinking, "no decent director auditions solo," am I right?'

'It is unusual.'

'Well, you know what? I'm an *actor's* director. I like to know what *I* think before the bean counters tell me what *they* think. Make sense?'

'Sure.'

'You play guitar?'

'A little,' Milo lies. 'It's been a while.'

'Have you ever been in love?'

'Sure,' Milo says, although he isn't sure. Unless his chronic longing for Tanis's approval qualifies, or his desire to lick her legs. Or his pining for Zosia, and his need to fondle her silk scarf. He keeps imagining he sees her on the street, keeps hoping for that chance encounter in which he'll be able to explain his feelings.

'Okay, soldier, here's the thing. You are *so* in love with this woman you get hard just thinking about her. 24/7 you're thinking about her.'

'I'm hard 24/7?'

The director touches his youthful hair as though to make sure it's still intact. 'That's funny. I like it. I've heard about you. You come from theatre, is that right? Do something for me.'

'Excuse me?'

'Hamlet or something. Can you do Hamlet? The slings and arrows bit. That's a good one.'

A trained classical actor, always prepared, Milo begins the *to be or not to be* soliloquy but the director stops him at *a sea of troubles*. 'Okay, now do it like it's a comedy.'

'You're insane,' Milo says and starts to walk out.

'Okay, okay, sorry, see that cell?' A cellphone is propped against an Evian bottle on the table. 'The woman you love is on the phone, gazing at you from that little screen and you want to fuck her in half. But instead you grab your guitar.' The director points to an electric guitar. 'And you play your lust out to her. Can you do that?'

'It's not plugged in.'

'Whatever, act it. Think *bitch in heat.*'

Milo, feeling the inevitability of gradual decline pressing upon him, grabs the guitar and starts wailing, 'Baby, baby, I want you ... ' He hops around, jabbing the neck of the guitar at the phone. He howls and yowls, repeatedly thrusting his pelvis, and yanks his shirt open. All of this excites the director who also hops around howling and yowling and thrusting his pelvis. 'Baby, baby, I need you. Baby, baby, love me too ...'

Milo grabs the phone and starts licking it. The director, sweating below his puff of youthful hair, stands back. 'They warned me you were wild.'

Milo starts to shove the phone down his pants.

'Okay, okay now, cool it,' the director says, holding up his hands. 'I get it. You win.'

Milo doesn't know what he has won. The casting director, probably alerted by the howling and yowling, squeaks open the door and says, 'How's everything going?'

'We're done here,' Milo says and walks out into the exhaust-scented morning.

...

Travis, the sports fan, is asleep but still his TV drones. Christopher doesn't seem surprised to see Milo. 'Look who it isn't,' he remarks.

'I'm sorry I couldn't bring Robertson.'

'Did you even try?'

'I told Tanis we'd been to see you. Did she call you?'

'She did indeed.'

'Is she going to bring him?'

'She hasn't decided. She's seeking professional guidance. As I have no time for professionals our conversation was brief.' How can a man trapped in a bed have no time?

'You're in the care of professionals here.'

'Yes, and look how well I'm doing. A man with multiple fractures fell off a gurney last night outside this very room. We heard his anguished cries. Apparently he was left unattended because the professionals were otherwise engaged. And yet I am expected to make it to rehab where professionals will roll me around on an exerball. That's what they do, I'm told. Sit you on a big rubber ball and watch you crash to the mat Humpty Dumpty-style over and over again until you figure out how to balance. It takes weeks apparently. I couldn't be more excited.'

'Well, it's good they're talking about rehab,' Milo says.

'It's all good. That's what my roommate here says frequently. *It's all good.* My wife has informed me that our marriage is over, and that she may or may not let me see my son. My body is broken in many places and the only person who visits me is you, Milo. It's all good.'

Frantic garbling over the intercom suggests another patient may have tumbled from a gurney.

'I might have killed Billy,' Milo says. 'It was an aneurysm. I might have caused it.'

'You can't cause an aneurysm. It's already there. It's like a ticking bomb.'

'Yeah, but me roughing him up might have caused stress that made it rupture. That's what Tanis thinks. She thinks I killed him.'

'Oh, well, in that case, bring on the executioner.'

'I think she wants me to turn myself in.'

'Yes, well, her world is black and white.'

'You don't think I should?'

'To what purpose?'

'A clear conscience.'

'We don't live there. Is my associate asleep?'

'I think so.'

'Turn the TV off before I go postal.'

Milo sneaks around the curtain and presses the power button. Travis, on his back with his mouth open, snores. Strewn about his bed are sports sections and empty pudding cups.

'A few months ago,' Christopher says, 'Robertson developed an interest in a girl at school. He swore me to secrecy but couldn't have been hiding his crush very well because Billy broadcast it in cyberspace detailing the sick and perverted things "the retard" planned to do to the girl. Then Billy took her to a movie and shoved his fingers up her vagina. I know this because the father of the girl was one of my clients. Like me, he didn't want to put his child through the humiliation, stress and futility of seeking justice. And so the Billies of this world go on damaging lives until nature takes its course, or someone accidentally kills them. No matter how hard my left-of-centre mind works at it, I can't perceive his demise as a tragedy and nor should you, unless, of course, you enjoy wearing a hair shirt.' He sucks on a straw sticking out of a large Styrofoam cup. 'But there's no denying I'm not the best person to judge, given that I am the father, and up close and personal with nature's course myself. All the lines that used to be clear to me have become blurred. Like any good atheist I've always considered the Earth, the intractable world of matter, to be the basis of consciousness. Our births are real, but after that, all bets are off, randomness rules. Of course now I'm hoping for wings and pearly gates. Very predictable and disappointing.' He sucks on the straw again. 'So the field is open, Milo, if you want to fuck my wife.'

'I wish you'd stop saying that.'

'You know what I find extraordinary? I didn't think it was about *us* anymore. Didn't think our relationship was that important. When you have a kid, you just don't matter that much anymore, to you anyway. I found this liberating, not being bound by my ego and needs and aspirations. I lived for Robby, did everything for Robby. Meanwhile my marriage was ending without me knowing it.'

'But you left.'

'At her insistence. And because I was afraid I might hit him again. Now I know I could never hit him again. My understanding was that the arrangement was temporary.' Christopher starts his laughing/crying combo again. 'But whaddayaknow? The wife says it's over. Finito. Kaput.'

'Who turned off my TV?' Travis demands.

'I did, asshole,' Milo says, suddenly incensed at the injustice of it all. He strides around the curtain. 'Wear fucking headphones. You're driving him nuts. *Me* nuts. You don't want me nuts.'

'I'm calling a nurse.'

'Oh, I'm sure she'll rush to your side, after she lets some poor fuck fall off a gurney. Wear headphones, dickwad.' He points to his ears. 'The hospital provides them.'

'All right already. Just back off.'

Milo realizes he is leaning over Travis's bed rail. 'Call your mother,' he quips before ducking around the curtain where Christopher gives him two thumbs up. Milo slouches in the chair.

'You've got no place to go?' Christopher asks.

'Not really. Do you mind?'

'Turn the chair so you're not staring at me. Face the window. I spend days watching the sun move across the sky. I'd like to say it's comforting but really it just reminds me of my infinite insignificance.'

Milo settles in, resting his feet against the windowsill. A small plane cuts across the sky dragging a banner that says, *Melissa, will you marry me?* Air whistles through Christopher's busted nose.

'What happened to that Russian girl you were dating?' he asks.

'Latvian. She dumped me.'

'Why?'

'I coast.'

'Really? How interesting. You know what she told me about you?'

'She talked to you about me?'

'We had a brief chinwag when you locked yourself out and had to borrow a ladder to climb in a window. She said, "Milo is disappointed in his oyster."'

'What's that supposed to mean?'

'That you're disappointed in life. But look at it this way, at least you have one.' He winces and clicks the button on his morphine pump. 'I think everybody's a little disappointed in their oysters, Milo. It's an unavoidable flaw in the human psyche. She was a nice girl, smart. Too smart for you, probably.'

'I don't know where she is. Even if I wanted to, I couldn't see her. I'm quite worried about her. Her mother's sick back in Latvia. She actually loves her mother.'

'Some people do.'

Milo is about to ask Christopher if he loves *his* mother but then remembers that she's dead and that Christopher's father married his twenty-something personal assistant who spawned two neuro-typical children younger than Robertson.

'Hello, Mother,' Travis says. 'Yes, it's me ... I said I'd call, didn't I? ... Not to worry, the doc says I'm doing just fine ... No, really, it's all good.'

23

*m*ilo walks stealthily up the walk, hoping to arrive undetected but, of course, Sammy Sanjari is on the couch in deep conversation with Tawny. Doubtless he is considering the potential of a reality show set on the res. Maybe her dead abusive father could show up and blow kisses.

'Milo,' Sammy says, jumping up and extending his arms. Milo heads for the kitchen. 'Why don't you return my calls, my friend?'

'I'm not your friend.'

'You should always return calls as a courtesy.'

'Fuck that noise.'

'Tawny tells me your father has settled in bootifully.'

'He's nuts, okay, *nuts*, all he does is fix things.'

'And cook,' Tawny adds. 'You should try his cabbage rolls.'

Milo smears Vera's cream cheese on crackers. 'Has Vera come down?' Tawny shakes her head. 'Did you take some food up to her?'

'Gus took up some goh-ron-tseh mleh-koh.'

'Some *what?*'

Gus appears from the basement. '*Gorące mleko*,' he clarifies, nodding and smiling. 'Hunny vit meelk.'

'He means milk and honey,' Tawny interprets.

'Varm dreenk,' Gus explains.

'Gus, my friend,' Sammy says. 'How well you are doing with your English.'

Gus nods. 'Eengleesh. Noh prrroblem.'

'Bootiful. Well, Milo, I would say you are ready to wrap things up.'

'I'm not wrapping up anything.'

Sammy's cell rings 'Where Is the Love?' He pulls it out of his jacket. 'Yes, I'm with Milo now. No worries. It's looking very good, very promising. Although he is a little reluctant ... A little, yes ... I understand, but are you sure you don't want to leave it with me? ... I understand.' He hands the phone to Milo. 'Birgit for you.'

Milo takes the phone only because he can't think of what else to do. 'Milo?' Birgit says. 'Milo, are you there? What's this about reluctant?'

'I want out.'

'There is the matter of a contract.'

'I'll give you back the money,' he says, knowing he has already spent the initial grand on utility bills.

'There are two kinds of people in the world,' Birgit says. 'The finishers and the quitters. Which one are you?'

A man who can build a debris hut is no quitter. 'I'm just not comfortable with this,' he says.

'Sammy will *make* you comfortable. That's his job. Let him do his job or I'll sue your ass. Give me back to him.' Milo hands the cell back to Sammy who listens to Birgit, periodically saying, 'I understand' and 'no worries' and, finally, 'bootiful.'

All the while Gus has been making tea and slicing lemon. '*Herbata*,' he says, lifting the teapot.

'It's called tea, asshole,' Milo says.

'Milo, is that any way to talk to your father? Come and sit with me.'

'I don't want to sit with you.'

Sammy grips his arm. 'Come, we can fix this.' He guides Milo to the couch and sits beside him with his arm firmly around his shoulder. 'I know this has been hard for you, but you know, sometimes we run away from the very thing we need most in the world. Sometimes our heart's desire is within our grasp but we don't see it because we have been blinded by our past. The past is over, my friend. Bury the past or it will bury you. You have a brand-new future with your father who is so good at fixing things and making cabbage rolls. Do you know how much I would give to be able to sit down to dinner with my father? I would be so happy to just be with him, healing old wounds and accepting that the past is past.'

Cotton balls plug Milo's lungs again, pushing up his throat into his mouth and nostrils. Why fight it? Resistance is futile. 'What do you want me to do?'

'Tomorrow night you'll have dinner together. A nice Polish dinner. Gus will do the cooking and we'll pretty up the house. No worries.'

'Have you spoken to Gus about this?'

'Get Pablo to ask him,' Tawny says. 'He speaks Polish.'

'No he doesn't.'

'Whatever, he communicates with him.'

Gus walks in with a tray and sets it on the table. He arranges Annie's 'special occasion' teacups and saucers that have been ignored for years and begins to pour. He has never done this in his life. Milo can't stand it.

'Vera?' He knocks. 'Vera, can I come in?' When she doesn't answer he nudges the door open. Pablo's sandwiches are untouched, although the teacup is half empty. He replaces it with a fresh cup and the crackers and cream cheese. He pats her hand. 'Vera? Vera, have some tea.'

'Goodness gracious, what time is it?'

'Late. Have a cracker.' He offers her one that she takes but doesn't bite.

'Did Wally come home? He was here, wasn't he? And didn't pop in to see me. He doesn't care one bit.'

'Oh, I think he does. He's just been incredibly busy at the office. We told him you weren't feeling well. He didn't want to bother you.'

'What codswallop. Why do you lie like that, Milo?'

This stalls him. He flops onto the marshmallow bed. 'It's not just me who lies, is it? Doesn't everybody make stuff up to make everybody else happy?' That word again.

'It doesn't make us happy if it's a lie.'

'You're not supposed to know it's a lie. A good lie can keep the masses happy for ages.'

'It all comes out in the end. Might as well sort it at the beginning, save yourself the trouble.'

'Okay,' he says, 'if that's how you want it. But don't tell me I didn't warn you.' He stares at a crack in the ceiling so he won't have to see her face as her world implodes. 'Wallace is sexually disoriented, has erectile dysfunction and hasn't had sex with a woman in years. I don't know if this means he's a pansy but I do know he's afraid of passing on the Parkinson's gene, and that he doesn't see the point of having children on a planet with seven billion people on it.'

'He said all that?'

'He did.'

'There's a certain sense in that.'

'I agree.'

'Why doesn't he just come out and tell me then?'

'He's afraid he'll worry and disappoint you.'

'What tosh.'

He still can't face her but hears her sipping tea. This is a good sign.

'They advertise pills for that on the telly.'

'I don't know if he's tried medication.'

She sips more.

'And there's something else,' he says.

'Yes?'

'He's not an accountant. He's a junk remover.'

'A what?'

'He removes people's junk.'

'That's his lorry, then, with *Friendly Junk Removal* on it?'

'It is.'

'He doesn't have a motor in the shop?'

'He does not. Just the truck.'

'Is that a good living then, junk removal?'

'Definitely. Seven billion humans produce a lot of junk.'

'Why would he lie about it then?'

'I think he thought accounting was more dignified. He didn't want to worry or disappoint you.'

'What tosh.'

Downstairs the misfits munch on black bread with cold cuts. '*Musztarda,*' Gus says, passing around a jar of mustard.

'Moosh-tar-dah,' Pablo repeats. 'Hey, Milo, look what we bought.' He holds up another jar. 'Genuine Polish horseradish.'

'*Chrzan,*' Gus explains.

'Hshan,' Pablo repeats.

'And pickles,' Tawny adds. 'Real Polish ones.'

'*Ogóorki kiszone,*' Gus explains.

'Oh-goor-kee kee-shoh-neh,' Pablo repeats. 'Is that right, Gussy? Oh-goor-kee kee-shoh-neh?'

'Ya,' Gus says, laughing his hahaha yoga laugh.

Milo escapes to the living room and searches for the remote.

'Tanis wants you to go over,' Pablo calls after him.

'What? How do you know?'

'I was over there doing some caulking.'

'Caulking?'

'Yeah, she's worried about the mildew around the tub. She thinks it might be bad for Robertson.'

'Is he home?'

'He's still at the centre.'

This is madness. The boy should be home by now. He raps on the glass doors. She pulls them open as though she has been waiting for him. She is newly showered, her Medusa hair soaking the shoulders of her bathrobe. She takes his hand and slides it inside the robe and onto her breast.

'My husband says you want to fuck me. I haven't been fucked for a long time, so let's get at it.'

'Are you crazy?' He feels her nipple hardening and all he wants in the whole world is to put his mouth around it.

'Pick me up,' she says. 'I can't walk.'

With his rib straining he carries her to the futon couch. He lays her down awkwardly, afraid that he will injure her ankle. 'Does it hurt?' he asks but she is unzipping his jeans, massaging his groin.

'I'm so ugly now,' she says.

'No you're not.'

'I've turned into a witch.' Her mouth feels foreign, so accustomed is he to the memory of Zosia. He slides his lips down her neck to her breasts, which have been hidden for years behind a good marriage and an abnormal child. She spreads her legs and puts his hand between them.

'I can still get wet,' she mumbles, exhaling relief or despair, he's not sure which. She guides his penis into her vagina, puts her hands on his ass and pulls him into her, forcing him to adjust to her slow, rhythmic movements. He tries to kiss her again but she turns her face away. He sucks and caresses her breasts while she manipulates his pelvis until his response is beyond her or his control and he comes fast, as though it is the first clumsy time, and he knows that whatever relief or distraction she was seeking in him has been spent, that he is just another premature ejaculator, failed actor, lover, friend. *Longing for fulfillment means you are not living in the moment.* Who said that? Sarah fucking Moon Dancer? Wait a minute, didn't he long to lick Tanis's legs? And now here she is, open before him. His tongue slides down her thighs in search of her clitoris. While she moans, exposed, he adds more pressure and speed to his oral gymnastics until her pelvic movements become more urgent, beyond the limits of her black-and-white world of right and wrong. Her cry of release he has heard before, through the wall when she has been with Christopher. Within what feels like seconds she pushes him away and rolls onto her side. He pulls up his jeans and sits on the edge of the futon, baffled. Does she want him to hold her? How can he on such a small couch? He tries stroking her back but she is unresponsive. 'Are you okay?' he asks.

'I forgot for a few seconds,' she says.

'That's good, isn't it?'

'People take drugs to forget.'

Screams crash through the wall.

'It's your father,' she says.

'I know.'

'You better go to him.'

'Why?'

'Because that's where you belong, not here.' She stands, cinching her robe. He doesn't want it to be over, even though he doesn't know what 'it' is. She hobbles to the door and opens it for him.

'I'll come back,' he says.

'Please don't.'

His father's suffering resembles his own: a writhing, screeching, relentless torment.

'Give him the pills, Milo,' Pablo says.

'What pills?'

'His pills that make him sleep.'

'I don't know where they are.'

'You must know where they are. You had them last night.'

'Go look for them. Check the medicine cabinet.'

Milo hid the pills, fearful that he would shy from this moment and not have the courage to endure his father's wrath. Gus, the junkie, scowls at him spouting Polish gibberish, with no recognition beyond *this is the idiot who gives me drugs, give me my fucking drugs.*

'Try *living* with your demons, asshole,' Milo tells him. 'Try being who you are, you selfish prick, you cruel, unfeeling, stupid fuck. What did you do to my mother anyway?' He shakes his father's shoulders. 'You fucked her to death is what you did. How does it feel to fuck someone to death? Get your rocks off now, dickwad, I hope they shove a stick so far up your ass it kills you. Because you don't deserve to forget everything and become a dumb-fuck Polish farmer. You killed her slowly, year after year, till she didn't know who she was anymore, who *I* was. You were her whole world, you fucker, she tried so hard for you, *lived* for you, and you killed her.' Tawny slaps Milo. He tries to fend her off but Pablo pins his arms behind his back.

'Where are the pills, Milo?'

'I have no idea.'

'Where did you hide them?' Tawny demands. 'It's not fair what you're doing. He doesn't know what you're talking about.' Gus, out of Milo's range, scrambles from the bed and down the hall.

'That's good, old man, you run away again, but don't expect me to come looking for you this time.'

Pablo charges after Gus but Tawny maintains her hold on Milo. 'Sit down,' she says.

'Who the fuck are you to tell me what to do?'

'I'm a friend.'

'You're not my friend. You're Gus's friend. And Pablo's. Everybody's Pablo's friend. Has he fucked you yet?'

Wallace looms large in the doorway. 'Cool it, buddy.'

'I'm not your buddy. You're a bunch of fucking freeloaders and I want you out of my house by morning.'

'Quit using bad language,' Tawny says. 'It makes you look stupid.'

'I am stupid.' He tries to step past Wallace but he blocks his path.

'Where are those pills, man? None of us are going to sleep tonight unless he gets those pills.'

'Who are you to talk? You're letting your mother starve herself to death. All she wants is for you to talk to her and all you can do is lie, lie, *lie*. What are you so fucking scared of? She's a little old lady.'

'And Gus is a little old man,' Wallace says.

It all seems so pointless, this last skirmish on the gallows.

Vera appears, waving Gus's pills. 'He hid them under his pillow. Where's Gus?'

'Pablo went after him,' Tawny says. Vera heads downstairs with purpose. This gives Milo comfort.

No longer restrained or needed, he treads to his parents' room and collapses on the marshmallow bed, succumbing to its cushiness, drifting down, down, down into the abyss where randomness rules. What must be tears leak from his eyes, although he isn't certain, so unfamiliar is he with the act of crying. This feeling that something is erupting inside him and must be purged, coughed up, is it grief? For what? What never was? What might have been? How much of it is real? Nothing is real.

'I made you a rum toddy,' Vera says. 'He's asleep now.'

'He'll wake up tomorrow and it'll start all over again.'

'That's good, isn't it? He seems happy.'

'Yes, yes, yes, as long as he's *happy*. How can he be happy with those nightmares scaring the shit out of him? And does he really forget it all day long or is he just in denial?'

'I think denial works wonders. I've never understood why everyone's so dead set against it.'

'But you were in denial about Wally and now you know the truth. Don't you feel better knowing the truth?'

'Not in the least, but what's to be done? You have to give things up, Milo, as you get older: dreams, smooth skin, good eyesight. Grandkiddies. Have *you* ever thought about having children?'

'God no.' His chest wrap has loosened as a result of the twisted sex and the tussle over the old man's pills. He pulls up his T-shirt and hands the end of the bandage to Vera. 'Can you help me unravel?'

'Don't you think the doctor should do that?'

'The doctor's two hundred miles away. It's not doing any good anymore anyway.'

'Stand up then, and turn around slowly.' He does, becoming mildly dizzy as he rotates, enjoying the tingling of his newly exposed skin, the freedom from his hair shirt. 'Why don't young men want babies anymore?' Vera asks.

'Same old, same old. Fear of responsibility, being tied down, although in my case, and I think Wallace's, it's got more to do with this no longer being a world of opportunity. The poor get poorer and the rich get richer trashing the planet.'

'What nonsense. You remind me of those bellyachers after the war. Nothing for it but to get on, Milo.' She hands him the bandage. 'We're all watching telly, would you care to join us?'

'Now? It's three in the morning or something.'

'It's that picture about Mr. Mandela and the rugby player. Quite inspiring really. Mr. Mandela was very keen to forgive the white people who locked him up for thirty years. Imagine that. He thought hatred was a frightful waste of time.'

Milo has seen this movie. Morgan Freeman says, 'One team, one Africa,' and everybody, black and white, stands up and cheers as Matt Damon kicks the ball around. No doubt Pablo will cry at the end of this movie, never mind that black and white are back to hating each other in that sports-loving nation, while the poor get poorer and the rich get richer trashing the diamond continent.

'Why don't you have a kip here then?' Vera says. 'I can sleep on the couch.' And she's off to join the deniers. Milo pitches the bandage in the wastebasket and lies back, gingerly touching his rib. *All life forms are connected.* Who said that, the Buddhist harmonica player? *We're all just an arrangement of atoms. Atoms that will cease to exist.* No pearly gates then. Just The End. So why bellyache and suffer guilt? Surrender to the marshmallow bed, savour your freefall into the void, feel the interconnectedness of all living forms, the circularity of it.

'I fucked your wife.'

'I figured.'

The intercom announces a code red in the Cardinal wing, fourth floor.

'It won't happen again,' Milo says. 'She says I don't belong there.'

'Who does? Just the dog.'

'I hope she's feeding the hamster. I forgot to remind her.'

'It's hard to remember things like hamsters when you're fucking.'

Sybil, in chartreuse today, pushes her face around the curtain. 'Would you mind not talking *smut*?'

'Is *fornicating* a better word?' Christopher asks. 'It's hard to remember things like small rodents when you're fornicating.'

Milo resumes his station in the chair, facing the window. 'So do you hate me now?'

'Not right this second. It might take a few minutes to sink in.'

'I'm sorry.'

'Oh, don't say *sorry*. It is such an utterly useless word. Be glad you got it out of your system. It is out of your system, isn't it?'

'I was a lousy lay.'

'Yes, well, we've all been there.'

'I don't understand why she hates me.'

'That makes two of us.'

The intercom repeats that there is a code red in the Cardinal wing, fourth floor.

'I remember years ago watching her from a distance,' Christopher says. 'We were supposed to meet at the St. Lawrence Market. I arrived early and spied on her as she fondled fruits and vegetables and negotiated with vendors. She was in command of her world. The world was her oyster, Milo. It bent to her will. Then she had Robertson and even though she never said it, I suspect she believes that I am the cause of his problem, that had she fornicated with someone of brawnier stock, she would have had a normal, bouncing boy. She had a tubal ligation, by the way, so don't worry that you might have impregnated her.'

Sybil pushes her face around the curtain again. 'You are *disgusting*. No wonder she ditched you and that freaky boy of yours.'

'Why,' Christopher asks, 'is my friend Travis not joining in this discussion?'

'He's wearing headphones, you jerk.'

'So why are you here, Syb? Can't hubby watch sports solo?'

Sybil sighs heavily and drops the curtain again.

'Hospitalization,' Christopher says, 'forces one to share the most intimate details with complete strangers. I know when Trav pukes, craps, pisses, farts. We've formed an inescapable bond.'

'Likewise, jerk-off,' Sybil says.

'It's all good,' Christopher says.

'When you can get in the wheelchair,' Milo says, 'I'll take you out.'

'Oh, to the Tim Hortons. How dreamy. No, Milo, you are under no obligation to look after the cripple.'

He still doesn't know if Christopher remembers that he called his name, causing him to turn away from the cab. 'You're my only friend.' How lame this sounds but utterly true.

'I guess that's why you fucked my wife.'

Sybil jerks the curtain. 'Enough already. There is a lady present, if you please.'

'I guess that's why you fornicated with my wife. All best friends share spouses. Maybe you could find that nice Latvian girl and I could fornicate with her.'

'You told me the field was open.'

'Oh, come on, Milo, how often do people mean what they say? Anyway, it's all *so* yesterday. The reality is when you're strung up like I am, not sure if you will ever walk again – or live, for that matter – intently focused on things like sitting up and not spilling food on yourself, small matters like fornication don't hold much sway. You know what Nietzsche said?'

'Didn't he say a lot of things?'

'He said *amor fati,* which means *love of fate.* That was his philosophy: as torturous as his life was, he embraced it. He accepted life's inevitable limitations, no matter what fate had in store for him. "*Amor fati,*" he said, "is not merely to endure necessity, still less to deny it ... but to love it." He called it his "formula for greatness in a human being."'

'What pretentious prattle,' Sybil says.

'Milo, I want you to bring Robertson back. I don't care what she says. Do you understand me? Don't come here again unless you bring him. This may require some aggression on your part. Can you do that, Milo?'

'Of course,' he says, although he can't imagine it, charging in to the centre and removing the boy by force, fighting off the yoga-panted and Birkenstocked women.

'I need you to do that.' The plaintiveness in Christopher's voice causes Milo to face him. So many tears pour from his eyes he makes Milo think of a candle dripping wax, dripping and dripping until nothing remains but a puddle.

'I will do that,' Milo says. *Amor fati.*

24

*H*e finds Pablo and Gus in the Zellers restaurant eating pork schnitzel with fries and sauerkraut. 'Can you believe it, Milo? Polski food at Zellers? It's good, eh, Gussy?'

'Goot,' Gus says, daintily eating a fry. Gus never dines among the old and infirm at Zellers. Gus never dines out, prefers home-cooking because 'you know what's in it.'

'They give you free refills,' Pablo says. 'Sit down, Milo. You want something? They got Montreal-style smoked meat on special with coleslaw and fries plus your choice of beverage.'

'Aren't you about to be arrested? Where's the security guard?'

'That's why we got him to call you. We knew you'd fix it.'

'What? What happened?'

'Gussy shoplifted. Well, he didn't mean to, he got spooked.'

'What do you mean "spooked"?'

'Didn't the guard tell you nothing?'

'He said there was "a situation." He didn't give details.'

'He told us to wait here or he'd call the cops.'

'Where did he go?'

'For a smoke.'

'Oh, for chrissake.'

'Everybody's allowed a smoke break, Milo.'

'What did you steal?' Milo demands of Gus who pays him no mind so intent is he on cutting his schnitzel.

'He didn't steal nothing. He got scared 'cause they put a siren on and this, like, flashing light they use when they're doing a demo. It's, like, this big flashing light, and a guy talks on a loudspeaker about the promotion. And everybody starts running to the big flashing light because the guy says the first ten people win a free gift. So Gussy had just come out of the change room to show me his jeans. Stand up, Gussy, show him your jeans.' Pablo nudges Gus who stands, still holding a fry. 'Turn around.' Pablo grabs the old man's hips and turns him around. 'Cool jeans, eh, Milo? Guess how much?'

Gus never wears jeans.

'Guess how much?'

'I have no idea.'

'Eleven ninety-nine. And the cowboy shirt, guess how much?' The shirt has snaps for buttons and horses' heads and lassos embroidered on the collar and cuffs. 'Nine ninety-nine. Can you believe that? You know how much this would cost in Cuba?' Gus never wears cowboy shirts.

Milo sits because his legs feel unable to support him. 'He's wearing clothes you've *stolen?*'

'Shit, no. I paid for them later, plus his underwear.'

'Un-dehr-vehr,' Gus clarifies, nodding.

'So what's the problem?' Milo asks. 'Why are you still here?'

'Because I don't got no driver's licence or nothing, and neither does Gussy. The guard wants to make sure we're no criminals. I said you'd tell him Gus is your dad.'

What if he doesn't? What if the Polish farmer in the cowboy shirt is whisked away to prison to await bail that no one will post? *I've never seen him before in my life.*

Pablo pokes Milo. 'Try the avalanche cake. It's got chocolate all over.'

Using the back of his chair for leverage, Milo manages to stand. 'I'm going to find the security guard. Does he have a name?'

'He's got a uniform.'

Milo heads for the entrance to Zellers where, presumably, the smokers linger, but he stops in the toy section stacked with junk for future removal. The shelves stand so high Milo can hide among the Barbies. Ernie Batty, the boy in foster care, and Milo dismembered some Barbies that belonged to his foster mother's spiteful daughter. They stacked a pile of Barbie limbs and tried to set them on fire but Gus caught them at it. Milo had never seen his father so red in the face – even his ears glowed. He grabbed Milo's arm and yanked him into the house. 'I've seen children burn,' he said. '*Never* play with fire.' Gus didn't spank Milo but sat him in front of the macaroni casserole left behind by Mrs. Cauldershot.

'What children?' Milo asked.

'What?'

'What children did you see burn?'

'Eat your dinner.'

Milo wanted to ask questions like Did they smell? How long did it take? Was there just a pile of ashes afterwards or were there still bones? But Gus descended to the basement to chisel stone.

Did the Zellers siren and flashing light evoke memories of burning children?

A hulking man with *Daddy* tattooed on his forearm talks on a cell while fondling the Barbies. 'The great thing about heavy-duty garbage bags,' he says, 'is you can put stuff like screwdrivers in them.'

Beyond Daddy's hulk, in the electronics department, a massive flat screen displays a freed Colombian hostage. Milo has already seen her on a morning show in which the big-haired hostess repeatedly leaned forward and said, 'It must have been very painful for you.' The hostage looks too normal to have lived for years in the jungle on gruel, tied to a tree by her neck. She kept track of the passing years by remembering her children's birthdays.

'They've got Kitty Care Vet Barbie,' Daddy says. 'Has she got that one?'

When Milo looked for Tanis and Robertson this morning, Gus was scraping the Muskoka chairs. How is it possible to forget a son but remember how to scrape a chair?

'What about Ballerina Barbie?' Daddy inquires. 'Or I Really Swim in Water Barbie? I'm not shitting you. It says she really swims in water. They've also got Ballroom Dancer Barbie, has she got that one?'

Milo walks past the toys, through pet supplies, past housewares, until he sees the glass doors opening onto a Gus-free world. He walks swiftly past the sidewalk-sale tables and across the parking lot.

When the Colombian guerrilla who tied the hostage by her neck to a tree was executed, the hostage confessed that she was not sorry to hear about his death, but she did forgive him. Just like Mr. Mandela forgave the white-asses who locked him up for thirty years. All Gus did was hit Milo occasionally, and forget about him. What's to forgive? The chin-up bar incident? Milo had desperately wanted one, imagining that daily chin-ups would transform his noodle arms into Stallone-like weapons. Gus said the bar would damage the door jamb. 'You won't use it anyway,' he added. 'Too much work.' Milo saved his lawn-mower money until he had enough for a bar. He installed it in his bedroom doorway, regularly forgetting it was there and slamming his head into it. He tried to use it but hauling his body weight up to the bar was agony. His neck muscles burned from pulling when his arms and shoulders gave out. Usually father and son avoided crossing paths in the hall but one evening Gus appeared just as Milo was slamming his head into the bar for the fifth time that day. Gus grabbed Milo's hair and repeatedly thumped his head into the bar. 'How smart is that, Mr. Universe?' he demanded. 'Are the girls chasing you yet?' With one swift movement Gus collapsed the bar and pointed to the indentations the rings left on the door jamb. 'How can my son be such an idiot?' he asked the walls. Bumps swelled on Milo's head. He considered going to the police and having Gus charged, but then Milo would have to admit that he'd failed in the chin-up department and frequently slammed his head into the bar.

A small boy points at him. 'Mummy, Mummy, look! It's the Canadian Tire Man.' The mother, weighted with bags and responsibility, tries to grab the boy's hand, but he scoots towards Milo. 'Can I have your autograph?'

'Sure. Do you have a piece of paper?'

'Mummy, do we have a piece of paper?' He hops up and down while she sets her bags on the pavement and searches in her purse. One of the bags tips, revealing many packets of Kraft Dinner. Apparently embarrassed, she immediately starts to shove them back in.

'I'll do that,' Milo says, righting the bag and collecting the packets.

'Thanks. They're on special, that's why I got so many.' She finds a pen and a scrap of paper and hands it to Milo. He squats so he is level with the boy. 'What's your name?'

'Thomas. I saw a wolf earlier.'

'Really?'

'Or it might have been a fox.'

'It was just a dog, Thomas,' his mother says.

'It might have been a wolf dog,' Thomas suggests.

Milo writes: *To Thomas, Watch out for wolf dogs, and don't lie to your mother. With warmest regards, The Canadian Tire Man.*

'Your writing is messy,' Thomas observes.

'Thomas, what do you say?' his mother prompts.

'Thank you.'

Not wanting to reveal that the Canadian Tire Man is a mere mortal, Milo walks in the opposite direction from Thomas and his mother, back to Zellers. He asks the sickly clerk at the Customer Service desk to page the security guard.

'You were amazing, Milo,' Pablo says, leading the way to the produce section. 'Totally Clint Eastwood.'

Gus sniffs mushrooms, grumbling as he examines then discards them.

'He shouldn't sniff the vegetables,' Milo says.

'It's because he's a farm boy,' Pablo explains. 'I don't think he likes the mushrooms. Are the gzhibs no good, Gussy?'

Gus shakes his head and throws up his hands. 'No goot. *Prawdziwe grzyby rosną w lesie, na mchu i na słońcu, to rośnie w szopie na końskim gównie.*'

'That bad, eh?' Pablo says, looking at the list Gus wrote in Polish in a childish hand completely unfamiliar to Milo. 'Okay, Gussy, take it easy, we'll go check out the meat counter and see if they've got cot-let s-habo-vyh pah-nyeh-roh-vah-nyh.'

'What the fuck is that?' Milo says.

'*Kotlet schabowy panierowany*,' Gus clarifies, nodding.

'And zhiem-nyah-kamee,' Pablo adds.

'*Ziemnikami*,' Gus says, nodding.

Milo trails them as they search for pickled herring and sour cream, and deliberate over pork tenderloin and pickles. 'Who's supposed to pay for all this?' he demands.

'Sammy gave me cash. I like that guy. He's a forward thinker. You should be nicer to him, Milo.'

He walks like Clint Eastwood into the Child and Parent Resource Centre but there are no yoga-panted women at reception. Should he wait for one to appear or should he stride to where the Curlys and Robertsons are secluded in quiet rooms? On the walls are photos of autistic children, some facing but not looking at the camera, others ignoring it entirely, and some looking normal, smiling mechanically, no doubt at the photographer's urging. *Say cheese.* Milo spots a photo of Robertson solemnly building a tower with Lego. Milo pulls the shot off the wall and slips it in his pocket.

'Oh, it's you,' the Birkenstocked woman says. 'Robertson isn't here.'

'Where is he?'

'When he isn't here, we don't know where he is.'

'Did he run away?'

'His mother took him. Please don't cause another disturbance.'

'She must have told you something.'

'We don't pry into our clients' private lives. We are here to offer relief, not to pass judgment.'

She holds the door open for him, smiling judgmentally. Milo smiles back. 'Cheese,' he says.

Facing the window, he listens to air whistling through unconscious Christopher's nose. Travis's father, Earl, talks loudly about a bowling partner who is not playing like a gentleman. 'I guess it's to be expected of a guy like that,' Earl admits. 'He grew up on tough street, end of the block.'

'That's no excuse,' Sybil, in apricot today, says.

'Syb,' Earl says, 'sometimes you gotta cut folks a little slack.'

'He told me I was the worst bowler in the league,' Travis whines, 'just because my average is a hundred.'

'Milo?' Christopher asks.

'Here.'

'Zowee, you really do have no life.'

'I tried to bring Robertson. She'd already taken him. I've checked the house twice.' Milo speaks too fast and too loud, like Robertson when he is trying to justify himself. 'They're not there, and she's not picking up, even when I call from a pay phone.'

'She brought him here,' Christopher says.

'She did?' Milo expects joy or relief to lighten Christopher's expression but he only looks haggard.

'I know for a fact he goes to titty bars,' Travis says.

'That's degenerate,' Sybil says.

'Lots of fellas go to titty bars,' Earl points out.

'Yes, but do you want to *bowl* with them?' Sybil demands.

'Why not? He's good. We win.'

Milo hovers by Christopher's bed rail. 'How was it? Seeing her?'

'It's like I haven't been seeing her. All this time I haven't been seeing her. It's the old see-what-you-want-to-see syndrome. She's old, she looked old. I'm surprised you fucked her.'

Sybil jerks the curtain. 'Oh, don't start that again.'

'Sorry, Syb. I'm surprised you fornicated with her, Milo.'

'Those two do nothing but talk smut,' Sybil advises Earl.

'Well,' Earl says, 'I guess he's not up to much, strung up like he is.'

'Anyhoodle,' Christopher says. 'It's all good.'

'What is?'

'The plan. Tanis has one.'

'I thought you were tired of her plans.'

'I'm tired of life, Milo. I have lost my joie de vivre.'

'So what are her plans?'

'I can't remember. I play a small part in them. She's going to call me. Oh, and she's selling the house.'

'What? She can't sell the house.'

'Why not?'

'It's Robertson's house.'

'Well, she wants to get him a new house in a new neighbourhood with a new school.'

'It'll be the same. It'll just start all over again. Is she moving because of me?'

'Because of you?'

'What happened between us.'

'What happened between you? Oh, you mean is she moving because you fornicated with her?'

Sybil sighs heavily. 'Two supposedly mature males. Unnn-believable.'

'I never said I was mature, Syb,' Christopher says. 'No, Milo, she didn't mention you.'

'She probably didn't want to upset you.'

'On the contrary, she loves upsetting me. Perhaps she forgot that you put your penis into her vagina. *Penis* and *vagina* aren't dirty words, are they, Syb?'

'You're pathetic,' she says.

'I couldn't agree more.'

'You can't let this happen, Christopher. It will damage Robertson.'

'Fascinating how everyone seems to know what will damage Robertson, a boy who forms emotional attachments to nothing and no one, who lives entirely in his head. Do you know what he was doing while he was here? Measuring my piss and asking how I shit. Not "How are you, Dad?" or "Are you feeling any better, Dad?"'

'Is that important? I mean, just the fact that he's here and curious about you, isn't that enough?'

'You're fortunate in that you don't have a child, Milo. Having a child is like having one of your vital organs outside your body. You spend every conscious moment trying to protect this vital organ from harm, but it keeps growing and doing things beyond your control, exposing itself to all manner of danger. And as it suffers, so do you, until, I guess, you die.'

'That is *so* maudlin,' Sybil says.

'Not at all, it just is. As Robertson just is. The truth is I don't really matter to my son. The question then becomes does it matter that I don't really matter? Why do I need to matter? I haven't come up with an answer to that one.' Christopher covers his face with his hands. 'I'm very tired now. You don't need to come here anymore, Milo. In fact, I'd prefer you didn't.'

Milo lingers, hoping for some indication that Christopher doesn't really mean this. The thought of never again sitting in the chair facing the sky causes waves of wretchedness. Milo understood his role here, he thought. He would bring Christopher back to the living, wheel him into the sunshine, take him to the AGO and show him the model ships made by nineteenth-century prisoners of war. Incarcerated in hulks offshore, the prisoners constructed the ships out of scavenged bits of wood, and bone from food scraps. 'They built them with only needles and knives,' he would explain, implying that if a half-starved prisoner of war, stranded at sea, could produce astonishingly intricate model ships, Christopher could learn to walk again.

'Can't you take a hint?' Sybil says. 'He wants you to buzz off.'

Tears spill around Christopher's fingers. The Canadian Tire Man puts the photo of Robertson building with Lego on the dresser.

...

Tanis doesn't answer the door. He finds her on the deck watching Gus and Robertson lay patio stones. 'Christopher says you're planning to sell the house.'

'Don't you find it odd that you're so invested in our lives?' she asks. 'It's as though you don't have one of your own.'

'Please don't sell.' He can't imagine strangers in the house, a normal family with noisy children throwing food at each other. 'I won't bother you anymore. I won't even come over, just please, don't do this to Robertson.'

'Or to you. Don't you mean to you?'

'To me or Robertson. Have you told him?'

'No. I have to talk to some agents first.'

'I'm sorry about the other night.'

'I instigated it. Please don't apologize.' She sits on the steps, keeping her eye on Robertson and Gus. 'Your father has the exact same focus. They've been at it for hours. Robertson even let him dig up stones that weren't set right. If I did that, he'd go ballistic. He never lets me disturb his order of things.'

'So you're allowing him to stay in the yard with my brain-damaged father but not with me?'

'I've been watching the whole time. He seems nice, your dad. Pablo really likes him.'

It feels as though he is being shoved into a small box. 'That's not my dad. Or anyway, not the dad I knew.'

'Maybe you didn't know him. I'm finding out I don't know people I thought I knew. You, for example.'

'He was a shitty father.'

'What is he now?'

'A stranger.'

'So, maybe you should get to know him.'

'I don't want to get to know him.'

Pablo bounds towards them. 'Sammy's bringing over all kinds of food, like, Polish stuff. I told him Gussy don't want to cook because we couldn't find no pickled herring and he don't like the store mushrooms. Sammy said "no worries." He's even bringing vodka.'

'What's the occasion?' Tanis asks.

'Gus's rebirth,' Milo says.

...

Val has transformed Milo's room into makeup and wardrobe and Dina, a wild boar of a woman, is 'staging' the house, adding ruffled curtains and God knows what. Milo forgoes the preparations for *The Reunion of a Lifetime* in the basement, imbibing vodka and telling himself he is in charge of his own happiness, and that once he scores the remaining ten Gs he'll skip town and leave all this behind. He hears hahaha yoga laughs from above. Sammy has invited the barbarians to take part in *The Reunion of a Lifetime*, it will be bootiful. Their ugly mugs are being refurbished by Val, who is accessorizing their attire, adding jackets, ties and scarves and whatever other accoutrements will lend an air of sophistication. She's 'gussying' them up. Hahaha. Vera enthused about a pale pink scarf Val draped around her neck. 'How grand,' Vera said, swishing the scarf to and fro. How easily these chumps can be bought. Not Milo. They're all avoiding him anyway; even Pablo is giving him a wide birth and has stopped offering tutelage in the school of life. 'Fuck you very much,' Milo mutters. He paces like he did before stage performances. Less accomplished actors, prior to the show, talk about who got laid or who auditioned for what, but not Milo. Before he forgot how to act he would pace backstage, immersing himself in the emotional reality of his character. The hack American sitcom star who slowly killed Marlene Temple in *The Death of a Salesman* called him Marlon. 'Hey, Marlon, you inside your character yet? What's your motivation, big guy?'

But what is he to play tonight? Devoted son? Lost son? Found son? It's all too vague; even bad acting requires lines and direction.

'Milo?' Sammy calls. 'Are you down there, my friend?'

Milo retreats to a dark corner, stumbling over a box. 'Fuck!'

'Are you okay, my friend? Val is ready for you.' Down the maniac clambers. 'How are you? You seem subdued this evening. Did you see the food we brought? Very authentic. Dina is making everything look bootiful. You won't recognize your house.'

'It's not my house.'

'What's that?' Sammy points to the box that Milo has inadvertently overturned. On the floor are Milo's lost Polaroids.

'Didn't I tell you there are always photos, my friend?'

'I'm not your friend.'

Sammy squats and begins to sort through the pictures.

'Don't touch those.'

'Why not? They might help him remember.' He holds up the shot of Gus in Niagara Falls with the grasping widow. 'Is this your mother?'

'No.'

'What about this one?' Many of the photos are of Gus with women who tried to snare him. Gus forced Milo to take these shots. Having his son take a Polaroid proved that he was middle-class. Regardless of whether or not he had any intention of marrying the clinging women, he wanted to impress them with his house and his business and his son. 'Gus looks so very different,' Sammy observes. 'I wonder if he will recognize himself.'

'Don't show them to him.'

'Why not? It might be the key to his memory, my friend. Don't you want him to remember?'

Milo isn't sure anymore. As each sordid memory surfaces, he wants to sink it.

'Oh, is this you?' Sammy holds up a shot of Milo at his high school graduation. 'Nice hair. Very eighties.'

Gus was late to the grad ceremony because he'd been arranging expensive rocks for a Rosedale matriarch with more money than brains. He arrived dirty, and ashamed of his son who didn't make the honour roll. Gus took him to an Italian restaurant anyway, decorated with wickered wine bottles. While bullying Milo about his future plans, he griped about the meat being dry. Who wants to remember this?

'I don't want you showing these to him,' he says.

'Please, Milo, it will be great for the show.'

'There's nothing in the contract about photos. You can't have the photos.' He quickly collects the pictures and drops them back in the box.

'My friend, do you know how happy I would be if I found lost photos of my father?'

'You don't live here. Fuck off.'

Birgit shouts from the top of the stairs. 'Get Milo's ass up here. Val's waiting for him.'

'You first,' Milo says. 'Go, my friend, or you won't have a show at all.' He snatches the grad shot from Sammy. Once the psycho is up the stairs, Milo swigs the last of his vodka and shoves the box under the workbench, covering it with oily rags.

'You look a treat,' Val says. 'What's the matter with you?'

'Nothing.'

'How's the rash, do you need a pill?'

'Nope.'

'We're doing it straight, are we?'

'Is that unusual? Do you normally drug your participants?'

'Only the neurotics. Okay, so we're going with earth tones today, to complement the food.' She thrusts barf-coloured garments at him and points to the folding screen.

'Did you dress my father as my identical twin again?'

'He's put on weight. I had to find larger pants.'

'That's because he's a happy person.'

'You're fat and you're not happy. Have you been sleeping? You've got craters under your eyes.' Milo doesn't bother to respond. 'Pablo's cute,' Val says. 'He'll look hot on camera.'

'Did you manage to get a shirt on him?'

'T-shirt.'

'Really? Normally he eats naked.'

'Invite me for dinner sometime.'

As she sponges foundation on his face, Milo tries to formulate a plan, adopt a role, find the path of least resistance. 'Cheese,' he says, smiling at his reflection.

'What?'

'Do Poles eat cheese?' he asks, still grinning. 'Will there be *cheese* at this banquet?'

'Fuck if I know. Count yourself lucky the food is real. Sometimes Dina puts fake stuff out, turkeys and hams to make it look fancy.'

'Couldn't they find any fake pig's knuckles?'

'They really eat every part of the critter, don't they? We had Poles down the street. They were always eating cow's tongues and sausages stuffed with blood.'

'Why aren't you smoking?'

'I don't smoke in private homes.'

'Don't hesitate to burn this one down on my account.'

The momentous evening begins with a toast. Gus, rosy-cheeked from vodka, seated at the head of the table as per Sammy's instructions, holds up his glass. '*Na zdrowie.*'

'Say that again, Gussy?'

'*Na zdrowie.*'

Pablo holds up his glass. 'Nah zdroh-vyeh.'

'Nice driveway,' Milo says, also holding up his glass.

'*Qué?*'

'Isn't that what you just said, nice driveway?'

'Nah zdroh-vyeh,' Pablo repeats.

'Right. That's what I said, ni-ce dri-ve-way.' Sammy prods him from behind. 'It *is* a fascinating language,' Milo adds. 'And fascinating food. I sure hope there's blood in those sausages. Do we have any pig's knuckles? Gosh, to think I spent all those years gnawing on Mrs. Cauldershot's Salisbury steaks when I could have been eating cow's tongues.'

'Have some dill pickle soup,' Vera urges.

'Did you say dill pickle soup?' Wallace asks, looking worried in a blazer that fits for once.

'It will be delicious with a dollop of sour cream.' Vera dollops cream into her dill pickle soup.

'*Zupa ogórkowa,*' Gus says, pointing cheerily at the soup.

'Zoo-pah ogoor-koh-vah,' Pablo says.

'Is there an echo in here?' Milo asks.

Pablo points his spoon at him. 'You don't even try to speak Polish, Milo, what kind of son are you?'

'That's an excellent question. What kind of son am I? Gustaw, what kind of son am I? Our home viewers would like to know.'

'Cut,' Birgit says, then stands so close to Milo that he could easily nuzzle her breasts. 'What do think you're doing?'

'Having a reunion of a lifetime. Isn't it fabulous?'

'We never refer to home viewers. Don't be a wiseass.'

'Sor-reee.' He looks at Pablo, Vera and Wallace, who all stare back with anxious eyes. Of course they're on edge; this is, after all, their big moment on network television. They only get one shot at dazzling viewers, whereas Milo, a seasoned professional, has dazzled many with his acting skills. To him, being in front of a camera feels quite natural, quite mundane, in fact. He is, after all, the Canadian Tire Man. He drinks more vodka.

'You've had enough of that.' Birgit snatches the glass from him. 'Dina? We need water here.'

'I'm not drinking water.'

'Oh yes you are, asshole, now eat up and behave.'

'Okay, fine, so what am I supposed to say? He doesn't speak English.'

Birgit snaps her fingers. 'Sammy?'

Sammy crouches beside Milo's chair and whispers. 'Remember your childhood, my friend, those lazy days of summer. Talk about the good times. Baseball, did you ever play baseball with your dad? Catch in the backyard on a summer's evening?' Sammy pats Milo's shoulder and steps back. 'Leave him for a moment,' he murmurs to Birgit. 'Give him a chance to remember.'

'Are you remembering yet?' Birgit demands. 'Let's move on.'

With the cameras rolling, Milo dons his fond-remembrances face. 'Remember, Dad, when you insisted on coming with me to Dads on the Diamond Day? I said, "Dad, you don't know how to play baseball, you don't need to come." I think I even said, "*Please* don't come, Dad." But you were determined, probably because you thought you could network with some potential clients and sell some patios. Anyhoodle, off we went, me in my *Miami Vice* T-shirt and jeans, and you in your stonemason clothes because you didn't dig cowboy shirts and denim in those days. And guess what? Do you remember?' Gus, still permitted vodka, stares hazily at him. 'You threw like a girl,' Milo says. 'The other dads thought you were faking it and figured you were hamming it up because your pitches totally sucked. They were laughing and slapping their thighs, oh, it was hilarious. But you kept throwing girly pitches until, finally, silence fell on the diamond as all the boys and their dads realized that you weren't faking it, that you were, in fact, throwing like a girl. Dean Blinky nudged me and said, "Who the fuck is that?" And you know what I said? I said, "I have no fucking clue." Then I took off, and when you came home you tore into me. It didn't occur to you that you'd embarrassed me, that I was mortally ashamed of you, because, as usual, you had your head so far up your own asshole you had no idea what I was feeling. In fact, as usual, you didn't want to know what I was feeling. You *sucked* at baseball, old man.'

'I think it's time we tried the pork,' Vera says.

'That's cot-let s-habo-vyh pah-nyeh-roh-vah-nyh,' Pablo explains.

'*Kotlet schabowy panierowany*,' Gus agrees, looking warily at Milo.

'And zhiem-nyah-kamee,' Pablo adds.

'*Ziemnikami*,' Gus says, nodding.

'It looks delicious,' Vera says.

'Can we stop this?' Milo asks, turning and staring into a camera lens. 'Can we cut this bullshit? I mean, seriously, it's not funny anymore.'

'It never was funny,' Birgit says.

'I can't do this,' Milo insists, 'this ... this farce. He was a horrible father and a horrible man. Ask Wallace, he stole his pucks. So what if terrible things happened to him in the war and in camps and God knows where else, that doesn't make him a better person. So what if he watched children burn, and bigger boys shoved things up his ass? I'm sorry he has nightmares and screams in the night but that doesn't make it okay that he was a mean son of a bitch.' He stumbles over some cables to Gus, who jumps out of his chair and backs away from him. 'I'm not Mr. Mandela,' Milo says, 'or the Colombian hostage, or Sarah Moon Dancer, or Mother-fucking-Teresa, I'm Milo, and you fucked me up and I *don't* forgive you.'

'Once more with feeling,' Wallace says.

'And why don't *you* tell your mother how you really feel? Why did *I* have to tell her that you haven't fucked a woman in years and work in junk removal? Why do you lie to her all the time? Why can't we be *honest* with each other? Why all this collusion and deceit?' To Milo's horror, he feels himself choking up as his losses mount: Christopher's rejection, Tanis's rejection, Robertson's disinterest now that he has bonded with Gus, Zosia's rejection, the clubbiness of the three musketeers and Gus – good god, even Tawny has taken his side. Everybody likes Gus. Everybody likes Pablo. Why is it that Milo is always on the outside? Not that he wants to be on the inside with the deadbeats but somehow, somehow he wants to belong somewhere; there must be somewhere. He starts to sing plaintively, 'Somewhere over the rainbow, bluebirds fly... ' They all look at him as though he has gone completely mad and maybe he has. He can't remember the rest of the words to the song so he hums into the satisfying stillness around him, enjoying the slight buzzing in his sinuses caused by the high notes. His singing coach told him he had a range of two octaves. She was ancient with flame-red hair and a bulging diaphragm that she forced him to feel to comprehend its power. He hated touching her, and the songs she made him sing, upbeat show tunes about gals and fellas. '*Smile* when you sing,' she insisted. 'Show your teeth.' Sometimes she took her foot off a piano pedal and kicked him to remind him to show his teeth. *Cheese.*

And then it clicks. *None of it matters,* and it doesn't matter that none of it matters. It doesn't matter that Milo doesn't matter. Nothing matters. It's all just an arrangement of atoms that will cease to exist. *Amor fati.* And he approaches his father slowly, carefully, because he is just an old man who has lost his marbles and wants to chow down on pigs' knuckles. Milo puts his arms around him, inhaling the stench of pickled herring on his breath, feeling his fear and frailty and says, 'It doesn't matter.'

25

*A*ll morning Gus and Robertson work on the patio. Neither of them respond to Milo's 'Hey, guys.' Even Sal doesn't bother to sniff him. When Milo sets fire to the box of Polaroids, Gus merely glances in his direction, untroubled by memories of burning children. It seems only his tormentors survive in his dreams. Bullies rule even in the subconscious.

Pablo hurtles out the back door. 'Milo, you won't believe it ... '

'You're being deported.'

'Maria wants me back.'

'Why?'

'She loves me. She told me she can't stop missing me even if I don't believe in God Almighty.'

'Go fig,' Milo says.

'We're just going to have a simple wedding, like, at city hall, no priest or nothing. She's downloading a licence. What are you burning?'

'Garbage. What about Fennel?'

'Oh she's totally busy with Vitorio. Painting will always come first with Fenny.'

'And you think you will always come first with Maria?'

'Of course.'

'Good luck with that.'

'Oh, this is for you.' He holds out a disk in an envelope.

'What is it?'

'Zosia left it.'

'Zosia was here? Why didn't you tell me?'

'You weren't here, Milo. It was when we were all getting ready for the show.'

'I was in the basement, you dumbass.'

'Before that, when you were out.'

'Did she say anything?'

'She said, "Give this to Milo." Her number's on it. Listen, are you serious about us having to move out, like, today?'

'Dead serious.' He isn't but wants to be obeyed for once.

'It won't be easy for Vera.'

'Vera can stay.' He can't have her passing out in some dank hotel room. 'Until she goes back to England.'

'She's not going back.'

'Since when?'

'Since her and Wally talked. He's going to find her a place.'

'They talked?'

Pablo nods. 'And Tawny don't got nowhere to go. Her alcoholic mama shacked up with her alcoholic uncle and he don't like teenagers.'

'Tawny can stay too.'

'What about Gussy?'

'It's his house. I'm leaving anyway.'

'Where are you going?'

'Haven't decided yet.' He emailed Sammy demanding payment but doesn't expect to hear from the head case. Birgit threatened to sue Milo's ass while the crew decamped and Dina, the wild boar, tore down her ruffled curtains. Only Val seemed sympathetic and insisted that Milo keep the jacket. 'You smoke in that,' she said. 'One of these days you're going to want to look hot.'

'Can I stay till me and Maria get stuff figured out?'

'Did you not say, a mere forty-eight hours ago, that Fennel was all the stars in your firmament?'

'Things change, Milo. Please. Just a few days.'

'Whatevs.'

Flames lick Gus and his widows. The shot of Mrs. Cauldershot's spider veins takes the longest to burn.

'Vera?' He can hear her packing. 'Can I use the computer for a minute?' He moved it to his mother's dresser when Tawny took over his room.

'Of course. Come in, Milo.'

'You don't have to leave.'

'Wally's going to find me a nice flat with a balcony, he says. I've always fancied a balcony. It'll be splendid with pots of geraniums. I could have my tea on it.'

Milo boots up the computer. 'Yeah, but he's not going to find the flat right away, is he? Stay till he finds it.'

'Are you sure I won't be any bother?'

'Quite sure.'

'I must admit, the good thing about Wally not being the marrying kind is he's got more time for his mum.'

'There's an upside to everything.' He inserts the disk and waits for it to load.

'Gus and the boy next door are the best of mates, aren't they? Tanis says she's not going to sell just yet.'

'When did she say that?'

'This aft. She said she's never seen the boy so at ease with anyone. She's going to home-school him till things get sorted.' This should mean something to Milo but his feet remain set in concrete. Tanis will avoid him and he will avoid her, and Robertson will build with Gus. It doesn't matter.

'Hel-lo,' Vera says, 'whose is that?'

'Whose is what?' On the screen a grainy image reveals a trapped creature.

'That's a baby in its mum's tummy.'

Milo leans closer to the screen and begins to decipher a head and limbs.

'It's sucking its thumb,' Vera says. 'Cheeky little bugger, finding his thumb already.'

A general trembling overtakes Milo. 'What makes you so sure it's a boy?'

'A girl wouldn't do that,' Vera says. 'It's marvellous what they can see these days. My nieces always get videos and we all wager on the sex. Five quid that's a boy. Who sent it?'

'Nobody.' Sweat trickles down his temples. He ejects the disk and staggers downstairs where Pablo is making a protein smoothie. 'What did Zosia tell you?'

'She didn't tell me nothing.'

'Do you know what this is?' He wields the disk, convinced they're all in this together. One big fucking joke on Milo.

'I don't know nothing. We was busy getting ready for the show. She didn't want to talk anyway. She looked tired.'

'Was she fat?'

'I don't know, she was wearing a raincoat, Milo. What's the matter with you?'

He walks fast, out of the house and into the ravine in search of muggers or anything that will offer distraction. What was she thinking? She who carries condoms on her person, the pragmatist, the problem solver, the career woman, the smartest person in the room, what was she *thinking*?

He clambers through the woods and undergrowth until he finds the debris shelter he built with Robertson. Though still intact, empty beer bottles and trash are strewn on and around it. Milo crawls into the hut, gagging from the stench of piss. A newspaper swats his head.

'Who are you?' a ragged voice demands.

In the poor light Milo is able to make out a man with matted hair, covered in blankets. 'I built this shelter.'

'Just because you built it don't mean you own it,' the man says. 'It's city property. Nobody owns it, just the city. You got no right.'

'I just wanted some peace and quiet. I'll go now.'

'D'you have a smoke?'

'No.'

'Spare change?'

'No.'

'Gum?'

'No.'

'Cough drops?'

'No. I have a disk.'

'A disk?'

'Yeah.'

'What's on it?'

'An ultrasound of a baby.'

'Yours?'

'I have no idea.'

'What you carrying it for then?'

'I don't know.'

'And I thought *I* was fucked. You can sleep here if you want. Nobody bothers you. And it's pretty dry. Sorry I hit you, but you can't be too careful.'

Bunking with the vagrant will not ease his mind. He crawls out and rushes on through the ravine, heedless of the branches and potholes. All his life he has taken precautions with women, even when they told him it wasn't necessary. AIDS was big news during his teens. Emaciated men with scabs on their faces haunted the theatre world. His first summer job was working the box office for a gay theatre company. Pasquale, who ran it, believed that Milo was gay but didn't realize it yet. 'Always wear a rubber, pussycat,' he advised. So this cannot be Milo's baby. This is a scheme. Like Wallace said, she's after his fucking wedding vows, forcing him to fix someone else's mistake. Not this time.

Someone tugs on his arm causing him to spring into Bruce Lee mode. He will not let the fuckers flatten him again.

'What are you doing?' Tawny asks.

'What are *you* doing?'

'Following you.'

'Why?'

'Because you're freaked out.'

'Who says I'm freaked out?'

'Chill for a second. It's peaceful here in the woods. It reminds me of home. Too much trash though. People shouldn't litter.'

'People shouldn't do a lot of things.' He trudges onward with no destination in mind. The effort required to climb over uneven ground shakes the numbness from his legs. Tawny keeps pace with youthful ease.

'So I guess you think it's your baby,' she says.

'How do you know about the baby?'

'Vera.'

'Which means she's told the whole crew. Thank you so very bloody much.' The wind picks up, bullying branches overhead.

'I'd like to have a baby someday,' Tawny says.

'Why?'

'To love. And maybe if I don't screw up too much, it'll love me back.'

'If you don't screw up too much. Ah, there's the rub.'

'This whole thing with your dad is a little retarded. I mean, everybody always thinks a miracle might happen and their parents will change into the people they wish they were, or back to the people they used to be. But that's not going to happen. And even though everybody knows it's not going to happen, they still hope it will. It's retarded.'

Milo squats on a fallen trunk. She sits beside him while the city grumbles and belches beyond the trees.

'Did you hear about that guy who killed his father with a crossbow?' she asks.

'What guy?'

'A Chinese guy. He hated his father so much he drove all the way from Ottawa to kill him with his crossbow. Shot him in the library, right in front of everybody. That's how much he hated him, he didn't care if he got caught, he just wanted him dead. That would take a lot of energy, hating somebody that much.'

'What did his father do to him?'

'The usual. Physical and psychological abuse. Plus he beat his mother. They moved to Ottawa to get away from him, but I guess that wasn't enough. The son had to come back and kill the guy. He shot him from behind. The father fell forward over a table with the arrow sticking out of his back. Now the son will go to prison for, like, forever.'

Milo imagines Gus flopped over a table with an arrow sticking out of his back. The image does not please him. Maybe he doesn't hate him that much, or anyway, doesn't have the required energy.

'Could you show me the baby?' Tawny asks.

'Why?'

'I've never seen an ultrasound. On the reservation only high-risk pregnancies get to have ultrasounds, and they have to go to Sudbury for them.'

High-risk? Is that what this is about? Is the trapped creature fighting for its life? Does Zosia fear she will die from complications in childbirth, leaving no one to care for her bastard? Has she turned to Milo because he is a nice guy, a suck, who will do the right thing? Whatever was propelling him is spent and torpor takes hold. Budging from the log becomes unfathomable.

'A rabbit,' Tawny says, pointing at bushes. 'Did you see it?'

'No.' Another unsinkable memory bobs towards him. He was five and wanted a bunny. Dean Blinky's sister had one. Since the moment he could talk, it seemed to Milo, he'd begged his parents for a pet and been told 'maybe when you're older.' Annie was allergic to cats, scared of dogs and repulsed by rodents, so why not a rabbit? 'Your daddy had a bad experience with rabbits.'

'What experience?'

'On his farm.'

'What on his farm?'

'Rabbits. They ate them.'

This dampened Milo's enthusiasm briefly but he understood that farmers ate some of their animals, which was why he didn't want to be a farmer. 'So?' he said.

She sipped more Bailey's Irish Cream. 'He loved those bunnies, gave them names and talked to them and stroked their ears. Every Friday night he had to pick one and hit it with a stick till it stopped moving. He always cried and sometimes barfed, but no matter what, he had to choose a bunny and hit it with a stick until it was dead so his mother could cook it. Otherwise his father would hit him with a stick. If he didn't eat the bunny, his father would hit *him* with a stick anyway.'

Milo tried to picture his father as a boy, crying and barfing and thwacking a rabbit with a stick. Then being forced to eat the bunny.

'Don't tell your dad I told you,' Annie said. 'It's just that rabbits upset him.'

'He wouldn't have to kill *my* rabbit,' Milo pointed out.

'Silly boy,' she said, brushing hair out of his eyes. 'You need a haircut, monkey.'

He loved it when she called him monkey, and didn't want to alter her mood by pushing the rabbit issue. He never raised it again.

'What are you going to do if it's yours?' Tawny asks.

'It's not mine.'

'Why would your girlfriend send it then?'

'She's not my girlfriend. To force me to marry her, duh.'

'Showing you an ultrasound of your baby isn't forcing you to do anything. It's just letting you know about it, giving you the opportunity to be part of its life. Some men want babies. My cousin and his wife can't have any. They've done all kinds of tests and she takes fertility drugs that make her even fatter. Every time she has her period she cries like her baby died. Your girlfriend's lucky she got pregnant, especially if it's yours.'

'How is she lucky?'

'Because you're a decent guy. A little mixed-up maybe, but you'll get over it.'

'What?'

'The father thing. I was pretty mixed-up about my mother hooking up with my dad's brother. I mean, I thought it was just going to be her and me from now on. I mean, she's old. She used to say, "I'm done with men." Then she goes and shags my uncle. I was pretty upset but I got over it. Maybe being a father would help you get over your father thing.'

Of course they all want to see it and lean over him to peer at the screen.

'Ten quid it's a boy,' Vera announces.

'It's dollars here, Ma.'

'That's a girl,' Pablo insists. 'Look at her little hands and feet.'

'Why is its head so big?' Milo asks.

'They always have big heads,' Vera advises. 'Think of what has to be packed into that noggin before they pop out.'

'I can't get over her not breathing,' Pablo says. 'Can you believe that, Milo? I mean, everybody knows babies don't breathe in the womb but to see her wiggling around like that and know she's not breathing.'

'It's fucking mind-blowing,' Wallace concedes. He is much more interested in the ultrasound than Milo would have expected. 'It jerked, did you see that? It *jerked*.'

'Those are hiccups,' Vera says. 'They all get them. And the mum can feel them, before she feels the kicks, she feels the hiccups.'

'Fucking unreal,' Wallace observes.

'It's like,' Pablo elaborates, 'she's a fish and then suddenly she's a human.'

'It looks trapped,' Milo says.

'No way,' Pablo says, 'that's her world, man, that's her space capsule.'

'That's why you swaddle them when they come out,' Vera explains. 'Imagine how strange it must feel to suddenly have your arms and legs all akimbo.'

'And breathing,' Pablo emphasizes. 'It must feel totally weird, being underwater then suddenly you have to, like, breathe polluted air. That must be why they cry. The polluted air must burn their little lungs.'

'And they must be fucking freezing,' Wallace adds. 'I mean, the womb must be warm, right, then all of a sudden they're out where it's cold and bright and they have to breathe and their arms and legs are flopping all over the place.'

'I'm surprised they don't die of shock,' Milo says.

...

He attempts to dial the number several times before finally completing the call. Her voice mail sounds officious, which means she must be job hunting again. He doesn't leave a message but tries again several times before muttering, 'It's me, Milo. Call me.'

With the musketeers downstairs he watches the video repeatedly. The raw vulnerability of the creature causes an unexpected heaving and shifting in Milo's intestines. 'Don't come out,' he whispers to it. Between hiccups it holds up its hands as if to ask *why*? 'Too complicated,' Milo tells it. Its legs look cramped, as though it wants to bust out, and its big head is being forced downward in the tiny space capsule. Maybe it should come out – who wants to hiccup in a cramped swamp? But if it's high-risk, what awaits it on the outside? Incubators, injections, tubes and wires leading in and out of every orifice? The phone rings.

'Hello?'

'Milo,' she says. She always begins their phone conversations with 'Milo.' The other women in his life immediately held forth about their feelings or worries but Zosia just said, 'Milo.'

'I got the disk,' he says.

'Good.'

He can't even hear her breathing. 'Why did you send it?'

'Why do you think?'

'I think you want me to think it's mine.'

'You don't think it's yours?'

'How could it be?'

'I'm seven months' pregnant. Do the math.'

'But there've been other men.'

'What other men?'

'The bartender at the Copper Pipe, with the moustache.'

She doesn't respond, which is not unusual. Unlike the other women in his life, she is comfortable with silence. The alien creature hiccups and holds up its hands again, *why*?

'He got shot,' Zosia says.

'Who?'

'The bartender. He was my friend, not my lover. The fact that you are questioning me tells me I made the wrong decision. I should not have contacted you. I'm sorry. Goodbye.' And she's gone, poof, just like that. He redials immediately but she doesn't answer. What was he thinking? Shot dead? Was she kneeling by the fallen man's side while his brains leaked onto the terracotta tiles?

'Milo?' Vera calls. 'Come have a sanny. You haven't eaten a scrap all day.'

The creature holds up its hands again. 'I'm sorry,' Milo whispers to it while his guts heave and shift. The creature shrugs as if to say, *it's okay*, and suddenly Milo is awash in an ocean of entitlement. It is *his* baby, is it not? She has no right to prevent him from having *his* baby. It needs his help, his protection in a violent world, and this gushing well of emotion that might be love. Seven months? No wonder the head is so big compared to the rest of it. Those little stick arms and legs will fill out, the tiny shoulders and chest will broaden against the onslaught of human ignorance. And Milo will be waiting for it, ready to do whatever it takes to protect his vital organ outside his body.

He can't sleep, of course, and calls her countless times between bouts of twisting himself into contortions on the couch. He managed to eat a peanut butter sandwich, understanding that Vera's right: faced with new responsibility, he must keep his strength up. He has told the musketeers nothing. They think he hasn't returned Zosia's call, that he is experiencing typical my-girlfriend-got-pregnant angst. Tawny has disappeared again, padding off soundlessly.

The Lay-Z-Boy creaks. 'Milo? Are you still awake?'

He plays possum.

'Do you want to talk about it?'

'Definitely not.'

'Maria's cousin freaked when he found out his girlfriend was pregnant. She was working in a flower factory so he was scared the baby would be born with flippers from all those pesticides. He told her to abort it, said he'd pay for it, but getting safe abortions in Mexico is hard. Anyway, she didn't want to.'

Milo waits for the blabbermouth to finish the story but no, the muscle-head unwraps a stick of gum and chews on it. 'What happened?' he asks, finally.

'It was stillborn.'

'Oh my god.' The thought of the little trapped creature being born dead causes a crack in Milo's foundation that expands with every breath, widening into a chasm. In seconds, everything he has ever cared about is sucked into cold, dark infinity. Only the little creature remains, teetering at the edge of the precipice, hiccupping and holding up its hands, *why*?

'I think you should call her Valentina,' Pablo says. 'Then you can call her Tina or Val. Or Teeny. Teeny's nice for, like, when she's little.'

'Shut up,' Milo says.

He sleeps fitfully, dreaming of rabbits spurting blood as Gus thwacks them with a stick. He hears noises in the kitchen and finds Tawny back at the books. 'Did you call her?' she asks.

'I pissed her off. Now she won't answer my calls.'

'How did you piss her off?'

'I questioned its paternity.'

'Bad idea.'

'I realize that.'

'You want me to call her?'

'You?'

'I could call her from a pay phone. She won't know who it is.'

Is he really so desperate that he will put his life in the hands of a fifteen-year-old? 'Okay. When?'

'Whenever you want.'

'Now.'

'You want me to call her at four in the morning?'

'She's an early riser.'

As they plod to the pay phone, she asks about Gus, and Milo realizes that the old sadist has not screamed for dope. Is it possible that the patio project has calmed his core as it has Robertson's? Not once in the past twenty-four hours has Milo heard screaming through the wall or head-banging.

'What's the number?' Tawny asks. He points to the envelope, sweaty from his grip. She punches the numbers then shoves him out the sliding doors. 'Don't listen. I have to tell her honestly that you're not listening. Go over there.' She points to some newspaper boxes.

'The whole point in you calling her was so *I* could talk to her.'

'I have to talk to her first.' With the receiver pressed against her ear, she shoos him with her free hand. He stands by the newspaper boxes, a man on a deserted island hoping for a passing ship. Tawny turns her back on him as she talks. He can deduce nothing from her body language. This child of alcoholics, possibly suffering from the lasting effects of fetal alcohol syndrome, is toying with his fate. What was he *thinking*? Should he snatch the phone and demand to be heard? It is his right, is it not, as the father of the child? *Father of the child.* The very words cause his ribs to jam. A child who might love him if he doesn't screw up too much. Isn't he screwing up too much already? But who will care for the child if not him? Liquid explodes behind Milo's eyeballs, enabling the confusion inside him to spew out and pool around his feet. Like Christopher he will burn and drip until nothing remains but a puddle.

Did she laugh? What's so funny? Are they *laughing* at him? He takes a step towards the phone booth but shame and fear harness him. More rejection he cannot endure.

She hangs up. *Hangs up?* And steps out of the booth.

'You were supposed to let me talk to her,' he protests.

'She doesn't want to talk to you right now. She has to think about it and wants you to stop calling her.'

'But ... but ...'

'But nothing. Quit stalking her. She has to think.'

And that's it. Poker-faced, the fifteen-year-old pads back to base camp.

26

*P*ablo operates a squeezeball in his right hand to cope with the stress caused by his impending nuptials. His cell died so Maria has been calling him on Milo's phone to make arrangements. Milo rushes to the phone each time it rings hoping, of course, that it is Zosia. But no, it is Maria.

'You going to have some yah-jetch-nitsah nah botch-kuh with us, Milo?'

'*Jajecznica na boczku*,' Gus clarifies, nodding.

'What is it?'

'Scrambled eggs with bacon. Gussy makes it better than anybody.'

The bacon does smell good, and Milo can't be alone right now with cold winds howling in and out of him. He quit looking at the video in an attempt to stop forming an attachment to the trapped creature, and has begun conversations in his head re the impracticalities of having a child – financial and psychological – particularly if it's high-risk.

'*Miłosz*,' Gus says, holding a plate of eggs out to Milo.

'*Coño*,' Pablo says, 'did he just call you Mee-wosh?'

'I have no idea.'

'Hey, Gussy, who's that?' Pablo points to Milo.

'*Miłosz*.' Gus pulls a chair out for Milo and gestures for him to sit.

'That must be your Polish name, Milo.'

'I don't have a Polish name.'

'That's so cool. Mee-wosh. I wonder what Pablo is in Polish. Hey, Gussy, what's Pablo in Polski?'

'Pablo,' Gus says.

Milo shoves Pablo's naked feet off a chair. 'I thought you were supposed to be the martyr. Get off your ass and make us some kah-vah.'

'See, Mee-wosh, you're learning Polish.'

The phone rings again. Milo runs for it. 'Is Pablo there?' Maria asks.

Vera comes downstairs waving a letter. 'The dog ate Ettie's false teeth. Imagine that. She was sleeping over for Freddie's party and she left her teeth by the bed and the dog ate them. Must have thought they were a bone. Poor Ettie.'

'Poor dog,' Milo says.

'Has anybody seen Wally? He's taking me to look at flats this afternoon. Isn't it grand?'

'Very.' She looks enviably spry.

'How can I help?' she asks Gus, and the two of them begin a breakfast dance, beating more eggs and buttering more toast. Milo leans back in his chair, tipping the front legs off the floor, a habit that irritated his father, but reborn Gussy doesn't seem to mind. Tawny, newspaper in hand, pulls a chair up beside him. 'That Chinese guy's father had a brain injury. He was hit by a car and part of his brain got damaged. It totally altered his personality. That's why he turned violent.' She points to the headline *Crossbow Victim's Trauma Revealed.*

'So now the abuser becomes the victim,' Milo says.

'His lawyer says he had severe cognitive, language and functional impairments.'

'You can always trust a lawyer.'

'He says he was destitute and homeless. His clothes were dirty and he smelled terrible. He got on his knees and begged the lawyer to take his case. He said he had been thrown out of his matrimonial home without notice and was living in a shelter.'

'Poor guy, no wonder he had to beat the crap out of his wife and son.'

Vera spreads jam. 'There are two sides to every story, Milo. Did we finish the marmalade?'

But really, it's not so bad sitting here with pig frying and the septuagenarians bustling around him. He could never sit idly like this with the old Gus. The old Gus would assign a task: laundry, floor washing, vacuuming. *You don't have Mrs. Cauldershot to clean up after you anymore.*

What was the story with Gus and the old witch anyway? Did he not realize she was enamoured of him, that she was the woman of his dreams, willing to sacrifice all to serve the great man? On her last day she left Milo a small dish of jelly beans. For nine years she had forbidden him candy in the house. At thirteen, jelly beans held considerably less value than when Milo was five. He sucked on a green one anyway as she traipsed down the walk. When she looked back with a wobbly smile, Gus said, 'Look after yourself,' then marched back to the basement. Only Milo stayed to see her off, waving limply. Once her back was turned, he flipped her the finger.

Pablo returns a weakened man. 'Maria wants to decorate the wedding chamber at city hall. We only get thirty minutes in there for a hundred bucks and she wants to decorate it.'

Already Milo can smell irreconcilable differences. 'That's more than three bucks per minute,' he warns. 'I hope it's an epic wedding chamber.'

'And that don't include tax,' Pablo adds.

'Well, a few cheery flowers will do the trick,' Vera says.

'You don't understand, she wants to, like, *decorate* the walls. How do you put up decorations *and* get married in thirty minutes?'

The phone rings. Milo lunges for it. 'Hello … ?'

'Milo.'

His heart sticks to his jammed ribs.

'Milo?'

'Yes.'

'Are you all right?'

'Fine. I'm … I'm having bacon and scrambled eggs.'

'Good for you.'

'Can we … ? Are you … ?'

'You wanted to talk.'

'Yes. I'm really sorry I said what I said.'

'What do you want to talk about?'

'Well, I … I was hoping we could meet and, you know, talk in person?'

A *Titanic* of a pause sinks between them.

'Where would you like to meet?' she asks.

He has already planned to suggest the Magic Bean where they held hands and played footsy while drinking five-dollar coffees. 'How 'bout the Magic Bean?' His voice jumps an octave on *bean*.

'Whatever,' she says. 'Two o'clock?'

'Two o'clock would be excellent. I'll look forward to it.'

'Okay.' She hangs up. They're all staring at him, except Gussy who is busy scrambling and humming a Polish folk tune.

Still three hours to go. To stop himself from thinking he resumes scraping the Muskoka chairs while Gussy and the boy lay patio stones. Why does time drag its ass when you want it to move, and travel at the speed of light when you want it to loiter? Gussy interrupts his masonry briefly to inspect Milo's handi-work. The son waits for the father's criticism but all Gussy says is 'Goot,' nod-ding and smiling.

And then Tanis is there hanging laundry and, to Milo's amazement, he has no desire to lick her legs. He watches her as though through a telescope. What an interesting specimen. Her system of holding pegs in her mouth, thereby freeing her hands, and then clasping the edges of two garments with one peg impresses him. Why use two pegs when one will do? How could he have failed to notice this demonstration of human ingenuity before? Does lust blind you? Of course it does.

He can't imagine touching Zosia again, so undeserving is he of her trust. He could tell from the way she said 'whatever' that it is over. She is agreeing to meet with him because she wants to end it. One of her favourite North American phrases is 'no loose ends.' When you're seven months' pregnant, single, on a temporary visa, unemployed and your mother is sick in Latvia, can there be looser ends? Could not Milo take her in his arms and offer comfort at least? Maybe he should try this, skip the dialogue and cut to the action.

'Are you ignoring me now?' Tanis asks.

'Not at all.'

'Just preoccupied.'

'A little.'

'Christopher's been calling. We're talking.'

'I'm glad.'

'It's because of you. Thank you.'

Her sincere gratitude as she stands gripping wet socks punches the breath out of him and once again liquid explodes behind his eyeballs. He keeps his head down and scrapes at chipped paint while what feels like his innards drib-bles onto the grass.

•••

Milo changes tables again, scoring a window seat. This way he'll spot her before she sees him. He has refrained from rehearsing in his mind how he will act, intending to be completely spontaneous. He distracts himself with crossword puzzles and horoscopes, checking the door only about every ten seconds. She has been known to arrive early, although usually exactly on time.

Virgo: Be decisive and dynamic and take full advantage of the new opportunities coming your way. Everything will work out for the best if you believe in yourself and if you believe that the Universe wants you to succeed.

Tanis told him one of Christopher's legs is healing half an inch shorter than the other. They might have to refracture it, the doctor said, or he could try wearing a lift.

'Is he upset?' Milo asked.

'He's beyond upset. He's in another zone.'

'Are you going to go see him?'

'It's not like we're getting together again, Milo.'

'I wasn't suggesting you were.'

'You want that, you want things like they were. You know what my father says?'

Her father is a businessman who uses terms Milo doesn't understand like *securitization, de-leveraging* and *structured investment vehicles.*

'He says long-term results are usually determined by short-term decisions.'

'I have no idea what that means,' Milo said and walked away, yes, walked away from Tanis to get on with his life, *his* life.

When he sees Zosia he feels emotions gurgling again and tries to appear preoccupied with the newspaper, although really, to maintain an even keel, he would prefer to lie on the floor.

'What can I get you?' he asks, hoping she'll request one of the decadent creamy coffees they used to share.

'A small decaf. Black. Thank you.'

He orders at the bar, assuring himself that all is not lost, even though she looks pale and worn and without hope. He sets the cup before her and tries to smile, *cheese*, but he is so jittery he spills some coffee. 'Sorry,' he says, grabbing napkins and mopping it up. She says nothing, only sits, waiting patiently while he disposes of the soaked napkins. 'Is there enough left?' he asks. 'Do you want me to get you another one?'

'This is fine.'

'Okay, well, just say the word if you want another one.'

'Sit down, Milo.'

He does. *Be decisive and dynamic and take full advantage of the new opportunities coming your way.*

She points to the newspaper. 'What are you reading?'

'Oh, nothing, just a bit about another suicide bomber. A woman this time. She only managed to blow up twelve people. Wonder if this means they'll give her a hard time in the afterlife.' Why is he babbling? Zosia's skin seems almost translucent. Is all the blood going to the baby? He read somewhere that the fetus's needs override the mother's, draining the life out of her.

'You had a haircut,' she says.

'Yeah, well, it was for a part.'

'What kind of part has hair like that?'

'A Nazi guard. It was a small part, a glorified extra really.'

'Good for you.' She sips what's left of her coffee. 'What did you want to talk about?'

'Is it a high-risk pregnancy?'

'Why do you ask?'

'The ultrasound.'

'What about it?'

'They don't do ultrasounds on normal babies, do they?'

'Of course. Between five and six months it's routine.'

What a magnificent word, *routine.* Milo grips the table, steadying himself as relief sloshes through him.

'Is that what you wanted to talk about?' she asks.

Wait a minute. Routine between five and six months and she didn't contact him till the seventh? Which means she took *a month* to think about it. 'No, I mean, yeah, I was just ... worried.'

'Don't worry.' She always says this, the woman who watched her father being dragged off to Siberia. 'Milo, I shouldn't have phoned you. It was a mistake. You don't need to worry.'

'I want to worry,' he blurts. 'I mean, I want to be part of its life.'

'Why?'

This hits below the ribs. *Why?* 'Because ... because it needs me and because ... I have no life.'

'It doesn't need you, and you have much life. Always Canadians think they have no life. They should stop watching TV and look around. There is much life here.'

'Are you going back? How's your mother?'

'Sick. And my sister can't help. She wanted to be Britney Spears. Now, if she is alive, she is a whore in Western Europe.'

'I'm so sorry, that's ... that's terrible, I mean how ... ?'

'They inject them with heroin. Drug addicts don't care what perverts do to them. If drug traffickers get caught, they serve years in prison. Human traffickers get months. Better to risk small time in prison playing the talent scout with stupid girls.'

'How horrible.' Can he really think of nothing more helpful to say?

'She was always stupid, always singing, looking in mirrors. But my mother doesn't want to live anymore. I'm going back but I can't help. She wants her baby daughter.'

'Aren't the police involved?'

Zosia snorts. 'It's not like TV, Milo. They don't catch the bad guys.'

'What about the fetus? Isn't plane travel dangerous for it?'

'I must go back now because I don't want her born there. It's no place for a young girl.'

'It's a girl?' Suddenly suffused with lightness, Milo sits erect. The creature has a face now, a mini Zosia, full of wit and wisdom, piss and vinegar.

'I should go,' she says.

And out the phrase pops, not tugged gracefully across the sky by a plane but sputtered from lips that have trouble forming the words. 'Zosia, will you ... marry me?'

'Not a good idea.'

'Why not? She'll be safe then. They'll *have* to let you back here. Divorce me later if you want.'

A bald man at the next table, clutching a *Cucina Italiana* magazine, complains to a hairy man about his old pot lights leaving holes that have to be drywalled to fit his new, smaller pot lights.

'I don't believe in marriage,' Zosia says.

'Me neither.'

'Somebody always loses.'

'I agree. I think it's an institution that has served its purpose. Now that we don't need Ma and Pa working together to keep the farm going, who needs it? But the fact is it would make you Canadian. And her Canadian.' Referring to 'her' causes a light-headedness that he tries to stabilize with a slug of caffeine. Zosia sighs as only a European can, a sigh weary from thousands of years of turf wars, slaughter and strife.

'We'd have to live together for two years,' she says.

Already he can feel the ground steadying beneath him. 'That's no problem. I have a house.' He doesn't tell her it's full of squatters.

'It's not that simple.'

'Sure it is, unless we complicate it. My friend Robertson doesn't like it when things get too complicated and I agree with him.'

'Did you build towers with him?'

'Yes.'

'Good for you.'

'It's simple,' Milo says, trying to believe it is. 'We download a licence, get married at city hall. You go to Latvia and see your mum then come back and have the baby. We play house for two years then you can leave.' He adds the *can*, hoping to suggest that she might also stay. Not that he wants this, he doesn't think, having never understood how two people can live in each other's faces and beds for years on end.

'I would need an agreement on paper. I would want sole custody of the child.'

'Of course,' he says, although he isn't sure about this either. *Everything will work out for the best if you believe in yourself and if you believe that the Universe wants you to succeed.*

'But don't most people usually share custody?' he asks.

'I'm not most people.'

'Right. Well, anyway, we don't have to decide that now, do we?'

'Yes. We do. No loose ends.'

He can agree then fight her later. Anyway, once she sees what an über-dad he is, she'll change her mind. 'Fine,' he says.

'I don't want to sleep with you.'

'I understand.'

Zosia stands. 'I'll think about it.'

'Can I walk you somewhere?'

'No. I'll call you.'

And she's gone. The bald man says to the hairy man, 'The problem is not everybody wants the same thing. Everybody has to want the *same thing*.'

The pet store has the fetid smell of caged and dejected animals. Behind dirty glass they lie limp or display obsessive-compulsive behaviour. A puppy chews on its paw, a monkey swings its head, a parrot plucks its feathers. 'You should try talking to it,' Milo tells the dull-eyed sales clerk.

'What's that?'

'Parrots pluck their feathers when they're stressed. They need attention. You should try talking to it. They enjoy Thai food, particularly lemon grass.'

The kid checks his cell.

'Do you have any rabbits?'

'Rabbits?' The kid squints as though trying to remember what a rabbit is. 'There might be one left, at the back.'

Milo walks down the aisle crowded with pet clutter until he sees the rabbit behind dirty glass. It doesn't wiggle its nose or twitch its ears. It sits with empty eyes, its ears flattened against its skull. Milo returns to the sales clerk.

'What happened to the other rabbits?'

'What rabbits?'

'You said there was only one left. What happened to the others?'

'Guess they got sold.'

'Does that mean this one's sick?'

'Why would it be sick?'

'It looks sick.'

'No way.' The sales clerk slouches down the aisle with Milo trailing him and stares at the rabbit. 'It looks all right.'

'It's not moving. It's not twitching its nose or ears, or even its tail.'

'It's resting.'

'Its eyes are open.'

'So?'

'Do they rest with their eyes open?'

'Cats rest with their eyes open.'

Milo tries to remember if cats rest with their eyes open. A cat-loving ex-girlfriend – named Cat – had cats that lay around staring. He snapped his fingers at them in an effort to make them blink. He taps the glass, hoping for a response from the rabbit. 'I've always wanted a rabbit.'

'Looks like today's your lucky day.' The kid checks his cell again.

'I always wanted one that looked like Peter Rabbit.' The resting rabbit is primarily white with black patches.

'Peter who?'

'How much is it?'

The kid points to $29.99 scrawled in marker on the glass. 'It's on special.'

'I'll take it.'

'What is that?' Pablo asks.

Milo sits with the boxed rabbit on his lap. He has lifted one cardboard flap, enabling the rabbit to adjust to the unfamiliar smells and lighting. On the walk home the rabbit barely moved in the box and Milo is still somewhat concerned that it might be terminally ill. The sales clerk said if it died in a week he could return it and get a credit. 'Sometimes pets expire and we don't know why. Make sure you give it water or it'll dehydrate.' He tried to sell Milo a cage but Milo has no intention of caging the rabbit. Dean Blinky's sister let Hoppy hop all over the house except at night when she put it in a pen built by Mr. Blinky. She and Dean were expected to pick up Hoppy's turds but Dean inevitably found excuses to avoid this task. Milo thought the little round turds remarkably clean and neat, and won't mind picking up after Patches. This is the only name he can think of so far.

'So what's in the box, Mee-wosh?' Pablo persists.

'Stop calling me that.'

'Can I see?'

'Bug off. It's a rabbit.'

'Are you joking me?'

'No.'

'To, like, eat?'

'God no, to hold, to love.'

'To love?' Pablo starts to giggle. 'You mean, like, a rabbit girlfriend? Your own personal bunny?' Pablo, wildly amused by his own wit, chuckles so hard he tumbles on the couch, gripping his sides.

'Quit it,' Milo says. 'You're bumping the box,'

'Sorry, so sorry.' He dons a serious face. 'Can I see it?'

'Forget it. If you push your big mug in there, you'll scare him. Or her.' He forgot to ask if it was a boy or a girl.

'Why'd you get a rabbit?'

'I've always wanted one.' As a child, even though Milo never mentioned the rabbit again, he fantasized about bringing one home and witnessing his father's reaction. 'Is Gus on the stationary bike?' he asks. The old man has been using it regularly, no doubt increasing his life span by decades.

'No, he went with Robertson and Wallace to buy more patio stones.'

'You mean they just got in the truck and went? Tanis said it was okay?'

'Tanis is at the hospital with Christopher.'

Why does everything run smoothly when Milo is not around? It's as though *he* is the problem.

'What did Zosia say?' Pablo asks.

'What do you mean, "what did Zosia say"?'

'No way would I go to that Magic Bean joint. What a rip-off.' He kicks off his boots and peels off his socks. 'So, is it your baby?'

'None of your fucking business.'

'Maria wants babies. I don't mind. I like *bambinos*.'

'You don't have a job, you dumbass, how are you supposed to afford *bambinos*?'

'Gus and me are going into business.' Pablo tosses his socks on the floor. 'Friendly Handy Men.'

'Since when?'

'Since we talked about it. Cash only. Wallace already has a couple of jobs lined up. He'll help us with his truck if he gets a cut. And you could work with us too, Mee-wosh, be our legit front man and make nice with the customers.'

'Am I missing something here? You don't speak Polish. How can you go into business with someone who doesn't speak your language?'

'It's not about language.'

'What's it about then, asshole?'

'Action talks larger than words. Vera says that. You should talk less and act more, Mee-wosh.'

'Excuse me, but did you not, days ago, accuse me of being Action Man? Did you not tell me to chill?'

'That was before.'

'Before what?'

'Before you went psycho on the TV show.'

'Oh, so that's what this is about.' He knows the musketeers are peeved because they will not be on television. The rabbit springs out of the box and bolts from the room.

'*Coño*,' Pablo says. They both chase after it but it has vanished. 'It must be really scared,' Pablo observes.

'No shit, Sherlock.'

Tawny pads in, books in hand. 'What's going on?'

'Milo bought a rabbit and it escaped.'

'A rabbit?'

'Yes,' Milo says, 'it's a small animal that hops and has floppy ears.'

'Are you going to roast it on a spit? That's really good.'

'Nobody's roasting the rabbit, okay? The rabbit is a pet.'

'It's Milo's personal bunny,' Pablo explains, collapsing into giggles again.

'This is serious,' Milo says. 'I mean, what if it doesn't come out and gets dehydrated and expires?'

Vera stomps downstairs. 'What's all this then?'

'Milo bought a rabbit and it escaped,' Tawny says.

'A rabbit? Is Gus putting it in a stew?'

'It's not to eat, it's a *pet*.'

'Mee-wosh's personal bunny,' Pablo says, convulsing on the couch.

'Goodness gracious. Well, it won't come out with all this commotion about.'

'Exactly. Quiet,' Milo commands but, of course, no one pays him any attention. Tawny rummages in the fridge and Pablo, whose cell is now working, takes a call from commando Maria.

'Everybody vacate the main floor,' Milo orders, shoving Pablo out the door.

'Has anybody seen Wally?' Vera asks.

'I'll call you when he gets back. Go up and rest.'

'I don't need to rest, Milo. I need a nice cup of tea.'

'Later. I'll bring it up.'

'You shouldn't talk to her like that,' Tawny says. 'White-asses don't respect their elders.'

'How 'bout you take your books upstairs and improve your mind?'

'Can I eat these?' she holds up cheese slices. 'I like peeling off the plastic.'

'Be my guest.'

Finally he is alone, listening for rabbit rustlings. He takes a carrot from the fridge and lies on the floor to be eye level with the rabbit. If he remains still, it might become curious about the carrot and venture out for a sniff. It has probably never seen a carrot, only little brown pellets of dried rabbit food. Milo places the carrot within arm's reach. Beatrix Potter based Peter Rabbit on a real rabbit, which suggests that rabbits do, in fact, have curiosity, although this one's probably less inclined to take chances having spent its life behind dirty glass.

When he hears the truck in the driveway he jumps up to stop them from barging in and terrorizing Patches further. 'You can't come in,' he tells them.

'Why the fuck not?' Wallace demands.

'There's a rabbit loose in the house.'

'A rabbit?' Robertson asks.

'Is it for some weird Pollack dish?'

'It's a pet.'

'Can I see it?' Robertson asks.

'When I find it. It's scared. Pablo was doing his usual blabbing and bouncing around and it scared the rabbit.'

'*Wszystko dobrze?*' Gus says.

'I need a beer, man,' Wallace says. 'Bring us out some beers.'

Milo moves stealthily into the kitchen to get the beers but, of course, has to dig around in the fridge crammed with animal parts.

'Okay?' Gus asks, startling him.

'Okay, just please, go back outside.'

'*Po co?*'

'Oh, for chrissake, I don't speak Polski, you know that.'

'*Niewazne.*' Gus starts to go back out.

'Wait, take the beers.' He finds a couple and tries to hand them to Gus but the old man is looking past him at the darting rabbit.

'*Ale cudo!*,' he says, '*Królik*,' and walks quietly into the living room, whistling softly and calling, '*Truś, truś.*' He picks up the carrot then kneels to look under the couch, still whistling and making kissing noises. Milo has never heard him make such sounds. Gus lies on his side in front of the couch, sliding his hand holding the carrot under it. '*Truś, truś.*' Completely focused, he looks as though he could maintain this position for hours. Milo takes the beers out to Wallace. 'He's seen it,' he says. 'Now we just have to wait and see what happens. Don't make any noise.'

'How hard is it to find a fucking rabbit?'

Back inside, on his hands and knees behind the La-Z-Boy, Gus talks more softly than Milo has ever heard him speak. '*Cicho maluti, cicho*,' he says. Milo kneels on the floor, ready to play goalie should the rabbit make a run for it. '*Truś, truś. Cicho maluti, cicho.*' Gus starts humming one of his Polish tunes and Milo, sleep-deprived, becomes drowsy. 'Sing to me, Daddy,' he'd say after his mother died, in an attempt to postpone the dreaded bedtime moment when his father would leave him alone with his terrors. 'Mummy used to sing to me.'

'I don't sing.' Gus ruffled Milo's hair but didn't kiss him, or make kissing noises. 'Big boys don't need songs,' he said. 'Go to sleep.'

'*Piękne, kurwa*,' Gus says, gently pulling the rabbit from behind the La-Z-Boy and settling it on his lap. He strokes the bunny's ears and continues to talk to it with a tenderness Milo has never witnessed, or felt.

He calls her even though he knows he shouldn't. 'Milo.'

'Hi.'

'Are you okay?'

'I bought a rabbit.'

'Good for you.'

'I thought it might make a good companion for the baby.'

She says nothing, of course.

'Zosia.'

'Yes.'

'I don't think my father ever loved me. I mean, like, ever, even before the brain damage.' He wishes she'd say of course he did, he just didn't show it. That's what Annie used to tell him.

'Did your father love *you*?' he asks. 'I mean, before they took him to Siberia?'

'He loved politics and vodka.'

'Did he love your sister?'

'She was a baby, what's not to love?'

'The thing is, I was his only child, how could he not love me?' This perplexes him even more now that he has felt his innards shifting and his emotions gushing in regards to his daughter.

'Some people don't know how to love.'

'Why not?'

'There are no rules. Many people grow up without fathers. They do okay.'

Is this the preamble to banishing him from his daughter's life? Already he can feel the lightness leaving him. He is circling the drain. In seconds he will be sucked into slick, dark hell. 'Please don't take her away from me. I don't think I could stand it.'

'You said you thought she was somebody else's.'

'I was an idiot. Please forgive me.'

He can hear her radio in the background. She listens to the all-news station to improve her English.

He treads water, spluttering. 'I'm so sorry, I mean about everything, and I ... I didn't realize how late it is. Were you sleeping?'

'I don't sleep much anymore.'

'Me neither.' There must be something insightful, or at least amusing, to say. He tries to sound easygoing, as though he is not about to expire. 'Are you okay, Zoz? You sound beat.' She doesn't respond and he feels himself dissolving. 'Please talk to me.'

'About what?'

'Anything. What you're feeling, what you ate for lunch, anything.'

He waits as the radio spews news of oil prices, floods and Third World uprisings.

'Everything is impossible now,' she says. 'I used to think anything was possible.'

He can't assure her that anything still *is* possible, knowing that it isn't.

'I thought it would be different here,' she says.

'It is. There is much here. You said that yourself. I mean, you don't hear about human trafficking.'

'You don't hear about it.'

'Maybe the trick is not to think about whether things are possible or impossible. Maybe the trick is to just go ahead and do whatever it is you're doing. Deciding that something is possible or impossible might just be a waste of energy. I mean, who knows what's possible? All we know for sure is we're going to die.' There's insight for you. What an asshole.

'What is it that you are doing, Milo?'

'Well, I'm ... I'm thinking of going into the construction business, small stuff, you know, patios and decks.'

'Good for you.'

'I don't think it would hurt to have some steady cash coming in.' He is hoping to impress her with his new no-coasting policy, and his determination to protect his organ living outside his body. But he can no longer conceal the truth for fear of disappointing her. 'Zoz, I did a terrible thing.'

'What thing?'

'I roughed up a kid who bullied Robertson. He body-slammed him and stole his cell and kept hitting him in the head with a basketball. He called him a fag and a retard and said online that Robertson wanted to do perverted things to a girl he had a crush on. Then the bully sexually assaulted the girl.'

'Not a nice boy.'

'No. The thing is, after I roughed him up, he fell down. He died two days later.'

'Why?'

'He had a brain aneurysm. I might have caused it to rupture.'

'How?'

'By roughing him up.'

Zosia doesn't speak and he feels the pull of the slick, dark drain.

'Do you often rough up little boys?'

'Never. I mean, not since *I* was a little boy. I wouldn't have done it except Robertson was miserable. He was getting worse and nobody was helping him.'

'How is he now?'

'Better. He's building a patio, and his mother's home-schooling him.'

'There will be more bullies.'

'I realize that, and I won't touch them, I promise. I could never, ever, assault a child again.'

The radio rambles.

'I'm going to eat something now,' she says. 'I have nausea. I have to eat small portions regularly.'

'Of course, okay, well, can I call you tomorrow?'

'Whatever.'

He sits stranded by the phone not knowing what to do other than wait until tomorrow when he can call her again, plead with her again.

Gus appears from the shadows cradling the rabbit. '*Wszystko dobrze?*'

'Whatever,' Milo mutters, understanding that the rabbit, like every one else, prefers to be with Gussy.

'*Miłosz,*' Gus says. '*Chcesz ją potrzymać?*'

'I have no idea what you're talking about.'

'Okay?'

'Fine. I'm okay. I'm glad you didn't kill it.'

'Rah-beet,' Gus says. '*Królik. Potrzymaj ją.* Rah-beet, *królik.*'

'Kroo-leeck,' Milo repeats.

Gus nods, carefully placing the rabbit on Milo's lap. 'Okay?' he asks. '*Pogłaszcz ją.*' He gestures for Milo to stroke the rabbit. Milo does, astonished by the softness of its fur and the feeling of life in the creature that looked lifeless only hours ago. '*Podrap ją w uszko.*' Gus gestures for Milo to stroke Patches' ears, which he does. Gus nods, smiling. '*Ona to lubi.* Goot.' He leaves Milo alone with the rabbit and Patches doesn't seem to mind, doesn't immediately hop off his lap in pursuit of Gussy. It twitches its nose and tail and keeps an eye out for predators, but it stays with Milo.

27

*I*mmediately after the security guard unlocks the door, the Mexican and Cuban soon-to-be in-laws swarm the wedding chamber. Armed with masking tape, the women hurriedly stick plastic flowers on the concrete block walls. Several of the men struggle with streamers that tear easily and are caught underfoot. A fleet of Mexicans puff out their cheeks as they inflate heart-shaped balloons. Pablo, wearing a pale blue rented tux, struts about offering decorating tips. Maria, for no reason that Milo can understand, is tearful, although she looks fetching in a flamenco-style dress, with ruffles at the hem and a mantilla veil. The rumpled officiant, Mr. Gunby, waiting to perform the service, watches the Latinos with some apprehension, periodically stroking his goatee. Milo is unclear as to Mr. Gunby's credentials but Pablo has assured him that he is 'legit' and not too expensive and 'totally Canadian.' His Canadian pedigree was of great importance to Maria, who has recently been granted Canadian citizenship.

Gus, with Vera's assistance, takes over in the streamer department and within minutes the beige walls are aflame with scarlet, lemon yellow and magenta – colours chosen by the bride, which complement her dress. Wallace, in his too-small blazer, kicks a ball around in a corner with some small ruffians. Tawny, as per Pablo's instructions, is in charge of the boom box, playing tracks from old John Travolta movies. The noise level in the windowless room is rising as is the aroma of body odour. As expected, Zosia is nowhere in sight and Milo's 'hot' jacket, donated by Val, is making him sweat.

Several stocky grandmothers herd the crowd into seats, scolding and slapping the non-compliant ruffians. Finally Pablo and Maria stand before Mr. Gunby, who has been instructed, according to Pablo, not to mention God.

'In the presence of God,' Mr. Gunby begins.

'No God,' Pablo protests, which causes Maria to gasp and the guests to titter. 'We agreed, *cariño*. Didn't we agree? No God.'

She nods meekly, her expression hidden by the veil, and Mr. Gunby continues: 'Do you, Pablo Suarez, take Maria Ortega to be your wife, to have and to hold from this day forward, for better or for worse, for richer, for poorer, in sickness and in health, to love and to cherish until death do you part?'

'Totally,' Pablo says.

'Just say "I do," please.'

'Totally. I do.'

Mr. Gunby asks the same of Maria but she falters under the veil. Pablo tries to console her with gentle embraces and quiet words until finally he looks at Mr. Gunby and says. 'Okay, say God in her part.'

Mr. Gunby pulls a handkerchief from his pocket and mops his brow. 'In the presence of *God* do you, Maria Ortega, take Pablo Suarez to be your husband, to have and to hold from this day forward, for better or for worse, for richer, for poorer, in sickness and in health, to love and to cherish until death do you part?'

'I do,' she says and the crowd ignites, throwing streamers and cheering. Maria has insisted that Pablo memorize a vow she wrote in English to prove that they are Canadians. Pablo has been rehearsing it in front of the bathroom mirror, omitting the references to God. Maria speaks the vow first: 'I will never leave you, and you will always follow me. For where you go, I shall go and where you stay, I shall stay. And my family will be your family and this new country our country, and my God your God, and we shall never be parted, even in death because where you lie dead, so shall I. And may the Lord punish me if anything but death parts you from me.'

All this sounds ominous. Milo looks around again for Zosia, a dull throbbing overtaking him.

Pablo manages the first part of the vow but stumbles over the God word, forgetting that he had chosen to omit it. Sweat appears on Mr. Gunby's upper lip. He dabs it with his handkerchief.

'And we shall never be parted,' Pablo improvises, 'because when you're dead, I'll be dead too, and we'll be buried together because nothing but death will part you from me.'

So much death.

Jorge, the best man, hands Pablo the ring purchased with a high-interest loan from Wallace. He slides it on her finger and the in-laws vibrate with anticipation.

'You may kiss the bride,' Mr. Gunby says, clearly relieved. Pablo lifts the veil and they smooch. Celebratory havoc ensues and then Zosia is tugging on Milo's sleeve. Although Pablo booked the wedding chamber for two half-hour slots, the decorating has left time short. Milo and Zosia sidestep the rejoicing Latinos and approach the altar, not hand in hand but like two prisoners awaiting sentence. Mr. Gunby keeps it very brief as directed and within seconds, despite the mayhem, Milo and Zosia have agreed, metaphorically speaking, to join hands in the state of holy matrimony.

He doesn't expect her at his backyard reception where the revellers hastily unfold tables and chairs and a pig, yes, an entire hog with an apple in its mouth, is being roasted on a spit built by Gus. According to Pablo, Gus does not believe a wedding is a wedding without a slaughtered pig. Thanks to the internet, a butcher who sells entire carcasses was found and the corpse bought. It has been roasting for several hours, guarded by Robertson, who, every half-hour, rotates the spit to cook the pig evenly. Milo expects fire trucks to arrive.

He spots Zosia sitting on a folding chair and strolls, he hopes casually, towards her. She watches sombrely as Pablo and Maria exchange Mexican vows, draping a *lazo* – a cord decorated with ribbons – around each other's necks to form a figure eight. This symbolizes, Pablo informed Milo over Shreddies this morning, eternal love.

'Nothing about humans is eternal,' Milo said. 'Except, of course, their stupidity. Einstein called it infinite.'

'Oh, stop that rot, Milo,' Vera said.

'The *lazo*,' Pablo elaborated, 'is a symbol of our commitment to always be together, side by side.'

'More like strangulation,' Milo said.

With the cord around their necks, the newlyweds make out while Gus chants, '*Gorzko, gorzko,*' several times, clapping his hands.

'Nice jacket, Milo,' Zosia says.

'Thank you.' In a summer dress, minus the raincoat, she really does look pregnant. 'Can I get you some sangria?' he asks. 'It's pretty tame.'

'Do you have any orange juice?'

'Of course,' he says, delighted that he can actually provide something she desires. He squeezes past tables and chairs and bodies until he makes it to the kitchen where the grandmothers have taken charge. Even Vera has surrendered her post by the stove and taken her G&T outdoors, where she adjusts the flower arrangements. Patches, however, sits in a corner contentedly nibbling veggie bits discarded by the grannies.

Orange juice in hand, held high above the crowd, Milo wends his way back to Zosia. Gus, still in congratulatory mode, chants, '*Sto lat, sto lat, niech zyje, syje nam.*'

Milo hands her the glass and sits on the folding chair beside her. The guests who aren't munching tortillas line up to dance a merengue that looks more like an out-of-sync bunny hop as they grip each other's hips and quickstep. Zosia's foot keeps time with the music.

'If they play salsa later,' Milo says, 'you and me are going to tear up some grass.' She snorts. They took a salsa class together but were never able to match the whirling speed of the instructor and her assistant.

'We weren't that bad,' he says. 'We just need practice.' And then, without warning, as though it were perfectly natural, she takes his hand and holds it against her swollen belly. He feels the pulse of her as she keeps her hand over his, and, for the first time, the startling, soft and swift determined force of his daughter's foot. The daughter he already loves more than breathing.